TRUCK STOP TANGO

KRISSY DANIELS

Published by Kiss Me Dizzy Books

Cover Design by:
Damonza.com

Editing by:
Madison Seidler
www.madisonseidler.com

Proofreading by:
Georgia Macey
www.georgiamacey.com

Formatting by:
Elaine York
www.allusiongraphics.com

TRUCK STOP
TANGO

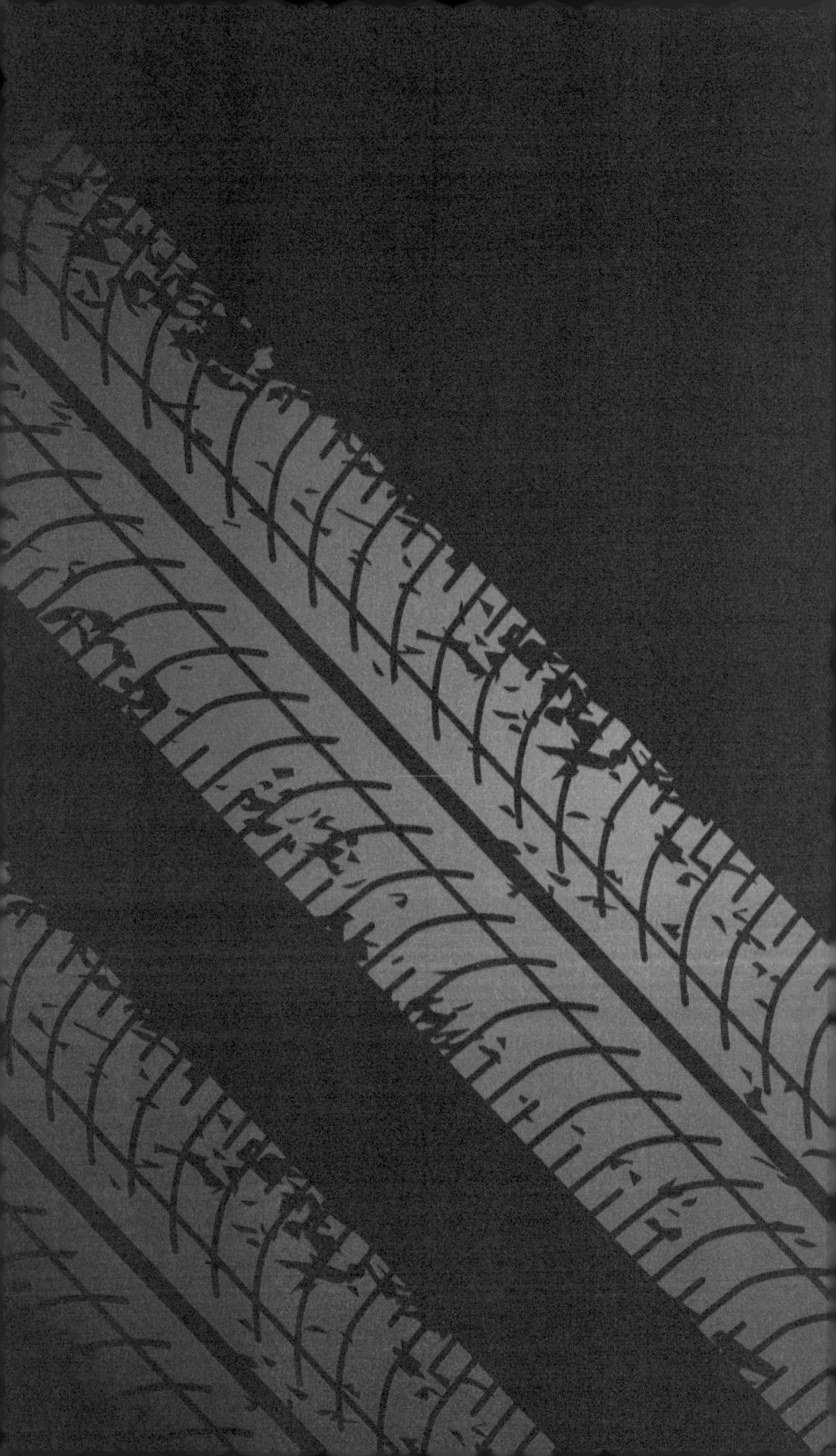

For Amanda K Byrne.

I'm a better writer because of you.

Rest in peace my sweet friend.

PROLOGUE

"GET UP AND DANCE, PRETTY BOY. These bloodthirsty fuckers paid a small fortune to watch me kick your ass tonight. Let's say we give 'em a good show." Rafael Turner bounced from foot to foot, circling my head, pumping his fists, taunting me, working the crowd.

I hated lying down for anyone, especially this prick. Unfortunately, vulnerability was a necessary ruse. I'd allowed him to land one, for show, but one would be all he'd get. I'd learned to toy with my prey before going for the kill—fool my opponent, and the voracious crowd, into believing the fight was fair.

The noise in the stadium drowned out the rhythmic thumping in my head. I peeled my cheek from the mat, sticky with sweat and blood. My jaw popped when I tested its mobility, but I ground my molars together regardless, using the pain to stifle the eager beast.

The colorful mob surrounding the ring blurred into a kaleidoscope of blues and grays—a scene that'd become less invigorating, and more blasé over the years.

Planting my fists on either side of my chest, I pushed hard, forcing my body to lift until I could find my legs and pull them under me. Rubbery bastards refused to cooperate.

Damn. Hadn't been hit that hard in years. The narcissistic fucker had been holding back when we'd sparred in the gym.

To my left, Tito yelled, "It's okay, T. Shake it off. Shake it off."

Code for *not yet*.

Christ. How much longer?

The crowd chanted, "Turner. Turner. Turner."

Rafael played to the cacophony of praises, one of his many weaknesses. He could grandstand all he wanted. Gave me time to gain my bearings.

"Turner. Turner. Turner," they continued.

Thirty seconds ago, it'd been my name rolling like thunder through the stadium.

No loyalty anymore. I was so done with this shit.

Pushing to my feet, I stumbled backward, the rope catching my fall. I chanced a glance in Tito's direction. Standing behind him, wearing a pinstripe suit, Luciano held a drink in one hand and his daughter, Aida, in the other.

My gut tightened. Bad shit was going down. Luciano never left the safety of his office.

Give the signal. Give the fucking signal.

"You good, pretty boy?" Rafael bounced toward me, planted a glove behind my head, and pulled me in for a kiss. A fucking kiss. Goddamn showboating motherfucker.

The crowd exploded.

Vibrating with rage, I shoved him away, clearing my field of vision in time to watch my boss saunter down the dark corridor leading toward the locker rooms, head hung low.

"I know you used to fuck her."

I snapped my attention back to my opponent.

His hazel eyes narrowed. Rolling muscle bunched and coiled under his dark skin. "Aida is mine. I'm gonna make sure you never forget that."

Possessive fucker. Aida belonged to nobody. Damn, I couldn't wait to take him down.

Tito yelled, "Give him hell, Rocky."

Code for *unleash the beast and end the cocky bastard.*

'Bout fucking time.

Shaking the tension from my arms, I blocked surrounding stimuli, dropped my walls of restraint, and zeroed in on my target.

"You're going down in two, douchebag," I said with a smile.

Rafael's smirk disappeared.

I lunged, Rafael dodged left, miscalculating, throwing himself into my right hook. I struck again, landing a blow that guaranteed he'd be drinking through a straw for the next two weeks.

Rafael's head hit the mat. Fight over. Three rounds too late for my liking.

Reveling in the uproar, I spun a slow three-sixty, taking in the view one more time. Then I closed my eyes, and pictured *her* face in the crowd, chanting, *Rocky, Rocky, Rocky.*

Fuck. I shook that fantasy from my thoughts and focused on the here and now.

One fight left. One win. Then freedom.

Luciano Voltolini would no longer own me. My debt would be paid.

I hadn't noticed Tito jump into the ring, but suddenly he was shoving me under the ropes, through waving hands and flailing arms, and down the dark corridor, his hand a firm pressure between my shoulder blades, not allowing me to slow for anyone.

Three of Luciano's whores stood at the entrance to my private room. Most days, I would've ignored the blonde and invited the others in. After taking Turner to the mat, I'd briefly considered spicing up the mix.

"Not today, ladies." Tito waved them away and opened the door for me.

My knees buckled when I crossed the threshold and absorbed the scene, the moment that would forever haunt me in its frightening simplicity. Luciano sat on my couch, elbows to knees, head to hands. No drink. No women. No bodyguards.

When I stepped closer, his eyes, always calculating, always fearsome, suddenly liquid and vulnerable, lifted to meet mine. In all the years I'd known Luciano, I'd never witnessed a lick of emotion on his face.

Things were about to get ugly.

Tito stepped beside me, clearing his throat. His eyes, too, were glassier than usual.

"What?" I managed to mumble through my foreboding.

Luciano Voltolini, the East Coast's most feared and elusive criminal, rose to his feet, cupped my shoulder with one hand, and wiped his eyes with the other.

"Tango, son. It's your mother."

Impressive, how my legs managed to hold me upright while Luciano, childhood friend of my father, explained the details of my mother's sudden death. Crazy, how I couldn't remember trashing my dressing room, but recalled the one thought roaring through my head.

I'm going home. I'm going home to my girl.

CHAPTER 1

Tango

I LIFTED MY FINGERS ONE BY ONE off the sticky grip of the steering wheel, then forced my hands to my thighs, fighting the urge to ball them into fists and make a punching bag of my dash. As her form took shape through the windshield, I pulled the bill of my Yankees cap lower and sunk into the buttery leather of my Range Rover.

Holy Christ, I couldn't take my eyes off her lean, muscular legs. Her frayed cut-offs could barely be considered attire at all, but I couldn't imagine her looking more beautiful. No designer in the world could improve on her small town, all-American girl beauty.

As she passed, her flip-flops smacked an annoying yet familiar rhythm between the sidewalk and the bottoms of her feet. I gripped the steering wheel again to anchor myself, because damn, was I itching to jump from the car, chase her down, and tangle my fingers through that blonde mess of coils cascading down her back.

Without glancing my way, Slade Mason trotted up the worn, wooden steps of her porch. The same weathered boards we had carved our names in as kids.

My stomach rolled at the sight of her. She was skinny. Too damn skinny. But those legs? Shit. Sweet, creamy skin stretched over lean muscle, no doubt carved from two decades of walking every-fucking-where she needed to go.

I laughed, remembering senior year and my many failed attempts at persuading her to buy a car.

"Walking makes me happy," she would always say. And that was that. Her driveway remained as it always had been— empty. Nothing but slabs of cracked cement posing as a dull gray, urban mosaic brightened only by veins of wild grass and dandelions.

As she fumbled with the grocery bags in her arms, and bent to set them down, my cock roared to life. I'd always loved that ass. High, tight, a perfect handful. Over the years, it had claimed the starring role in many late night jam sessions with my right hand and a hot shower.

I glanced at the time on my dash. Nine-fifty. Shit. Forty minutes to get to the church. My stomach knotted. Why wasn't she dressed? Surely she'd attend Mom's funeral. A volatile mix of dread and regret billowed through me. I rubbed my temples to quell the oncoming headache. God, as much as I hated to admit the truth, and despite the fact that I hadn't seen her in six years, I needed her to be there. I'd counted on it.

I drew a deep breath and gripped the door handle. I had to do this. Would she forgive me? Fuck it. Didn't matter. I wouldn't forgive me. But, damn. I needed to face Slade before I could face the town.

Sucking in a breath of courage, I pushed the door open and dropped one foot to the asphalt. I heard a squeal as the front door of her house swung open. I paused, heart in my throat, and watched a little shit jump into her arms and tackle her to the ground. His raven hair, a sharp contrast to her blonde waves, pointed every which way on his head.

"Mommy. You're home!" He hugged her tight.

Mommy? Impossible. The kid was tall. Six or seven, by the looks of him. Slade was a virgin when I'd left six years ago. I would know. I was the reason she'd remained untouched.

Slade's arms wrapped in a protective cage around the boy, and she rolled to her side, planting kisses up and down his face.

My heart dropped to my gut. Motherfucker. A kid.

I scratched the nagging tingle at the base of my skull. A child. Hadn't considered that. Was there a husband? Didn't matter. Not like I came to proclaim my love and beg her to take me back. Just needed to clear my conscience of the damage I'd done all those years ago.

Maybe then, I could go back to being the Tango she'd once known. The Tango I wanted to be again.

That was what I told myself, anyway. Truth? I needed to convince her to come with me, walk into the church, hand in hand. Hell, she could walk ten feet in front of me, wouldn't matter. Just needed to know those blue eyes were out there watching me.

I stood frozen, one foot glued to the ground, the other still inside my car, arms perched over the top of my door. *Move, jackass. Move. It's now or never.*

I was about to call her name, when a stout, older woman, waddled onto the porch with a knitting bag over her shoulder.

"Thank you, Marion," Slade shouted, tickling and kissing the little shit in her arms.

"Any time, sweetie." The woman carefully maneuvered the steps and shouted a goodbye before cutting through the neglected lawn toward the house next door.

Slade pushed to her feet, grabbed the grocery bags, and then finally, her gaze fell on me. Those eyes. Those fucking eyes. My crack. Lighting me up from head to toe. I lifted a hand, offering a pathetic wave, all confidence lost.

Smile. Smile for me. Please.

Slade's beautiful face dropped, along with her shoulders. She shook her head back and forth in a slow *no*. Warning me to stay away. Gutting me.

I watched, wrecked beyond comprehension, while her boy opened the door and gestured for her to go in.

"What a gentleman. Thanks, babylove," she said, glancing back at me one more time before disappearing behind the door.

Babylove. Bile rose in my throat. I hadn't heard or spoken that word since the day I walked out of her life, a hotheaded, selfish coward. My pet name for Slade. An endearment she shared with her son, as if it had never been special, had never meant anything to her at all.

Like I'd taken a punch to the gut, I crumpled into my seat, and closed the door. Deflated. Disgusted. Dangerously close to losing my shit.

"Fuck. Fuck, fuck, fuck," I roared, pounding the steering wheel, releasing the rage before it could boil over. "Babylove," I grumbled, testing the name. My tongue soured.

I revved the engine, and rolled down the street, away from the only girl I'd ever loved.

Slade

The only man I'd ever loved. Parked on my street. In front of my house. Waving hello like he'd only just returned from a trip to the corner gas station. Was he insane? Had he forgotten that he'd shattered me into a million pieces, then disappeared? For six years.

Ouch. I knew there was a chance I'd see him while he was home for the funeral. I'd no idea it would kill me. And it was killing me.

I stood with my back pressed to the door, struggling to breathe, eyes closed tight to keep the tears at bay, fighting a tidal wave of nausea.

He can't hurt you again.

Tango Rossi had broken me. With time, I'd glued the shattered pieces back together. Some of them had fit. Some hadn't. I'd stuck them together anyway, a morbid, mosaic human sculpture. I was happy with the outcome.

My mom used to say that the glue we used to repair our broken hearts made us stronger. I'd always believed her, because no matter what, Mom had always held her head high, always smiled through the pain, and loved harder than anyone I knew. Of course, Mom had suffered a new broken heart every week, and her glue had come from a bottle filled with eighty-proof liquid.

What she'd failed to mention, what became painfully obvious while I trembled against my front door, was that glue was useless against the very thing that broke you in the first place. I was living proof. Because after seeing Tango's face, my put-together pieces were crumbling to the floor one by one.

For the first time in my life, part of me—well, most of me ... okay, a tiny bit of me—wished he'd never existed. The knot in my stomach, formed of nostalgia and worry, wreaked havoc on my sanity.

I glanced at the time. The funeral would start soon. Had he expected me to attend? It made no sense. But why else would he have come to my home?

"C'mon, Mom." Rocky pulled on my pinky finger.

Rocky. My glue. The reason I could never break again. I shook my head, hoping to clear the image of Tango's face from my thoughts, and forced myself to follow my son into the kitchen.

"Marion made a pancake stack," Rocky shouted and jumped into his chair, eyes wider than the sticky, buttery heap piled in front of him. The boy rarely ate more than two pancakes, but Marion loved cooking for Rocky, and insisted that pancakes weren't pancakes unless they were piled at least ten high.

"She did?" I asked, shoving milk and yogurt into the fridge. "Think you can eat the whole thing?"

He nodded and stabbed his fork into the fluffy pile.

I reached for the cupboard to grab a coffee mug, unnerved by the tremble in my hands. After filling my cup, I sat next to my beautiful boy and stared long and hard at his brilliant green eyes. The color, a tad darker than his father's, should've haunted me, but instead offered a solace I hadn't experienced in years. "Have you danced today, babylove?"

"No, Mom. I waited for you," he mumbled with a mouth full of flapjack.

God, I loved my kid. My heart swelled. I scooped him into my arms, sticky face and all, and spun around the kitchen to the tune he hummed. Together we jumped, shimmied, wiggled, and laughed. We never let a day go by without dancing together, even if for only a few, short seconds on the kitchen floor. Breathless, but happy, Rocky climbed back into his seat.

For the first time in ages, I wished I didn't have a business to run. I'd given my waitresses the day off for Marta Rossi's memorial service. They had both attended her dance classes for over two years. They adored her. Everyone did. Everyone but me.

"Mommy?" Rocky reached for the syrup bottle. I snatched it before he made contact.

"No more. That's too much sugar. I need you on your best behavior today. You have to help me at work."

"I do?" He bounced in his chair, and, just like that, the pancakes were ancient history and Rocky was all business, hands to hips, brows pinched. "How come? I thought you didn't like to bring me with you."

"Sweetie, I love having you with me. It just isn't right to make you hang out for the whole day." Truth was, I enjoyed bringing my son to work. The older patrons loved him. The younger crowd treated him as one of their own. Those my age, the people I'd gone to school with, those who knew my history, they made me wary. Six years had passed, and I still heard the occasional whispers and taunts. People believed I had done something to run Tango out of town.

"Biker whore," was the most common term I'd heard whispered. I could handle it, but I sure as hell didn't want Rocky asking questions. Besides, the rumors were far less damaging than the truth.

"But I like playing at The Stop. Especially when I get to help."

"Honey, today shouldn't be too busy. Tucker said he'd stop by and pick you up later this afternoon. Take you fishing. That sound good?"

Rocky squealed and trotted down the hall. "Fishing! I'm gonna catch the biggest one this time."

I sighed and gulped my coffee before cleaning our breakfast mess. I wondered what Tango would wear for the funeral. A nice suit? Maybe a dress shirt and slacks? Would he cry at the service? I hadn't shed a tear for his mother. That fact saddened me more than her passing. I'd known her my whole life. I should've wanted to mourn. I just didn't have it in me to care about someone who'd turned on me the second her son left town.

The last time I had laid eyes on Tango, he'd worn a suit. A brand name label that had cost over a grand. I'd saved my tips for two years to buy a dress. It was pretty, but might as well have been a burlap sack next to Tango's designer threads.

I shivered at the memory of that night. The one and only time I'd worn heels. The last time I'd worn my three-hundred-dollar dress. The night I'd learned the toughest lessons in love. Boys would break you, and even the best of friends couldn't be trusted.

I shook away the unpleasant thoughts, pushed START on the dishwasher, and headed upstairs to find my uniform.

"Mom!" Rocky shouted from his room. "Where's my work shirt? I can't find it."

"Did you look in your shirt drawer?" I snickered and pulled my own red tee over my head. The words "truck stop" lay in bold, white font over my left breast. The back of the shirt bore a vintage photo of the building, in its prime, when the diner was an actual truck stop, before the new highway was built, directing traffic around town instead of through it.

"I can't find it," Rocky whined.

"Honey, look again. On the left side." I wiggled my feet into my Keens, then grabbed my handbag and Rocky's backpack off my bed.

I heard the scrape of his dresser drawer opening. "Oh, there it is."

My son sprinted down the hall, half-dressed, and pulled black high-top Chucks from under my bed. His hair stood thick and tousled atop his head, his face alight with excitement. I stared, in awe, as he tied his laces, then swallowed the lump in my throat. Despite the fact he was the spitting image of his dad, Rocky was, and always would be, mine.

And I would die to protect our secret.

Tango

It was no secret, Mom's cause of death. Intentional overdose. No one, including me, especially me, could wrap their head around the harsh reality of her shameful demise. The woman was stubborn as hell and too damn proud to take her own life.

In the lakeside town of Whisper Springs, Idaho, everyone knew everything about everybody. If you were somebody, as was my mother, Marta Rossi, the town came together, like one big family, to offer support, to make sense of the senseless, to talk, gossip, and celebrate the life of a woman everyone had held in esteem.

Mom looked peaceful, and as beautiful and put together as always, lying in the quilted, champagne silk bedding of her gold-trimmed casket. Trembling, I stepped behind the small oak pulpit and lifted my gaze. The church overflowed with mourners. I scanned the rows of people one last time, slowly, deliberately, checking the face of each and every attendee.

The weight of an anvil pressed on my chest, suffocating me. Slade hadn't come. *She didn't fucking show up.*

I held the speech I'd written for Mom. Violent tremors shook my hands, making it impossible to read the words. *This isn't right*, I thought. None of it made sense.

A reassuring hand rested on my shoulder. "Son, would you like a moment?"

I met Pastor Davies in the eye, handed him my wrinkled piece of paper, and cleared the gravel from my throat. "I'm sorry. I can't do this."

He nodded in understanding and waited for me to exit stage left before continuing with the service. I walked past my seat in the front row of pews and made my escape, feeling the sting of pitiful stares. I tuned out the whispers and focused on the stained glass image of Jesus above the hand-carved wooden doors.

Once outside, I loosened my tie and drew a drag of fresh air deep into my lungs. My head spun, my skin buzzed, and I squeezed my eyes closed, forcing images of my dead mother out of my head. On a slow exhale, I lifted my face to the warmth of the sun. God, I'd missed home. Clean air. Quiet, except for the occasional buzz of a critter or chirp of a bird. Blue sky that stretched an eternity.

Twirling my key ring around my index finger, I made my way to the car, fighting the urge to rush back to Slade's house and beg her forgiveness.

Anger rose in my core. Had she avoided the funeral because of me? Six years was a long time to hold a grudge. Then again, six years was a long time to wait for an apology.

The caterers were hard at work when I arrived at Mom's dance studio. The place had been decorated to the hilt. Dad wouldn't have it any other way. The hardwood floor gleamed under the sparkling lights hanging in layered streams across the ceiling. Round tables topped with white cloths, flowers, crystal, and shiny silver lined the walls of the large studio. The French doors opened to the newly rebuilt deck out back. The slate and wood structure stretched halfway across the lawn.

The lake danced and sparkled in the background, beckoning. I made my way through clusters of seating areas to the bar that had been set up at the far end of the property. I helped myself to a bottle of Jack before continuing down the steep set of stairs leading to the beach.

It was early still, but the sun already promised to be a scorcher. I walked to the end of our private dock, stripped down to my boxer briefs, and dove into the cool, soul-cleansing lake. I swam underwater until my lungs protested, then came up for air. Memories flooded my psyche, weighing me down with unbearable guilt.

It seemed a lifetime ago, when Slade appeared out of nowhere, jumped off my dock, and right into my soul. She had nearly drowned. I'd saved her. I'd taught her to swim. We'd shared dances, and kisses, and stories. At the end of our now-refurbished pier was where I'd made her a promise. The promise I'd broken on the night I'd broken Slade, before leaving and never looking back.

What a shithead.

I swam a few laps across our little bay, then pulled myself onto the bleached wood and stretched in the sun. I pulled a long swig of amber liquid from the bottle, and stared across the bay, to the small structure that stood out like a sore thumb above the shoreline of Lake Willow.

The Truck Stop Diner. Its rusted three-tier sign stood high above the tree line. Through a clearing in the tall pines, I could make out the white brick of the building itself.

I swallowed another mouthful of Jack and pretended I could see her inside. Working. Working. Always fucking working, that girl. Smiling without fail.

Dad's canoe butted the side of the dock. I entertained the idea of taking it across the bay, to the small beach below the Truck Stop, but opted to nurse my bottle instead. My insides were beginning to untangle, my thoughts slowly numbing. I hadn't slept in days. Thanks to the peaceful slosh of water, mixed with the massaging fingers of the sun's rays, combined with the warm buzz coursing through my veins, courtesy of Mr. Jack Daniel, I closed my eyes and passed the fuck out.

"That your boat?" she asked, splashing through the *water toward me.*

"It's a raft. And yeah, it's mine. Come on." I stretched my arm and helped her in.

"Can I steer?"

I snorted. "No."

She reached over and grabbed an oar. "Why?"

"Have you paddled a raft before?" I asked, reclaiming the handle.

"No."

"That's why."

She giggled and wrestled a clump of wet hair off her face. "I can't go far. My mom might see."

Her mom wouldn't see. Her mom never noticed when Slade snuck down to the beach.

"No problem. Today, we'll stay on this side of the bay. Next time, I'll take you across to my house."

That made her smile. Her smile made my insides feel weird. But I liked it.

I handed her a lifejacket. "Here, put this on."

"I don't need it. I'm a better swimmer than you."

"You can't be in my raft without it." I looked across the bay. Maria, my nanny, stood on the dock, waving her arms like a freak. I had been warned not to go past our dock. Her voice didn't carry far enough for us to hear, but I knew she was yelling at me, in Spanish, which meant I was in big trouble. "Maria will pop the raft when I get back if we don't wear lifejackets."

Slade looked across the water, laughing when her gaze rested on my nanny. She shook her head, rolling her huge, blue eyes at me. That, too, made my stomach do weird things.

"Fine," she said, grabbing the jacket from my hand. "I'll put it on, but I get to steer."

"Yeah, yeah." I waited for her to adjust her straps, then handed her one oar. "You are not a better swimmer."

"Whatever, Rocky Balboa. I'm pretty much better than you at everything. Except for boxing. Which is fine with me, because hitting people is stupid."

Hitting people was stupid. But it felt good. I'd teach her how to hit people the right way, too. "I'm gonna be better than Rocky ever was."

Slade smiled. "Yeah. You are. You are."

Slade

"There you are," I said, thankful to see his playful grin.

Tucker strode through the diner like he owned the place. Jeez, those blue eyes and moppy blond hair were the perfect accessories to his sun-kissed skin. He'd put on a few pounds since moving to Whisper Springs. He wasn't overweight by any means, but he'd definitely bulked up since I met him over five years ago.

I couldn't help but smile whenever we shared space. Tucker was my best friend, my confidante, the only father-figure Rocky had ever known.

"Rockster!" he yelled, falling to one knee and spreading his arms wide to catch the excited boy barreling toward him like a runaway train.

Their usual greeting consisted of a bear hug, then Tucker hanging Rocky upside down by his ankles. Today was no different.

"Hey, Tuck. I'm ready to catch some fish!" Rocky squealed, his hair dusting the checkered tile. "Mom said I can make a milkshake to-go, do you want one?"

Tucker righted my boy and set him on his feet. "Dude, have I ever turned down a Rocky's Special Peanut Butter Chocolate Shake?"

The boys high-fived, and Rocky hopped to the kitchen. Tucker turned to me, brow raised. "So, loverboy show up yet?"

I pulled the coffee carafe from its dock and shook my head no. The diner only held two guests. I filled their cups and returned to the counter. "Oh, Tuck. I don't think my stomach can handle much more of this. What if he walks in here?"

"You'll be strong. Like you always are." He crossed his arms and glared down at me. "Everyone in town is at the Rossi gathering, where there's free booze and food. Just close early and go home."

"What about Charlie?" I asked. "He can't afford a whole day off." He totally could. I paid him a high-level manager's salary. I just didn't look forward to being alone with my misery.

Tucker's grin stretched ear to ear. "C! Wanna go fishing with me and Rockster? Take the afternoon off?"

Charlie, my cook, and second-hand man, peeked his round, rosy face through the swinging double doors. "Give me twenty to clean up?"

Tucker nodded.

"Hot damn and hell yeah. Gear's already in my truck." Charlie glanced my way with a face full of little boy charm. "That okay with you, boss?"

"Go." I waved him off. "Have fun."

Tucker winked at me and strode to the front door to flip the sign to CLOSED. My guests stood, tossed a few bills on the table, and waved goodbye before slipping out the door.

"Go home. Take a bath. Pop open a bottle of wine and a good book. That's what girls do, right? Read and drink in the tub?"

"Maybe I'll go fishing with you," I teased. I hated fishing. Tucker had dragged me along on a couple of occasions. Both times I'd ruined his trip by stripping down to my undies and jumping in the water. Why be on the lake if you couldn't get wet?

Rocky backed through the double doors with two drippy styrofoam cups. "C'mon Tuck. Let's go."

"Hey, babylove. Go set those down outside, then come back to give me a squeeze."

"'K, Mom." Rocky backed into the door and pushed it open with his butt.

I hugged the burly blond. "Thanks, again. Don't know what I'd do without you."

Tucker stepped back and held me at arms' length. "I got a call from Dad this morning. He suggested I bring you guys along on my visit. I know you can't get away, but would you consider letting me bring Rockster? He's the closest thing to a real grandchild my mom's ever gonna get."

A dull pain settled in my chest. Thanks to a freak accident, that he refused to discuss, Tucker would never be able to father children. It also left him horribly scarred in the one place most men are proud of. I'd always suspected that was the reason he didn't date.

I'd never been away from Rocky for more than a day, but I did adore Tucker's parents, Lettie and James. They spoiled Rocky, like I'd always imagined a grandma and grandpa would. Plus, for the first time since he was born, letting him out of my sight, sending him out of town, seemed the safest option. Avoiding Tango would be hard enough without having to worry about protecting my boy.

"I'll think about it."

He flashed a knowing smile and hollered for Charlie to meet him outside as Rocky came back in.

"'K, bye Mom." My son wrapped an arm around my thigh and tipped his head to me.

"Oh, no you don't, mister." I squatted to his level. "I need a real, two-arm hug."

His hair tickled my nose when he squeezed me around the neck.

"Be good. I'll see you tonight."

"I will, Mom," he yelled, already halfway through the door.

I watched them drive away before braving a glance across the lake, which was eerily quiet for early July. The Truck Stop sat on twenty acres of lakeside property and boasted a million-dollar view. The gas pumps had been removed years ago, so now the property behind the diner resembled a barren wasteland. Mom had always dreamed of building a small bed and breakfast or roadside hotel on the vacant lot. Life, unfortunately, had other plans.

I could see lights from the Rossi estate across Lake Willow from the front window. No doubt, Marta Rossi's memorial would be a full-blown celebration. Everyone would dance, and drink, and share stories of Marta's generosity, her grace, her philanthropy. I knew the monster behind the mask. I hated her, but I refused to dwell on the negative.

I pictured Tango dancing, taking turns with the ladies, giving everyone a quick spin across the floor. I wanted to join the party, pretend I belonged there, to feel his arms around me one more time.

Instead, I locked myself in the diner, pulled the shades, cut the lights, cranked the stereo, and danced alone. I shook my moneymaker across the dining area, through the kitchen, and back to the counter. Then shit got real, and I jumped on top of the bar. I danced and sang into a spatula until I had no breath.

It was silly and immature, but I didn't give a flying frog's ass. I'd had to grow up too fast when Rocky came along.

Who could blame me for unleashing the inner child once in a while?

Dancing was a great stress reliever, and heaven knows I needed to decompress. The threat of running into Tango while he was in town had my intestines tangled in knots.

After wiping the counter again, I headed to my office. Just before I sat down to tackle bills, I heard the front door of the diner rattle. I peeked my head around the corner. All I could make out through the uncovered bottom of the glass were a pair of thick-soled, black boots. Whoever it was shook the door one last time and stomped away.

I had never closed early. Guilt settled in my gut, until I heard the terrifying roar of a motorcycle. Sounded like a large bike. The engine was loud enough to rattle the window. Whoever was driving the beast circled the diner twice before driving away. Nerve-rattling fear froze my limbs.

It's not them. It's not them. They can't hurt my son.

Motorcycles were everywhere, I reminded myself. It meant nothing. I decided to leave my paperwork for the next morning and headed home, double-checking the locks before I left.

CHAPTER 2

Tango

"TANGO ROSSI," A DEEP VOICE startled me from behind. "Sorry about your mom, man."

I'd heard those same words three hundred times too many since the funeral. I didn't turn to look. I'd spent the last fifteen minutes tracking the pattern of ice twirling in my tumbler. It was better than watching the town spin and gyrate across Mom's dance floor.

"It's me. Brett."

I snapped my head up to meet a pair of feisty, gray eyes. A wave of relief washed through me, clearing some of the funk from my fuzzy head. "Thank fuck. A face I actually want to see." I hugged my old partner in crime. I hadn't seen him at the church. Then again, I'd only searched for one face in the crowd. "Get me the hell out of here," I grumbled, sliding off the stool and aiming for the door.

Hooking an arm through my elbow, Brett swung me toward the rear exit. "Back door might be a good idea. Kaylee Martin was looking for you up front."

Hadn't heard that name in years. Sure as hell didn't want to see the face belonging to it. The chick had been a thorn in my side since seventh grade. Had arranged marriages been legal, Kaylee would've become the ball to my chain the day I'd turned eighteen. Mom had never stopped trying to shove the poor girl down my throat.

We stayed in the shadows and made our way down Cherry Lane. Whisper Springs was deserted. The silence haunted me with memories of stolen kisses, fingers tangled in blonde hair, and running wild while the rest of the town slumbered. I hadn't been home in six years, yet my body was attuned to the landscape, the smell, the comfort, as if I'd never left. Twenty minutes later, we cut through Lakeside Park and headed toward Whisper Springs High School's football field.

Brett's voice cut the nostalgic musings pricking at my skin. "How is New York treating you?" he asked, then stopped and planted his hands on his hips. "I don't understand why you threw away a full ride, dude. You had it made."

"Didn't want it," was the only explanation I could offer.

"Didn't want it, huh? I'm calling bullshit on that one." He tucked his hands in the pockets of his slacks and continued walking.

My friend wanted to pry. I changed the subject. "I hear you're assistant coach now. Pop says you'll be top dog in a year or two."

"It's a great gig, T. I love those boys. If you're sticking around for a while, you should come by. Summer practice is in full swing." He stopped and turned to me, head hung low.

I knew what was coming. Knew it would sting.

"I haven't heard from you in, what, six years? What the hell, man?"

I ran a hand over the top of my head. "I had shit to work out. I'm sorry." I didn't know what else to say. He wouldn't understand why I'd left and never returned. Hell, I didn't understand completely.

"Sorry? Six fucking years. Not one word from my best friend. No goodbye. Nothing. I only knew you'd gone to New

York because I overheard your mother talking to my mother, and then I was sworn to secrecy." His gaze dropped to the grass, then lifted back to my face. "You talk to Slade yet?"

Ouch. Okay, maybe he did get it. "No."

Our subject matter needed to change. And fast.

"She's got a kid, you know. Bitch got knocked up the second you left town."

My left hand found his throat, and I raised my right fist to strike. "Don't talk about her like that."

His laugh and crooked smile set my blood on fire. Brett batted my hand away. "There you are. Thought I'd lost you for a while."

"Fuckin' prick." I huffed and headed toward the fifty-yard line.

The guy had always known how to rile me. Great skill on the field. Dangerous when it came to Slade.

"I saw her this morning. The kid, too," I confessed, swallowing hard. "Is she married?"

"No, man. Single mom. She left town a couple months after you took off. Came back almost a year later with the baby. Mom had seen her hanging with Addy and her uncle. You remember that creepy fucker, right?" he asked, crossing his arms.

How could I forget? Drug dealer, racist. Ran around with a scary-as-fuck MC. "Yeah, I remember." The Satan's Slayers stayed at his place when they came through town.

Brett nodded, dropped his gaze, and sucked in a breath. "Rumor was, Slade had hooked up with one of those douches. Mom had seen her on the back of one of their bikes more than once."

Envy choked the air from my lungs. Regret weakened my knees. I dropped my ass to the cool grass. Shit. I was supposed to be the one. The only fucking man to touch her.

Should've been my kid. I buried my face in my hands and scrubbed the seething anger away.

Brett's cell blared an annoying ring from his pocket.

"Gotta get this, give me a sec." He rolled his eyes as he walked past me to answer.

That was when I looked up, and the earth fell away from me.

In an instant, I was pulled back to my glory days. Me on the field, Slade in the bleachers. Same row. Same bench. Same damn smile on her face.

Slade lay in her favorite spot. The seat she'd claimed as her own, during my first high-school football game, a million lifetimes ago. Stretched across the top row of bleachers, legs crossed at the ankles, her head and feet bobbed in sync to a tune I couldn't hear. Her hair bounced in a mess of waves splayed across the bench. Large white headphones clung like headgear to her ears.

Through the dark sky, the moon appeared to shine only for her. I jumped to my feet. Brett turned and caught sight of her. He nodded her way, sporting a smile too big for his face, then waved me off. "Good luck, tiger. I'll catch ya later."

I took off at a jog that turned into a sprint. My fucking palms were sweaty, my face burned like a son of a bitch, and a loud boom, boom, boom bounced between my ears. Good God, what she did to me.

I took the stairs two at a time and paused to catch my breath before stepping closer. Who was I trying to fool? I could never breathe right when she was near. We'd done things, shared things on those bleachers, on her special bench, that were forever scorched into my memories.

Eyes closed, voice barely a whisper, she sang along to words I couldn't decipher. Probably some sappy ballad. She'd always had a thing for those cheesy love songs. Her lips were moist, pink, and full. I could still taste them. I needed to taste them again. Her bright red flip flops matched the polish on her nails. Slade and her flip flops. I never understood her love affair with those hunks of rubber.

Bending low, I studied that gorgeous mug. Flawless. Soft. Feminine. Peachy. Fuck, how I'd missed her organic beauty. "Slade," I said, bringing our faces inches from each other. I ran the back of my finger down her cheek.

Her scream was punishment enough for the sneak attack, but she followed through with a punch to the face and a simultaneous foot to my knee. Thank fuck she hadn't worn real shoes.

Wild-eyed and bewildered, she jumped to her feet. I opened my mouth to speak, but she silenced me with a hard slap. Followed by another. I let her have those strikes. Hell, she could hit me all night, as long as I got to stare into those stormy eyes.

"Tango! You fucking bastard!" she yelled, ripping off her headphones. "You scared the shit out of me." With hitched breaths, she pounded at my chest.

I couldn't contain my smile. Feisty as always. One of my favorite things about her.

Before I had time to process my thoughts, Slade dug her fingers into my shoulders, pushed up on her toes, and crushed her lips to mine. The way she kissed me? Hot damn. I could've taken her right then and there, a million different ways.

Slade

A million different scenarios had played through my head, in preparation for the possibility of his return. I'd practiced a speech. I'd considered leaving town, or going into hiding until he'd gone back to wherever he'd been living. I'd imagined emotional, drawn-out conversations, most of which ended with me crying and making a fool of myself. None, not a single one, had ended with me kissing Tango Rossi.

Dammit! I was such a girl.

After the shock of finding him towering over me, in the last place I'd expected to see him, I was drawn straight back to my seventeen-year-old self. Pre-prom. Like that night had never happened, and he'd never ripped my heart and guts out and left me to bleed.

My Tango was home. Years of bottled anger, hurt, and frustration disappeared as if they'd never been there. It came naturally, pulling his lips to mine, pressing my body tight to his. That connection was what I knew, what I needed, more than explanations or apologies, more than atonement.

I kissed six years into his mouth, hugging his neck to pull him closer. His groan made my soul dance. Strong arms, bigger than I remembered, snaked around my middle and hoisted me off the ground. My legs, reacting to muscle memory, wrapped around his waist. I was dying inside, yet never felt more alive, like I had fallen into a coma and his touch jolted me back to life.

True, I'd instigated the lip-lock. By no means, though, was I in control of it. Tango had my full compliance. His tongue slid across my own, tangled, invaded, explored. Dear God, I'd missed his mouth.

I wasn't sure how long the exchange lasted, but when he pulled away and pressed his forehead to mine, I squeezed my eyes closed. I'd be lost forever if I looked. I didn't want to accept reality. Unfortunately, there wasn't a choice. There was too much at stake. My heart, for one. I had to protect that, for my son.

I clung to him like a frightened child. Held on longer than I should have. Earlier, I'd been afraid to face him. After that kiss, I feared letting him go again.

"Have you danced today?" he asked with a rasp. His voice, deep and rich, was a harsh reminder of the years that'd passed. He was no longer the boy I'd known. Tango Rossi was a man.

Have you danced today? If he only knew.

I sighed, lacking courage to meet his gaze, but forcing eye contact anyway. His words hurt, but I loved hearing them, craved them, clung to them.

"Look at me, please." A pained set of eyes stared down at me.

"Hi," I whispered, because that was all I could do.

"There's so much I need to say to you." His brows drew tight, and he shook his head. "But I can't think straight right now."

Gulp. "I know what you mean." I studied the curve of his full lips, the slant of his nose, the thick brows framing his deep green eyes. His lashes, so long and thick, gave the illusion he wore eyeliner. They'd always been the feature on his face that had fascinated me the most. Hard as I tried, I couldn't avoid getting sucked into the heady gaze he'd mastered not long after puberty had struck.

A fading bruise surrounded his left eye, enhancing his beauty.

His mouth curved to a crooked smile. "It doesn't help, having you wrapped around me like this. Makes me want to keep kissing you."

Oh, crap. A wicked heat swelled in my cheeks, and I unclamped my legs from around his waist. Tango held tight until I found my footing, then pressed a kiss to my forehead before letting me go and taking a step back.

He dropped his butt to the metal bench. "Jesus, you're beautiful."

I studied the sky above his head. My eyes burned. Dammit, I could not let him see me cry. "I'm sorry about your mom," I muttered. "Why aren't you with your family?"

I plopped my rear next to him, pressing our thighs together. From the first time we had met, it had always been a thing with us, touching, whenever we were within touching distance. Bumping shoulders, rubbing feet, hooking pinky fingers.

"I had to get away. Needed room to breathe. I know I should be celebrating her life with the rest of them, but it didn't feel right." He slid his hand over my thigh and draped his long fingers over my knee. "It didn't feel right without you there."

I didn't know if he was fishing for an explanation. I wasn't about to give him one. His mother was dead. I wouldn't talk ill of her.

"How long will you be in town?" I asked, steering the conversation another direction.

He turned, straddled the seat, and pulled my hand into his own. "That depends. How long will it take you to forgive me?"

"I forgave you years ago. We were stupid kids. It's ancient history." Truth was, I hadn't forgiven him. I should have. What I'd done in those weeks and months after prom night was unforgivable. I knew holding a grudge made me a hypocrite. His sin had been no more damaging than mine. Still, I was human. I'd been hurt, with the kind of hurt that was difficult to let go of. "I don't want to talk about that night, Tango."

"I need to talk about it." He searched my face with a curious scowl. "You may have gotten over it. I haven't."

I had never been able to lie to him. I'd mastered the art of fooling my mother at an early age. Hell, I'd fooled everyone in town for years, but if Tango probed, he'd discover things that would destroy me and Rocky. I couldn't let him dig.

I pulled my hand from his grip and cupped his cheeks, drawing his face closer. "That's your cross to bear, not mine. Too much time has passed. Don't you see? Nothing you can say would make a difference now."

My hands tingled, sending bursts of giddy energy down my arms and straight to my damn female parts.

The man was beauty. Plain and simple. Every part of me ached to connect with every part of him. I let go of Tango and stood to back away. I'd thought my heart had healed. Apparently not. A wave of pain rushed through me, flooding me with fear, hurt, confusion, and suddenly I was drowning. Drowning in magnificent green eyes, memories of lost youth and broken promises. Suffocated by guilt, anger, and fierce, protective motherly instinct.

I wanted him. Still. After everything. But because I'd been greedy, and jealous, and because I'd sold my soul to hold on to one little piece of Tango Rossi, I'd lost any chance, any hope, of ever getting him back.

Tango

I would get her back. Didn't have a choice. The girl was my missing rib. How the hell had I forgotten that?

I watched the spark fade from her eyes—the brilliant energy that danced and sizzled and filled whatever space she occupied. I hated being the one to extinguish her fire.

Slade took a step back, slipping away, away from me again. Fuck, it hurt watching her retreat. That woman still had the power to bring me to my knees. She said she forgave me. What a crock of shit. Why lie? She'd never been able to pull the wool over my eyes.

I leaned forward, elbows to knees, hands clasped, and studied her expression. She was working something out in her head, and, by the look on her face, it wasn't tipping in my favor. I had a fight on my hands. Good. I loved a challenge.

"Slade, I—"

"I have a son," she blurted, nibbling on her thumbnail.

My gut shifted. "I know."

She shivered and wrapped her arms around her middle. "I need to go. He'll be home soon."

No way in hell was I letting go yet. "I'll walk you."

She stared long and hard at me. My chest, my shoulders, my forehead, my nose. When she found the courage to look me in the eye, she nodded and offered a hand to help me up.

"I'll be fine. You should go back to the party. Be with your dad."

She was right. Pops needed me. It wasn't cool to slip out the way I had. Now that I'd talked to Slade, the party didn't seem so daunting. "I'll go back. After I walk you home."

Hand in hand, we headed down the bleachers, across the field, and started toward her house.

"How's your mom?" I asked, squeezing her fingers, appreciating how soft and delicate they felt between my own.

Slade stopped, releasing her grip, and studied me, brows pinched. "She died. Three years ago."

Aw, fuck. "I'm sorry. I had no idea."

With a sigh, she continued walking. "Car accident. She'd been drinking."

"I'm so fucking sorry. I didn't know." Because I'd never asked. Because asking, and hearing, and acknowledging that she'd survived without me would've meant facing demons I hadn't been ready to confront. "Mom and Dad never said a word to me about it."

Her cheeks turned crimson. A low, angry chuckle escaped her lips, and after a long pause and loud exhale, she continued, "As you know, there was only one thing Mom loved more than men."

Our eyes locked, and we spoke at the same time. "Vodka."

A sad smile graced her face. "She died with a man at her side and a belly full of Grey Goose."

Ah, yes, there she was, my brave girl. Smiling. Even when she'd been kicked in the gut. Her mom had always been a drinker. A functioning alcoholic, and a floozy, for lack of a better word. There wasn't a night I could remember that she didn't bring a man home. Even after working a double shift.

Slade deserved better. She'd never complained, though. All the years I'd known her, she'd never spoken ill of her mom.

We walked in silence most of the way, making small talk here and there, avoiding personal bits. The smack of her flip flops against her feet soothed my jagged emotions more than the liquor had earlier. Or maybe it was just Slade. I'd been back in town for two days, but I hadn't come *home*, not until she'd kissed the hell out of me.

I walked her up the steps of her front stoop, ignoring the tightness in my chest. When she opened the door, without a key, I nearly lost my shit. "You didn't lock your door?"

"I've never locked it. You know that better than anyone."

Yeah, I knew. How many nights had I slipped through the unlocked door, tip-toeing past her mother, who was otherwise occupied, or passed out? How many times had I chastised her for leaving it unlocked? It wouldn't have kept me out. However, it would've been fun to have to sneak through her bedroom window once in a while.

I raked my fingers through my hair and pulled at the roots. "Jesus. We're not kids anymore. It's not safe."

Wrong thing to say, apparently, gauging by the daggers shooting from her eyes and aiming straight for me.

"Really? Thanks for that bit of information." She jutted her chin at me and crossed her arms. "You're abso-fuckin-lutely right. We're not kids anymore, are we? You were a stupid boy when you left." She stepped closer, fury brightening her eyes. "You gutted me, then you disappeared. Now here you are, all grown up. A man of the world. And here I am, a small-town hick who doesn't know better than to lock her own door." She poked a finger into my chest, stepping even closer. "Fuck you!"

I grabbed her wrist. With a grunt, she tried wrenching free. Silly girl. Fighting was useless. I wrapped my other arm around her waist and hoisted her up. "God, I've missed that spunk."

"Let go—"

I smashed her mouth to mine, maybe a touch too hard. She whimpered. My blood warmed. Her lips parted for me, despite the wriggling to free herself. Damn, the woman could kiss, and that was what she did. Kissed me hard, then soft, then ate my mouth with hungry lips. My cock hardened between us. I pulled her tighter against my hips, because damn, she felt good.

That was when her teeth sunk into my flesh.

I dropped her, shocked but even more turned on. "Holy shit. You bit me," I half-laughed, half-yelled, wiping blood from my lower lip.

She pushed away and found her footing. "Like I said." She slipped backward through the door and poked her head out. "Fuck you." With impressive dramatic flair, she slammed it in my face.

I stood, dumbstruck, and stared through her window into the dark house. Couldn't see a damn thing, but I heard angry footsteps clomp up the stairs.

My heart swelled when she stomped back down, then deflated when she turned the lock and disappeared into the darkness.

I scratched my head, lifted my hand to knock, then changed my mind. "Game on, babylove," I mumbled to myself.

Not a chance in hell she'd forgiven me. I had work to do.

Frustration, elation, and arousal—mostly arousal—pumped through my veins, inflating me with wicked energy. I pulled out my cell, trotted down the steps and across the lawn. I dialed the number of the only other person on earth I wanted to talk to.

My cousin, Tito, answered on the first ring. "T. What's up?"

The gruff voice centered me. "I need more time."

After a long silence, he huffed. "You lost your mom. Take as much time as you need. I can handle things on this end. I'll talk to Luciano. I'm sure he won't be too upset."

Upset? He'd be irate. Probably kill me, but shit, Slade wasn't over me, not by a long shot. I sure as hell wasn't over her, evident by the tight knot in my chest, and the fact that I hadn't felt this alive in years. I'd welcome a thousand deaths for one more shot with my girl.

"Sorry I couldn't be there, man," he said, interrupting my musings.

Tito managed Luciano's underground fights. His was a respected position in the Voltolini family that, unfortunately, didn't allow for time off, even to pay last respects to his aunt.

"Don't sweat it. Don't want Luciano pissed at both of us."

Tito chuckled. "Tango, I gotta ask, did you see your girl?" Tito had spent three weeks every summer with my family. He'd had a thing for Slade, too. It had never bothered me though. Even then, he'd known she was mine, and he'd never crossed a line.

"Yeah." I scrubbed a hand over my face. Seen her. Felt her. Tasted her.

"She as hot as I remember?" he asked, ruffling my feathers whether he meant to or not.

Heat rushed through me. "You have no fucking idea." I had to get home before I turned around, climbed through her window, and blew off steam the good old fashioned way. "Listen, I'll call you tomorrow."

Slade

"See you tomorrow. Thanks, Slade," Maurice McReary shouted across the dining room. He slipped through the door, giving the old cowbell an extra rattle, as was his custom.

I waved goodbye and plucked the quarter and three pennies off the corner table. Twenty-eight cents. Every morning, for as long as I could remember, Maurice would drink two and a half cups of coffee—sugar, no cream—and leave a twenty-eight cent tip. When we'd ask him about it, he'd laugh and say, "Everyone needs their secrets."

Someday, I'd get him to tell me the story behind the twenty-eight cents. Not today. Today, it drained all my energy to smile at people.

I yawned and passed the empty mug and saucer across the stainless steel partition separating the dining area from the kitchen. Charlie's crooked grin greeted me. "Why so sleepy, boss? It's not like you to drag your butt the way you been doin' today. Rough night?"

Oh, if he only knew. Tango Rossi. Slimy bastard. Why the hell had I kissed him?

"Rocky was too wired after all the soda and candy you guys let him eat. He kept me up half the night," I lied. Truth was, my little guy had crashed before I'd wrestled him into his pajamas.

Charlie chuckled his deep, throaty chuckle I loved so much. "That wasn't my doing. I warned Tuck. Told him he'd suffer the wrath of big, bad mama bear if he gave the cub too much junk food."

"Oh, yeah? I'm mama bear now?" I played along. "What'd he say?"

"Something about you being nothing but a soft, fuzzy bunny." Charlie cracked two eggs on the grill with one hand and flipped pancakes with the other.

I rolled my eyes and turned to greet the guest who had just entered. Had I not been surrounded by customers, I would've yelled something like, "Holy fucking shit. What the hell are you doing here?" Instead, I croaked, "Oh, good morning, Kaylee. Haven't seen you in, like, forever."

"Hi, Slade." She surveyed the restaurant.

I took the opportunity to check her out. The girl had certainly matured physically. If I wasn't mistaken, she'd gotten a boob job. Her nose looked smaller, too. "You look good," I exclaimed, in my sweetest voice. My least favorite thing about owning the Truck Stop was that I had to be nice, all the time, no matter who walked through the door.

"Thanks, girl." She stopped perusing the patrons and gave me a once over. "How are you? Working hard, I suppose. The place looks great." She smacked a pink wad of gum between her lips. "I didn't see you at the funeral yesterday.

Of course, it was packed. Everyone in town was there. Maybe we just missed each other."

"Yeah." I nodded. I wasn't about to explain to anyone, especially her, why I didn't go. "Are you meeting someone? You want a table, or the counter?"

Her eyes met mine with a snap. "Just grabbing a cup of coffee, on my way to see Mr. Rossi. I'm taking over Marta's classes at the studio until he decides what to do with it."

"Oh, hey. I watched you on that dance show last summer. Wow." I shook my head for dramatic effect. "You blew me away. Third place. I mean. Holy crap. That's pretty amazing, right?"

Her cheeks reddened. "Yes. Just got home from the tour a couple weeks ago."

"Are you staying in town for a while?" I asked.

"I think so." She lifted her cell and thumbed the screen. Clearly, I wasn't worthy of her attention anymore.

"Alrighty, then." I rolled my eyes. "Let me get your coffee."

I filled a to-go cup. She turned to look out the window and shifted nervously in her red flats. I stared in awe at her powerful legs. Her poise. Her perfect figure. She was a beautiful dancer. I used to watch her for hours at the studio while Tango and I studied. Too often, Marta would ask Tango to partner with Kaylee. He hated dancing with other girls. I hated watching him dance with other girls, but hot-damn, the boy could move, and when he was moving, I had no choice but to watch. The two of them together were breathtaking.

His mother had thought so too. She'd made it clear from the beginning that Kaylee was the girl Tango should've given his heart to.

"Here you go." I pushed the coffee across the counter. "On the house. Good luck with your meeting."

"Thanks." She didn't even glance up from her phone. "Tango looks amazing, huh?"

Damn. I'd rather she slapped me in the face than bring him up. "No. I mean. I don't know."

Hard to tell what shone brighter, her eyes or her smile. "Wow. You two haven't seen each other, have you?"

Her question fell under the category titled: *None of Your Damn Business*. I sensed what would come next and braced for impact.

"God, Slade. That breaks my heart." She had the gall to slap her right hand above her left breast. I wasn't fooled. The glimmer in her eyes didn't reflect heartbreak. Not even a little bit.

"I guess he truly is over you. No wonder he was so sweet and attentive last night. Felt good having his arms around me again."

I took a step back. Fire licked my cheeks. "Arms around you?" I gripped my shirt hem to keep from clutching my chest. Who stuck the sword through my heart? Why did her petty words hurt? I needed Tango to be gone. He could have his arms around any woman he wanted, as long as it was not her and not in my town.

Kaylee tucked her bright pink phone into her fuchsia Gucci bucket purse and slapped her perfectly manicured hand to her cheeks. Surprise, surprise, her nails were painted a lively shade of rose, same shade as her shiny gloss. "Seriously, he danced like he wanted to fuck me."

I stumbled back a step and raised my fingers to my lips. They tingled, still sensitive from the impromptu workout Tango had given them last night. Apparently, his lips needed more stimulation, seeing as he had run to her the second I'd chased him away.

She'd always been jealous. A snide, catty opportunist. Never before had she weaseled her way under my skin.

The pink bitch stepped closer. "Does it hurt, knowing you're not his girl anymore? Nobody could believe he had just up and left you. What'd you do to him, anyway?"

A deep voice boomed behind me, thick with anger, "I told you last night, it was none of your business." Strong fingers encased my trembling hand, offering an assuring squeeze, or perhaps a warning not to rip her pretty throat out. "And Kaylee, Slade will always be my girl. Don't ever fucking forget that."

She stared over my head at the man pressed firmly against my backside. First confusion, then defeat darkened her features. "Okay. Your girl." She nodded and quirked her brow. Without so much as a glance at me, she turned on her heel and plowed through the door.

I reclaimed my hand, whipped around, and came nose to chest with the hard body I wanted to both jump and dismember at the same time.

The bastard smelled like he'd been in the sun for hours, reminding me of the summer days we'd spent on the lake. "How'd you get in?"

Tango hooked a finger under my chin and urged me to look up. I did, dammit. Oh, if only I could trade my vagina for something less girly—like a bear trap.

He shrugged his shoulders. "Charlie let me in through the back. Just like old times."

"He's fired." I realized I hadn't moved, and stood too damn close to the enemy. The restaurant fell eerily silent. I looked over my shoulder. Every eye in the place was on us. "Great, just great," I mumbled and pushed at him. "I'm working. You need to go." He didn't budge. My butt smashed into the counter behind me.

He stepped closer, invading my personal space, and cupped my cheek, brushing a thumb across my lip. "I can't go yet," he said, leaning closer than should be legal. My mouth parted on exhale, opening for him. Our eyes locked, rendering me speechless, breathless, helpless. Dear God, if he kissed me again, I'd be done for.

His lips hovered over mine, then a crooked smile broke the trance. Tango reached around, grabbed a menu, and wiggled his brows. "I'm hungry. Think I'll stay for breakfast."

I was about to protest when Rocky barreled through the door. "Mom! Guess what?"

The blood in my head whooshed to my feet as if I were a giant toilet that'd just been flushed. I gripped the counter for balance.

Rocky stopped dead when he spied Tango. "Whoa!" he shouted. "You're ginormous."

Tango crossed his arms and looked down. Hard to tell whether it was disgust or dismay scrunching his face. He studied my boy, then crouched and extended a hand. "I'm Tango Rossi. Who might you be?"

Rocky stepped closer and gave him a high five in place of a shake. "Rocky James Mason."

Oh dear God, my worst nightmare. Played like a horror movie right before my eyes.

Tango glanced my way, then mussed Rocky's hair. "Great name, kid." He stood and backed away, burning a hole through my skull with his scrutinizing glare.

Marion waddled up. "I'm sorry, Slade. My mother slipped and fell. I need to get to the hospital." Marion was nearing seventy. Her mother had celebrated her ninetieth birthday last summer and had only recently moved into a retirement home.

"Oh, Marion. I'm sorry, go. Go. Rocky's fine with me today."

Talk about epic, shitty timing.

Marion pulled Rocky in for a hug and scurried back through the door.

Rocky's shoulders slumped. "Aw, man. We were gonna go to the park and the beach today."

"I'm sorry, babylove."

Tango stepped between me and Rocky. "You know what? I was planning on going to the beach today. How about I take you?"

No! No! No! I'd never fainted, but I was pretty sure it was about to happen.

"Can I, Mom?" Rocky jumped up and down. "Please, please, please."

I opened my mouth to speak, but when Tango scooped Rocky into his arms, like it was the most natural thing in the world, I lost my voice.

"Mom says yes. Is that your gear?" He patted Rocky's backpack.

"Yup." My son, in all his dangerous, youthful innocence, straightened his spine and nodded his head.

"It's settled then," Tango proclaimed, his hard biceps bulging as he squeezed my boy tighter.

"Wait—" I started to protest.

Tango shut me up by pressing a finger to my mouth, smashing my already tender lips. "What time you off?"

"Four," Charlie shouted from the kitchen, betraying me in ways he couldn't fathom. Ooh, he was so fired.

"We'll be back by four." Tango didn't let me respond. Before I could make my jaw move, the boys were halfway out the door. Tango stopped and turned to me, an unholy fire lighting his smile. "I'm on to you, girl. We're gonna talk."

With that, Tango left. With my son.

I stood, helpless, speechless, boneless, and I knew, because life hated me, I knew, that moment was the beginning of my end.

CHAPTER 3

Slade

SUCK IT, LIFE.

Six o'clock in the freaking morning. I stood on my porch, waving goodbye to my little man, scrunching my face to fight the tears.

You're doing the right thing, I reminded myself. The sooner Rocky was out of town, the better. I needed him safe, and far away, so I could think straight and navigate the damn nightmare I was living.

Letting Rocky go away for two weeks was harder than I'd imagined. Not running after Tucker's Jeep as they drove down my street took will power I hadn't known existed. Yay me.

My house was eerily quiet and achingly empty. I dragged my butt up the stairs and buried myself under the blankets of my queen-sized bed. Facing the day seemed an insurmountable task.

Last night, Rocky had talked non-stop, retelling stories from his beach day with Tango. He'd come home with a new football, too, and had made me play catch for an hour after dinner.

Tango had spoken two words to me when he'd dropped off Rocky. "Hey," and "goodnight." His scrutinizing glare had spoken volumes. He knew. I mean, how could he not? And if he hadn't put two and two together, it was only a matter of time.

I'd never been able to lie to him, and I used to love that he knew me so intimately. Now I hated how our lives were like an overgrown patch of blackberry bushes—tangled, massive, and impossible to separate. We were intertwined, and it'd take a miracle to unsnarl us. Or, a herd of ravenous, angry goats.

Thank Heaven it was my day off. It'd been years since I stayed in bed all morning, and I couldn't think of a safer thing to do. It was time to initiate *Operation: Avoid Tango.*

I rolled over and slid my nightstand drawer open. My hand shook when I reached inside and felt for the framed picture. My eyes blurred, overflowing with pesky tears. I wiped them away with my sheet and studied the old photo.

In the glossy five-by-seven, I stood between Addy and her cousin, Dane. Addison's arm hung lazily around my neck. Auburn hair fell in chunky layers over her shoulders, framing her round, hazel eyes and perky button nose. My mom had taken the photo the morning before Senior Prom. Addy and I had spent the day getting "beautified," as she'd liked to call it. Not that she'd needed any help. That girl was a natural beauty, and she had learned how to work her sex appeal. There wasn't a guy in school who hadn't tried to get in her pants, or at least brag that they had, whether it was true or not.

I never thought it'd be possible to love someone with all your heart, and at the same time, hate them with your entire soul, but those were my feelings about her. Addy had betrayed me, on the most important night of my life. Bad as that memory was, it wasn't the worst of what our friendship had endured.

"You're not over me."

I knew the source of the deep, rich voice without having to look up. How pathetic was it that he hadn't even startled me?

"You haven't forgiven me."

I slunk deeper into the sheets, pulling them up to my chin. "What are you doing here?" I asked, embarrassed by the quiver in my tone. Did he come to tear my world to shreds? I couldn't blame him. I'd have done the same, had the tables been turned.

Tango stood at the foot of my bed, legs apart, massive arms folded across his chest. Navy running pants hung low on his waist and stretched around his legs, highlighting the dips and bulges of his matured, and remarkably virile thighs.

I was screwed. "I'm trying to sleep. Come back later if you want to chit-chat."

He huffed. "I'm not going anywhere."

"Fine. Stay if you want. Just be quiet. I haven't slept past five-thirty AM in five years. Don't you dare ruin this beautiful moment for me."

Tango responded by kicking off his shoes.

I rolled to my side and pulled the sheet over my head.

The mattress dipped behind me.

Why was he torturing me? Why didn't he just say what he came to say?

"You didn't lock your door."

I whipped the sheet off my body and rolled with a bounce to face him. "Oh my God. Enough already. Why are you here? You're killing me."

Tango lay on his back, hands clasped behind his head, legs stretched long and crossed at the ankles. The boy who had left six years ago with my heart and guts had returned a man. From head to toe he radiated power, sexual prowess, and control.

"The kid looks like me."

The axe was about to fall. I prayed he'd be merciful.

"The kid has a name," I said through gritted teeth. A name Tango knew well.

"Green eyes, dark hair." He laughed and shook his head. "Hell, he even has my throwing arm."

A thick lump swelled in my throat.

"Brett told me you'd gone away and returned with a son."

My hands trembled. I bunched them in the blankets on my lap.

"Did you give yourself to the first guy you could find who looked like me?"

What? My heart stopped beating.

"Was it a revenge fuck? Were you trying to get back at me? Kind of backfired, don't you think? The shit head couldn't even stick around and be a father to his child?"

Relief washed through me, along with a cleansing breath. "Tango. I … I—"

"Let me finish," he interrupted, and sat up, pulling my hand into his. "I need you to listen."

I nodded.

"I fucked up that night. I fucked up in the worst way. Shit. I can't even explain what happened. I drank too much. I was graduating with honors and a full ride. I was the fucking man." He huffed and shook his head. "I had been looking for you. You had said you needed to talk to me and you'd looked nervous. Addy showed up. She said you'd left, and she gave me the note. I was too shit-faced to read it. She read it for me. Addy said you were letting me go, that it hurt too much that I was leaving for college, leaving you behind. Said you didn't want to see me again. I couldn't believe what I was hearing. I looked everywhere for you. And then I saw you. On the back of Dane's bike. Your arms around him. Tore my fucking heart out. I was angry, and drunk, and—"

"Shut up, Tango. Shut the fuck up. I can't hear this right now." I wiped the moisture from my cheeks. Hearing Tango replay the events of that night sliced deep. I didn't want to talk about it.

He looked up with tear-soaked lashes. "I'm so goddamned sorry. So fucking sorry that I was weak, and cocky, and out of control. I just wanted the pain to go away. When I saw you standing there, with that look on your face—"

"No more," I screamed, yanking my hand free. "Are you trying to break me all over again?"

"No." He raised a palm to my face, dropping it when I jerked my head away.

His wide shoulders slumped in defeat. "What else can I say? What can I do to make it right?"

I stared at my hands, because the pain in his eyes was too much to bear. "There's nothing left to say."

Tango

There was so much I needed to say. So many words, six years' worth, each syllable superglued to the tip of my tongue.

"What do you want from me, Tango?" she asked, such delicate strength in her voice.

"Forgiveness," I whispered.

I wanted her, I left unsaid. I wanted Slade Mason to be mine again. I needed to wake up to her smile every morning. I'd missed my best friend. Missed her every godforsaken day I'd been gone.

"I already forgave you. You can go now." The cold snap to her reply sent a shiver through me. Not much could do that anymore.

"No, you haven't," I argued, leaning closer.

She turned her head and picked up the frame she'd been holding when I walked in. When I spied the subject, wicked anger, mixed with shame and a shit ton of regret, slithered through me. I snatched the photo away.

"What the hell?" She grabbed for the picture. I held it out of reach.

"Did you forgive *her*?" I asked, pointing at the image. "Did Addy get a second chance?" That name was acid on my tongue.

"That's none of your damned business." Slade rose to her knees, chin held high, and claimed the photo back.

"Why Rocky?" I asked, forcing my gaze, with great restraint, to stay above her shoulders.

"What?" Her eyes widened.

"Why did you name him Rocky?" Fuck. Saying the name out loud brought back an unwelcome flood of emotionally charged memories.

"Don't make me do this," she pleaded.

"Why Rocky? To spite me?" Growing up, Rocky had been her nickname for me. It was our secret. I'd always hated my name, the moniker given to me because my parents had fallen in love in Argentina, over a tango. I'd confided in Slade once that I'd wished I'd been given a badass name, like Rocky, after my favorite movie. She'd loved it. It stuck, and on numerous occasions, she had teased that our first child would be named Rocky, regardless of gender.

Slade plopped her butt next to me and placed a hand on my thigh, tempting the beast in ways she couldn't fathom. "God, no. Not to spite you. To remember you."

I was jealous of the tyke. I wanted to murder the man who fathered him. "How could you give another man's child our name?"

"That name was all I had left of us," she whispered, running a finger over the length of the plastic frame.

I had no right to be angry, or envious. If only someone could explain that to my wounded ego.

She turned her head my way. Her body trembled against mine. "You took everything from me when you disappeared." As she rose to stand, her voice rose, too. "I had nothing. You stole my future." She flung the frame across the room and screamed, "You ruined everything," before storming out of the room and leaving me to process her outburst.

Finally. We were getting somewhere.

I found her in the kitchen, fighting with a box of coffee filters. "You want me to forgive you?" she asked, stabbing the cardboard with a knife and prying it open.

"I *need* you to forgive me."

"Then you're going to listen. I'm only saying this once." Slade pointed the knife my way, then to the door. "When I'm finished, you need to go."

I dropped my ass into a chair, and rested my elbows on her well-worn kitchen table. Instinct screamed at me to go to her, to hold her, to dance the fight clean out of her, to beg, and scream, and cry until the past six years disappeared and there was nothing left but Tango and Slade.

"I can't even begin to describe how deeply you destroyed me that night. You left. No explanation. No apology. Did you even try to contact me?" she asked, pacing and waving the box in the air. "Never mind. I don't want to know. You were gone. Your parents wouldn't talk to me. I had no one. *No one.* I was lonely. I did things I'm not proud of. Things I thought I needed to do to feel better, to make sense of everything. We were supposed to be together forever. You were my rock, my best friend, my family, my future. Then you were gone. It was like waking up and being the only person alive on the planet."

"I'm sorry," was my pathetic response.

Slade slammed the coffee filters onto the counter and turned to face me. "*Sorry* doesn't mean shit anymore."

Fuck. I hated seeing her so undone. I hated being the cause of it. I rose from the chair and pulled her into a tight embrace. Words couldn't patch her wounds. Words, and not even good ones, were all I had.

"I'm sorry," I repeated, kissing the top of her head, "I'm sorry. I'm sorry. I'm sorry."

"Why didn't you reach out to me?" she asked, wiping her tears on my shirt and burying her face in my chest. "Why wouldn't your parents tell me where you were?"

A vicious anger brewed in me. "I knew nothing about that." My parents had told me they'd made efforts to talk to Slade, only to be rejected. Dad had some explaining to do.

"What now?" she whispered. "What if I can forgive you? You want to be friends? I can't do that. It hurts too much. Right now, you being here, it's making me physically ill. My stomach is a mess. I can't think straight." Slade tilted her face up to meet my eyes. "You're not my future anymore. Rocky is."

Her words ripped me to shreds. Didn't matter, though, because I knew, deeper and truer than I'd ever known anything, I was supposed to be her future. I was her future. I was her past. I was her right-fucking-now. Whether she could see it or not. She was, and always would be, my girl.

"Rocky is my life now," she muttered, unconvincing.

Again, shitty as it was, the little green monster reared his ugly head. "Where is the munchkin?"

"He's gone for two weeks with his—" Slade coughed. "He's at summer camp."

Summer camp? He was only five. Fuck. I hated that she was lying to me. "Where is his father?" I asked, biting back the anger.

"He's gone," she mumbled.

"Does he help? Does Rocky even know him?"

Slade pulled away and leaned against the counter. "No. And I'd like to keep it that way."

"That isn't right, Slade. Jesus." I paced the length of the kitchen, hands to hips, sucking in a few calming breaths. "What kind of man walks away from his kid?"

She seemed to study something on the floor. A smudged crayon drawing, maybe a dinosaur. "The kind that doesn't know he has a child."

My gut tightened like she'd hit me with a two-by-four. I couldn't believe what I was hearing. "You didn't tell him?"

"I couldn't tell him, and I won't talk about him. Not with you." Slade wouldn't look up.

She was hiding something.

I fucking hated secrets. If she was keeping things from me, it was out of fear, and damn if that didn't piss me off. Swear to Christ, if Rocky's father had hurt her, I'd hunt him down and kill him.

"Did he hurt you?" That thought alone made my hackles rise. Instinct took over and the urge to protect had me breaching her personal space.

We were too close. My body reacted the way any healthy man would, by sending a shitload of blood and desire straight to my cock. Shit, she was a sight. Messy, fuck-me hair, pink cotton boxers, a black clingy tank top with no bra.

Angry eyes pierced me when she said, "I'm done talking about it."

I stepped closer, taking a cleansing breath. Forcing my shit to cool. I could let the conversation lay for a while. What I couldn't do was leave without her knowing that she still owned me.

I leaned close and claimed her lips. Then I cupped her ass and lifted it to the counter. My girl was too light in my arms, but there was a roundness to her hips that hadn't been there before. I pushed my body between her legs and yanked her hard against me. Made sure she felt my arousal between her thighs.

Our tongues brushed, and she opened wider for me, softening in my arms. She slid her hands around my waist and under my shirt, scorching my skin everywhere her fingers traveled.

I kissed her deep and with no restraint. Apologizing. Reacquainting. Reclaiming. When I'd given everything to her mouth, I grazed on her neck, her shoulder, every delicate, soft patch of skin I could find. It wasn't enough. I needed all of her, everything, body and soul. Fuck, I needed *her*. I needed us. Together was where we belonged. Slade was my home.

Sliding her hands down to my waistband, then under, she danced and teased her fingers across the top of my ass. Holy shit, the rush of sensation made my head spin. I brushed my thumb across her breast, over the thin, stretchy fabric, groaning when a tight bud formed underneath.

She pulled away from my mouth and looked down, watching me stimulate first one taut nipple, then the other. With hitched breaths and parted lips, she let me play, and it didn't go unnoticed that her thighs had tightened around my hips.

Arching against me, she moaned and let her head fall back. Fucking hell, she was perfect.

I curled one hand around the back of her head, pulling her lips back to mine. I was ravenous. Insatiable. I pulled away, gasping for breath, stealing a moment of sanity. She braced her arms behind her and stared up at me, lids heavy with lust, chest heaving.

Blood pounded through my cock. Pressed tight against her warm core, I suffered an excruciating, beautiful hell.

Slade

I was in a hell of my own making, brutal, beautiful, and so wrong. What was I doing? Sex with Tango was not an option. I wanted him. More than I'd ever wanted anything in my life. He kissed like he was claiming me, marking his territory. His erection pressed hard and thick between my legs, prompting an ache in my gut and a fire in my cheeks. I couldn't breathe. I couldn't see through the desperate need eating me alive.

But I could not let him in. He would know. He would discover the one lie I could not talk my way out of. We had to stop. Tango needed to leave. I could never see him again.

With those impossibly perfect eyes, he gazed down at me. "I want you, Slade. I've never wanted anything more in my life."

"No." Despite my mental commands, my arms wouldn't move to push him away. "I can't do this."

Dropping his forehead to mine, he released a frustrated sigh before asking, "Can't? Or won't?"

"Tango. I can't—"

His lips brushed my cheek, sending sparks up and down my spine. "I've missed your soft skin, your scent, how you shiver every time I touch you."

I wanted him. Oh God. I needed him. I hadn't been touched for so long. My body sizzled and crackled with the overload of sensation, with the heady feeling of want, of being wanted. And, oh my, he wanted me. I could feel it, smell it, taste it, get drunk on the thrill of it.

"Your body is so attuned to mine. Do you feel that?" he asked, dragging the back of his knuckle down my cheek, my throat, and resting his hand over my bleeding heart. "Just say the word and I'm yours."

"No."

"Please. Let me in." He pulled my hips closer to the edge. Closer to him. When he lowered his head to my chest and dropped a kiss on the exposed skin, I started to cry.

"Fuck. You're perfect," he whispered, his lips traveling lower.

How many nights had I fantasized that scene? His mouth on me. Mine on him. Pleasuring. Loving. I'd always known he'd be tender and selfless in bed. That was who he was.

We couldn't go any further. If we did, I'd be helpless to stop, and I would destroy everything. I shuddered with emotion, frustration, regret. Tears fell freely down my face, and I raked a hand through his hair.

He moaned.

I pulled tight. "Stop."

Tango snaked his arms around my middle and pulled me closer. His mouth crashed to mine, his erection nestled snug and tight into the aching spot between my legs. I writhed against him, unashamed, unconcerned with the past, or the future, obsessed with the right now—the present that brought Tango and I together one last time before I had to let him go again.

It was shameful, really, how easily I melted into him, how desperate I was to cling to his warm body, knowing that the longer I held him, the more danger I was putting myself in. Oh God, I had to let go.

"You have to leave," I mumbled into his mouth, bracing my hands on his shoulders. "Please," I begged. "You have to walk away, because I can't seem to let go right now."

"I don't know if I can," he whispered, his arms tensing.

The pain in his voice cut me to the core.

I buried my face in his neck and cried through the onslaught of emotions. Cried for the years he'd stolen from me, cried for the loss of my best friend. Cried because I wanted him to stay forever. Cried because I loved him. I loved him so hard that every part of me ached.

There would never be another man for me.

We would never be together.

I wanted to tell him everything. But I could never confess, because when he'd disappeared, on the night I was supposed to give myself to him, he'd set in motion a series of events that made it impossible for me to ever be honest with him again.

Tango carried me, coiled around him, up my stairs, and back to bed. He held me tight until I fell asleep, emotionally drained.

"Addy." I brushed an oily chunk of hair away from her eyes. "Did they turn the water off again?"

My friend nodded.

We headed up the stairs and into my room.

"Can I use your shower?"

"Of course you can. Where is Walt?"

"He's with them." She shivered. "Took Dane to Montana, for some rally. Walt is stupid enough to think they want

him in the club." Addy pulled her shirt over her head and shimmied out of her jeans.

I could count her ribs. "When was the last time you ate?"

Naked as a jaybird, Addy headed down the hall toward my bathroom and shrugged. "Yesterday morning."

I followed behind and stood in the doorway. "You don't have to stay there anymore. Mom says you can live with us. We can share my room."

Addy laughed. "And have to watch you and Tango rubbing against each other all the time? No, thank you." She rolled her eyes, then turned to reach for the shower faucet. Fading bruises marred her pale skin.

I waited, holding in the cuss words that I wanted to scream on her behalf. When she disappeared behind the curtain, I snagged her dirty clothes and headed downstairs to throw them in the wash, but not before I heard her say, "I'm gonna snag me a rich boy-toy, like you. Then I'm getting out of this shit town."

Tango

Shit. This town. My town. I'd missed it so goddamned much. I listened to the group of kids, all squeals and giggles, spraying each other with a hose two houses over, and mourned the years I'd wasted by running from my fuck-ups.

A dog barked incessantly somewhere in the distance. Next door, Marion sat on a wobbly stool, brushing white paint on the fence that shared a property line with Slade. I'd only just finished the fresh baked blueberry scone she'd brought me earlier. *This is the life*, I thought to myself, unsure what to do with the contentment flowing through me.

I finished tightening the screw in the strike plate of Slade's front door when the loud revving of a motorcycle engine drew my attention to the street. I looked up just in time to see a large bike slow down in front of the house. Its driver, hidden behind dark glasses and a half helmet, nodded my way, then disappeared around the corner. At the same time, I heard footsteps padding down the stairs behind me.

My ticker kicked into high gear.

I turned to face my girl, hungry for a slow gander. The summer heat had already choked the cool morning air from the house, but the sight of Slade had me melting into the floorboards. Hair in a messy coil on top of her head. Blue eyes bright, despite the redness around them from her breakdown earlier. Long, lacy tank top. Jean shorts. Those damn legs. Bare. Long. Delicious. And of course, flip-flops.

"I thought you would've left by now," she said, crossing her arms and resting a hip on the shaky banister.

I pulled two screws out of my back pocket. "I did. Then I came back."

"What are you doing?" she asked, gaze bouncing from my face to my naked torso.

The girl was killing me with that damn blush. I flexed my abs, not enough to be obvious, but enough to rile her. The glow in her cheeks spread. Yeah. Too easy.

"I'm installing new locks." I hit her with a warning glare and pointed the screwdriver her way. "And you will use them. You have a child to worry about. There are dangerous people out there. You can't leave your doors unlocked anymore."

I waited for her to argue. Instead, with a smile, she said, "Thank you," and hopped off the last step.

Slade disappeared down the hall. I watched her retreat, willing my dick to behave, and forcing myself to stay put. By the time I'd finished my job and dropped the last screw back into Slade's tool drawer, a plate of eggs and toast waited for me on the kitchen table. I wasted no time digging in. Nothing better than a home-cooked meal. Especially when the chef was more edible than the food.

"Damn, girl. You've always made the best scrambled eggs." I wiped my mouth on a napkin and sat back in my chair, more at ease than I remembered feeling in years.

"Rocky loves them, too," she said, grabbing my plate. "That boy eats like a horse."

She wasn't exaggerating. I'd experienced his bottomless-pit firsthand on our beach day together. "He's a great kid. You've done a good job with him."

Slade's eyes liquefied. She turned to rinse the plates, and I watched, helpless, as she wiped her cheeks with the backs of her hands. "Thank you," she said, voice strained. "It's hard. I never know if I'm doing things right. I'm always second guessing myself, wondering if I'm doing more harm than good."

Goddamn. I sat, speechless, battling rage and pointless regret. Had I stayed, Slade and I would most likely be raising our own children together. Man and wife. Mother and father. A family. Like we were supposed to be.

Instead, I'd left her to fend for herself—a pure, white bunny dropped dead center into a wolf's den. Hardest part? She'd thrived.

Without me.

I wanted to be angry at her for moving on, despite the fact that I'd left her no choice. Anger had become as much a crutch as it had been a weapon. I couldn't bring that into Slade's home. So I sucked up my wounded ego and said, "For what it's worth. I'm proud of you."

No response. Couldn't blame her.

I offered to help with dishes. She turned me down. So I watched her move about, graceful and gorgeous, offering me little more than an occasional thoughtful glance.

"Can I ask you something?" she finally asked, crossing her arms, cocking her head to the side.

I straightened in my chair, eager for any interaction. "Anything."

"Are you okay? I mean, you haven't talked about your mom. I know how much it hurts to lose a parent. My mom's death was an accident, but your mom..." Slade winced, then shook her head in apparent disbelief. "No way that isn't twisting you up inside."

As much as I loved hearing the genuine concern in her voice, I wasn't ready to discuss my mother's death with anyone. "Sure. I'm okay."

Slade quirked her brow, letting me know she wasn't falling for my shit.

Yeah. That was my cue to leave. "Listen. I should head out. I need to spend some time with Pops." I retrieved two keys from my pocket and set them on the kitchen table before getting up. "Use these. Promise me."

She nodded. "I promise."

"I have to go," I said, forcing my legs to move.

"Okay," she mumbled, turning around to busy herself at the sink, as if my leaving meant nothing. *I had to mean something.*

I stared, disbelieving for a moment, before making my exit.

Turn around, babylove. Turn around.

She didn't. I left. Wounded ego? Fuck that shit. Mine had just been decimated.

CHAPTER 4

Tango

DAD STOOD, IN ALL HIS REGAL GLORY, staring out the window of his home office, no doubt admiring the view. He hadn't heard me come in.

Phone to his ear, he said, "That property is not for sale. Even if it were, Styles, I wouldn't sell to your client. Sorry. No. Keeping my hands clean on this one." Dad released a loud sigh and ran a hand over the top of his head. "They are not an organization I want to be tied to."

He must have caught my reflection in the window. He whipped around and gestured for me to sit. "Styles. That's low, even for you. A negotiator? No. There's nothing to negotiate. Is that a threat? This conversation is over."

Dad ended the call. Rolled his shoulders. Pinched the bridge of his nose.

"Styles still ruffling your feathers?" I asked, admiring his physique. Had to admit ... the man looked damn good for his age. Lean. Fit. Few wrinkles, but not enough to give away his age.

"Fucker keeps pushing me to sell our mountain acreage. Thinks he can twist my arm."

"You haven't been up there in years. Why not sell?"

"Styles sounded desperate." He blew a long breath, cheeks puffed, and combed fingers through his hair. "His clients are shady, at best. I'm not lying in bed with criminals."

My stomach twisted at the mention of *criminals*. "Who are they?"

"Doesn't matter." Dad shook his head. "How ya holding up, son? Ready to discuss my offer?"

The Rossi Corporation. Built from the ground up by my father. Real estate, hospitality, media, publishing, advertising, restaurants, golf. Carlos Rossi had carved himself a mini-empire in our little corner of the Pacific Northwest. It would be mine someday. Dad was eager for me to take some of the weight off his shoulders.

"You and I have some shit to hash before we talk business." I made myself comfortable on the leather wingback next to his bookshelf.

"Sure, T. What's up?" Dad asked, tucking into the chair behind his desk.

"It's about Slade," I said, ice filling my veins.

His face paled. "You've seen her?"

"Did you think I wouldn't?"

Dad cleared his throat, straightened his back, and poured himself a shot of Johnnie Walker Blue.

"Why did you lie? Why'd you keep me from contacting her?"

He didn't hesitate. "She was no good for you, son."

"That was never your choice to make."

"Sure it was. Your mother and I weren't going to sit back and watch our only child throw his life away over some white trash waitress."

I could feel my monster clawing to make an appearance. "Pops. Don't talk about her like that."

Dad studied my face briefly before dropping his gaze to his drink. "You had a future. She didn't."

"Did you know she had a scholarship, too? That girl worked her ass off in school. Earned a free ride through smarts and sheer determination, not because she could throw a football."

Without a lick of regard, he replied, "Look where that got her. Single mom. Working at the same diner as her whore of a mother. Leaving her was the best move you ever made. Your mother and I tolerated your friendship, because we knew it was a passing fancy. People grow up, T, become a product of their environment. There was no hope for her, but you—"

I needed to hit something. Or better yet, someone. "Slade owns that damn restaurant and the land it sits on. Kept it running for her mother, doesn't owe a dime on the mortgage. It's hers, and she's managed to deflect your attacks and attempts at getting your greedy fingers on her property. Pretty damn successful for a twenty-four-year-old single mom. That white trash girl of mine has more gumption, more class, than everyone in this fucked-up family put together."

Dad slammed his glass down and pushed to his feet. "Watch your tongue, Tango."

I rose to full height, bringing me a head taller than my father. "I'm not a boy anymore, and I'm not your punching bag. We're not gonna duke it out like we used to."

My parents had been old-school disciplinarians. Spare the rod, spoil the child. When I was old enough, rather than bend me over his knee, Dad would strap a pair of boxing gloves on my small hands. It had always ended with me getting a stern lecture before he'd knock me on my ass, but along the way, I'd learned to love boxing. It wasn't until my late teens that I realized it was Dad's way of bonding with his only son.

"I love you, Dad, but I'm only going to say this once. I loved Slade with everything I had in me. You will never speak ill of her again. If you see her on the street, you'll damn well show her the respect she deserves."

"Or what?" he asked, face turning a menacing shade of red. "You threatening me now?"

"That's exactly what I'm doing. You, better than anyone, know what I'm capable of."

Dad's glass hit the wall across the room and shattered. He slumped back into his chair, elbows to his desk, head resting in his palms. "What happened to you?"

"I'm a product of my environment, like you said." I stalked closer, pressed my palms on the smooth wood, and leaned toward him. "I fucked up six years ago, in too many ways to count. Been fucking up ever since. It's time for me to make it right."

"Make what right? You've got a promising career ahead of you. That's what you should focus on. Not your childhood sweetheart, who, as you just pointed out, has been getting along fine without you."

"I cheated on her." I had never told my parents why I'd left so abruptly. They had been so thrilled that I'd chosen New York over Texas they hadn't given my last minute change of heart much consideration.

Dad loosened his tie, shuffled papers, then blinked up at me.

"That's why I left. And that, Pops, is why I didn't come back. Like father, like fucking son. You must be proud."

A soft knock broke the thick tension.

"Yeah!" Dad shouted.

The door opened, and Kaylee walked through wearing a short little number that showed entirely too much skin. Her eyes widened at the sight of me. "Oh, Tango. I'm sorry to interrupt." She glanced at Dad. "Mr. Rossi, I brought the swatches you requested."

Dad pushed back to his feet, cleared his throat, and straightened the hem of his shirt. If I wasn't mistaken, he was nervous. "Enough with the misters, okay Kaylee? Just Carlos."

"Sure," she said, studying her feet.

Dad cleared his throat again, and loosened his tie. "Tango, can we continue this conversation later?"

"Yeah." I looked at my father, who hadn't taken his eyes off Kaylee. "Sure, Popo. Later." I stormed out and headed for my bedroom.

Kaylee caught my arm before I made it to the stairs. "I, um ... I want to apologize for the other day. You know, at The Stop."

"Slade is the one you owe an apology to," I said without hesitation.

She crinkled her nose. A new nose, if I wasn't mistaken. "Are you two a thing again?"

Protective fury churned through me. I grabbed her shoulders and squeezed hard enough to make my point. "Slade and I will always be a thing. You'll be wise to remember that. You fuck with her, you're fucking with me. I put up with your shit in high school because I had to, for Mom. I'm not that guy anymore."

My intention was to scare her. Sure, it was a shitty move. Problem was, it only seemed to turn her on.

"Who are you now?" she stared at my mouth and sucked her bottom lip between her teeth.

This girl had tried to wedge herself between Slade and me for as long as I could remember. Apparently, she had no intention of relenting. A habit she'd learned from my mother, no doubt.

Without offering a response, I dropped my hands, took the stairs two by two, and kicked the bedroom door shut behind me. I fell back on my bed and stared at the vaulted ceiling. Hard as I tried to wrestle away thoughts of Mom, memories bombarded me.

Tango. I know it hurts. It's just a bruise. Get up. You don't quit. You never quit.

What do you mean they didn't put you on Varsity? No, you aren't quitting football. You get back in that gym, and you train harder. Rossis are not quitters.

You don't stop until you're irreplaceable.

Rossis don't quit.

Mom had quit.

I hated her for it.

Truth was, Mom and I had been estranged from the moment I'd told her I would choose Slade over my family if they forced my hand. That was the same day I had threatened to stop dancing. It was also the day I had decided to buy Slade a ring and make her mine forever. I still didn't know what had upset Mom more, hearing I might never perform for her again, or realizing I loved Slade more than anything or anyone.

I would never know.

I was okay with that.

Slade

"Are you okay?" Maurice asked.

I studied the weathered hand resting atop mine. Blue veins pulsed beneath graying, wrinkled skin. I detected a tremble, but it didn't stop those spindly fingers from holding me tight. "Please. Sit for a minute."

I sighed and looked around the dining room. The Truck Stop was at capacity, but my waitresses, Margie and Kim, had everything under control. They always did. I had the best employees. So good, in fact, I never had to work the floor if I didn't want to.

Maurice winked at me and gestured to the seat. "Do an old man a favor, will ya?"

How could I say no to him? "Okay, but only if you buy me a cup of coffee," I said, dropping my butt into the chair opposite his.

It wasn't the first time Maurice had invited me to join him. I enjoyed our visits. The man was our oldest and most loyal patron. I was pretty sure he'd been coming to The Stop long before my mother had bought the place.

"How are you today?" I asked. He looked chipper for a man nearing eighty.

"I couldn't be better. The sun is shining, my ticker still works, and I'm enjoying a cup of coffee with the most beautiful girl in town."

"You're too sweet." I tilted my head and batted my lashes. It always made him laugh when I did that.

His grin faded too quickly. "You seem different today. Your eyes are sad. You haven't had sad eyes for a very long time."

"What do you mean, Maurice?"

"I've known you longer than anyone in town. Watched you grow up. Watched you take care of your mother." His eyes glazed and puddled. "I was there when a certain boy broke you, and I watched you fake a smile every day for a very long time. It was only after Rocky came along that your joy seemed genuine again."

My tongue failed when I tried to respond. He was right. I'd been a walking corpse for months after Tango had left.

Rocky had given me a reason to go on. He'd become my sole focus, and it was impossible to be sad around that beautiful boy.

My eyes burned with the threat of tears. Memory lane was a bitter bitch, and I'd walked its beaten path too many times since Tango's mother had died.

Maurice rested his forearms on the table and leaned closer, lowering his voice. "Secrets are a terrible thing. They'll rot you from the inside, and by the time they work their way out, the damage that's been done is irreparable." His voice quivered and broke. He squeezed his eyes shut.

I fought off a terrible shiver. What was he trying to say? I'd never seen him so somber. I reached over the table and squeezed his hand.

"I lived without the love of my life for fifty years, because I wasn't man enough to tell the truth. I was weak. That lie cost me a family. I thought I was protecting them, but they suffered, and now, I'm an old man, bent and deformed under the weight of too much regret."

"What about Elizabeth?" I asked, half afraid of the answer. Maurice's wife had died a few years ago. He had never brought her to the diner, despite the fact that they lived a short distance away, sharing a property line with The Stop. I could see his house from the west window, a large Tudor-style home overlooking the lake from atop a hill. He talked about his wife every day—his sons and grandchildren, too. They'd been married for as long as I'd known him. I'd always believed she was the love of his life.

"My dear Beth was an angel, and I couldn't have asked for a better companion." He pulled his hand from mine and covered his face. His shoulders bobbed, and he drew two deep breaths.

When he looked at me again, the pain he wore cut my heart wide open.

"You can love more than one person in your lifetime. Very few of us are lucky enough to experience soul-changing, undeniably fated love. I had it and walked away from it. You had it, and it slipped through your fingers. If ever any two people were meant to be together, it's you and that Rossi boy. I've sat in this very same booth, every morning, watching your story unfold. I know you love him, I know what you did for him, and I know you think he won't be able to live with the truth."

I couldn't believe what Maurice was saying. He couldn't possibly know what I did for Tango. My body flushed with heat. "What do you mean, you know what I did for him?"

"I pay attention," he whispered, and the hard set of his face, the knowing in his light blue eyes, assured me he was not bluffing.

A high-pitched scream, followed by laughter, drew my focus outside. A group of kids were unloading their car, no doubt headed down the trail toward the swimming area. I owned the property directly above the water's edge, but not the beach itself. However, the Truck Stop parking lot was the only way to access the foot-worn trail that led down the short cliff to the secluded swimming hole. I didn't mind that people used my lot. It brought a steady trail of summertime customers.

A man stood next to the kid's car, cigarette in hand, leaning against one of the guard rails. His dark T-shirt and black leather vest revealed skinny, tatted arms. He hid behind dark glasses and a baseball cap pulled low over his eyes. My stomach soured.

The man flicked the cigarette butt as if he were aiming for me and turned to get on his motorcycle. My heart exploded in my chest. The back of his vest read Satan's Slayers.

Suddenly I was falling through a dark tunnel, shadow and light passing by in a nauseating whirl. From somewhere far away, I heard laughter. Addison's crazed cackle. Then Rocky. Then horrible cries, begging for mercy.

Kill me. Please. Make it go away. It hurts so bad. Make it stop. If you love me, you'll make it stop.

Slade

"Stop. Stop pushing. I got her. What happened?" someone shouted above me.

An arm curved around my shoulders, another under my knees. I tried opening my eyes, but my face was smashed against soft cotton.

Charlie's voice sounded far away. "Bring her in here, T."

I jerked my head up and bumped into a hard chin.

"Ouch, shit," Tango grunted.

"Hey, she's awake." Charlie patted my shoulder.

Tango lowered himself onto the worn couch that decorated my office and held me tight in his lap, stroking my arm. "You scared the shit out of me," he whispered, his lips grazing the top of my head.

I put my hand on his chest with the intention of pushing myself away, but he was hard and electric beneath my fingertips, and I lingered a moment before deciding to stay put.

A warm hand covered my cheek. "You okay?"

I glanced from Charlie to Tango. They wore the same worried frowns. "I'm fine. What happened?"

"I got her, Charlie. Can you give us a minute?"

Charlie waited for my approval. I smiled, nodding, and he slipped through the door, closing it behind him.

"What the hell is going on with you? You're keeping something from me. I can see it's scaring you. Now you're fainting at work."

I couldn't have read that man's vest right. The Satan's Slayers never came near our town. And Dane had promised. Promised they would never come back. I was just tired, and stressed. My head screamed at me to get up and get my ass far away from Tango. My body, my heart, wanted to curl into the man holding me, crawl inside him, let him carry me forever.

"You were mumbling Addison's name," he said, his voice deep and pained.

"I was?"

"Yeah. Just before you came to."

Shit. "What are you doing here?"

"I came to see you. Walked in as you went down."

God, he smelled good. "I have to get back to work."

"You're not going anywhere. Not until you tell me what's going on."

"I didn't eat this morning. My blood sugar must be low, that's all."

"I don't believe you. Try again."

I reached up and cupped his clean-shaven jaw. "Okay. Okay. We've established that I can't lie to you. So here's what we'll do. There are things I am not going to tell you. You can pry until you're blue in the face. I won't bother trying to lie. It's exhausting, and really, why do I have to answer any of your questions? You're not my father. You're not the police. I don't owe you anything. You don't get to know my business. From now on, when you feel the urge to get personal and in my face, I'll give you this signal." I flipped him the bird. "That'll be your reminder that it's none of your damned business. How about that?"

"You're a feisty little shit." He captured my wrist and pulled my offensive finger into his mouth, sliding his silky tongue to my knuckles then back to the tip.

Thank goodness nobody could see my toes through my shoes, because they were doing serious yoga moves.

We shared a long, challenging stare-down, and he sucked hard before releasing my digit with a pop. "I missed you so goddamned much," he groaned, before bending down and smothering my mouth with his own.

I was caged in a tight embrace, my arms pinned between us. I didn't fight to free myself. Kissing him was wrong; deep down I knew there'd be consequences. There were always repercussions. But Tango was here, holding, kissing, wanting me. So I let him, and I returned the favor, softening for him, fisting his shirt, pulling him deeper into my mouth. I kicked guilt aside, dropped my walls of self-preservation, and allowed myself to indulge, to feel, to take what I needed—and oh God, did I need to get lost in the powerhouse that was Tango Rossi.

My insides warmed and opened to him, like a flower blooming for the first time. He was the sun, calling me to life, awakening a part of me that had lain dormant for far too long. Although I knew it was wrong, I savored every breath, every stroke of the tongue, every moan, and I let him breathe new life into me.

His cocked swelled, pressing into my hip. I shifted to straddle his thighs, settling my core against his erection. Tango moaned into my mouth. Oh, how easy it would've been to take him. To be a woman—not a boss, or a mom, but a soft, vulnerable, horny female. Take back what was stolen from me.

What Tango had stolen from me.

Oh, dear God, what was I doing?

I flattened my palms against his chest and pushed, breaking the kiss. Through thick, black lashes, his eyes blazed with desire.

Tango drew a sharp breath and gripped my hips, holding me still. "Slade. Christ. I didn't mean for that to happen again."

I don't know why, but it made me smile, knowing I'd unnerved him.

He pushed my hips, moving me away from his arousal, but he didn't let go of me. "I'm sorry. I shouldn't have kissed you." His fingers tightened, curling painfully into the soft flesh of my backside. "I'm sorry about everything. For letting you go, for hurting you." He squeezed his eyes shut and dropped his forehead to my chest. "I'm a fucking idiot for not fighting for you, and I'll have to live with that regret for the rest of my life." He sighed, long and deep, trembling against me.

I cupped his face, pulling his head up to look at me. The Tango I remembered wasn't there. A man, broken and lost, met my gaze.

"I'm not sorry that you kissed me," slipped out of my mouth before reason could stop such nonsense.

"I need more time with you. I can't leave yet. I don't know why. I just need more time. Need more you." He slid his hands up my back and tangled his fingers in the hair at the base of my skull. "A few more days, then I'll leave you alone ... or not. Whatever you want."

What did I want? I wanted Tango Rossi to have never broken my heart. I wanted to not have been forced to make impossible decisions. I wanted Tango.

It was selfish and dangerous to want him, to even consider another day, or week. Every moment I spent with him, every passing tick and tock of the clock, brought me closer to losing everyone else I loved.

I put my finger over his wet lips to make him stop talking. "You have to go. You know we can never go back to what we were."

The longer he stayed in town, the weaker my defenses. The pull between us was too strong, too intense. I didn't know how long I could bear the strain of pushing him away. It wasn't a matter of *if* I'd give in, but a question of *when* I'd crack.

CHAPTER 5

I COUNTED CRACKS in the ceiling for the umpteenth time. Slade's house needed a major facelift. It hadn't been painted since ... well, shit, it was the same color as when I'd met her in first grade. I was convinced only divine intervention held together the bones of the neglected structure. Despite its haggard appearance, the tired Victorian was more a home than mine had ever been.

My phone buzzed with an incoming text—Aida Voltolini. *Where r u? Have a situation.*

I hadn't said goodbye to Aida. My intestines knotted. Not the reaction one should get from his ex-fuck buddy. I hadn't touched her in months, but mine was still the number she dialed when she was lonely, or whenever she wormed herself into a jam. Christ, I needed to leave that world behind.

I shot back a short but sweet:

Out of town. Sorry, princess, gonna have to get yourself outta this one.

Tito and I worked for Aida's father, a childhood friend of Dad's, who'd been all too eager to nudge his daughter my way. Luciano Voltolini was not a man you said no to. He suggested you took his daughter on a date, you obliged. Lucky me, the girl gave good head. What red-blooded, single male wouldn't take advantage of that? Did it make me a dick? I didn't give a shit. Keep the boss's daughter happy, keep your head attached to your shoulders. It was a matter of survival. That was how things worked with the Voltolini family.

"What are you doing?" Slade's voice bounced off the walls of her bedroom. "How'd you get in? I locked the damn door."

Sweet mother of mercy, what a sight. Hair pulled back, loose strands framing her delicate face. Her work T-shirt pulled tight across a pair of fabulous breasts. Blood filled my cock.

"I'm counting the cracks in your ceiling. There are twenty-seven. It's a miracle the damn thing hasn't caved in yet."

Her glare sliced to the longest crevice, then back to me. She shifted her weight onto one leg and folded her arms. "Yeah? Well, raising a child and running a business tends to suck up your free time *and* your disposable income."

I curled my fingers into tight fists and bit my tongue to stifle the expletives trying to escape. My girl shouldn't be a single mother, and sure as hell shouldn't have to work so goddamned hard to make ends meet. I was supposed to take care of her.

"How's Rocky?" I asked, testing the waters, hoping she'd come clean.

Slade dropped her worn handbag to the floor and stomped to her closet. As if I wasn't there, she pulled her shirt over her head and tossed it into the small laundry basket by the door. Her jeans followed suit. She had never been modest around me, and my dick was happy that hadn't changed.

"He's..." She shook her head. "He's having so much fun." Her voice trembled. When she turned to face me, her tits bounced in her thin, cotton bra, and tears splashed the beautiful exposed skin.

"Shit." I jumped from the bed and pulled her against me, squeezing tight so she couldn't pull away. Slade didn't cry often. Well, not before I'd left anyway. When it had happened, I'd always known there was something genuine backing her tears. "What is it?"

"It's the first time I've been away from him. I miss my baby," she mumbled into my shirt. "I didn't know it would hurt this bad."

I held her steady, nose in her hair, while she pulled herself together. She smelled like cooking grease and bleach. Fuck me, but I'd take that over expensive perfume any day.

Slade lifted her head. Despite the black shit smeared under her eyes and her red, drippy nose, she was the most soul-gutting, beautiful creature I'd ever laid eyes on.

"Thank you," she whispered. "Sorry about that."

"Never be sorry for needing a shoulder, especially when it's mine." Dear God, I wanted it to be mine. Forever. I needed her to need me, more than I required oxygen.

"Seriously, how'd you get in?" she asked, pushing away from me and wiping under her eyes.

I had snagged my own set of keys—a detail I'd failed to mention after I'd installed her new locks. A fact I decided to keep to myself a while longer. "I'm not saying I snuck through the window, but that's always been a fantasy of mine."

Her lips quirked on one side. Amusement, or maybe annoyance, flashed in her eyes before she turned and headed down the hall. "I guess I'll have to put locks on the windows now, too."

Yeah, like that would stop me.

"I'm taking a shower," she yelled. "There isn't a lock on the bathroom door, but if you come in, I'll cut you with my razor."

I'd no intention of following her, but shit, was it tempting. I'd crossed a line by kissing her, numerous times now, and I didn't want to push too hard.

The photo of Slade, Addy, and Dane lay picture side down on her bedside table. I picked it up and studied the subjects. Well, one subject in particular: Dane Reynolds. Addison's cousin. Scary as fuck. Body piercings. Tats. Dropout. In and out of juvie. Hated his father. He seemed to be the only person, aside from Slade, who gave two shits about Addy. Far as I could tell, he was the only other guy besides me who didn't fall for her bullshit.

He'd had a thing for Slade back then. Everyone did. Only reason he didn't go after her was because I'd warned him off. Well, me backed by the Whisper Springs High football team. He had seemed to respect that I had her back and had assured me his only concern was protecting Addy from his father's piss poor choices and dangerous as fuck associates.

I looked closer at the photo. Green eyes. Dark hair.

Mother. Fuck.

There was a resemblance.

It couldn't be. If Dane were Rocky's father, Slade would have no reason to keep that fact from me.

I needed to discover what Slade was hiding. I couldn't move on until I knew she was safe. I had turned her house upside down earlier, looking for anything that could clue me in to her troubles. Found nothing of significance except for Rocky's birth certificate. No father listed, but he was born in Montana, which made no sense to me. Why Montana?

I'd also found boxes buried in her basement, jam-packed with everything having anything to do with me. Photos, mementos, every gift I'd ever given her, every note passed at school, every poem or stupid joke I'd written, every article of clothing she'd "borrowed," including my football jersey, all buried in a dark corner of her musty basement.

I headed downstairs and into the kitchen, stopping at the fridge. I studied the photo pinned to the door with a magnet. Rocky stood proud, holding a trout. A large, blond man squatted next to him, smiling wide, arm around the little boy.

Couldn't be Rocky's father. The two looked nothing alike. Still, the fact that he'd spent time with her son, and that the photo claimed center spot on her refrigerator, meant the man was significant somehow, and fuck if that didn't amplify the annoying boom, boom, boom in my chest.

Slade

I felt the boom, boom, boom underneath my feet before I could discern the source. When I shut off the water, Salsa music blared through the house and the smoky scent of bacon wafted up the stairs.

I should've thrown him out when I'd found him lounging on my bed. Scratch that. When I found the Rover parked in my driveway, I should have run the opposite direction.

Truth was, just like when we were kids, finding him in my room had filled me with a sense of comfort. Hell, he'd spent more time in my home than his own back then.

On a normal day, I would've pulled my hair into a bun, climbed into my pajamas, and called it good. Having a sexy man cooking in my kitchen made me feel extra girly. So I fluffed my waves, put on some mascara, and dug my Kimchi Blue baby doll dress out of the closet. It was cool, and comfy, and I didn't have to wear a bra, because it was just tight enough across my chest to offer support. Bonus. Because who wanted to wear a bra on a hot summer afternoon after working ten hours?

Although it wasn't necessary, due to the wall-thumping volume of the music, I tiptoed down the stairs and into the kitchen. A shirtless Tango stood at the stove, whisking something, and shaking his rock-hard ass to the music. Dear Lord, the way the muscles in his back rolled, the way his jeans hung low on his waist, it was like he was meticulously designed to inspire procreation.

The man could dance, that was for damn sure. Marta had taught him well. Except the way he moved seemed less like dancing and more like he was making love to the stove. Seriously, I was jealous of my oven.

The bodice of my dress tightened around my boobs. Not good. Not good at all, but I couldn't turn away. Tango had been mine once. I was no stranger to his outrageous physique. I fantasized about his body on a regular basis. When he had been mine, I had been able to touch. Now I could only watch, and hope he didn't turn around for a long time, because my eyes were greedy bitches and they could ogle him for days and days.

When he turned to grab two plates from the counter, he froze, and a wicked smile spread across his face, highlighting his dimples. Then he reached for the remote and turned down the music. "Sweet Jesus." He whistled, his gaze traveling from my chest to my feet and back up. "Are you trying to kill me with that dress?"

Darn, I needed an icepack for my cheeks. I shrugged my shoulders.

Tango set the plates back down and stood toe to toe with me, snaking his right arm around my waist and scooping my right hand into his left. "Have you danced today?"

Dear God, those words. His voice. His heat. How could they hold such power? Whatever scent he wore—wasn't sure if it was deodorant or cologne—blended perfectly with the smoky tang of bacon, cocooning me in homey, masculine comfort. He guided me around the kitchen, stealing my breath, resurrecting buried memories. We had to stop. I couldn't get sucked into the whirlwind that was Tango. I couldn't afford to lose myself in him.

I pulled away and made myself comfortable at the table. And I swear, with everything I had in me, I tried to keep my eyes off the half-naked man as he prepared a meal for me. No one had cooked for me, not since Mom had passed. I decided to enjoy the hell out of both his culinary skills and his bare torso. Then I would get rid of him.

"Smells good. What're you making?" Duh. The heavy aroma of bacon and the bowl of eggshells sitting next to the sink made that a dumb question.

"Being as you don't have a lick of food in your cupboards, I settled for the old standby. I'm going to feed you, because you're too damned skinny. After that, we're going out."

No. Hell no. I was supposed to avoid the man, not hang out with him. "I can't Tango. I have to get up early tomorrow." My stomach growled. "And who the hell are you to tell me I'm too skinny?"

His cheeks reddened, and his eyes narrowed. He turned back to the stove and dumped scrambled eggs on each plate.

Damn, that pork fat smelled good. "We'll eat, then you are cordially invited to leave."

He chuckled and set a plate of crispy heaven in the center of the table. I wasted no time digging in. I was starving.

"You expect me to believe you put that dress on just so you can kick me out?"

Busted. "This old thing?" I teased, and promptly filled my mouth with food so as not to say something I might regret, like, *Damn right, I want to drive you mad with lust so I can kick you out and make you suffer the world's worst case of blue-balls.*

Tango settled himself in his chair and eyed me warily, forking a heap of bacon over his own scrambled eggs. The more I ate, the more his shoulders seemed to relax.

"You know what?" he blurted, breaking the silence.

"What?" I raked my gaze from his chest to his eyes. Why couldn't he put on a shirt? It'd make digesting my food much easier. Where was his shirt, anyway? "What?" I repeated, because he was smirking, apparently pleased by my blatant gawking.

"I'm not leaving until I break you." He pointed his fork my way and wiggled his brows.

I choked and coughed, spewing food across the table. *Could someone shoot me now, please?* Fear and fury swirled through me, two tornadoes wreaking havoc on my insides. "Break me? What exactly do you mean by that?"

Tango flicked a chunk of chewed meat off his chest. "Yes, Slade. I'm cracking your shell. Not leaving until I know what's eating you, and before you get self-righteous and tell me it's none of my business, you need to know, I don't give a fuck. Despite what went down between us, you're my girl. That alone makes whatever you're going through my concern. I'll be damned if I'm going to sit back and watch you suffer because you're too damned proud to ask for help."

Oh, fuckety-fuck-fuck. I'd forgotten how protective he was. My plan to push him away exploded in my face. I'd have to change my line of defense.

We needed to be somewhere public. Public and full of distractions. So I wasn't tempted to jump his bones, and those unreal muscles. "Your cooking sucks," I said, pushing from the table and grabbing my plate. "You wanna help? Take me for a burger. Where's your shirt?" I dropped my plate in the sink, and he followed right behind.

"In your washer. You know, on account of the snot and tear stains." He laughed and smacked me on the ass before heading for the laundry room.

CHAPTER 6

Tango

I NEVER WANTED TO BE A FRENCH FRY so bad in my life. Lost in thought, or some kinky food fantasy, Slade rubbed a potato stick across her bottom lip, her glossy eyes aimed somewhere over my shoulder.

"You gonna eat that?" I teased. "Or is that a new lip gloss trend?"

"Hmmm?" She continued with the slow rub across her mouth.

Dear God, I wanted to jump across the table and lick the grease off her fingers. I'd chosen a booth in the darkest corner of the bar, for privacy, and because I was selfish and didn't want to share her with anyone. Damn dress made it difficult to remember what I'd wanted to discuss. The floral print fabric squished her tits into two perfect, succulent mounds. It well and truly sucked that someone else had tasted those glorious breasts. That thought alone filled me with murderous rage.

"Slade." I flicked a chunk of ice at her chest, hitting her cleavage dead-center.

She jumped and dropped the fry on her plate. "Sorry. What?"

"Where were you just now?"

"Oh. Um." She dabbed her breasts with a napkin, unconsciously sliding her foot against mine under the table. "Do you remember the first time your mom caught us making out?"

"We were hiding in the utility closet." I'd never seen Mom look so disgusted with me. "She told Dad to take you home, but you said, *No, thank you. I've got my own ride,* and then you stole my bike."

"Borrowed," she corrected. "Yeah. How old were we? Eleven? Twelve?"

"Twelve." I remembered that day well. I'd jerked off in my room three times that afternoon. A new record.

Her eyes danced. "When I got home, Mom was laughing hysterically. She said Marta had called and told her to keep her whore of a daughter away from her son."

I cringed. Slade had never shared that story with me.

"My mom hugged me and said, '*He's a keeper, sweetie. Even I can see that. You hold on tight to Tango. Marta Rossi can kiss our white-trash asses.*'"

"Your mom said that?"

Slade nodded and gestured to the waitress for another beer. "Do you want to know why we never locked our front door?"

I nodded and sat back in my chair. I'd always assumed they'd left the door open because her mother was too inebriated to care. Or, that she'd left it open so her nightly visitors didn't have to ring the doorbell and wake Slade.

"She left it open for you. She knew we couldn't stay away from each other and didn't want you hurting yourself by climbing through the window. That's why she left the door unlocked."

"No shit," I mumbled. A dull ache rolled through my stomach and rose to my chest.

"Part of me always thought you'd come back. Hoped, maybe, that you'd sneak back into my room in the middle of the night and make everything okay. I never got into the habit of locking it." She shook her head and fiddled with a napkin. "It's stupid, I know. We could've just given you a key."

She may as well have stabbed me with a jagged knife. After I'd ripped her heart out, in a drunken, self-pity fueled tantrum, then disappeared, she'd still wanted me to come home to her. Fucking hell.

"It doesn't matter anymore. Maybe it's a good thing. I mean, not the way it happened, but the fact that you left. I relied on you too much. You were my everything. You would've taken care of me, and I would've let you. I would've always been *your girl* and would've never known who I could be on my own."

The waitress brought our beers, and I drew a long drink, waiting for her to clear earshot before calling bullshit. "That's a fucking lie and you know it. I *tried* to look after you. You took care of yourself, your mom, that piece of shit house you live in. You even took care of me. If anything, you made me want to work harder." I shook my head and took a cleansing breath. "Do you have any idea how hard it was to keep up with you? To be worthy?"

"Worthy?" She leaned forward, pressing her chest against the table. "Are you kidding me? You were king of the high school. The town's golden boy. Football star, valedictorian, mister popularity, Carlos Rossi's son. Nobody understood why you wasted your time with me."

That pissed me off. I clenched my fists under the table so as not to break my glass. "You understood why, and that's the only thing that matters. Everyone else can go to hell."

She glared at me for a long, uncomfortable spell. "Seems they were right all along."

"Don't say shit like that. We loved—"

"We were young," she interrupted.

"We were lucky," I countered, then shook my head. "Not lucky. Blessed. We were fucking babies, and we knew. We knew we were it for each other." I stopped there, because arguing was pointless, and I was only making myself angry. I'd fucked everything up. Nobody but me. Being home, facing my demons, only confirmed how desperately I needed to win her back.

Slade turned her head and chewed her bottom lip. Her eyes fixed on something behind the bar. I averted my gaze, too. The longer I stared at the blonde beauty, the more savage my hunger grew.

"I'll be right back," Slade interrupted my downward spiral of thoughts. "Need to use the ladies' room."

She got up, and I watched her sway, with her natural sexy glide, toward the restroom. I wasn't the only one appreciating her, either. She didn't seem to notice any of the lewd comments directed at her as she passed between tables of drunk assholes.

I heard buzzing and looked down. Her cell phone sat next to her plate, lit up with a picture of the large blond douche holding Rocky upside down by his ankles. Seeing a picture of another man on her phone made my blood boil. The fact that he was holding her son downright pissed me off. Naturally, I did what any responsible dickhead who needed to size up the competition would do, and violated her privacy. I pressed the answer button but didn't say a word.

"Mom?" Rocky's raspy voice cut straight to my heart. Hadn't expected him to be on the other end of the call.

I cleared my throat. "Hey, Rocky."

"Uncle Tuck. Uncle Tuck. You dialed the wrong number," Rocky shouted, panic in his voice.

"Rocky. It's me, Tango," I said, trying to calm him.

"Tango?"

"Yeah. Your mom went to the bathroom. She'll be right back. How's it going, buddy?"

"Oh." Short breaths blew through the receiver.

"How's camp?"

"Grandpa said we can't go camping, but he's taking me fishing."

My heart rate spiked. "Grandpa?"

"I'm at Grandma and Grandpa's house with Uncle Tucker."

A man's voice ordered him to hand over the phone.

"No," Rocky shouted. "It's my friend, Tango."

I heard a door slam, then pounding.

"Guess what, Tango. I brought my football with me. I can throw it through the tire swing now."

"That's great, Rocky. Listen. I gotta hang up, but I'll tell your mom you called, okay?" I tapped the end button and squeezed the phone.

Secrets. Lies. I fucking hated them. Coming from Slade? Betrayal had never cut so deep.

After disassembling her phone, I dropped it on the floor at my feet, smashed it under the heel of my boot and kicked it across the floor. I slipped the battery behind my seat and tucked the SD card into my pocket.

"Camp, my ass," I grumbled under my breath. Grandparents? Uncle Tucker? Far as I knew, Slade had no living relatives.

What the fuck was she hiding? What was she afraid of?

I would get to the bottom of this shit if it killed me. I owed her that much.

When she returned from the bathroom, I met her halfway and dragged her to the dance floor. She didn't protest, but judging by the grimace she wore, she wasn't too pleased either. I didn't give a shit, honestly. Other men ogled her like the star attraction at a strip club. She was with me. I'd make that clear to every dumbass in the place.

Then, I'd make it clear to Slade.

I'd prove to her that side by side was the only place we belonged

Even if it took the rest of my life.

Slade

Life certainly had a way of slapping you upside the head with ugly reminders of the past. Growing up, I'd hoped to be Tango's dance partner during his mother's classes. To make him proud. To make her proud. I'd worked extra hours to afford the lessons. I didn't love ballroom dancing—too many rules. Nonetheless, I'd loved dancing and I'd loved Tango. His mother had made him assist after school in her studio. Where he'd been, I'd wanted to be. I'd also hoped that if I'd participated and worked hard, Marta Rossi would see past my social status and fall in love with me as her son had.

What a naive fool.

Marta had never let Tango partner with me during class. She would scold me for wearing the wrong shoes, or some days ignore me altogether. She had made me dance with Donnie Simmons, the kid with the perpetual cold and runny nose. She had forced Tango to demonstrate with Kaylee over and over, saying in her heavy accent, "See Slade. That's how you do it. Good Kaylee. Very good."

It was only after Tango had threatened to stop dancing that Marta had backed off. He had jeopardized his relationship with his mom for me. I had never asked him to, had never voiced how much she'd hurt me, but he knew and had put a stop to it. That was how he had loved me. That was the kind of boy Tango had been.

As I now did with Rocky, Tango had never let a day pass without stealing a moment for a dance. Despite his mother's attempts at keeping us apart, he had always found a way to sweep me off my feet. Sometimes slow and close, but most days wild and crazy.

He had often surprised me in the hallway between classes, sneaking up behind me and whispering, "Have you danced today?" Then he would make a show of it, for the world to see, kiss me, and be on his way.

I stood on the dance floor of Jackson's Pub, in the arms of the only man I'd ever wanted to dance with, pulled tight against the hard planes of his body. It was home. My home. Painful emotions taunted me. The more we danced, the more those bad thoughts faded, and before long, I was filled to the brim with nothing but good memories. The games we'd played. Dancing on the docks under the moonlight. Stolen kisses in the bleachers of the football field. Our marathon study sessions in my room. Swimming, laughing, planning our futures.

Heavy techno music played on the speakers, but Tango held me close and moved to a rhythm all his own, rolling his hips, guiding me through the tangle of sweaty bodies. Power. Grace. Sexuality. He was all those things and more. So much more.

I could let go for one night. I could pretend, for a few hours, that I, like most people my age, didn't have the weight of the world on my shoulders. Right then, right there, I had my best friend back, I had a buzz, and I was surrounded by people who just wanted to dance. I needed to let loose. I deserved a night of mindless bliss.

I pushed away from Tango, not too far, and let go—of the worry, the fear, the sadness. I danced, like I did when alone at The Stop. I closed my eyes, absorbed the harsh beat, and I fucking danced. I didn't care what I looked like, who watched, who I bumped into or ground my ass against.

When I looked up at him the first time, Tango stood with arms crossed, shock and awe on his face. I didn't care. When I looked up again, he was right there with me. Moving like he needed the release as much as I did, wearing a carefree smile full of teenage charm. Before long, I was in his arms again, his lips were on my neck, his hands tangled in my hair, and then he kissed me. Hard and rough. Sweaty. Hungry. I fisted his shirt, pulling him closer. I didn't care. Fuck being the good girl. I wanted bad, lustful, greedy passion. Needed him. Ached to be wanted by him again, to show him that I wanted him, too.

The music stopped. The DJ announced he was taking a break, and Tango's lips left mine. He wrapped his hand around my wrist and led me back to our table.

The waitress brought two shots of dark liquor. "From your fan club." She nodded to a table of girls.

Tango had always been a chick-magnet. It had never bothered me. He was the kind of beautiful that made your heart ache. He had also been the kind of loyal that never gave me cause to question who his heart belonged to.

Until prom night, anyway.

I didn't ask what the shot glass was filled with. I threw it back and ordered more.

"Take it easy, babylove," Tango warned.

"Don't call me that," I snapped at him. "You don't get to call me babylove anymore."

I ordered another round of drinks, and Tango handed the waitress a fifty-dollar bill. "Bring water too, please. Bottled if you have it."

When she returned, I grabbed the hard drinks, while she set the bottles of water in front of Tango.

"Don't worry, I know my limit," I lied. I'd never been drunk, but I liked the way it made me feel brave. I cared about nothing but the here and now. I stood and moved to his side of the table. I straddled him and settled on his lap, my knees pushing into the vinyl of his bench seat. His hand slid around my waist, and he pushed the table back to make room. Then he gripped my ass and squeezed.

"What are you doing?" he moaned, tilting his chin to bring our mouths dangerously close to touching.

"We are going to toast." I handed him the shot and clinked our glasses together. "To our past. To our futures. You're going to kiss me. Then you're going to take me home and you are going to make love to me. I need you. Just once, to get you out of my system."

"Slade," he whispered, shaking his head. His erection swelled beneath me. I imagined what it would be like to take him there, in our dark corner of the bar. No one would be the wiser. I could unbutton his jeans, pull my panties to the side, and slide his cock inside me. No one would know.

I pressed my finger against his thick, moist lips. "Shhh. Please, Tango. Do this for me. For goodbye."

"No." He brushed my hand away. "Not when you're drunk."

I slammed my drink, choking on the burn, and dropped the empty glass on the floor. He set his aside, untouched.

I watched the inner struggle play out on his face. Lips drawing tight, brows crinkling, gaze darting from my eyes, to my chest, to my lips. He wanted me.

He cupped my cheeks with large, warm palms, and pulled my face closer to his. "I'm going to drive you home now. I won't come in, and I will not kiss you, because if I taste you again, I won't stop at your lips. But I'm not saying goodbye. Not yet."

His noble rejection was a hot poker to my chest. I slid off his lap and helped myself to his shot glass. The liquid burned my throat, my stomach, made my head spin. I knew I'd regret behaving irresponsibly, but I didn't care.

I smiled at the boy, the man who owned my heart and soul, and backed away, narrowing my eyes at him. The music started back up, and I wanted to be young and free for a while longer. I blew Tango a kiss and made my way through the sweaty, sexed-up bodies to the center of the dance floor.

I'd make him regret telling me no.

Tango

What man in his right mind would tell that girl no? It was obvious Slade was shitfaced, or well on her way, but she wanted me, and were I not certain she'd regret it in the morning, I could've taken her right there in our dark little corner. My every fantasy come true.

My plan was to watch her dance until my dick deflated, then take her home before she passed out drunk, but the horny bastard wouldn't cooperate. Damn, the girl could move, and neither one of my heads worked right when she stood front and center.

The vultures circled her on the crowded dance floor. One had already swooped in for a peck. She'd held her own and swatted him away. I waited and watched, from my dark perch, my heart swelling every time she glanced my direction. She danced for me. My own private show.

A commotion at the bar's entrance drew my attention away for a nanosecond. People gathered around, but the bouncers seemed to have things under control.

No way was I about to take my eyes off Slade. The way her hair fell around her neck and bounced along with her tits made my balls tighten. When she smiled, I swear it was like Christmas, my birthday, and winning the State Championship all rolled into one. My heart damn near exploded in my chest.

I had to get her home, tuck her safely in bed, and get my ass far away. I needed to screw my head on straight. I wouldn't hurt her again, but shit, how long would I be able to resist my blue-eyed beauty? I was a man, after all.

Giving zero fucks about my erection, I rose from the chair. As I made my way toward her, a tattooed motherfucker stepped behind Slade, wrapped his arms around her middle, and pulled her ass against his groin. The room around me turned red, as I watched her struggle to push his arms off. My inner switch, the one I hadn't engaged since my last fight, toggled from calm to nuclear rage.

His hands slithered higher, and when she tried wiggling free of his grip, he pressed his mouth to her ear. Fear darkened her gorgeous features, and I charged, fury slamming through me. Blood was about to spill.

One strike knocked him to the ground. Unfortunately, the dick was nothing but coward, pulling Slade down with him, using her first as a shield, then a cushion. Her cry of pain sent a whirlwind of blind rage from my core to my limbs.

Before he could gain his bearings, my fingers tightened around his throat, and I pulled the fucker off my girl. Slade rolled out of the way, clutching her right hand to her chest.

I dropped hard, forcing my knee into his gut. Blood spewed from his mouth, and I hit him again, for good measure. "What the fuck is wrong with you?" I asked, striking the other side of his face.

The dude tried to look at me, but it was clear he couldn't focus by the way his eyes danced in their sockets. I wiped my bloody knuckles on his shirt. It was then that I noticed his cut. Black leather vest, patches up and down each side. My boiling blood cooled to ice in one heartbeat. Shit. Satan's Slayers. Livingston chapter.

I stood and scanned the room. Didn't see any more of them, but a larger crowd had gathered at the front door. People continued to thrash and gyrate around me as if nothing had happened. I turned a three-sixty, searching for my girl, and caught a flash of golden hair pushing through the back exit at the same moment I heard gunshots.

Two pops.

Chaos erupted. Screaming, pushing, crying.

I fought my way through the crowd and toward the door, fear and rage blinding me to anything but heads of blonde hair. When I spied her against my car, doubled over, I damned near fell to me knees in relief.

The police had already arrived on the scene, but I wasn't about to get caught up in that mess. I lifted Slade into my Rover, foregoing the safety of her belt, and ran to the driver's side. Three Harleys tore down the back alley. Thank fuck none of them had seen what I did to their friend. I jumped into my seat and hightailed it the opposite direction.

Not until we'd cleared a few miles did I pull over to check on Slade, who hid behind the shield of her hands. Before the engine stopped, she hopped out of the car to purge her burger and fries. Holding her steady, I gathered her hair to keep it clear of the line of fire.

As soon as the heaving stopped, I pulled my shirt over my head and wiped her face. Cupping her shoulders, I helped her stand. "There," I said, kissing her forehead. "Good as new. Ready to head home?"

"Why was everyone running out of the building?" she asked, swaying where she stood.

Shit. Drunk as a skunk.

"Didn't you hear the gunshots?"

"Gunshots? No. I had to get out. I needed air." Slade rested her palms and forehead on my chest and moaned. "I lied to you."

I snaked my arms around her middle. "Yeah? About what?"

"I don't know my limit. I never drink. Now I made a fool of myself and you. I'm sorry." She turned her head, pressing her cheek to my heart, and wrapped her arms around my waist. "I wanted to feel like a girl again, just for one night."

Holy fuck, the way she clung to me. My brain short-circuited, but I managed to ask, "Did you have fun?"

"I did. Until that asshole showed up," she mumbled against my chest. "Stupid biker fucker. Bashed his head in with a baseball bat and crushed his ugly fucking skull. I should've killed them all."

"Baseball bat? Killed them all?" Damn. She was beyond drunk. Wrapping an arm around her shoulder, I nudged her toward the SUV.

"Yes. Killed them." She pulled away from me and faked swinging a baseball bat. Then she winced and rubbed above her right wrist. "My arm hurts."

A nasty bruise marred the perfect skin across the top of her hand and wrist. "God damn. I should go back there and kill the guy."

"No." She patted my arm. "You can murder him another time. I need to go home."

"Okay," I chuckled. "Murder later. How about we swing by the hospital before I take you home, in case that's broken."

"Take me home. I just want to sleep. Promise me. No hospital. I'm not my mom. They'll think I'm like Mom…"

Slade curled in the seat, her head on my shoulder. Out cold.

I understood why she didn't want to go to the hospital. She'd always promised not to follow in her mother's footsteps where men and alcohol were concerned.

What the hell had I been thinking bringing her to a bar?

Slade

What the hell had I been thinking? I had been raised by an alcoholic. I'd worked hard my whole life to prove I was not my mother. Yet there I lay, curled in the fetal position on my couch, cursing God for creating beer and liquor in the first place.

A pair of bare feet stepped into my field of vision. I didn't bother raising my head. I hadn't been able to move since I woke an hour ago.

"I brought you something for the headache, and some dry toast. Try to eat; it'll settle your stomach." Tango set a plate and glass of water down on the floor next to me.

"What time is it?" I asked, struggling to speak. A moss garden must have sprouted on my tongue overnight.

"It's noon. I called The Stop for you this morning. Charlie said not to worry, he's taking care of everything. I think he likes bossing everyone around."

"Thank you." I forced myself to the sitting position and choked down the ibuprofen. "How do I look?" I asked, patting my hair and lifting my chin to meet Tango's smirk. I vaguely remembered him helping me into my boxers and tank top last night. "'I feel like death, wrapped in a dirty diaper."

He forced a half-hearted laugh, and sat next to me on the couch. I jumped when he pressed a bag of frozen peas to my wrist. Dark circles framed his eyes. "I don't think it's broken, just beat up a bit. I iced it for you while you were sleeping, to keep the swelling down." He dropped his head against the back of the couch.

"Did you sleep at all?" I asked.

"Little bit," he mumbled through a yawn.

"Because you were taking care of me?"

His insincere, lopsided grin grated my nerves.

"You didn't have to do that."

He huffed. "Yeah, I did."

"You need to go home, Tango. Don't you have a job to get back to in … in … Where the hell have you been, anyway?"

He drew a long sigh. "Slade."

"Where have you been living, Tango?"

"New York."

"The Big Apple. Hmm. I never would've guessed. What were you doing there?"

"This what you want to talk about?"

"I don't know. Yeah, maybe. I just don't understand. You're here, and you should be there. Getting back to your life."

Even in my nauseated, self-imposed misery, I could feel the air thicken around us.

Tango's chest rose and fell. "New York isn't good for me. It changed me, and not for the better. When I'm with you, I feel like I can be the old me again."

"You haven't changed."

"You don't know the things I've seen, done…" His eyes glazed over before he shook the thought away. "I have to know you're okay. Because if you're okay, I can be okay, too."

"I'm okay, but the longer you're here, the less okay I feel. That's why you need to leave. God, look at me. I got drunk last night, and I liked it. I won't be that kind of mother to Rocky."

He chuckled. "You were quite amusing, I must say. Mumbling about bashing skulls with a baseball bat, cussing up a storm."

His words sent prickles down my spine. "What?" Oh, triple fuck. "Baseball bat? What did I say?"

"Some biker got cozy with you on the dance floor…"

Tango continued to speak. I didn't hear a word, because I remembered. I felt the man's hands on me, smelled his rancid tobacco breath, cringed at his words—*How's that little boy, Blondie? You raising him right?*

Maybe I hadn't heard him correctly. None of them had seen my face that night, aside from Walter, and dead men couldn't speak.

"…then you said you should've killed them all." Tango snapped his fingers in my face. "Slade? You okay?"

I had to leave. They were coming for me.

"Babylove. Talk to me. Did you know that guy at the bar?"

I shook my head no, afraid to open my mouth for fear of vomiting my confession all over Tango.

"Brett told me you and Addy had been hanging out with an MC at her uncle's place. Please tell me that was just a rumor."

"I feel like shit. You need to go home."

Tango stiffened next to me. "Slade. I've known you for damn near twenty years. I know you better than anyone." Leaning closer, he pinched my chin between his thumb and forefinger, and stared me down. "You're scared. You're lying, keeping secrets, pushing me away. Let me in. Let me help."

"Fuck." I shrugged him off and screamed into my hands. "You don't get it." I threw the blanket off my body and turned to face him. "You are the problem. Everything was fine. You came back and stirred up these damned feelings. Now I'm questioning every decision I've made since you left. You have to leave. You have to go home and never come back."

Tango closed his eyes and clenched his fists at his sides. "Where's Rocky?

"He's at camp."

The muscles in his jaw protruded. "Slade, please don't lie to me."

I spoke the words, despite knowing he'd see right through them. "He's at camp for two weeks."

"No. He isn't." Tango rose from the couch and wrestled his feet into his boots. After drawing a deep breath, he rubbed his chin. "You dropped your phone last night. It's toast. I put it on the kitchen table."

Halfway out the front door, he paused and shot a quick glance over his shoulder. "You should've told me the truth."

The door slammed behind him, vibrating the walls. A prickly chill rocked my body. Oh my God. Had he looked through my phone? I scrambled to the kitchen, ignoring the bile rising in my throat. My smashed cell lay lifeless and unrecognizable on the table. No way could he have read anything through that cracked screen.

Did Tango know I was lying, or was he calling my bluff? The expression he wore, before making his dramatic exit, told me I was screwed.

I dragged my sorry, hungover ass upstairs and tucked myself into bed, but not before sneaking a peek at the photo on my nightstand.

Bad idea.

I hated Addy. I hated Marta Rossi more, for what she'd forced Addy to do. What she'd forced me to do. One thing I knew for certain: my world, the life I'd worked so hard to build, was about to crumble.

I needed sleep before I could pack. How did my mother do this every day of her life? I closed my eyes and gave in to exhaustion.

"Slade, I don't have anyone else. Dane is MIA." Addy swayed on unsteady legs, wiping black streaks of mascara from her bruised cheek. "I'm scared. They told me if I didn't take care of it, they would." She wrapped an arm around her stomach and doubled over, falling to her knees at my feet. "I was so stupid. I don't want this. Help me, please."

CHAPTER 7

THE PARING KNIFE AIMED at my throat, no doubt intended to thwart my advance, did little more than remind me that I'd skipped breakfast. The fire in Slade's eyes, however, raised a shit ton of hot, hard trouble in my pants. Had she not had a mouthful of apple, I would've given those juicy lips a morning workout. "You're not getting rid of me that easy. Come on. I already called Charlie. He's happier than shit to run the joint."

"I can't. It's summer. Busiest time of the year," Slade argued.

"And you've hired the best people," I countered.

Slade dropped her arm, and set the knife, along with her apple core, on the door side table. "You can't waltz back into town and start running my life."

Damn she looked delicious standing there in her cut-offs and pink tank top, all pissed and full of defiance.

"You need a break. I need to drive. Come on. Blue sky, fresh air. I'll even let you pick the radio station."

"No, Tango. We can't. I can't." She started to close the door.

I leaned against the frame, blocking her attempt to shut me out. "I need this. You're the only person I want to spend my time with." Because I was going to get the truth, one way or the other. I'd break her. Even if it meant she would hate me more than she already did.

"I'm sorry. No. Just no. Go home. Go back to New York. Stay out of my life." She pushed at my chest.

I stood my ground. "No isn't an option, I'm afraid."

"Go away, Tango." She stepped back and threw her arms out wide, practically inviting my tackle.

I crouched, snapped my arms around her hips, and threw her over my shoulder. Damn, she was lighter than the punching bags back at Tito's gym. I'd make it my life's mission to put some meat on her bones.

"We're going. Got me?" I smacked her ass. "Got anything you need to turn off? Oven, lights, curling iron?"

"No." She slapped her palms on my ass.

"Good. Let's go."

"I meant, *no*, I don't have anything to turn off because I'm not going anywhere. Put me down."

Ignoring her protests, I carried her outside, turned, and locked the door. She kicked and screamed all the way to the car. I stuffed her into the passenger seat, dodged a right hook, and threw my bodyweight across her lap to hook the seatbelt.

"Dammit, Tango. Let me go." She pulled at my shirt, my hair, punched and kicked. I did the one thing I knew would calm her down. I pulled her face to mine and kissed the fight clean out of her.

As I'd suspected, she softened against me and melted into the seat. Pliant lips mimicked mine. Her slender fingers curled in my hair, tugging and twisting. Sweet moans. Heavy breaths.

Shit. She'd turned the tables. Now I wanted nothing more than to carry her back inside and get her naked. I'd never lost control with a woman, but with Slade, I was nothing but a damned puppet.

I had to get my shit together. Snagging her bottom lip between my teeth, I nibbled, just enough to get her attention. When I broke contact, the corner of her mouth curled.

Her fingers slowly untangled from my mane. She raised her sleepy lids and smiled. "That wasn't fair."

"I play dirty. Now, are you coming quietly, or do I have to pull out the big guns?" My weapons were safely stashed in the hidden compartment in my trunk. However, I wasn't above using them to get my way.

Her gaze darted back and forth from me to her front door. "Just a day trip?"

I smiled and kissed her again.

"Damn it. Stop," she half-whined, half-laughed, pushing me away. "Okay. I'll go. On one condition."

"Name it."

"You cannot touch me. No kissing. No hugging or holding hands, no dancing. Definitely no dancing."

"Come on, now." I tilted my head. "You know damn well you'll be the first one to break that rule."

"Arrogant dickhead, much?"

I laughed. Slade smiled, that fucking wide, brilliant smile that could end wars, power cities, bring the deadliest of men to their knees.

"I need to get a new phone today."

"We can do that together."

"I need to do it first thing. In case there's an emergency with Rocky and the camp needs to get a hold of me."

Fuck. Again with the lies.

"They have your work number, right?" I asked.

Slade chewed her thumbnail and nodded her head.

"I gave Charlie my number. If the camp calls, he'll have them call my cell." I refrained from telling her that Charlie knew nothing about Rocky being away at camp.

"You're a presumptuous ass."

She had no idea, but she'd learn, soon enough. When confident she wouldn't bolt, I shut her door, jogged to the driver's side, and situated myself behind the wheel.

"My presumptuous ass, your white-trash ass. What a pair of asses we are, huh?" I winked, and her cheeks flushed.

Chin raised, she snatched my Oakleys off the dash, slipped the oversized, green frames over her eyes, and turned her head from mine. "Where are we going?"

"I don't have a fucking clue. Just gonna drive." Gravel crunched under the tires of the Range Rover as I backed out of her driveway. The neighborhood was quiet, save the bark of the Shih Tzu two houses down, and distant roar of a lawnmower. The sky hung above us, blue and vast, and the air was ripe with the aroma of gasoline and freshly cut grass. Our possibilities were endless, my endgame vital.

I navigated the streets of town, heading toward the interstate. Slade poked my arm. "Take the old highway. Please? Let's get lost in the mountains."

How could I say no to anything she asked? I wrenched the wheel to the right, performing a brilliantly executed, illegal U-turn, and caught the on-ramp to I95. It would take us past The Stop, and I was certain that was why she'd asked me to go that route. The girl had been raised in that damn restaurant. I could imagine it was hard for her to leave it behind, even for what she believed to be only a day trip.

Words weren't necessary with the windows down and the radio tuned into the local country station. We drove, I sang along to the cheesy lyrics, and Slade eventually joined in. Just like old times.

"When are you going back to New York?" she asked, when we'd driven deep enough into the mountains to lose the radio signal.

"I'm going back in a few days to get the rest of my things, and I have one job to finish." One more fight. A quick knockout that'd make Voltolini millions. He'd postponed the fight once already, giving me time to mourn.

"Get the rest of your things?" Hands clenched in her lap, Slade turned her head toward the passenger window, hiding her reaction to my news, no doubt. "You're coming home." It wasn't a question, but a vocalized realization. She shifted in her seat and the tremble in her hands made my blood boil. "Why didn't you tell me sooner?"

I hadn't wanted to tell her yet. I'd wanted her to want me to stay, maybe even beg me to stay. "Slade. Listen. I was going to tell you. I. Shit. I don't know. I wanted to make things right with you before I broke the news."

"But why leave New York? You have better opportunities there. Why would you come back?"

Stupid question. Slade Mason, my girl, my heart, didn't live in New York.

The Big Apple had made me a shit ton of money, no denying that fact. I had to sell my soul, however, and that was no longer an acceptable exchange. "I don't belong there."

She didn't respond. Not verbally. Instead, she gnawed the corner of her thumbnail, unwittingly giving away her state of emotions, her level of worry.

My hands tightened around the wheel. My chest caved in. I wanted her to be happy I was back. And fuck me, it hurt like hell knowing she wasn't.

I would do everything in my power to change her mind.

Slade

I would do everything in my power to protect my lie.

With the Satan's Slayers hanging around Whisper Springs, and Tango moving back home, my only option was to leave. I wouldn't have the strength to avoid Tango, and he would eventually discover the truth. He still owned my heart, and my life was built on a shaky foundation of secrets, lies, and wishful thinking. If he tugged the right string, the world I'd built would come crashing down, burying not only me, but the others who'd risked everything for my son.

I had a back-up plan. One I'd hoped, prayed even, that I would never have to implement. I didn't want to leave everything behind. I loved my town, but I could make a new home, with Rocky. We'd have a better life, some place far away. I could buy us a brand new house. One that didn't have a crumbling foundation, peeling paint, squeaky floorboards, or a lifetime of bittersweet and treasured memories.

The thought should have saddened me, but instead, worry left my body on a deep inhale and exhale, leaving my head and heart lighter than they'd felt in forever. I no longer feared spending an entire day with Tango. I would enjoy our day. Enjoy him one last time. Rocky was safe with Tucker for the time being. When I got home, I would pack my essentials, rent a car, and head to Montana. Then? Tit for tat. My turn to disappear.

I turned to face the man who had built me up, broken me, and shown me how far I could fall in the name of love. The man I had committed crimes for. Five years ago, I sold my soul to the devil for Tango Rossi. I would do it again. For that reason alone, I had to leave.

For one more day, I would take what I wanted from him. Let him fill me, fuel me, make new memories to carry me through the next chapter of my life.

"Isn't Moss Lake up this way?"

"Yeah." His eyebrows crinkled as he slid his gaze my way then back to the road.

"Let's go there. That's where I want to go."

His lips curled, engaging those deep dimples. "The family cabin is up there."

"I know." I wiggled my brows at him, biting my lower lip.

He lifted his right hand off the steering wheel to scratch the stubble on his chin. "I was strictly forbidden to ever take you up there."

"I know," I whispered.

"You remember?" He dropped his hand and shifted gears, his foot weighing heavy on the gas pedal.

"How could I forget?" When Tango had received his driver's license, and his first car, a gift for his sixteenth birthday, his mother had given him the now-infamous *no girls allowed in the cabin* speech. She'd made a point to do it in front of his friends, to slut shame me, most likely, which was laughable. I was one of a handful of girls at school who hadn't already lost their virginity. After Marta Rossi's speech, I was the *only* girl who hadn't been introduced to the Rossi cabin.

Just to stick-it to his mom, Tango had made sure every guy on the football team had taken a turn or two sneaking their dates to the remote location. He'd made quite a killing, renting the shag shack to his horny teammates over the years.

We stopped at the only gas station within a forty-mile radius of our destination. I made a quick trip to the restroom around back while Tango ran inside to pay. He returned balancing three large bags in his arms.

"What's all this?" I asked, snagging one of the brown paper sacks. It overflowed with crackers, cookies, and chips.

"We gotta eat, right?"

"That's a ton of food for one day."

Tango just smiled and plopped the groceries on the back seat. I climbed back into the SUV. The leather seat burned the back of my thighs—a welcomed distraction from the man climbing into the car next to me. His light blue T-shirt clung to his chest and arms and pulled tight in all the right places.

My gaze drifted down to the large, strong fist wrapped around the gear shift. I anchored my fingers under my legs to keep from tracing the veins mapping the top of his hand. My throat tightened then shriveled. A bead of sweat rolled between my breasts.

Sweet Jesus, I wanted him to touch me.

Cool air blasted through the vent when he started the car, and I leaned forward, pulling my shirt low to dry the collection of moisture in my cleavage.

We reached the cabin almost an hour later. I jumped out of the car and stretched my legs before taking in the grandeur of the Rossi family cottage. For crying out loud, it was bigger than three of my houses put together. It sat next to, well, practically on top of the lake. The wraparound deck stretched over the water and connected to a small dock.

"This is what you call a cabin?"

Tango shrugged. "Dad doesn't do anything small." He handed me a bag, snagged the other two, and headed for the front door.

I followed behind, wishing I'd brought another pair of shoes. When I looked back at the driveway, I noticed several fresh tire tracks. "Who else comes up here? You guys rent the place out?"

Tango gave the driveway a once over. "Those look like motorcycle tracks. Maybe someone turned up our road by mistake." He continued inside, unconcerned.

I ignored the ice picks jabbing my spine and trailed after him.

I'd expected the inside of the cabin to be dusty and dark. Silly me. Everything sparkled—the dark wood furniture, stainless steel kitchen, heavy ceiling beams. The scent of lemon and ammonia tickled my nose.

"You have a maid staff here too?"

"Dad pays a local couple to keep it clean. Sweet people. Maybe you'll get to meet them." He dropped his load on the dark granite counter, then relieved me of my sack and set it with the others.

I shoved my hands in the back pockets of my cut-offs to hide their tremble. Then I reminded myself to breathe. "How much did you pay them to keep quiet about your parties?"

Tango stepped closer. "They liked me better than they liked my parents. Bribery wasn't necessary."

That didn't surprise me in the least. Tango could charm a trout away from a hungry grizzly.

"So." I surveyed the massive open layout of the kitchen, trying my best to avoid eye contact. "What shall we do with ourselves?"

Tango took another step toward me. My insides churned and warmed. I faked interest in the fireplace. The rustic stone structure took up half the living room and housed several large antlers. Clearly, the Rossi cabin was nothing but an oversized man-cave. I couldn't find one touch of female inspiration in any of the decor.

"Slade."

Oh God. His voice.

"Look at me."

I had to keep my cool. I needed to get through this day, pretend everything was okay, so I could get home and start packing. I forced my gaze up the length of his lean torso, carved chest and shoulders, irresistible lips. My nerves settled the moment our eyes met. He'd always had that effect on me. When he smiled, it fed my soul and I found strength. *I can do this.* I could enjoy one day with him and be okay.

I pulled my shirt over my head.

Tango's nostrils flared. Lips parted.

Forcing my fingers to move through the tremors, I popped the button on my shorts and slid them down my legs. Despite the heat, goosebumps covered my skin.

I can do this.

Tango

I can't do this.

I'd promised our trip would be a hands-off excursion. My goal had been to get her away from her day-to-day responsibilities, help her de-stress enough to open up. Talk to me. Unburden, and allow me to help.

No way in hell would that happen. Not when she was standing inches from me in nothing but a cotton bra and panties.

I was a man, after all, and holy shit, Slade was a woman. No fucking way would I deny her what she wanted.

Judging by her naked state, she wanted my hands all over her. I stepped back to admire the goddess who'd claimed the starring role in every fantasy I'd conjured since puberty.

"You know what I want to do?" she asked, kicking her shorts across the floor.

Hot blood filled my cock. Lust stole my voice. I'd waited my whole life for that moment. Slade Mason, mine, in every sense of the word.

Her lips curved in a half-wicked smile. A gesture I knew all too well. She was up to no good. I was more than ready to be her bad.

I yanked my shirt over my head. Holy fuck, the way she looked at me. I felt like a king.

"What do you want to do?" I asked, manipulating the top button of my shorts.

"Skinny dip!" she squealed, turning on the balls of her feet and sprinting toward the back door. She opened the slider and shot me a wink over her shoulder before running across the deck and hopping down the stairs. I watched, hands still working my button, as she dashed to the end of the dock and cannonballed into the water.

Well, shit.

I took my time joining her, on account of my dick and its refusal to deflate. By the time I dove in, Slade had made it to the floating dock in the center of the private lake. She hoisted herself up and turned to look for me. Then she threw her arms out wide and lifted her face to the sun. Hell yeah, definitely a goddess.

When I reached her, she was lying on her stomach, absorbing the late morning heat. I settled next to her, on my back, and crossed my arms behind my head.

"It's beautiful here," she said, staring across the water.

"Yeah. It is." Never gave the serenity of our summer home much thought before that moment. I supposed I had taken it for granted, much like everything else in life.

"Tango?" she whispered.

"Hmm?" I hummed, throwing an arm over my eyes to shield them from the sun.

"Do you suppose things would've turned out different if your parents hadn't hated me so much?"

That rage I'd learned to suppress bubbled and churned in my gut. "I don't know if things would've been different. What happened that night had nothing to do with my parents and everything to do with me being an asshole."

Slade sighed. "Asshole is right. King of the assholes. Ruler of Assholeville."

God, I loved my girl. I turned to face her. Her eyes were fixed on the water. I wanted her attention on me. Nowhere else. I broke my promise about no touching and reached over, brushing her cheek with the tip of my finger.

Slade tilted her head, resting it on her arm, and slowly brought her gaze to me. "Oh my God, Tango!" She rolled to her back and hid her face behind the shield of her hands. "You're naked." Laughter erupted, and her breasts bounced erratically beneath her wet bra.

"You said you wanted to skinny dip."

"I know, but..." She peeked between her fingers, then turned her head. "Oh my God. Cover yourself." Tears rolled down the sides of her face.

Fuck, I'd missed that laugh. "Cover myself with what?"

"I don't know."

"What's the matter? You've seen it before."

"We were kids, in the kiddie pool, and if I remember right, your mom left a welt on your ass for exposing yourself in public."

"Slade. Come on now. We're adults," I teased, rolling to my side and snapping her bra strap. "I don't know why you bothered keeping this on. I can see right through it."

Begging to be sucked, her pink nipples puckered into tight little buds under the thin white cotton.

Slade huffed, drew her knees up and crossed her arms over her chest. "There. I covered mine. You cover yours."

"No." I gestured down to my semi-erect woody. "He hasn't seen the sun for years. Think I'll let him get some air."

"He?" Laughter erupted again.

I couldn't help it. I leaned over and kissed a tear from her cheek.

Her body relaxed, and she closed her eyes. When she dropped her arms to her sides, I studied the curves of her hips, the rise and fall of her breasts, the stretch of skin over her taut abdomen.

"You don't have any stretch marks."

"What?" Wide-eyed, she lifted her head to meet my gaze.

"No stretch marks." I broke the no touching rule again and traced a figure-eight pattern over her stomach. "None here." I dragged my finger upward and between her breasts. "None here."

Slade sucked in a sharp breath before smacking my hand away and rolling onto her stomach. "No. I didn't get stretch marks. Just lucky I guess."

Her butt wiggled as she settled into a comfortable position. Fuck, I wanted to gnaw on those ass cheeks. Curl my fingers into her soft hips and pound her from behind.

"What was it like?" I asked, steering my thoughts in a direction that didn't include coitus.

"What was what like?"

"Being pregnant. Growing a baby."

Slade turned her head away from me. "It was fine, I guess."

"Fine, I guess?" I hated that she wouldn't look at me.

"I don't know. I was moody and mean. Hungry all the time."

God, what I wouldn't give to see her with my baby growing in her belly. I couldn't imagine anything more beautiful. "I can't believe you did that alone."

She shrugged her shoulders. "Women do it all the time."

Not my woman. Never should've been my woman. "Who is Rocky's father, Slade?"

She huffed and buried her face between her arms. "Nobody you know. Can we change the subject?"

"Why are you afraid to talk about him?" I asked, running a finger along the curve of her waist.

"I'm not," she mumbled.

I sensed her agitation, but continued to push. "Was it Dane? Did he hurt you?"

With a sigh, Slade turned to look at me. *Finally.* "No."

"Did you love him?" I had to know.

"God, Tango. Stop. I don't want to talk about this." Slade pushed to her feet. Again, those glorious tits bounced, scrambling my thought pattern.

"Did you love him?" I repeated, curiosity, and envy, getting the better of me. Her heart had belonged to me once. If she'd shared it with another man, it would kill me, but I supposed I deserved nothing less.

"Yes," she yelled, throwing her hands to the sky. "Is that what you want to hear? I loved him."

I hated the fucker. Whoever he was, I wanted him dead. "More than you loved me?"

"You're an asshole." With that, she turned and dove into the lake, ending the convo, leaving me alone to cool my shit, and once again, wait for my cock to deflate.

Slade

Dear Lord, the man had a beautiful cock. I needed to get away, clear my head. Skinny dipping? What the hell had I been thinking? Stupid, stupid, stupid girl.

I barely pulled myself out of the water before Tango's naked body covered mine. Out of breath from the swim, I lacked the energy to protest. In all honesty, I didn't want to.

On hands and knees, he straddled me and lowered his nose to mine. Wet hair fell over his forehead, dripping water on my face. "Sorry," he laughed, showing off his brilliant white teeth. Running a hand through his hair, he slicked it back and squeezed out the excess moisture.

Helpless to resist his sun-kissed skin, I reached up to trace his deep dimple. Dammit. Irresistible bastard.

He gripped my wrist, turned his face into my palm, and landed a kiss on my finger. "I'm sorry I pushed. I didn't mean to upset you. I just need to know you again. I want to know everything I missed."

I wanted to know him, too. But what was the point when I could never see him again, when we had no future?

I sucked in a deep breath, building courage to tell yet another lie. "I only have room in my heart for one man, Tango. That's my son. The past doesn't matter anymore. You had my heart once. It belongs to him now."

Remorse darkened his eyes, and his fingers tightened around me. "It sounds like you're saying goodbye."

Just one more day. "We broke the no touching rule," I whispered, desperate to change the subject.

"When have we ever followed rules?" he asked, twisting a finger through my hair.

"Good point."

A lazy grin spread across his face. "I'm about to break another one."

Oh God. My heart. "You are?"

He nodded, fixing his gaze on my lips. He was going to kiss me.

Please kiss me.

I was bad. Very bad. Because I wanted his lips too much.

Then again, kissing was better than talking. I wouldn't have to make up lies if my tongue was busy doing other things.

I snapped a hand around his neck and pulled him down, smashing our mouths together. *Oh yes, I can do this.* All day long. Goodbye could wait until tomorrow.

Anger welled inside me. I didn't want his affections for only a day; I wanted his lips, his mouth, his attention every day. Until we were old and wrinkly and stinking of mint and Depends. But because of one desperate decision made on one bad fucking day, I would never get my happily-ever-after. Not with Tango Rossi, anyway.

Anger turned to rage. Rage to need. Need to desperation. I tangled my fingers through his wet hair. He forced a knee between my thighs, nudging my legs apart. When they opened, he nestled nice and tight between them, pressing his hips to mine, positioning his thick erection in the soft spot between my legs.

He kissed me, wet and fierce, with tongue, teeth and lips—and when Tango kissed, he not only gave with his mouth, his entire body got involved, rolling, gripping, and trembling. With every suck, every nibble and moan, he moved, dancing against me. And his hips, dear sweet Jesus, his hips undulated between my legs, working the heavy weight of his arousal against me. I rocked with the little movement his solid body would allow, my thin panties the only barrier between us.

How I wished there didn't have to be a barrier.

Tango slid a hand down my ribcage, my waist, my hip. My body melted into the rough wood of the dock, my worries dripped between the cracks, dissolving and disappearing in the cool, cleansing water. My skin was on fire, my muscles aching and needy.

He gripped underneath my knee, guiding my leg up and around his waist, still rocking, working with perfect pressure. I dug my nails into his ass. He moaned into my mouth.

His cock rubbed against me harder, faster. Fucking. Fucking without penetration. I writhed beneath him, curled around him, mindless, boneless, wanting, needing this, him, us. Oh, my fucking God, how I wanted us. He thrust against me, releasing my mouth, blowing heavy breaths into my ear.

Grinding our bodies together, he rasped, "Come with me, babylove. Let go." He reached down and slipped a finger under my panties, between my folds, opening, entering me, driving me insane. "Let go for me."

My heart burst, my body exploded, my insides spasmed around his finger as he drove it deeper. "Oh God. Shit. Shit. Shit." I moaned, arching against the sweet agony.

"Fucking hell," Tango rasped into my neck, thrusting one more time before shuddering and spurting semen between us, hot and thick. He moaned and collapsed, his full weight on top of my limp and sated body. Wet lips pressed against my collarbone, and he rolled off me with a deep sigh.

I couldn't move, couldn't talk. My head floated above us, somewhere between a billowy cloud and heaven, I think.

"You are so goddamn beautiful." Tango sat up, scooped lake water with his cupped hand, then poured it over my stomach. He did it again, this time wiping away the sticky mess.

I watched his eyes widen, then soften, as he inspected my breasts, my stomach, my thighs. He splashed me with another handful of water and massaged it into my skin, the tips of his fingers skimming the top of my panties, sending shivers through me.

"We should get out of the sun before you burn," he mumbled, pushing to his feet.

I accepted the hand he offered and sighed as he pulled me up and coiled his strong arms around me. Resting his chin on my head, he whispered, "Have you danced today?"

I shook my head *no* against his bare chest, and locked my arms around his waist. Tango swayed, I followed, and I danced with the only man I would ever love. The one man I could not have.

This would be our last dance.

CHAPTER 8

Tango

"HOW MANY PARTIES did your friends throw up here, anyway?" Slade asked, before popping the last bite of her sandwich between her lips.

"I think the real question is, how many of the guys lost their virginity up here?" Twenty-five that I knew of, from my graduating class alone. Or so they'd claimed.

The pink in her cheeks darkened. Damn, that was cute.

"And your parents never found out?"

"The guys were terrified of Mom. Cleaned up after themselves. Usually left the place in better shape than they found it."

"I'm glad I finally get to experience the legendary Rossi shag-shack." She paused, her eyebrows scrunching and her head tilting in that adorable way that never failed to make my insides soften. "Why didn't you ever sneak me up here?"

I set my half-eaten bologna and cheese back on my plate. "Do you really have to ask?"

"I'm asking, aren't I?"

Not sure why her question irritated me, but it did. Arms crossed, I leaned my hip against the counter. "You weren't a conquest. You weren't a challenge. You were mine already.

What we had, who you were, meant more to me than getting laid."

"Oh," she said, picking at a potato chip.

"I wanted to do things right with you. I did do things right with you, didn't I? I mean, until that night." And there we were again, back on the last subject I'd wanted to bring up. "Fuck. I didn't want to go there again. Sorry."

"It's okay. It's hard not to reminisce." She offered a reassuring smile. "Tell me about New York."

That was why I loved her. She'd sensed my unease and changed the subject.

"What do you want to know?" I asked, claiming her hand and leading her to the living room.

"You said you didn't like who you were there. Why?"

I dropped my ass to the couch. In a perfect world, I would shield Slade from ever seeing that side of me, from ever knowing the truth about what I'd done in the name of honor, loyalty, and self-preservation. I wouldn't lie, though. Shit was shit. You could sugar-coat all you wanted, but eventually, the stench would seep through the pretty package and expose the ugliness inside. I wanted honesty from her, so I had to be truthful in return. "I hurt people. A lot of people."

"What do you mean?" Slade pulled her hand from my grip, faking interest in her fingernails.

"You remember Tito?"

"Your cousin? How could I forget? I dreaded his visits." She rolled her eyes. "The two of you were always getting into trouble."

"He worked for a childhood friend of my father, Luciano Voltolini. Voltolini runs underground fights, among other things. I was so angry after I left Whisper Springs. I needed an outlet. Tito hooked me up, I started fighting, and I won. Every fucking time. And it felt good. Too good." I swallowed, pausing to get my emotions under check. "Long story short, I got cocky."

"You? Cocky?" She faked a gasp. "I don't believe it."

Shit. I wanted to kiss that playful smirk clean off her face. "One night, Luciano asked me to throw a fight, said there was good money in it. I agreed, not that I had a choice. When the bell rang, and the shithead threw a dirty punch, I saw red. Everything after that was a blur. I nearly butchered the guy. Luciano could've killed me. Had I not been my father's son, he would've. Instead, he let me work off the money I'd cost him. Aside from fighting, I did things for him. Unpleasant things. I never let him down again. It took four years, but I paid my debt, and then some."

I searched her eyes for a reaction. She stared through me, unblinking, chewing the corner of her thumbnail.

"Say something," I whispered.

"I don't know what to say. I mean, are you talking about the mafia? Like organized crime?"

I nodded.

"You did all that, and still graduated?"

"Had no choice." Couldn't let Pops down any more than I could disappoint Luciano again.

"And he let you walk away?" Slade fell into the cushions next to me.

"I'm here, aren't I?"

"Tango. What the hell were you thinking? You could be dead right now. Or in prison. I can't believe you were so stupid. Why would you get involved with criminals?"

To feel. To hurt. To forget. Self-imposed punishment, perhaps. "We've talked about me long enough. It's your turn."

She stiffened. "There's nothing to say. My life is painfully uneventful."

Why did her confession thrill me? "Uneventful suits me just fine."

"What about girls?" she blurted, blue eyes fixated on my mine. "Did you date? Fall in love? How many hearts did you break?"

The only girls I talked to, besides Voltolini's daughter, were the whores on his payroll. Much like fighting, my sessions with them served only as an outlet. A form of therapy, I supposed.

"There were women. Nothing serious."

"Never mind," she said, shaking her head. "I had no right to ask."

"What about you? Any asses I have to kick?"

"Afraid not," she mumbled, dropping her head.

Lie. No way in hell Slade hadn't had men beating down her door. "You haven't dated?"

She cleared her throat, picked at a loose thread on her shorts, and sighed. "I've had my hands full."

Thank fuck. I couldn't stand the thought of sharing a town with any man who'd touched her. I'd have to add murder to my list of crimes. Hell, if I discovered who Rocky's dad was, I wouldn't give it a second thought. Which reminded me. "What happened with Rocky's father?"

Slade shifted in her seat. She turned her head to the left, and her gaze followed suit. "It's getting late. Shouldn't we head home?"

"No. We've got all night."

She rose to her feet. "I would like to go home."

"No." I gawked at her back side, appreciating the way her ass filled out those shorts before she turned around.

"No?" Arms crossed, she glared me down. "Tango. Take me home. Now."

I pushed off the sofa, meeting her toe to toe. "We're not going anywhere. Not yet."

"Fine. You stay. I'll go." She stormed to the kitchen counter.

As fast as she grabbed the car keys, I trapped her wrist in my fist. "What are you going to do? You can't even drive."

"I can drive. I just choose not to," she reminded me.

I wrenched the keys from her fingers. Not easily. She fought me every step of the way. I resorted to tickling to get her to release the damned key ring. When I won, which I always did, I stormed outside onto the deck and tossed the keys. They landed with a satisfying splash in the dark water.

"Oh my God. Why would you do that?" she screamed, slapping my back. "How in the hell are we gonna get home?"

Hot damn, Slade was gorgeous when she was angry. I turned and grabbed her shoulders, holding her at arms' length. It took all my willpower not to kiss her again. "Now you're stuck with me, and we're going to talk."

"Fine." She tried wiggling free.

I held her steady. Fuck, I wanted those lips.

Murderous eyes met mine. "You want the dirty details? How's this for dirty? You left. I was broken. I fucked the one person who was there for me. Then I learned he had a girlfriend and he disappeared, too. Pretty sure you can figure out the rest."

Ouch. Releasing her, I stepped back and scrubbed my hands over my face. I had betrayed her. Rocky's father had betrayed her. That would explain why she refused to date. "I'm sorry. Fuck. That's messed up."

Slade backed away, bumping into the counter. "You're sorry. I know. You've said it over and over. If you're sorry, stop asking me about it. I don't want to think about that night. I don't want to talk about Rocky's dad. Can you please let it go?"

"Okay." I threw my palms up in surrender. "No more questions."

Slade

"Well, I have a question. How are we supposed to get home now?"

Tango shrugged his shoulders. "Guess we're having a sleepover."

"No!" I shouted. "Absolutely not." I could not, would not, spend the night alone with Tango. "No. No. No."

I slipped my shorts off once again and headed for the door.

"What the hell are you doing?"

"Getting the damned keys." I'd swim all night if need be.

"It's too dark now. You'll never find them." He had the nerve to laugh at me.

"The water is shallow. I can find them. Where's your flashlight?"

"Slade. The keys are not going anywhere. We'll get them in the morning."

"Ooh!" I stomped my foot like an errant child. "I want to hurt you right now."

"Is the idea of spending the night with me that terrifying?"

"Yes. No. I mean..." Oh crap. What did I mean? The longer I was alone with him, the weaker my defenses. Why did he have to be so desirable? I rubbed the pain in my temples. "I don't know. This was supposed to be a day trip. I don't have clean clothes, no toothbrush, hair—"

Tango clamped a hand over my mouth. "Shh. You'll be fine. He turned me toward the front door. "See?"

My duffel bag sat next to his shiny suitcase. "What's this?" I already knew the answer. I'd been duped. The bastard had planned ahead.

"I knew you wouldn't come if I told you it'd be overnight."

"You lied to me."

"No. You asked if it would be a day trip. I didn't answer. I kissed you instead, remember?"

My insides heated to a nuclear level. "Screw you and your damn lips. Not fair, Tango. When did you have time to pack my stuff?"

"You're a deep sleeper. I snuck in this morning."

"I locked the doors." I had never been more frustrated in my life.

His crooked, prideful grin grated my every nerve ending. "I have a spare key to your house, you know, in case of an emergency."

That was the last straw. I snagged my shorts off the floor, tugged them back on and wiggled my feet into my flip-flops. I could not spend another second in the same space with that impossible man.

I shoved past him, giving the dickhead a hard bump with my shoulder, and stormed through the front door into the darkening forest. I'd head for the main road. I could get there in about thirty minutes, I figured. I was a fast walker. Someone would drive by eventually, and I could catch a ride back to town.

Okay, even I, the small-town hick, knew that wasn't smart, but I needed to be away from him. And it was either head toward the main highway, or into the woods. I wasn't properly equipped to handle any sort of mountain animal I might bump into, say a wolf, a bear, or Bigfoot, so highway it was.

I made it to the end of the gravel driveway before I heard footsteps behind me. My damn heart thumped faster, and not from adrenaline.

"Slade." My name rumbled like thunder behind me.

I marched forward, determined to hold my own, straining my eyes to safely place my steps between potholes and tangles of wildflowers and overgrown grass.

"For fuck's sake, stop."

I hadn't a nice word to speak. I sealed my lips.

The crunch of heavy feet drew closer. I hurried my pace. The toe of his shoe caught the back of my flip-flop, holding it in place while I propelled forward, landing with a crack on my right knee and the palms of my hands.

"Oh, shit. I'm sorry." He was kneeling at my side before I had time to register any pain.

I plopped onto my butt, defeated.

"Let me see." Tango grabbed my hands for a thorough inspection. He brushed off the dirt and dropped a soft kiss on each palm.

The sting of my injuries was nothing compared to the burn of his skin on mine. I looked down at my knee. Blood welled into a misshapen semi-circle before forming a warm trail down my leg. That didn't bother me so much. When I noticed my shoe was broken, I fought, with zero success, to stop the quiver of my lip.

With one hand, he smoothed hair off my face. With the other, he cupped my chin and brushed his thumb over my mouth. "Shit, babylove. How bad does it hurt?"

"Don't call me that. And it doesn't hurt." It did hurt. A loud sob broke loose. "You broke my shoe."

He fell back on his ass and draped his arms over his knees. "Seriously? You're crying over a damn piece of rubber?"

I picked up my mangled shoe, my Robart flip-flop, blue with flying pigs, and waved it in his face. "It's my favorite pair."

"Those aren't even shoes." He scrubbed a hand over the back of his neck.

"They're important to me. And you…" I whacked him in the shoulder. "You broke into my house, tricked me into spending the night with you, broke the no touching, no kissing rule, and now you've killed my favorite pair of shoes."

I mopped the annoying moisture off my face with the hem of my shirt and pushed to my feet. I could not afford to give this man another drop of my soul, yet it kept leaking through my eyes and rolling down my cheeks.

"I won't apologize." He looked up at me, head cocked to the side. "I want you in my life. You're forcing me to fight dirty."

I turned on my heel, kicked off my other shoe, and headed back toward the cabin. "Why did you have to come home?"

"What did you say?" he asked, voice deep, dark, and if I wasn't mistaken, sad.

I marched forward, barefoot, wishing I didn't want him to follow me, pretending I was strong enough to survive the evening unscathed. I didn't make it far before I stepped on a sharp stone. "Ouch. Shit."

I limped onward, cussing under my breath.

Tango grabbed my elbow. "Get on my back."

"I'm fine," I whispered, yanking my arm free.

"Jesus, Slade. Stop being so damn stubborn and let me help you," he shouted, stepping in front of me.

The sky had darkened enough that I could no longer see the ground. I'd never make it back on my own, not without slicing my feet to shreds. "Fine. Fine."

He turned around. I gripped his shoulders, hopped up, and snaked my arms around his neck.

"There. Not so bad, right?" he said with a grunt.

Not bad? It was terrible, because it was awesome. I felt like a kid again. I wanted to be this close to him for the rest of my life. Letting go was going to kill me.

Tango

The woman was killing me. She was hot, then cold, happy, then pissed. Soft and molten against me, then icy hard.

"Hold still." I clamped my hand over her thigh.

"It hurts, it hurts." She squeezed her eyes shut and sucked a sharp breath through her teeth. "And it's cold."

I emptied the contents of the peroxide bottle over her knee, let it bubble for a few seconds, then wiped her leg clean. There wasn't one bandage large enough to cover the laceration, so I dug through the multiple sizes in the box and patched her up the best I could.

"Why are those shoes special to you?"

"What?" she asked, sucking air between her teeth.

"You said they were special." I positioned the last bandage over her wound.

"They were the last gift my mom gave me, before she died. It was the first time she'd ordered anything online. She'd been pretty proud of herself."

"I see." Great. I did feel like an ass. "I am sorry about breaking them."

"She tried, you know."

"Tried what?" I asked. It gutted me, the way her eyes glazed every time she spoke of her mother. I ached to hold her, to comfort and kiss and chase away the sadness. I knew, deep down, I should be suffering the same loss, but when I thought of my mom, there was nothing but anger.

"After Rocky was born, she tried to stay sober. She loved him and was ecstatic to be a grandma, even if..." Slade's face reddened, her gaze dropped to the floor.

"Even if what?"

"Nothing. Never mind," she mumbled, shaking her head. "Anyway, her sobriety only lasted a month. I found her passed out in that shitty hotel on Eagle Point Drive. At least the man she'd hooked up with was decent enough to call me."

I tossed the bandage wrappers into the trash, then tapped her knee. "There, good as new."

Slade inspected my handiwork and hopped off the bathroom counter. "Thank you," she whispered, slipping through the door as if she couldn't wait to put distance between us.

I followed her to the kitchen. She grabbed a bottled water out of the refrigerator and tossed it my way before getting one for herself. When she made her way to the couch, I couldn't help but appreciate the softness in her glide and the way her hair swayed across her back. She fell into the brown leather and stretched her bare legs in front of her, plopping her heels on the knotty pine coffee table.

"Did you ever wonder what our parents were doing the day we met?" she asked, running a hand through her hair, pulling it away from her delicate face.

"No. I guess I haven't. What I remember about that day is looking out my bedroom window and seeing a girl who was nothing but skin and bones and wild, golden hair jumping off my dock."

"My mom told me to go play outside because she had an important meeting with Mr. Rossi. I was so excited when

I discovered the stairs leading down to the dock. The water was still and clear. I thought since I could see the bottom, it was okay for me to jump in. I sunk like a rock, and I couldn't breathe. I kept pushing off the bottom, trying to jump up for air. Then, there you were, pulling me to shore."

"And there you were, this skinny little thing, coughing up lake water, clinging to me like a scared cat. I thought for sure you would start crying, but you looked at me with your enormous blue eyes and laughed." I smiled at the memory. "Then you ran back onto the dock, did your funny dance, and jumped off again."

Slade put her bottle on the table. "And you pulled me to shore again, yelled at me, and said I wasn't allowed back on your dock until I had swimming lessons." She turned sideways on the couch and tucked her toes under my thigh. "God I was a stupid kid."

"Not stupid. Fearless." And funny, and happy, and full of life, and so over the top beautiful, I'd felt I'd been struck by lightning. I remembered thinking, that day I first met Slade, that maybe she was lost, like a stray kitten, and that maybe, if I begged my parents hard enough, I'd get to keep her, take care of her.

"Anyway, back to our parents. When Mom came looking for me, she looked ... weird. Scared even. And when she dragged me across your lawn and to your driveway, your mom was standing inside the front door with her suitcases, screaming at your dad in Spanish."

"No shit," I whispered.

"I told Mom I wanted to stay and swim with you, but she just yanked on my arm and walked faster."

"You don't think..." I couldn't say the words. The thought sickened me. I raked a hand over the top of my head, recalling the events of that day. "That's right. Mom had returned from

Argentina three days early. I remember now. After she got back, she was pissed at Dad, and he left for a week."

"That's why your mom hated me so much."

Slade may as well have punched a hole in my chest and squeezed the blood from my heart. "Damn. Why didn't you ever tell me about this?"

"I only remembered today, when we were on the dock."

"Dad couldn't keep his dick in his pants if his life depended on it." Unfaithful piece of shit. I refused to taint my evening with reminders of our parents' ugliness. So, after a few deep breaths and some serious concentration, I buried the anger.

"Mom couldn't keep a dick out of her pants," Slade retorted, laughing. Fucking laughing. God, she was amazing.

If she could keep it light, so could I. "It's a miracle we turned out so well-balanced, don't you think?" I raised my bottle in salute.

She snatched her water from the table and bumped it against mine, offering a half-hearted smile. When she sighed, I thought I was about to lose her again, until she set her drink down and crawled into my lap.

I couldn't keep up with my girl, but when she nestled her head against my chest, I didn't care. I wanted nothing more than to enjoy her, feel her, breathe her in.

I tightened my arms around her curves, rested my cheek on top of her head, and closed my eyes, shutting out the world so I could focus on her scent, her silky hair, her soft body curled against mine.

Aside from Mom's funeral, I hadn't stepped inside a church since moving to New York. Hadn't prayed much either, except before a fight. God and I were long overdue for a heart to heart. I offered Him what I had to give, and in that moment, it was gratitude, and the only words I could manage were *thank you, thank you, thank you.*

I pressed a kiss to the top of her head. "Slade."

"No talking, please. Let me absorb you for a while," she mumbled into my chest.

I could give her silence. I'd brought her here to talk, but my desire to keep her between my arms outweighed my bullheaded need to unearth her secrets.

I wanted her to trust me with the truth, with her heart and soul, with her son, with her life.

I had no right wanting anything from Slade. I didn't deserve her. I'd let too many guilt-filled years pass between us while I'd drowned in a world of anger, self-loathing, and cowardice. In spite of my mistakes, she clung to me, and I vowed to never let her go again.

"Okay. No talking." I squeezed her harder, absorbing her, too.

This is good.

Slade

This is bad. I was a horrible person. A detestable, greedy, manipulative bitch. Tango was tender, and caring, and trying to make amends. And dear God, how I wished we could conquer the monumental fuck-up that was my life. I wanted, more than anything, to hold him tight and never let go.

I had to remember, it wasn't about me, or my nonsensical fantasies. There was a bigger picture, and I had to keep a level head. To protect Rocky. To protect myself.

I fell asleep on Tango's chest. He was warm, and hard, and safe. He was my home. But I never should have let him back in.

I woke to a heavy arm tucked around my waist and a warm hand cupping my breast. A wool blanket covered us.

Minuscule dust particles danced and shimmied through the rays of sunlight pouring through the large windows of the cabin.

I yawned and stretched. My butt rubbed against an impressive erection. Tango pulled me closer. My insides warmed; my blood pressure spiked. I rolled off the couch. I couldn't get into another touchy, feely, make-out session with him. I enjoyed it too much and the chemistry between us was too potent.

Tango mumbled under his breath and rolled over, pulling the blanket with him. He was beautiful. Dangerously so. I watched him sleep, holding my emotions at bay. When admiring him became too much to bear, I headed for the kitchen.

He woke when the coffee percolated, wafting its aroma through the cabin. When he stood and stretched, in all his shirtless glory, I turned away. My body buzzed and hummed at the sight of him. I wanted him on top of me—touching, kissing, biting. Making love.

I pulled mugs from the cupboard and poured us both a cup. Before I could turn around, he snaked his arms around my waist and buried his nose in my hair, blowing warm breaths against my ear.

"Mmm..." He moaned, pulling my ass against his groin. "Good morning."

My knees weakened, and coffee sloshed over the rims of the cups. If he hadn't held me so tight, I would've dissolved into a puddle on the floor.

"Sleep okay?" he asked, releasing me and taking one of the drinks from my hand.

I hadn't slept that good in years. "I guess." I turned to face him and shrugged. "Why didn't you wake me up, make me go to bed?"

He lifted the coffee to his mouth and narrowed his eyes at me before taking a sip. He swallowed, then licked the moisture from his lips. "I couldn't let go."

I dropped my gaze to the floor, ashamed of leading him on the way I had. Tango hooked a finger under my chin, forcing me to look into his thoughtful eyes, reminding me why I had to continue my charade until I was able to leave town, leave him behind.

"Tell me you slept as good as I did." He leaned forward and stole my breath with a soft kiss. He slid his hand over my jaw and around the back of my head, tangling his fingers through my hair, and bringing our foreheads together. "I know you felt it. Every time I moved, you curled into me, clung to me like you were afraid to let go."

A sane woman would've chosen that moment to run like hell. Every second that ticked by, every touch and glance, every smile weakened my already pathetic resistance. Instead, I moved closer, seduced by the warmth and energy his body provided.

"We could sleep like that every night. Wake like this every morning. You just gotta let me in. All you have to do is ask. Please, say you want me. Say you'll give us a chance."

I did. I wanted him so badly my bones ached. Goddamn, why did life keep yanking the rug out from under me?

I took a deep breath, and a step away. "Are you going to fish the keys out of the lake, or am I?"

Tango's shoulders bunched. He dropped his head, scratched at the stubble on his chin, then released a sigh before slamming his coffee mug into the sink.

He reached around me, slid open a drawer, and pulled out a set of keys. "No need to get wet. I have a spare." Dangling them in front of me, he ordered, "Get your bag. Let's go."

Fire burned my gut. I wanted to rip him a new asshole, but what would be the point? I just needed to get home and away from the man.

We drove in silence for what seemed an eternity. I counted six times that his knuckles turned white with the force of his grip on the steering wheel.

When we stopped at the gas station, and Tango ran inside to pay, I snagged his phone off the dash, thumbed through his contacts and dialed the number I'd never thought I would have to call.

Carlos Rossi answered on the second ring. "Morning, T. What's up?"

"Mr. Rossi. Um..." I cleared the nerves from my throat. "It's Slade. Um. Slade Mason. Hi. How are you?"

"Surprised to hear from you." Not a lick of emotion in his tone.

I swallowed the last of my pride. "I'm ready."

"Those are the last words I expected to hear this morning. Are you sure?"

"Yes. How fast can we make this happen?"

"I have a few meetings to get through, but I'll get on it as soon as my schedule is clear. I'll have my lawyer call you this afternoon and set up an appointment."

"Good. Good. Thank you. And Carlos, I'm sorry about Marta."

"Are you?"

"Yes." It was only half a lie.

"Slade?"

"Um, yeah?"

"Does your sudden change of heart have anything to do with my son coming home?"

"Does it matter? You're getting what you want."

"Fair enough. We'll be in touch soon."

"Tango doesn't know!" I shouted into the phone, before he could hang up. "I'd like to keep it that way."

Carlos cleared his throat. "That's probably wise, Miss Mason."

"Thank you."

I ended the call and watched Tango walk toward the car with his innate confidence. Despite the perma-scowl, he moved in a way that incited lustful urges and suddenly the car was too hot. I shifted positions, squeezing my thighs together, ashamed of the throbbing sensation between my legs.

Tango folded into his seat and hooked his belt without looking my way. I shifted again and tucked my hands under my thighs to keep from touching him. Holy crap, I was a pressure cooker ready to blow.

He reached for the key and turned the ignition, highlighting the muscles in his forearm. When he wet his lips with a slow drag of his tongue, heat blasted my core, burning my cheeks, settling fierce and unrelenting between my legs. I scrubbed my hands over my face and tried to scrub the wretched desire away.

Dear sweet Jesus, what was wrong with me?

Tango

"What is wrong with you?" I killed the car and turned toward Slade.

"Nothing. Nothing. I'm fine." Releasing a nervous laugh, she dropped her arms to her sides and feigned interest in a spot on the passenger window.

I was done with the bullshit. "I don't fucking get you."

Her head snapped my way, and she had the balls to look offended.

"Why are you fighting this so hard? You want me. I mean, shit, look at you. It's in your eyes, your bright red cheeks, the way you're clenching your fucking thighs together." I didn't give her time to come up with another lie. "You're clinging to me one second, pushing me away the next. I'm getting whiplash trying to keep up."

Slade's fingers curled into her thighs. The red glow in her cheeks spread, reaching her chest.

Fearful of losing my shit, I sucked in a calming dose of oxygen. "Do you want to know why I came home?"

"To bury your mother," she said with a snap, eyes wild, challenging.

The steering wheel made a cracking sound under the force of my grip. Swear to Christ, had she been anyone else, I would've knocked that spiteful glare into the next county. But she was hurting. Hiding. Protecting herself. So I dug deep and buried the rage.

"I hated the lies. The manipulation. The bullshit. New York was dark, and the women were hard. I missed your softness, your bright smile, but more than anything, your honest heart. There was never any of that crap between us."

Slade wrapped her fingers around the door handle. Her breaths came rapid.

"I came home looking for my best friend. Didn't care if you were married. Dating. In love. It didn't matter. I just wanted that honest, pure connection again. I've never had that with anyone but you."

"Don't do this, Tango," she mumbled.

"Now there is a huge fucking lie between us. You know how I feel about being lied to."

"Leave it alone."

"What are you hiding?"

Her chest rose and fell, and she pulled on the handle. I grabbed her wrist to keep her from bolting.

"I know if I slid my hand between those sweet thighs, I'd find evidence of how badly you want me. Why are you fighting it so hard?"

"Enough!" she screamed, unbuckling her seatbelt and turning in her seat. She pounded her fists into my chest. "I want you. I want you. Is that what you need to hear? I want you so much it's killing me, but I am never, never letting you back in." Slade poked a pointed finger into my forehead. "Get that through your thick skull. We will never be together. I hate you for what you put me through. You need to take me home. Our perverted reunion is over. Understand? I don't want to see you again. Ever."

As she released her frustrations in the confines of my vehicle, I watched the walls slam down around her. First, with the dimming light in her eyes, then in the straightening of her spine. Her signals hadn't changed. When her giant heart needed protecting, she'd throw up the shields. Never had there been a need to put one between us, though. Until now.

We shared a stare down. Obviously, I wouldn't break through her barricade any time soon.

Slade yanked on the door handle and exited the car. I let her go. We both needed a minute. Slade, to cool her jets, and me, to tame my raging boner. I was turned on by her feisty spunk, but more so by the challenge she unwittingly laid down. I'd decimate that wall if it killed me.

Arms crossed, Slade leaned against the front of the SUV. I knew she was itching to walk, but the parking lot was dirt and gravel, and without shoes, she wouldn't make it far enough to burn off any frustration.

I heard the rumble of engines, felt the vibrations, before I noticed the gas station was filling up fast with one leather-clad gangster-on-wheels after another. Slade dropped her arms and froze in place.

"Get in the car, Slade. Now," I ordered before realizing the windows were up and she couldn't hear me.

With wild eyes, she scanned the Harley-riding motherfuckers, who, up until the point I tapped the horn to get her attention, hadn't paid us any mind. Slade didn't budge.

It was only a matter of time before they noticed her. I wasn't about to give them a chance to, either. If one of them liked what they saw, and they would, shit would get nasty. I couldn't take down twenty psychos to defend my girl. I'd give it my everything, but the odds wouldn't be in my favor.

I hopped out, dashed around the hood, and hooked my arm through her elbow, pushing her to the passenger side door. "Time to go."

From behind, I heard someone yell, "Hey, Blondie," followed by several loud whistles.

Fuck. Too late. I tucked her into her seat and hustled back to my own, wasting no time on a seatbelt or turn signal.

When we'd cleared a mile, and I was sure nobody had followed, my heart returned to its normal rhythm. Slade's skin was three shades paler. Her hands trembled in her lap, and she seemed to fight for air. "Babylove," I whispered, brushing her cheek with my knuckles. "You okay? You look like you saw a ghost."

She licked her lips, swallowed hard, then nodded, shooting me a nervous glance. "I'm fine. I thought I saw someone I knew. False alarm."

Voltolini conducted business with several MC charters on the East Coast. I knew too well what they were capable of. "Tell me you don't know any of those criminals."

"The only criminal I know is you, apparently." Shoulders tense, she raised her thumb to her lips and gnawed on the corner of her nail.

That stung. I let it slide. I had been a lawbreaker. No point in arguing. The past was the past. Slade was my future, and I'd be whatever she needed me to be.

Right then, judging by her body language, she needed me to be quiet.

CHAPTER 9

Tango

"DID YOU GET THE PACKAGE?" Setting my phone to speaker, I snapped it into the dock and turned the ignition.

"It's in my hot little fingers as we speak," Tito said, his voice gruff. If there was information to be procured, Tito Moretti was the guy to call. To him, my private job would be nothing more than a preschool game of connect the dots.

"Good. She got a call around nine, two nights ago. Find out who it came from."

"Sure thing," he mumbled.

In a momentary fit of insanity, I considered asking how Aida was getting along. Instead, I mumbled, "Thanks, Tito."

"How soon you need it?"

"Yesterday."

"Give me an hour."

"That's why I love you."

Only after I ended the call did I realize my palms were sweaty, despite the arctic breeze blasting from the vent. Slade would be pissed when I showed up. Probably cause a scene. But I wasn't ready to give up. Sure as hell wasn't going to run again.

When I rolled into the Truck Stop's gravel lot, my ticker dropped like a lead weight to my gut. Slade stood outside, next to a man in blue, who stood next to a police car. The back door of the diner hung crooked on its hinges. Charlie sat on a crate holding a towel to his head.

I parked around front and made my way into the diner, surprised to find it was open and full of customers. I'd intended to head through the kitchen to find out what the fuck had happened, but another officer blocked the way, scribbling notes while Kim rambled about being the last one to arrive at work that morning.

She turned and offered me a wink. "I'll be right with you, Tango. Find a seat."

I wanted to question her, but the cop shot me a glare and tapped his pen on his notepad. I searched the room for a place to park my ass, and smiled when I spied a familiar face. Maurice sat at the same table he'd occupied every morning since Slade and I were kids. He'd aged some in the past six years, but his steely blue eyes and deep dimple remained the same.

"What a surprise. Look at you, boy." He chuckled, and rapped his knuckles on the end of the table.

I took his trembling hand in my own and gave him a firm shake. "Maurice. Nice to see you."

"I knew I'd run into you again if I hung around long enough."

I'd always loved the guy. "Yeah. Took me awhile to find my way home. But here I am." I settled into the seat across from him.

"Last time we shared a table, you wanted advice about a ring."

"That's right." I'd wanted to marry Slade the day she turned eighteen. Maurice had encouraged me to wait until after college.

"Did you ever buy it?"

"No." Shame clogged my throat. "Never got the chance."

His boney knuckles rapped the table. "I know, son. I know."

The redheaded waitress topped off Maurice's coffee and poured a mug for me. "I'm sorry, boys. No breakfast this morning. The kitchen is out of commission for a bit."

"What happened?" I asked. "Slade okay?"

"Everyone is fine. Charlie's got a bump on his head. He came in early this morning and got clocked from behind, but he managed to wrestle them out the back door. Cops said he probably stopped a robbery in progress. Slade found him on the floor when she arrived."

Fuck. Every muscle in my body drew tight. Fists clenched under the table, I forced my rage to stay below the surface. It could've been Slade. What if she had arrived first? My body rumbled with unchecked anger. *Keep your shit together, T.* The last thing Slade needed was to see my monster. I was here to win her back, not scare the shit out of her.

"The paramedics have come and gone already. Said Charlie was fine. The big lug refused to go home. Soon as the cops clear the kitchen, we'll be up and running again." Kim shot me a wink and left to attend her other customers.

Maurice studied me for an uncomfortable spell with glassy eyes. "Slade is a good girl. Strong. Independent. Damn good mother. You don't need to worry about her."

I almost laughed out loud. Was I that obvious? "I can't help but worry."

"You love her," he stated, his voice softening.

Nothing like cutting straight to the chase. "Never stopped."

"Then what's the problem? She loves you, too. Get her. Fight for her. You three belong together."

We three? That statement threw me back for a moment. I hadn't considered that getting my girl back meant I'd be raising another man's child, living with a constant reminder that I'd failed her. That was a heavy load to carry. "That's exactly what I'm doing. I'm fighting, but she keeps pushing me away."

Maurice dropped his gaze to his coffee cup, wrapping both hands around the white porcelain. "She's a tough cookie. Doesn't want to depend on anyone, just like her mother. Don't give up."

"Make no mistake," I said, tapping my thumbs on the table. "I'll break through her wall if it's the last thing I do."

"You want answers. I get that." He tilted his head, drawing his brows tight. "What happens if you don't like what you find?"

He knew something. Damn. I should've come to him sooner.

"Maurice. If you had any idea who I've been working for, you'd understand there isn't a damn thing Slade could tell me that would scare me away. I've seen it all. Heard it all. Done unforgivable shit. I've beaten men to the edge of death trying to wipe away the pain of losing her."

The old bugger's eyes actually welled with tears. I'd always known he had a soft spot for Slade. Her mother, too. Never understood why. Guess I had never given it much thought.

He huffed. Opened his mouth to speak. Snapped it shut. Looked over his shoulder as if to make sure no one was listening. "Ask your father what happened to the other girl, Slade's friend."

"Addison," I mumbled, fighting a shiver. "What do you know about her?"

"That's all I can say. I'm sorry, son. You've got your work cut out for you. Slade won't be easy to break."

"I don't want to break her. I just need her back in my life. I want to help." I leaned forward, gripping the edge of the table. "Please. Tell me what you know."

"I can't."

We locked scowls for an uncomfortable spell, neither one backing down.

"What are you doing here?" Slade's voice broke our battle of wills, and I traded one game of stare-down for another.

Maurice dropped some change on the table and grunted as he pulled himself out of the booth. "I need to get home. I'll see you tomorrow, Slade."

"Bye, Maurice. I'll see you tomorrow." Her wide eyes darted back and forth between the two of us before settling on me.

I cleared my throat, ready for a fight. "Sit down. Please."

Brows pinched, she shot me a warning glare. "What were you two talking about?"

"You."

"Why?"

I tapped on the edge of my coffee cup. "You know why."

"What did he tell you?" she asked, her tone worrisome.

"He only stated the obvious. We still love each other."

"He's a stupid, senile old man. What does he know?"

Ouch. "Obviously more than I do."

"Enough, Tango. You need to leave. It's been a shitty morning, and you're the last person I need to see right now." Slade stormed toward her office.

I followed. She was not getting off that easy.

"Where do you think you're going?" she asked, attempting to shut the door before I could enter.

I blocked it with my foot. "Just want to make sure you're okay. Do you know who broke in?"

"No," she said, stepping back in defeat, looking everywhere but at me.

"Has it happened before?" Crossing my arms, I leaned against the door frame.

"Once. Years ago. I never keep money here overnight, so there was nothing to steal." Slade moved to her desk and shuffled through a stack of mail. "I'm busy, Tango." She came to a large white envelope and tucked it into her handbag, but not before I caught glimpse of the Rossi Corporation logo.

Interesting. I'd file that bit of information away for later.

"Did you hear me? I'm busy. That's your cue to leave."

I had no intention of leaving without answers. "Where's Rocky, Slade?"

Her leg bounced like a jackhammer under her desk. She gnawed the bottom of her lip before flipping me the bird. "Not your concern."

Any fool could see that fear dictated her actions. Fuck if that didn't make me need to push harder. "What happened to Addison? The truth this time."

Slade slammed her palms on the desk. "Get out of my restaurant."

"What are you hiding from me?"

"You are not welcome here anymore. Get out. Don't come back."

Charlie came around the corner, laying a heavy hand on my shoulder. "Hey, T. Everything kosher?"

"I'm having a conversation with my girl, Charlie. Give us a minute?"

Charlie cleared his throat. "Listen, Tango. You know I love ya, but Slade's had a rough morning. She asked you to leave. Don't make me ask, too."

Charlie had at least a hundred pounds on me. Most of them soft. I could take him down easy enough. But I liked the guy, and he did have Slade's back. Had to give him props.

"All right." I nodded, and stepped away from the door. "I'm sorry," I whispered before turning to leave. I would give her this round, but I hadn't lost a fight yet.

She caught me by the elbow halfway down the hall. Face flushed, breaths shallow, she begged, "Please. Please. If you ever cared about me, leave. Go back to New York. This town isn't big enough for both of us."

Ouch. That stung. Like a paper cut dipped in lemon juice. I only nodded, swallowing the lump of emotion threatening to choke me. I needed to drag her into her office, kiss her dizzy, and remind her of why I could never leave. Instead, I turned and walked away.

I dialed Tito's number as I retreated to my car. He answered on the first ring. "Yeah, bud."

"I want details on every personal contact on that card. Names. Addresses. Backgrounds."

"Done. I have one name for you now. The call she received the other night came from a cell registered under the name Tucker Slade. Thirty-two. Single. Moved to Whisper Springs a couple years ago."

"Slade? You sure?"

"Yeah, he and his father, James, own Slade Trucking based out of Billings, Montana. James's wife is an ob/gyn. Has her own practice. Tucker resides in Whisper Springs, runs the Idaho hub."

"You don't fucking say."

"There's one more thing. She made several calls to another cell number, twenty-six times in the past week. They all went unanswered. Took some digging, but I got a name. Dane Reynolds. I'm working on his rap sheet now. Send you the intel when I have it."

The Rover shrunk around me. Dane. Fuck.

"I need everything you can find on Dane Reynolds. His cousin, too. Addison Reynolds."

"Addison? Isn't she the crazy chick you—"

"Don't say it, Tito. Fuck's sake. Just send me everything you can on both of them."

"What's up with your girl, T? You retiring your dick? Luciano's ladies will be heartbroken."

"That's precisely what I'm doing."

"Sweet. More pussy for me." He chuckled. "I'll send a file when I have the other intel."

"Thanks, again."

My car heated a few thousand degrees, or maybe it was just me. I started the engine and blasted the air conditioning. James Slade. Was it possible she'd found her father? Why hadn't she mentioned him? Rocky had said on the phone he was with Uncle Tucker and his grandparents.

Fucking secrets and lies.

I dialed Dad's assistant. "Hey, Lisa. Yes. I'm good. You? Good to hear. I need a favor. Can you book me a couple flights? New York, then Billings, Montana."

Lisa put me on hold, giving me time to ponder my next move. Slade was not making things easy, but I was not about to quit.

Rossis didn't quit.

I considered Maurice's warning about not liking what I'd find, and decided that whatever it was, I'd deal. I would make things right for my girl. I would win her back.

I dropped my head to the back of my seat and closed my eyes, allowing the cool air to calm me the fuck down.

Addison. Dane. I had the pieces to the puzzle. I just couldn't get them to fit.

"What am I missing, babylove?"

Slade

"I miss you, babylove," I sighed into the phone.

"Mom," Rocky growled. "I'm not a baby."

"Right. How about ... pumpkin?"

"No," he said, cocky and pretentious like his father.

"Little man?"

"I'm not little."

Jeez. I hated this growing up crap. "Just Rocky?"

"Yes. Just Rocky. Grandpa says I have the coolest name ever. He used to be a boxer. He showed me his trophies. He even lets me beat up a punching bag."

"I'm happy you're having so much fun."

"I gotta go, Grandpa's waiting for me in the truck. We're going to buy a new fishing pole. Here's Tuck. Love you, Mom."

"Love you, baby ... I mean, Rocky."

"Slade?" Tucker sounded short of breath.

"Hi, Tuck."

"Shit. I thought Rockster would never stop talking." He blew a long breath into the phone. "What happened? I've been trying to call you. Charlie said you took a couple days off."

No need for Tucker to hear the hows and whys, so I skipped to the end. "I busted my phone. Took me awhile to get this new one figured out."

"Slade. Rocky called you the other night. Talked to Tango. Told him he was with his grandparents. I tried to grab the phone, but he locked himself in the bathroom."

I laughed, picturing that scene, then realized what Tucker had said. "Wait. What?"

"Tango answered your phone, said you were in the bathroom. Asked Rockster how camp was. Your baby-boy spilled the beans, lil sis."

"Fuck. Fuck. Fuck!" Tango knew I'd been lying the whole time. No wonder he'd been relentless in questioning me. "Oh fuck, Tuck. Shit. What am I gonna do?" I paced the width of the kitchen. "It's over. My life is over."

"Whoa, whoa, whoa. Slow down. Deep breaths."

"I can't breathe. I can't breathe, Tuck. He's going to find out."

"Snap out of it, Slade. He won't find out. If he knew anything, shit would've hit the fan already."

"I don't know about you, but I'm feeling pretty covered in crap right now." I pressed my butt against the counter and slid to the floor. Deep breath in, deep breath out. And again. In. Out. It wasn't helping. "I can't go to jail, Tuck. I can't lose Rocky. Oh my God? What am I going to do? I should never have come back to town. I should've moved far away, changed my name." I tugged at a loose thread on my jean shorts.

"Slade. Pull your shit together. I'll talk to Dad when he gets back. We'll figure this out. No one will take Rocky away from you, understand? I'll die before letting that happen."

I believed him. Tucker, James, Lettie. They loved Rocky like he was their own flesh and blood. We had each put our lives on the line for my boy. We all had something to lose.

I had to talk to Tango. I had to find out what he knew. I had to cover one lie with another.

Lies.

Lies.

Lies.

I would drown in them.

I dialed Tango's number. No answer. I couldn't wait for him to call me back. It took all the courage I could muster to pull myself off the floor and step outside.

When I reached the Rossi estate an hour later, my clothes were drenched with perspiration. It was the hottest day of the year. Ninety-seven in the shade. Why hadn't I called a taxi or borrowed Marion's car?

I stood at the arched entryway and shook out my nerves before pushing the doorbell. A petite, Latino woman greeted me.

"Maria?" I slapped my hand over my mouth. Maria had been Tango's nanny, and when he no longer needed a nanny, she had been promoted to staff supervisor. I'd always adored the woman.

A loud shrill pierced my ears. "Oh Dios mío. Look at you. My, my, my." Like an anaconda, her arms coiled around me, stifling my ability to inhale. "So beautiful." She dropped her arms and took a step back to inspect me head to toe. "Princesa. So lovely to see you," she said in her thick accent, grabbing my hand and pulling me into the house.

"Hi." Maria hadn't aged at all. Gorgeous olive skin. Jet black hair cut in a short bob and tucked behind her ear. Chubby cheeks. A smile wider than the Grand Canyon, and welcoming eyes that never let you down. "I'm here to see Tango. Is he around?"

"No. I'm sorry. Mr. Rossi left yesterday."

"Left?"

"Yes. His father drove him to the airport yesterday morning. Said he was going home to New York."

"Oh." I should've been elated. Instead, my heart and chest deflated.

"Would you like me to get a message to him?"

Had he given up? Had I convinced him to leave? Maybe the lying beast I'd turned into disgusted him, and he'd decided he didn't want me back after all. "No. No. That's not necessary. I have a long walk home. Could I bother you for a glass of water before I go?"

"Sí. Sí. Of course. But you shouldn't walk so far in this heat. I'll drive you."

"Oh no. I couldn't put you out."

"Nonsense." Maria dismissed my refusal with a wave of her hand and headed down the main hall toward the kitchen. The house was exactly as I'd remembered, except it didn't look as big as it did when I was a kid. Expensive artwork covered the walls. The wood floors were still polished to a reflective shine.

When we passed the grand staircase, I fought the urge to run up the steps and dive into Tango's bed, like we used to do when we were kids, before I was banned for being a white-trash whore.

Maria grabbed a bottle of Evian from the refrigerator, which I quickly and gratefully drained. "Thank you," I sighed.

"I have an appointment in town. Come. I'll drop you off. It will be so lovely to catch up."

We made our way past the back staircase when a familiar voice stopped us cold.

"Where are you going dressed like that? Get back in here."

"Carlos. Tango is gone. The staff know better than to talk. I'm tired of hiding."

I looked up the stairs in time to see a blonde head tuck behind the double doors that led to Tango's parents' bedroom. The voice and the head of hair belonged to Kaylee.

Hmm. I could've contrived a list of everything that was wrong with that scenario, but I figured they deserved each other, and neither of them were worth my brain juices.

When the lock clicked, Maria mumbled, "Esa puta" under her breath, compressing all of my thoughts into two simple words, and continued through the door leading to the six-car garage.

She led me past a Range Rover, a Porsche, then a Mercedes.

Oh God. *The* Mercedes.

My stomach flipped. My knees buckled. Visions slammed so hard and fast I fell to my knees.

Tango. Bow tie dangling from his opened collar. Hair disheveled. Eyes glassy and unfocused.

Addy. Hair bouncing. Skirt bunched around her waist. Riding. Moaning.

Kissing. Fucking.

Addy and Tango. In the back seat of his daddy's Mercedes.

I vomited on the pristine, tiled floor of Carlos Rossi's garage.

Far away, or maybe right next to me, Maria called my name.

I pushed to my feet and ran.

Through the door. Across the lawn. Down the long drive and through the security gate. I ran. When I couldn't run anymore, I walked.

I headed toward the Truck Stop. When I hit the parking lot, I made my way past the restaurant and headed down the trail to the beach. I kicked off my shoes. Trudged through the water. When chest deep, I floated onto my back and willed the current to take me away.

I lost my shoes somewhere between Maple Avenue and Sycamore Lane. Didn't matter. I never wanted to wear them again. I ran until my legs gave out, and I cracked my knees and palms on the asphalt. I stayed that way, on all fours, in the middle of the dark street, huffing, and faint, and blank.

Tango had seen me, seeing him.

He would come after me. Explain it all away.

I waited, shuffling through memories like a mad woman, desperate to find an excuse for his actions. Maybe it was a dream. Perhaps I'd misunderstood. Either way, I knew, I just knew, he'd find me and stitch my deadly wound.

I stayed where he could find me, my heart bleeding out, on that dark street.

He didn't come.

Lifetimes passed before the roar of a motorcycle startled me from my delusions. The engine cut and thick-soled, black boots stepped into my line of sight.

"Hey, Blondie."

A familiar voice.

"I found these down the road." He dropped my four-inch heels at my side. "Care to talk about it?"

I curled into a ball, the bite of the asphalt on my bare skin a welcome distraction. I never wanted to talk again.

Dane didn't ask any more questions.

Dane squatted, slipped my shoes on my feet.

Dane lifted me off the road and settled me on his bike.

Dane wiped the blood from my hands and knees.

Dane dusted the muck off my three-hundred-dollar dress.

Dane.

Dark.

Dangerous.

Dane...

Saved me.

Tango

I would not survive losing Slade again, but if protecting her meant going behind her back to uncover whatever she was hiding, I would risk pissing her off, and yes, possibly losing any chance at winning her love.

From behind the safety of my tinted glass, I watched Doctor Leticia Slade spin her graying hair into a neat bun and fasten it on top of her head. She slid her shoulder bag and briefcase behind her seat, then hoisted herself into the dust-coated Ford. Because she was petite, maybe a pinch over five feet, it took some muscle and gumption to settle behind the wheel.

I waited for her to roll a few cars ahead of me, then pulled onto the street. My light blue rental sedan was inconspicuous enough, but I didn't want to draw attention to myself, so I stayed a safe distance behind. I followed her through town until she turned off Garden Avenue onto a long dirt driveway that led through a sprawling property.

The house at the end of the drive was modest. Several fenced, unkempt fields surrounded the white rancher. The yard, however, was immaculate and landscaped to perfection. Bright red and fuchsia flowers hung in baskets across the wraparound porch. Behind the house stood a large red barn, its doors open wide. Parked inside was a shiny blue eighteen-wheeler. The sun bounced off its polished chrome, casting an eye-squinting glare my way.

Sure enough, when Dr. Slade hopped out of the truck, Rocky James Mason, flanked by a black dog twice his size, sprinted through the front door and barreled into her arms.

For some odd reason, seeing the little guy happy and safe warmed my insides.

I rolled past the property, parked under the shade of a juniper tree, and scrolled through the records Tito had emailed earlier. My guts knotted and unbidden anger heated my face at the sight of Addy's name. I'd never liked the girl. Tolerated her for Slade's sake. Such a shame; Addy had been every bit as smart and pretty as Slade, only she had chosen to use her intelligence to manipulate people. A costly lesson I'd learned firsthand.

Addy's mother had run off with a man when we were thirteen, leaving her in the care of her unstable uncle, Walter Reynolds.

According to Tito's findings, Addison had quit her job at the Dollar Tree and disappeared from Whisper Springs three months after graduation, around the same time Slade had left town.

Walter's son, Dane, had lived with them off and on. He'd been arrested numerous times—drugs and other petty crimes. The charges never seemed to stick. Slippery fucker was now running with the damn Satan's Slayers.

No doubt in my mind, it was his bike Brett's mother had seen Slade on.

To my core, and with equal measures shame and disgust, I knew that tattooed motherfucker had to be Rocky's father. I understood, respected, and was grateful for Slade's decision to keep Rocky a secret. If she hadn't, she'd have been lost to me forever. If Dane knew Rocky was his child, Slade would have zero say in her or Rocky's fate. Girls like her didn't survive long with men like Dane. Club life would have destroyed her.

The thought of her being afraid of anyone filled me with rage. I squeezed my phone until I heard a crack, then tossed it on the passenger seat. The other files could wait. I needed a shower and at least two cold brews before I could read further.

I turned the car around with the intention of heading to my hotel back in town. Had a plume of smoke not caught my eye, I might have missed the mountain of muscle wearing a black cut over nothing but tatted skin, leaning against a mean-looking Harley, ankles crossed, cancer stick hanging between his lips, attention aimed at the white house.

I slowed to a stop. Through the rearview, the skull and snake emblem and the white print on the back of his vest stood out clear as day. Satan's Slayers.

Faster than a flipped switch, I turned, from calm and cool to raging beast. In a fit of adrenaline-amped fury, I jumped from the car and was on the guy faster than he'd heard me coming. I struck. Once. Twice.

He grunted, but didn't teeter. His hand was at my throat. My back hit the dirt. We wrestled. I gained the upper hand, straddled his thick torso. Through his heavy beard, the fucker showed off a set of yellow choppers.

I struck again.

The man laughed, eyes fixed over my shoulder.

I realized my mistake. He wasn't alone.

I turned to block the oncoming strike. Not fast enough. With a flash of white hot pain, I was down for the count.

I woke, choking on the iron tang of blood, my face throbbing like the bass drum at a Slayer concert, in the driver's seat of the rental sedan. When I moaned in agony, cold metal pressed to the back of my skull.

"Drive, pretty boy," the man holding the gun ordered.

I wiped my bloody knuckles on my pant leg. My head buzzed like a son of a bitch, and the world spun around me. "Not doing shit 'til you tell me why the fuck you're casing that house." Through the rearview, I could see the man wore a baseball cap pulled low. With the aviator shades and his full beard, the only facial feature I could make out was the crooked blade of his nose.

The man leaned closer, his breath heating my ear. "Not your fucking concern." He tapped the side of my head with the gun's muzzle. "Drive."

I turned the key. Pressed the gas. Rolled onto the quiet street. Minutes passed in excruciating silence before my captor released a loud sigh.

"Where the hell am I going?" I asked through gritted teeth.

"Where are you shacked up?"

"Rimview Inn."

"Head there."

"What's your connection to the Slade family?"

The asshole pulled off his cap and glasses. With his long auburn hair and unkempt facial fur, he remained indistinct. Until he met my gaze through the reflection with a pair of wild, angry, and fucking huge green eyes.

I nearly choked on my rage. "Reynolds."

"Listen, pretty boy. No time for a reunion here. Tell me what the hell you're doing in Montana."

I wasn't telling that criminal shit. "Why the fuck you stalking that family?"

"Stalking?" He barked out a laugh that didn't contain a lick of joy, then turned his head to look out the window. "I heard the boy was here. Just wanted to get a look at him."

My heart rate spiked. He'd been keeping tabs. He knew about Rocky. "Get a look. That's all?"

He nodded, then sucked in a sharp breath. "That's all. Needed to see him living and breathing with my own two eyes." Dane shifted behind me, then leaned forward, resting his elbows on the two front seats, waving the Ruger around like he couldn't decide where the target mark was on my head. "Never thought I'd see your pretty mug again. Blondie send you?"

Fuck. He'd given her a nickname. "Nobody sent me. Slade doesn't know I'm in Billings."

He cocked his head to the side. "Interesting. I assume, since you're here, that you know about the boy. What I'm worried about is how much you know and what you plan on doing about it."

"I know enough, and I'm not doing shit. Unless you plan on going after my girl. That happens, you and me are gonna get bloody."

Dane's lip curled in a snarl. "Fucking rich-ass, pansy motherfucker. If I wanted Blondie, I could've taken her the night you fucked my cousin. Which reminds me." His fist met my jaw, my head met the window. I swerved. He grabbed the wheel and righted the car. "Keep driving. You pass out on me, I'll shoot all that pretty, clean off your face."

No need to ask what the cold cock was for. I deserved it.

I white-knuckled the steering wheel, forcing the murderous urges down deep. I'd be no good to Slade dead.

"So what's the plan, Reynolds? You get a look at your boy, you go back to the club, forget he exists? Can you really just walk away?"

"You got balls of steel talking to me about walkin' away. You privileged fucker. You should be thanking me. I've been shoveling your shit for six damn years. I can't walk away from something I never had. The club can't know he exists. I can't have anything to do with either one of them."

What the fuck was he spewing on about? "Help me understand something, Reynolds. What's so fucking special about that club to make you give up your son? What kind of man—"

"That club," he interrupted. "My brothers are the only family I got, which is more than I can say for..." Dane fell back into his seat and tapped the Ruger against his forehead. "Wait a minute. Wait a motherfuckin' minute." He dropped his forehead into his palms and rubbed his eyes. "*My* son?"

I turned into the hotel parking lot and slammed the car into park, more confused than ever. "You didn't know?"

Dane's shoulders bobbed, and a deep, menacing laugh tore from his throat. "You're as stupid as you are pretty." He pushed his door open, unfolded from the small space and proceeded to *help* me out of the car by wrapping a large hand around my throat, and tucking the barrel of his 9mm under my chin. "I should kill you right here, for bein' so damn ignorant."

Dane's buddy pulled into the slot next to us, cut his engine, and dismounted his bike. He ripped his helmet off with a jerk, revealing a bald scalp, a scar that stretched from mouth to ear, and a glare that promised a shitload of misery to anyone who crossed him. The guy was an inch shorter than Dane, but deadly all the same. "Get what you needed?" he asked Dane, never taking his eyes off me.

Dane grunted a yes and pushed me toward the entrance.

Baldy pulled a blade from under his cut. "We doin' him in the room?"

Slade

"We're doing this now," Dane yelled over the phone. *"It's your only chance. Shit goes tits up, it's over. Hear me? They're bringing the buyers in tonight. If they like what they see, that kid is gone for good. Understand? She's alone, but*

not for long. You got thirty minutes, give or take. And Slade, don't fucking ask her permission first. There's no nice way to go about this. The girl is jacked. Grab her, however you gotta do it, and get the fuck clear of that cabin."

I nodded, mindless to the fact he couldn't see me. Dane's words faded to garbled noise, and everything seemed to move in slow motion. I watched Tucker snag the keys from the counter and nod to James. When he tucked a gun into a holster under his shirt, my hands started to tremble.

"You hear me, Blondie? We can never talk again after this."

"Yeah. Yeah," I managed to mumble.

Tucker grabbed my arm and yanked me out the back door.

"Thanks again, Dane. I owe you so much." I waited for his response, but he'd already ended the call.

"Miss Mason."

"Yes," I said, shaking the haunting memory from my thoughts.

"Mr. Rossi will see you in just a moment. His conference call ran a bit late."

"That's fine. Thanks, Lisa." I forced a smile at the gorgeous redhead and watched her busy herself behind her desk.

Sweet Lord, my palms were sweaty. The manila envelope in my hands made for an adequate fan, I supposed, but my inner oven seemed to be on the fritz, melting me from the inside out.

I closed my eyes, sucked in a deep dose of oxygen, and blew it out nice and slow. I had nothing to fear. I'd faced scarier adversaries.

I reminded myself that I had the upper hand. Carlos Rossi had been after my property for longer than I could remember. He wanted it, he'd get it, but I wouldn't let him take advantage. He'd have to bleed for this win.

I rose from the white leather chair and looked out the window of the reception area. The view, as expected, was stunning. Downtown Whisper Springs, the city beach, the lake. The once quaint town was now vibrant and busy and teeming with tourists, beachgoers, and outdoor enthusiasts. New construction bloomed everywhere I looked. My hometown had grown so much I hardly recognized it anymore.

"Beautiful, isn't it?" The deep voice, although familiar, ignited prickly chills down my spine.

"It's become too commercial, if you ask me," I replied. "We're losing our small town charm." I wasn't about to make nice with a man I was prepared to play hardball with. The man who was responsible for the changing face of Whisper Springs.

He chuckled, placed a hand at the small of my back, and gestured toward his office door. I strode forward, steeling my spine, head held high. If only I could've controlled my wobbly ankles. I hadn't worn heels since that awful night six years ago, and the moment I stepped onto his plush carpet, my foot turned and gravity took hold.

Mr. Rossi caught my arm and held me upright. So much for my confident facade. I thanked him, after I steadied myself, and sat in the brown leather chair situated in front of his desk.

When he sat opposite me, I choked down my nerves and forced myself to meet his gaze. My eyes burned with threatening tears. His eyes. Dear God. So green. Like dewy moss enjoying its first rays of the morning sun. Eyes so familiar my chest ached.

"It's lovely to see you again, Miss Mason. Excuse me for staring. You look so much like your mother."

It took everything I had not to punch him in his smug face. "I could say the same for you and Tango." Aside from the wrinkles around his eyes, and the gray hairs, the two of them could pass for twins.

Carlos cleared his throat and folded his hands on top of the desk. "Thank you for meeting me without the lawyers. I wanted this to be a pleasant discussion. I know how much that diner means to you. Do you mind if I ask why the sudden change of heart?"

Imminent death at the hands of a violent gang. Life sentence for murder and kidnapping. So, so many reasons.

"It's time for me to move on." I licked the dryness from my lips and pulled my papers from the envelope. "This is the list of things I need from you, Mr. Rossi. You want the property, it's yours as long as you meet these conditions."

"Please. Call me Carlos. No need for formalities." He skimmed the stack of papers, brows shooting up in surprise more than once.

"If I don't agree to these terms?"

"You're not the only interested party."

Carlos shook his head, sat back in his seat, and laughed. "Styles?"

Oh, yes. Ray Styles. The thorn in Rossi's side. Former business partner turned rival. "I'm not at liberty to say."

Carlos pushed a button on his desktop phone. "Lisa. Would you mind ordering lunch for two? Santino's please. The usual. And please cancel my appointments for the rest of the afternoon. Miss Mason and I will be here awhile." He winked at me, a fresh twinkle in his eye.

"Certainly, Mr. Rossi," Lisa's voice rang through the speaker.

Carlos rose from his chair and crossed the room to his mini bar. He poured a drink and offered me one, which I declined. When he sat back down, pretty crystal tumbler in hand, his eyes narrowed on me. "There's a little bit of devil hiding behind that angelic mask, isn't there, Miss Mason?"

Oh, if he only knew. "You've no idea."

Tango

"You've no idea what the fuck's goin' on, do you?" Dane leaned against the bathroom doorframe and flipped through the Bible that he'd pulled out of the nightstand drawer. "Fuck. I've dreamed of this day for years. Prayed we'd run into each other."

I spit blood on the ground at my feet. "Wouldn't take you for a praying man."

Baldy pressed the sharp end of his blade deeper into my neck.

"I swore, if I ever got the chance, I'd cut off that dick and feed it to you." Dane threw the book on the bed and stomped toward me, fists clenched, cheeks red, eyes narrowed to deadly slits. "Problem is, pretty boy, I can't kill you." He pressed his nose to my cheek and released a frustrated breath in my ear. "Ain't that a bitch. 'Cause I got a hundred and one ways of makin' a pansy-ass fucker like you scream."

He shoved his hand into my crotch, grabbed my boys and twisted, indeed making me scream, and crumple to the floor, where I stayed until I could breathe again. When I pushed to my feet, neither one of my new buddies made a move toward me. They only watched, half amused.

"Sit," Dane ordered, pointing to the bed.

I only obeyed because my head was a fuzzy mess.

"I know where you've been, who you work for, what you're capable of."

"The fuck you talking about?"

"I've had eyes on you. I've had eyes on Blondie and the boy, too. I need to pull my men off her. Club's getting suspicious, and I'm done risking my life for your fuck-up. So here's the deal. I ain't gonna kill you. Long as I have your word you're gonna be her guardian angel. Hire your own damn men to watch out for them."

"What the hell did she do to need protection?"

"Only thing you gotta know is that she tangled with a brother. Club doesn't know it was her, but they find out? Nothing I can do to stop the natural progression of things. Got me? Anyone harms a hair on either one of their heads, I'll unleash the gates of Hell on your ass."

"Tell me something, tough guy. You hate me so much, why you trusting me with your son's life."

Dane threw his head back and laughed. Fell into a fit of hysterics. Tears and all. Baldy found it amusing and joined in. I watched, trembling with rage.

When composed, Dane headed for the door and turned to face me, one hand on the knob. "Fuckin' idiot. I tried to tap that ass, but the fuckin' cunt wouldn't spread 'em for me. The kid ain't mine. He's blood, but he ain't mine." He tapped his index finger to his temple. "Think, pretty boy. You'll figure it out. And when you do, I'm trusting you to do the right thing. You ain't gonna like what you find. But you'll damn well deal with it, that is, if you prefer keeping your head attached to your shoulders. Think," he said again, laughing. With that, he disappeared.

I couldn't think past the pain shooting through my head and groin. Somehow, I managed to shower and order dinner. When settled, I pulled up the other files Tito had sent to my phone.

When I opened the first folder, labeled *Slade Mason Hospital Records*, my blood turned frigid. The picture attached to the file wasn't Slade. It was Addison Reynolds. She looked two breaths short of death. Cheeks hollow, dark circles around her eyes, hair stringy and greasy. A gash stretched from the corner of her mouth to her ear. It'd been stitched, not by a professional. The Slayer's skull and snake symbol was tatted under her left eye.

Doctor Leticia Slade was listed as her physician. I struggled to decipher the notes and medical jargon, but it didn't take long figure out what the hell had happened. The mother had been brought to the emergency room in labor. She had given birth to a healthy baby boy. The last entry in her file stated the patient had been discharged from the hospital along with the infant the next afternoon. I looked at the date. It would've been close to nine months after I fucked Addison in a drunken stupor on prom night.

I'm done risking my life for your fuck-up.

He's blood, but he ain't mine.

Dane's voice rattled around my throbbing skull.

I couldn't read another word.

I tossed my cell across the room, fisted the hair on top of my head and released the boiling rage in a profanity-filled scream.

Slade

Addy's profanity-riddled scream ripped my heart wide open. "Slade, you self-righteous bitch. I hate you! I fucking hate your cunt ass! You can't make me do this. They'll kill me, do you understand?"

I understood. They'd kill me, too, if she didn't shut up and come with us. No way in hell was I letting that baby be sold to the highest bidder, or worse, raised by a bunch of sick criminals.

"Grab the Jeep, Slade. Dad and I got this." Tucker tossed me his keys. I heard the scary drone of engines in the distance. Oh shit. They were close.

"Hurry."

I looked down at her uncle one last time and kicked him in the gut, because it seemed like the right thing to do, and because I needed to release my anger and disgust. Sick piece of shit—trading his pregnant niece for a debt he'd never be able to pay. I hoped he was dead. When I'd hit him with the baseball bat, he went down like a rag doll. Judging by the amount of blood on the floor, he wouldn't be getting up anytime soon. Maybe never.

Fueled by fear and adrenaline, I sprinted to the Jeep and pulled up to the door. Addy kicked and screamed. With great difficulty, Tuck and my father managed to maneuver her into the small back seat. I joined her, locked my arms around her shoulders, and held on for dear life as we drove into the darkness and away from the nightmare.

"Slade."

I jumped, dropping the toothpick holder I'd been polishing for the past five minutes. I stared into the bright eyes of Maurice.

"Hi there." I shook my head. "Sorry, I was daydreaming. Jeez. How embarrassing." I grabbed a menu and hugged it as if it could offer support. "How are you this morning?"

"Come and sit with me for a minute."

I followed him to his table and helped him settle before sliding next to him. I nodded to Margie. She grabbed a pot of coffee and two mugs and set them in front of us. I poured. Maurice stared long and hard. Something about the way he studied me made my stomach sink.

"Maurice, I think it's time for you to fess up. You've been keeping a secret, and it's driving me insane," I said, hoping to break the tension.

"I'll tell you anything you want to know."

"What's with the twenty-eight cent tips?"

He chuckled, dropping his gaze to his hands. "Oh, that's an easy one. My daughter was born on the twenty-eighth. It was the first time I remember feeling like a man. A real man. It's my way of honoring her. She was a waitress for most of her life."

"That's beautiful."

He smiled. "She was beautiful."

"Wait. I thought you only had two sons."

"Sweet girl, you aren't the only one with skeletons in the closet." He shifted and rested his elbows on the table. "Let's talk about you."

"I'd rather not."

"I know firsthand what secrets can do to a soul. Maybe I can help."

Probably not. "The other day, you said you knew what I did. What, exactly, do you think you know?"

"Rocky isn't your son," he said, his voice low so only I could hear. "I know you rescued him from a dangerous situation. I know Tango deserves to know the truth."

A sharp pain pierced my gut. "I can't tell him the truth. I'll lose Rocky. I'll go to prison. Or worse, if the truth comes out, if those bastards discover what I did, they will hunt me down and kill me."

I didn't know if Maurice was bluffing. Maybe he knew, maybe he only had an inkling of what had happened. Regardless, I continued, because I knew whatever I said would never leave the table, and I would never suffer that man's judgment. "They tortured her for days before they dumped her body. She died because I pulled her out of that God forsaken place."

Maurice curled his weathered fingers around my wrist. "She was dead the moment her mother left her with her uncle, with those devils. None of it was your fault. You tried to save her."

"I don't understand, Maurice. If you've known all this time, why didn't you say anything?" I shook my head. "I killed Addy's uncle. I hit him with a baseball bat. He was going after Addy, and I lost it. I just swung, and he fell, and then I hit him again. And I wanted him to die, after everything he'd put her through." I clamped my lips together, ashamed of the ease in which my confession poured out.

Maurice huffed. "Sweet child. Walter Reynolds is serving time at Crossroads Correctional Center. For extortion, I think. There was a big write-up in the newspaper a few years ago. If I remember right, Marta Rossi was a witness in the case."

"What?" God, I needed to start reading the newspaper. "I didn't kill him?"

"You're not a murderer."

I'd been so sure, but too scared to confirm, hoping to leave that horrid night behind me. Five years of guilt left my body in one long, hard sob. I buried my face in my hands and cried. Maurice's warm arm slid around my shoulders. He scooted closer, tucked me against his chest, and held me while I purged five years of regret, fear, and anger.

I may not have been able to save Addy, but I saved Rocky. I gave him a good home. Grandparents. An uncle who adored him. I saved Tango's child.

And he could never know.

CHAPTER 10

Tango

I STARED, ONE MORE TIME, at the picture Tito had sent to my smartphone, and fought another wave of nausea. I'd bloodied a few faces in my day. It was unavoidable when you worked for Luciano. A rite of passage, some might say. Luciano had an unwritten rule about laying hands on women. It wasn't tolerated, and that was one of many reasons I respected the man. However, what the Satan's Slayers had done to Addison Reynolds made my faith in the human race waver.

On paper, the Slayers were no more criminal than the Voltolini Family. The list of crimes between the two organizations were comparable. What the bikers lacked was any sort of code. They'd beaten and tortured that poor girl past the point of recognition. Like a pack of wild dogs, they'd torn her apart, not to send a message, not to punish, but to unleash. They had crossed a line of sanity I couldn't fathom. Her body had been found along Interstate 89, left like roadkill, three weeks after she'd given birth. Her murder never made headlines. No one had claimed her body.

I replayed my earlier conversation with Maurice over and over. He'd tried to tell me. How the hell had he known? He'd told me to ask my father about Addison, and I'd written him off as a crazy old coot. Fuck all, if Dad knew anything about this, I'd kill him. If he'd kept a child from me … I clamped my hands behind my head and paced back and forth in front of the door. I needed to calm the hell down. If I entered the house with guns blazing, someone would leave in a stretcher.

Rocky had to be my child. How had I not seen it before? That gorgeous little shit was the spitting image of me. My eyes, my hair, my damn throwing arm. I'd spent a whole fucking day with him. How could I not have recognized my own flesh and blood?

And Slade? That girl was going to talk. If I had to tie her down and torture the truth out of her, I'd do it. No more trying to be the old Tango. That boy was dead and buried under a shitload of secrets and lies.

I took three deep breaths before walking through the front door. I should've taken a few more. What I walked in on knocked the air clean out of my lungs.

My father and Kaylee held each other in a tight embrace. His lips were pressed to her ear. One hand rested at the small of her back, the other kneaded her ass.

Dad's eyes lifted to meet mine, and he bolted upright, dropping his arms. "Son. You're back."

"You gotta be fucking kidding me. Mom hasn't been in the ground more than a couple weeks, and you've got this baby in her bed? A goddamned child? She's my fucking age, Pop. What the hell is wrong with you?"

Dad pushed Kaylee behind him. "Enough, Tango."

Fury unfurled inside me, clouding my vision. I was done trying to keep my temper at bay. "How long have you been fucking this girl, Dad? Did Mom know? Is that what pushed her over the edge, you cheating piece of shit? Couldn't keep your dick out of other women. No wonder Mom pumped her body full of pills."

"Tango!" Kaylee stepped between us, placing a hand on each of our chests.

I shot her a warning glare and pointed to the door. "Get the fuck out of here."

Eyes narrowing in protest, she huffed, "I'm not going anywhere."

"Kaylee," Dad chimed in. "Tango and I need to be alone."

She dropped her arms and stormed out the door.

"You drove her to it. You know that, right? She knew about the women, Pop. All of them."

"Enough!" he yelled. "Do you think your mom was perfect? She lived with her share of secrets too, son."

"Let's talk about secrets, Dad." I stepped closer, daring him to back down. "Tell me what you know about Addison Reynolds."

His face paled. "Who in the hell is Addison Reynolds?"

My hands balled into fists and my muscles coiled, ready to strike. "Aren't you tired of the lies? Aren't you sick and tired of the shit?"

I watched the fight drain from his eyes. Dad's shoulders slumped. "I need a drink."

I followed him to his office, shaking the tension out of my arms. He poured two glasses and handed one to me. "Tell me what you know."

I slid my phone out of my pocket and pulled up Addison's picture for him to see.

"Christ Almighty." Dad blanched and fell into his chair. "She came to us claiming to be pregnant with your baby."

"Fuck!" I threw back my drink. "And neither one of you bothered to tell me?"

"We knew she was lying. You'd been so smitten with Slade, we couldn't believe you'd messed around with anyone else. Your mother told me she would take care of it."

"Take care of it, how?"

"I didn't ask. I let Marta handle it."

"And that's it?"

"No. Your mother confessed months later that she'd paid the girl's uncle fifty grand to get Addison out of town. I only found out because he came back looking for more money. When I looked into the guy, I learned he was affiliated with a criminal organization in Montana. Bikers. I forbid your mother to have any more contact. We spoke with the authorities. Turned out, they were already building a case against him. He was arrested a short time later, for extortion, among other things, and your mom was a witness in the case."

"Shit. Why would you keep that from me?"

"Your mom didn't want you to know. Didn't want you to worry."

"And you turned a blind eye. Neither one of you followed up with Addison? No one cared enough to find out if she was carrying my child? What the fuck?" My head was about to explode.

"Son. Your mother said she had taken care of it. I had no reason to doubt her."

Innocence by ignorance. How convenient. I wanted to hit him. I wanted to crush him.

Instead, I raised my empty glass in salute. "Congratulations, Pop. You are now responsible for the deaths of two women. Have fun living with that." I dropped my glass on his desk and grabbed the bottle. Didn't know where I was headed. Just needed to be far away from the man.

My legs guided me to our private dock out back. I pulled a long swig of bourbon into my body, stripped my clothes and dove in.

"I think you should go, Rocky." She smiled up at me, teeth chattering, and threw a fake punch at my cheek.

I scooped up her towel and wrapped it tight around her body, dotting kisses over her wet hair. "It's too far away from you."

"It's important."

"I don't want to go if you're not coming with me."

"You know I can't leave Mom alone. I'll stay here, go to State. It'll be good for us. We've never been away from each other for more than a couple weeks."

"I don't believe it'll be good for us any more than you do."

She laughed. "Can't you see I just want you to follow your dreams? Don't let me hold you back. I bet there'll be a million different boxing gyms in Texas."

"Not sure there'll be much time for boxing. I'll be too busy with football."

"I'll be here. I'll always be here, waiting. You know that, right? Just promise me you'll come back. Promise me you won't fall in love with some horny freshman and forget about me."

I cupped her cheeks and forced her lips open with my own. God, I'd never get enough of her softness. "You are my heart and soul. There will never, ever be another girl for me. It's always been you. It will always be you. I promise."

"Tango?"

"Yeah, babylove?"

"Have you danced today?"

"That's my girl." I laughed, dropped her towel, and scooped her off her feet. The moon cast a bright glow across the smooth water. I spun Slade across the dock and kissed her hard, dancing to the beat of waves lapping against the rocky shore.

She didn't know it yet, but I was taking her with me. Wherever I went. Because wherever I traveled, if Slade Mason was by my side, I was home.

Slade

Home didn't feel like home without Rocky. I tried settling on the couch with a good book, but the house was too damn quiet. I tried reading through the contract Carlos Rossi's lawyer had sent over. The numbers only blurred on the pages. I tried to focus, but my brain was a jumbled mess. All these years I'd believed I'd killed Walter Reynolds. The sick fuck was alive and kicking in a Montana prison.

He knew where I lived. And that was exactly why I needed to get the hell out of Dodge.

I ran to my computer and Googled the Satan's Slayers. Bad news all around—hardened criminals and psychopaths. The list of charges against them over the past thirty years made me shiver, despite having witnessed their insanity firsthand. Rape, prostitution, drugs, murder. Extortion.

Next was Walter Reynolds. Aside from news articles highlighting his arrest and trial, I didn't find anything of significance. One article mentioned the fact that he was affiliated with the Slayers. What that meant, exactly, I wasn't sure.

We'd been damn lucky to avoid any backlash after dragging my pregnant friend out of their clutches. If we hadn't checked Addy into the hospital under my name, they would've found her, and who knows where Rocky would've ended up, or if he would've survived.

I needed to hug my boy. Hold him tight and never let go. As soon as I finalized the sale of The Stop, I would be on my way. I dialed Tucker's number and Rocky answered on the second ring.

"Hi, Mom!"

"Hi, Rocky. Do you miss me yet?"

"Yep."

"Have you danced today?"

"Yep. I danced with Grandma. She's not as fun as you, but I taught her how to do our booty shake."

"Did you?"

"She said I was silly."

"Will you dance with me now? I miss you, and I don't have anyone to dance with."

"Okay. Ready?"

"I'm ready."

I kicked my slippers off and jumped to my feet. Rocky hummed a tune I didn't recognize, and I danced around my room, shaking my head and ass, tossing my hair and flailing my arms. If anyone were watching, they'd think I'd been possessed. Rocky sang until he was breathless.

"Did you dance, Mom?"

I caught my breath and fell across my mattress. "Yes, baby. That felt good. I needed that."

"I gotta go. Grandma says dinner is ready. She makes the best noodles and cheese. She puts pepperoni in it."

"Okay, have a good dinner. I love you, Rocky."

"I love you too, Mom. And tell Tango I can't wait to play football with him again."

He may as well have punched me in the gut. "Goodnight. I'll see you in a few days." I ended the call and tucked my phone under the pillow.

Folding my comforter over my body, I rolled to my side. It hurt thinking about Tango. My heart ached more than it should. My blood pumped harder, too, especially between my legs. I hated how he affected me that way. Worse yet? I missed him. I wanted to talk to him about my problems. Only, he was my problem.

I buried my face in my pillow and screamed. I had to stop this. Tango Rossi was not mine. I had to get him out of my head.

I needed to hate him. Couldn't afford to love him anymore. It made me vulnerable. Made me drop my guard. If he knew that Rocky was his son, he'd take him away. It'd put not only me in danger, but my father, his wife, and my brother.

I closed my eyes and drifted to sleep.

"Let go of me, you fucking bitch. Do not take me to the hospital. They'll find us. They'll kill all of you. Ow. Oh God, it hurts."

"Shhh ... calm down, Addy. You're in labor."

I don't want this. It hurts, Slade. Make it stop. Kill me. If you ever loved me, you'll kill me now. I can't be a mom. I can't do it."

"It'll be okay, Addy. We'll take care of you."

"You stupid fucking bitch. They won't let me go. They'll find me. If they think I ran away..." She hunched over, digging her nails into my wrists. "Oh God, it hurts so bad. I can't do this. I can't. Let me out of the car. Stop the fucking car."

We pulled up to the emergency room doors. Addy shoved her hand into my hair and pulled hard. Her eyes danced in their sockets, frantic with fear and pain. "I hate you. I hate you for doing this to me. They'll find me. They will hunt you down and kill you." She held me tight, forcing my head back. Then, she started to laugh. "You think you're helping? I don't need to be rescued. They'll take care of me."

She wasn't the Addison I grew up with. I couldn't imagine what they'd done to her over the past few months. The girl was not sane. Her eyes were vacant. Where her bright spirit used to shine, there was nothing but a dull shell of the girl I used to love. I pulled at her arm, but she wouldn't loosen her grip on my hair. "You don't know what you're saying, Addy. Let's get you inside. You'll see. Everything will be better. We just have to make sure the baby is okay."

"I don't want this baby!" she screamed. "It can fucking die for all I care. They'll sell it anyway. Or kill it. One less Rossi in the world."

Her harsh remarks unhinged me, and I had no doubt that her unborn child was in grave danger. Refusing to listen to another word, I snapped my free hand back, curled my fist like Tango had taught me, and punched Addison Reynolds in the face, knocking her unconscious.

CHAPTER 11

Slade

"UGH," I MOANED. "What a long day."

I finished dividing tips and laid them on the counter for Charlie and Kim. I was just about to lock the door when Tango barreled through with a clumsy sway to his step. When he locked eyes with mine, my knees gave out, and I gripped the counter for purchase.

His face. His beautiful face. Swollen. Bruised. Battered.

Hatred and disgust burned behind his haunting glare.

Oh shit. My stomach rolled in warning. Before I could retreat, and damn did I want to slink away, his large hand wrapped around my upper arm. "You're coming with me." His breath reeked of liquor. His bloodshot eyes looked right through me.

Ignoring Charlie and Kim altogether, Tango pulled me into my office and slammed the door behind us. "No more lies. Tell me what the fuck is going on." He tossed a file folder at me, and papers spread across the floor at my feet.

Self-preservation urged me to back away. My calf hit the front of the couch and I fell onto it, losing any chance of standing my ground and putting on a brave face. He leaned over me, pounding his fists against the cushions.

I folded into myself. The only other time I'd seen Tango drunk was the night he broke my heart. I hadn't a clue what he was capable of in his inebriated state.

"You're scaring me, Tango."

"You haven't seen scary." He retrieved a photo off the floor and held it at eye level. "But you will if you don't explain this."

I snatched the grainy print from his hand. Addison's bruised and scarred face glared up at me. Oh God. My life was over. He knew. The room spun around me and my chest constricted, stealing my vital oxygen.

"Tango."

"Explain!" he shouted, spraying spittle on my face.

"I. I. Oh, shit. I'm sorry." I'd lose everything. My son, my home, my diner. I would go to prison. What would happen to my father and Lettie?

"Sorry for what, Slade? Say it. Goddamn you, say it!"

"I did it for you!" I screamed, losing my battle of nerves. "Addy was crazy, fucked in the head. She wanted to get rid of Rocky. I had to protect your son. Addy wanted him gone. Your mother wanted him dead. I protected him."

"And you couldn't fucking tell me? Why?"

"Because I thought I'd killed Walter." The room spun around me. "Because I lied to the hospital. I gave them my information instead of Addy's. I didn't want the club finding her. Then Lettie and James covered for me. I didn't want them to get in trouble. They were only protecting Rocky. I thought Addy would come to her senses and that we could reach out to you, but the second I took my eyes off her, she disappeared. She ran right back to those sick fucks. And they killed her. Tango. They killed her, just like they would've killed Rocky."

Tango stood straight and stumbled backward until he hit the wall. Wild-eyed, he scuffed his hands across his scalp and slid down the rough wood, dropping to his ass. "Am I supposed to thank you?" He fisted his hair and dropped his gaze to the pile of papers. "You stole my child. You kept him from me, for years. Am I supposed to be grateful to you? What the fuck were you thinking?"

If ever I'd wished for a black hole to open up and suck me into oblivion, that would be the day. Tango had been angry with me before, in the past, on more than one occasion, but never to the point where I'd feared retribution.

"I was scared. I had to protect James and Lettie. And I fell in love with Rocky. I fell in love with him, and I couldn't bear the thought of anyone taking him away from me. I know what I did was wrong. It's been eating me alive all this time. But I'd do it again. I'd save him again. I would die for that boy."

"My mother wouldn't turn away her grandchild. She was cold, but not heartless."

Oh shit. He'd just lost his mother. How could I reveal her ugliness? I slid off the couch and crawled over to him. God, how I wanted to touch him. "Your mother gave Addy money for an abortion, set the appointment and everything. I talked Addy out of it. When Marta found out, she was irate, kept calling, threatening to send Addy away if she didn't go through with it, calling the baby an abomination."

"No." His face crumpled. "Why would she do that?" he asked, shaking his head back and forth. "She wouldn't do that."

I pulled his trembling hand into my own and stroked his long fingers. "I took Addy with me to Montana to get her away from your mom. I'd only recently found my Dad. He took us in. Somehow, Addy's uncle found us. I don't know what he said to Addison, but she left with him. I searched for months."

Tango bounced his head against the wall, crazed and oozing anguish. "How the hell does Dane play into this?"

"Dane wanted her away from the club. He knew what they were doing to her, what Walter was forcing her to do. We planned for weeks, waiting for an opening, for a chance to pull her out of there. When we'd finally caught a break, it was too late."

Tango jerked his hand from under mine and pushed to his feet. He moved to the opposite corner of the room, pressed his head against the wall, and screamed into his hands. My heart shattered, exploding into jagged shards and piercing every nerve in my body.

"My God," he cried, shoulders trembling. "He's my son, and you stole him. You should have told me, Slade. You, more than anyone, should have told me." He turned to face me, his thick lashes clumped and wet.

"I'm sorry. I'm so sorry." I stepped closer. Tango moved away. "I tried, once. I tried to find you. Before everything got out of hand. But you weren't in Texas, and your parents wouldn't tell me where you'd gone."

"You didn't try hard enough," he said, low and menacing, pointing his finger as if he wanted to stab me through the heart. "I'm taking my boy, Slade."

"No. You can't. Please. He's all I have. You can't do that to him. Please." I ran to him and gripped his shirt, desperate to make him listen. "We'll figure something out; just don't take him. He's all I have."

Long, trembling fingers tightened painfully around my wrists. He turned, taking me with him, and flattened me against the wall. Tears rolled down his face. I wanted desperately to wipe them away. To erase everything.

"He's all I have left of you." I sobbed, sagging against him.

Tango slid a hand around my throat, then up to my jaw, forcing me to lift my face and meet his deadly glare. "You could've had me. You could've had me and my son. You should've trusted me, Slade."

He squeezed hard enough that a surge of panic pulsed through me. Slamming his eyes closed, he yelled "fuck" against my lips, and let me go. "I need air," he murmured, stumbling backward, then heading for the door. "I can't fucking breathe."

Tango

Slade stole my breath. Deadly pissed as I was, her mere presence sucked the oxygen from my lungs.

Highlighted by the dusty glow of the moon, her blonde hair lay fanned across the dark blue pillow, reminding me of angel wings. *How deceiving.* That beauty, the girl I'd once considered mine, was no angel. Divine beings didn't steal babies and claim them as their own.

A sliver of conscience urged me to comfort her—muscle memory, I supposed. Tenderness was the last thing I had to offer. Instead, I hid in the shadows and watched her bleed. Reveled in the knowledge that I wasn't suffering alone. Fuck, my heart was hemorrhaging.

When she cried her last tear and gave in to exhaustion, I settled on the floor next to her and leaned against the small bed frame. The room smelled of musty shoes and the beach. I wondered if that was a usual scent for a child's room, or unique to my son.

My son.

Fucking hell.

I had a child.

I turned around and slapped Slade on the ass. "Wake up."

She flew to the sitting position, kicking my shoulder in the process. "Ow. Shit." She grabbed her toe and rocked on the bed. "Jeez, Tango. What? You scared the hell out of me."

I snatched her phone off the nightstand and tossed it on the bed. "Call them. Tell them to bring Rocky home."

"What? No. No," she argued, swiping at the hair on her face. "He has a few days left. Let him enjoy them before you rip his world apart."

"Before *I* rip his world apart? Don't pull that shit with me." I stood and paced the room twice, then sat next to her. "I've missed five years. Bring him home. Don't make me wait another goddamned day."

"What are you gonna do, Tango? Tell him you're his father? Take him away from his mother, drag him to New York?"

The bite in her tone pissed me off. Had I not been on the downswing of drunk, I would've controlled my emotions, but this had been one shit-storm of a day and she'd plucked the wrong nerve.

I leaned in, too close for comfort, hoping to inject the fear of God into her. "I don't know what the fuck I'm gonna do. The only thing I know is that I have a child. I am his father, and he'll damn well know it. No matter how this shit plays out, he'll know who his father is. Don't fight me on this. You're lucky your ass isn't sitting in jail right now."

She held my gaze, her red-rimmed, swollen eyes thick and glossy with unshed tears.

"Pick up the phone and call them. Now."

Slade stretched a trembling hand across the mattress to find her cell. "What do I tell them?"

"The truth."

Lifting the phone, she paused, then tucked it against her chest. "Tango. Please, do what you have to with me. Just don't bring them into it. They're good people. They love Rocky so much. Please, hurt me if you need to. Not them. They were only trying to help. I sucked them into the lie."

"Shut up. Stop talking, and dial."

Slade made the call, talked to her father, James, for half an hour. She cried, apologized, reassured him everything would be okay.

My heart raced, like it wanted to fly.

"No," she whispered into the phone, wiping her eyes. "Tango won't do anything to hurt Rocky. He's drunk right now, and angry, but he's a good man."

I huffed. Good man? She didn't have a clue what I was capable of.

Turning her back to me, she mumbled, "Yes. I trust him."

I watched her shoulders slump, her body crumple to the floor.

"I love you, too. Good night."

Her cell hit the hardwood floor with a dull thud. On hands and knees she made her way back to the bed, curled under the blue and silver comforter and pulled it over her head. "Tucker will bring him home first thing in the morning."

"Why didn't you tell me you found your father?" I asked, collapsing onto the bed beside her.

"I don't want to talk right now."

"I need this. Talk me down, like only you can. My head and heart are buzzing so hard I want to hurt someone. Please."

"I didn't tell you because it didn't concern you. And I couldn't afford to give you any more of myself. I didn't want to let you in, because it would hurt all the more when you left again."

Bullshit. She'd only been trying to cover her lies. I didn't voice my opinion. Instead, I asked, "How did you find him?"

Head still buried, Slade told me the story. "I found a box of photos. There were pictures of a man. A lot of them. They weren't dated, but they were taken at The Stop before the new highway was built. James stood in front of his eighteen-wheeler in most of them. The Slade Trucking logo stood out. I knew it couldn't be a coincidence. Slade? I mean, seriously, who names a girl Slade? Mom must've had it bad for him, huh?"

"So you hunted him down."

"I did," she mumbled.

"How did he take it?"

Slade shifted under the blanket. "He knew about me. He wasn't surprised when I reached out to him."

"No?"

"He'd told his wife years ago about his affair with my mom. She'd actually encouraged him to look me up. He never did, but I'm not sure why."

Interesting. Our fathers had something in common. Unfaithful, fucking bastards. "He'd cheated on her, and she forgave him?"

"Apparently," Slade answered on a sigh.

"And she put her job, her life, on the line to help you and Rocky?"

"I told you, they are good people." Slade curled the comforter away from her face. "Tango?"

"Yeah?" I asked, avoiding eye contact.

"What are you going to do?" She sniffed, and I suspected, if I had it in me to look, I'd find a new wave of tears rolling down her cheeks.

Still, I lacked the compassion to care. "I don't know, babylove. I don't know. Right now, I want to sleep."

"Do you hate me?" she asked, voice trembling.

I rolled to my side, away from Slade, and studied the blanket of stars out the window. "There are no words for what I'm feeling right now."

CHAPTER 12

Slade

"MOM!" ROCKY SLAMMED against my chest, coiling his arms so tight around my neck I struggled to breathe.

"Hi, sweetie. I missed you so much."

"Me too." Rocky squeezed tighter, then gasped and wiggled free of my embrace. "Tango!"

I turned. Tango stood in the doorway, disheveled and looking like he'd survived a ride in a tornado. His hair stuck out every direction, his wrinkled shirt was half-tucked into his jeans. His bloodshot eyes, full of emotion I couldn't decipher, locked onto my boy, who ran toward him in a full sprint.

Rocky bounced up the steps and jumped into his arms. When Tango hugged him tight and buried his face in Rocky's neck, I fell to my knees, no longer able to bear the weight of my grief and worry. Tango's shoulders heaved, as if he were sobbing, and he turned and carried his son into the dark shadows of my house.

Tucker's arms came around me from behind. He rested his chin on my shoulder, pressing our cheeks together. "How you holding up, sis?"

"I'm not," I whispered, thankful for his strength, his solid body keeping me grounded.

"What now?" he asked, breath hitched.

"I don't know. It's out of my hands, isn't it?"

"We'll get through this. Whatever happens, I'm here for you." Tucker stood and pulled me to my feet.

"Did you see the way Rocky was drawn to him? It's like he already knows that's his daddy."

Calloused hands cupped my cheeks. "You are an amazing woman, Slade Mason." He kissed my forehead. "Come on, I need to meet this man. Make sure he knows where I stand on this situation."

I snuck a hand around his bicep. "Wait. Let Tango have some time to process."

Rocky appeared in the doorway. "Come on, Mom! Tango said he'd make me a pancake stack. After we eat, we're gonna play football."

Tango stepped behind Rocky, whisk in hand. His gaze met Tucker's, and he strode toward us, sucking the oxygen from my lungs, the blood from my veins.

Ignoring me completely, he offered a hand to my brother. "Thank you for bringing him home. I'm sorry I cut your vacation short, but I'm sure you understand."

Tucker stood only a hair taller than Tango, and he was definitely wider. Not as fine-tuned, but beefier, for sure. "How about we get a drink sometime soon."

"Sure." Tango nodded, sizing him up. "I think that'd be good." He turned and headed back toward the house.

I followed my brother to his Jeep.

"Call me later," Tucker grunted as he pulled Rocky's luggage out of his back seat. "If you need anything, don't hesitate. I mean it, Slade. I know you hate asking for help, but you are not alone in this, you hear me?"

"Thank you, Tucker. For everything." Our gazes locked, and I knew he understood what I meant by *everything*.

"I'd do it again. That little nephew of mine is worth every risk." Pulling my trembling hand into his own, he whispered, "And he is my nephew, I don't care if it's by blood, or circumstances. I love both of you more than anything." He kissed my cheek and pulled himself back into the driver's seat.

I stood outside until his Jeep disappeared around the corner, and took a few deep breaths before mustering the courage to face whatever destiny had in store for my lying, baby-stealing ass.

When I entered the kitchen, Rocky stood on a chair next to Tango at the counter. His butt wiggled back and forth as he whisked pancake batter with gusto. The sight of them, side by side, father and son, twisted my insides. Guilt burrowed its nasty fingers through my ribcage and squeezed the blood from my chest.

What would the past six years have looked like if Tango had known about the pregnancy, if his parents hadn't swept his indiscretion under the rug? Would he have come back to Whisper Springs? Would Addy be alive? The two of them would've made a life together, to raise their child. He would've married her, of that I was certain, because that was the kind of man he was. He probably would've insisted she follow him to college, because he wouldn't have wanted me to watch him raise a family with another woman.

Would I have survived that future? Perhaps I would've ended up like my mother, dependent on a bottle of vodka to make life's truths bearable, seeking reprieve from desolation and heartbreak through casual encounters with strange men night after night.

Cold, hard truth hit me like a frying pan to the face. I hadn't saved Rocky's life. He had saved mine.

"Mom? Why are you crying?" Tiny fingers wrapped around my pinky and tugged, snapping me back to the here and now.

"I just missed you like crazy, and I'm happy you're home." I scooped him off the floor and dotted his face with kisses. He giggled and squirmed, but clung tightly to my neck. He'd missed me, too.

"Mom?" he asked with his raspy laugh.

"Hmm?" I hummed into his neck.

"Have you danced today?"

The spatula Tango had been holding hit the floor with a ding. He gripped the edge of the counter, head dropping low between his shoulders.

"No, I haven't danced today. I waited for you."

"Let's do it now!"

Tango turned his head to catch my gaze, eyes flooded with remorse and recognition. He had always made me dance when I was sad.

I set Rocky back on his feet. "Okay, but only if Tango dances with us."

"Come on, Tango!" Rocky shouted. "I'll show you how." His small hand disappeared inside Tango's long fingers, and he yanked him to the center of the kitchen. "When we don't have music, I sing."

Rocky belted out the tune to his favorite cartoon, threw his hands in the air and wiggled his hips.

A swarm of angry bees buzzed in my gut, and I focused on Rocky, terrified of the emotion I'd find in Tango's eyes, afraid I'd shatter and never gather the pieces to put myself back together.

Even when Tango joined my son—his son—and hopped around my kitchen, I couldn't bring myself to look at him. Instead, I reached across the counter, plugged my iPod into the speaker, and started the dance playlist Rocky and I had spent hours compiling.

Rocky giggled, his bare feet slapping against the linoleum. I joined in, minding my personal space, and let the music wash over me, fuel me, and chase away the desolation threatening to consume my spirit.

We danced. We laughed. I pretended, for Rocky, that the world was bright and beautiful, and life hadn't just kicked my ass down another flight of stairs.

Tango

I couldn't tear my gaze from the pair of legs descending the creaky stairs. The roll of her thighs, the tight curve of her calves. My balls ached with the thought of those lithe limbs locked around my waist. Temptress. Nice play, wearing those frayed cutoffs and that clingy little top. How many times over the years had I pretended it was Slade I rammed my cock into, instead of Luciano's whores?

Slade paused at the last step and fiddled with the loose banister, picking at the chipped brown paint, avoiding eye contact. "I thought you were going back to your dad's."

I huffed. "Changed my mind." Not a chance in hell I was leaving her alone. I didn't trust her not to bolt. "We have shit to iron out." This was not the kind of shit I could take out on the punching bag, or some unfortunate dick's face. It spoke volumes that I actually wanted to talk to this girl standing before me, rather than fight or fuck my frustration away. Maybe I wasn't so far gone, after all.

"Coffee first?" She hopped off the last step, the same way Rocky did every time he came down the stairs. I should've offered to help make the java, but the sight of her retreating to the kitchen stole my fucking breath.

The loose waves of her hair swayed across her back, soft and dreamy, much like a snake under the spell of a charmer. Perhaps I was the one being charmed—seduced by a deadly beauty who had no idea I'd spent the past six years fighting or fucking anyone who crossed my path, pathetic attempts to purge her venom from my system.

Fuck. I shook the crazy thoughts from my head. Exhaustion made me delirious.

I had spent the day with Rocky. Playing catch, wrestling, watching ridiculous cartoons, eating. Damn, that boy could shovel it in.

Slade had stayed in the background, keeping herself busy with menial chores, out of the way, never out of sight. Giving me precious time with my boy.

Holy shit. My boy. I'd made a little human. I fucking loved the hell out him already. Emotionally and physically, I was drained. Entertaining a child was hard work.

She'd done it alone for all these years.

"Here you go," Slade offered a strained smile when she set my mug on the coffee table.

"Thanks." I rubbed at my itching eyes.

She paced from the couch to the kitchen door, and back, the same trail she used to blaze on those nights her mother would come home too late. I was certain if she didn't have a cup of coffee in her hands, she'd have her thumbnail half chewed off.

"Sit," I ordered.

She ignored me.

"Slade." I patted the cushion next to me. "Sit down."

With a huff, she plopped her ass next to mine, set her cup down, and turned to face me. "You were amazing with him today."

A cluster of words and emotions rolled through me, catching in my throat. Unable to speak, I nodded.

"I always knew you'd be a great father."

Goddamn. Why the hell were my eyes burning?

"What are you going to do, Tango?" she asked with a quiver to her voice that made my guts twist.

"What do you mean?"

"Are you going to take him away? Are you going to press charges? I know you have every right. You do. I just need to know what you're thinking. I need to prepare for what's coming."

"Press charges?" I set my cup down next to hers, to keep from throwing it across the room. "Jesus. I'm not a fucking monster." Not always, anyway.

"I. I. Just—"

"Just what, Slade? Thought I'd rip him from the only home, the only family he's ever known?"

"But last night, you said—"

"I was drunk, and pissed, and ... and ... fuck. I don't know. This is so goddamned fucked up," I hissed through gritted teeth, roughing my hands through my hair. "I have a son. And he's perfect, and healthy, and *alive*, and I had nothing to do with that. I hate that I wasn't here for him, but do you know what I hate most?" I asked, not waiting for an answer. "I hate how you didn't trust me to do the right thing."

"Tango." She rested a hand on my thigh.

"No. Let me finish." I pushed to me feet and crossed the room, fearful of my reaction to her touch. "Why didn't you tell me? I don't understand. I know I hurt you, but this? A child ... this is epic. And I'm angry. So goddamned furious that I missed five years of his life. Missed his first breath, his first smile. But then I look at him and he's alive and thriving and I'm so in love with him. I hate that you kept him from me. And I fucking hate how, right now, I want to make you hurt all over again."

I turned around, annoyed by the tears pooling in her eyes. I couldn't let anger control me. I slammed my palms against the wall and dropped my head between my arms.

Breathe, damn you. Breathe.

I stayed in that position, staring at the floor, unable to muster even a drop of empathy for the girl breaking behind me. "Jesus Christ, Slade, help me understand this because I can't wrap my fucking head around it."

She sniffed, and I heard her shift on the couch. "The anger you feel right now. The betrayal. The hurt. That's what I felt back then, when I watched you fuck Addy." She then let out a frustrated laugh. "When she told me she was pregnant? Amplify that pain by a million percent."

Her voice drew closer, but I didn't move. I pressed my fingers harder into the wall, vibrations of rage moving up my forearms.

"It wasn't my problem, and I wasn't going to help her, even when your mother, your flesh and blood, turned her away. Then Marta and Walter ordered her to get rid of the baby like he was trash, and that pissed me off. I hated Addy, but I wasn't going to let them kill your baby, Tango, no matter how bitter I was."

Her words sliced through me, swift and deadly. I sucked in a breath and watched a tear fall to the floor beneath me, followed by another.

"And by the time I convinced her to keep the baby and leave town with me, it took all of my energy to take care of her. The selfish bitch never even thanked me. Just pouted about getting fat. And it wasn't my place to tell you. Don't you see?" She sighed long and loud. "Then we rescued her from those monsters, and after that, I couldn't tell you. I couldn't tell anyone, because I needed to protect my dad and his family."

I heard her pad down the hallway and open a door. I pushed off the wall and swiped at the moisture on my face. When she came back, she shoved a pillow and blanket at me. "I know you hate me. I don't expect you to understand, because you weren't here. You don't know what it was like. Whatever happens, whatever you decide to do, I'm just happy Rocky has his father. He needs you."

I wanted to be angry. Needed to shelter myself with rage, because rage was easier to handle than the other emotions boiling inside me. I slammed my shields around me, like I did during my fights, and met her gaze.

Slade's eyes widened, and she took a step back, wrapping her arms around herself. "The couch is yours," she whispered. "For as long as you want to stay."

I watched her ascend the stairs. I ached to follow her, throw her into bed and work out my frustrations the old fashioned way. Pissed as I was, I knew she didn't deserve that kind of punishment.

Slade

Watching Tango sleep on my couch was the worst kind of punishment. A harsh reminder of everything I would never have.

Tight, fine-tuned muscles rolled under his olive skin as he stretched and shifted in his sleep. A small smile played across his lips before he buried his face in the pillow, hugging it tight. Oh, how I envied that pillow. Every cell in my body was drawn to the half-naked man on my sofa. I ached, craving his touch, the musk of his skin, his thick, strong lips. Dear God, those lips. Full and soft, like a warm, fresh-baked cinnamon bun.

I stole a few moments to admire his drool-worthy, pajama-clad ass before tiptoeing past and sneaking out the door. Tango had slept on my couch every night for the past week. He still hadn't told me why he'd left his father's house and crashed at mine. He hadn't talked to me much at all. I didn't push, and I sure as hell didn't mind. Tango Rossi belonged in my home. Whispers of him lived in every nook and cranny.

Rocky was in heaven, having a man around. They'd become joined at the hip, and the only time Rocky seemed to need me was during his bedtime routine.

I didn't know what to do with myself now that Tango knew the truth. I'd lived the lie, carried the burden of fear for so long, I hadn't noticed the kinks and bends it had caused, or the stifling effect it had on my life.

For years I'd avoided certain areas of town, afraid of bumping into the Rossis or any of their friends. I'd been certain they would know what I'd done after taking one look at Rocky. Christ, anyone who knew Tango, who cared about him at all, would see him in Rocky's eyes, his smile, his personality.

I hadn't dated. I'd skipped the county fairs, the annual fireworks show, Christmas tree lighting in the town square, all the things I'd loved to do with Tango when we were kids. I'd bent, twisted, and compromised my life to adjust to the lie. Now that Tango had assured me over and over he wouldn't take legal action, to protect my father and his wife, I felt like I'd woken from an extended hibernation, stiff and sore, and unsure how to rejoin the community. Other than the people who frequented the diner, I'd lost touch with the town I loved.

For now, I wanted to give Tango and Rocky time to get to know each other. I gave the boys their space, or at least told myself that was what I was doing. Truth was, I was avoiding his cold stares, and the way he'd move to the opposite side of the room when I was near.

Tango only spoke to me when absolutely necessary. He had a ton of harsh reality to process. He didn't want me anymore. I couldn't blame him, but sweet Jesus, I missed him.

All the attention he'd lavished on me before the baby-daddy-truth-reveal, was now being poured on my son.

Correction. *His* son.

He loved Rocky. Fiercely. The proof was in the way his eyes turned liquid every time they rested on the boy. Or in the way his chest puffed, or his smile spread so wide, I feared his face might crack.

As I mentally prepared for my first day back to work, I was surprised at how right it felt, leaving the boys sleeping at home. I locked the door behind me, trusting Rocky was in the best care.

I made it to the sidewalk when I heard the patter of feet drawing close. Warm arms enveloped me, and I struggled to turn.

I pressed my cheek to Tango's warm chest. His hair tickled my nose. It didn't stop me from enjoying the strong, spicy musk. I'd no idea what cologne he wore, but it wasn't overpowering, and it made me want to crawl inside him and snuggle up for a decade or two.

We held each other in a silent, intimate embrace for a long, perfect moment before I broke the connection. "What was that for?" I asked, surprised by the deep tone my voice had taken.

Tango stared down at me, his full lips slightly parted in a sexy smirk. He stepped back and lifted a hand to his tousled hair. His eyes seemed to lose focus before he shook his head and pounced. Wrapping his long fingers around the back of my head, he pulled me close and kissed me hard, dancing his tongue across my own.

My legs turned to rubber, collapsing under the heady power he poured into his kiss. Tango hooked an arm around my waist, holding me steady and too damn close. Oh God. I wanted to wrap my legs around him and never let go. Never spend another day away from his arms, his lips, his soul-warming gaze.

That was where I belonged. That was my home. That space between Tango Rossi and the rest of the world. It was my right.

I pulled away, breaking the sweet connection, held captive by the allure of his eyes.

"Have a good day," he murmured, taking a step back and roughing a hand across his chest, or perhaps rubbing his heart.

Was he feeling the same ache I suffered?

My lips tingled. "I'll see you tonight," I managed to whisper as I turned, brushing a finger over the heat on my mouth. I didn't look back. I forced my legs to move away, squeezing my eyes closed to keep the tears at bay.

I had to be strong. I couldn't bow under the incessant weight of emotion, want, or need. I had to be brave, a fucking woman of steel. For Rocky, for Tango.

I hadn't instigated the kiss, but sweet Lord, I would cherish it, wear it, and let it charge the rest of my day. It meant something. It meant everything. And despite the grief gnawing at my insides, it put a big, unflappable smile on my face and filled me with the courage to do what I had to do when I arrived at work.

Say goodbye. Again.

Tango

"Again. Again," Rocky commanded, climbing up the length of my torso, his toes digging into the tops of my thighs. Teeth chattering, he wrapped his small arms around my neck.

"Okay. One more time, then we need to head home." I wrapped my hands around his waist and tossed him up and into the lake. He landed with a splash and bounced out of the water, spitting and wiping his face. Damn, his smile made my heart swell.

I hoisted him onto the dock and caught him in his towel, rubbing him from head to toe. He laughed like my mom, deep and raspy, the only difference being Rocky wasn't afraid to share his joy. Mom had always hidden her smile, only giving it when the timing was right, only after I'd won a first place trophy, when the cameras were pointed her direction, or she was in the presence of someone she'd held in esteem.

I wondered if Rocky could've breached her walls.

He squirmed and giggled as I dried him one more time.

"Tango." My father's voice startled me.

My spine stiffened, and I tucked my son under my arm.

"Pop. I didn't expect you to be home."

"I'm happy to see you."

Rocky wrestled the towel off his head. "Hi!"

Recognition shimmered in Dad's green eyes and he squatted. "Hello. I'm Mr. Rossi, Tango's dad. What's your name?"

I didn't want to let him go, but Rocky wiggled free and stood in front of his grandfather. Carbon copies, from the tone of their skin, to the thick hair, to the brilliant green eyes the Rossi men were famous for.

Like a boss, my son held his hand toward Pop. "I'm Rocky James Mason. Nice to meet you, sir."

Pop's eyes filled with liquid, and he cleared his throat before giving Rocky a firm shake. "Very nice to meet you, Rocky James Mason." Rising to full height, he grabbed my son's hand and started toward the house. "You must be hungry after all that swimming. How about some lunch?"

"I'm starving. Do you like grilled cheese? My favorite is grilled cheese. Mom puts magic sprinkles in it." Rocky continued to rave about his mom's cooking. The two of them headed up the stairs, leaving me no choice but to follow.

I'd never seen my father cry. The sight of him tearing up had me clearing an annoying lump from my throat. Yeah, Pop and I were in for one hell of an uncomfortable talk. Good thing Rocky was with us, because he was the glue holding my shit together.

Rocky dominated our attention, and I'd never seen my dad more at ease. I'd never seen him cook his own meal either, but there he was, making fucking grilled cheese sandwiches, with magic, parmesan cheese sprinkles. It was evident Dad was already head over heels for the child who'd been dropped in our laps.

I couldn't deny the regret in his eyes when he managed a glance my way. For Pop, that was epic. He'd always been a master at hiding any emotion other than anger.

It wasn't until Maria offered to give Rocky a grand tour of the house that my father and I sat at the kitchen counter and dared to speak.

"So, T, what version of the truth am I going to get from you?"

"I've never lied to you, Pop."

"I know."

"Addison Reynolds wasn't lying either when she came to you for help. Now she's dead. Rocky could've been dead."

Dad squeezed his eyes shut and pinched the bridge of his nose. Head hung low, he sighed. It had to hurt, knowing he'd turned away his grandchild. "How did he end up with Slade?"

"She was forced to make an impossible decision. I'm not giving you details. Trust me, it's to protect you, but you need to understand something. She's my boy's mother. Got me? As far as you, or anyone knows, Slade Mason gave birth to my son."

I knew Dad could be trusted with the truth. He didn't want the Rossi name tainted any more than I did. True, he'd never encouraged my relationship with Slade, but the whole town had believed Slade and I would marry someday. A baby born out of wedlock with my childhood sweetheart would be easier to explain than the shameful truth—I'd revenge fucked a girl I hated because I was a hotheaded, selfish fool. I'd been too drunk to see through Addison's lie, too caught up in my own self-righteous bullshit.

Hell. I didn't even remember the actual fucking. I did recall knowing I'd been royally fucked the moment I looked up and met the most devastated eyes I'd ever seen. Slade's broken expression had sobered me enough to realize I had become everything I hated about my father. Unfaithful. Arrogant. Weak.

Slade Mason deserved a man who would never cheat, never get drunk and lose control. Never fucking hurt her.

"What are you going to do, son?" Dad slid off the tall stool and walked to the fridge.

Scrubbing my hands over my face, I stood and paced the length of the kitchen. "I'm staying in Whisper Springs."

Pop returned to the counter with a bottle of Riesling and two glasses. "And Rocky?"

I stopped my patrol across the cold, sterile floor and rested my elbows on the counter. "Slade and I will tell him when the time is right. I'm so in love with that kid, Pop."

Dad slid a glass of wine my way. "He is your child. You have every right to—"

I slammed my palms on the counter. "No. No. I won't take him away from his mother. That's not an option."

Lifting the glass to his lips, Dads eyes snapped to mine, then over my head. He finished the drink in one take and promptly refilled his goblet. Cheeks flushed, he met my gaze again. "I want to be part of his life, too, Tango." He cleared his throat. "I know you're disappointed in me, for countless reasons. I'm asking for your forgiveness. I need my boy. I need you in my life. With your mom gone..." Dad choked on his words and paused for a deep breath. "We only have each other now. Come home."

I didn't know how to respond. He'd never been the sentimental type. 'Sorry' wasn't a word that ever came out of his mouth. Was I ready to forgive a lifetime of infidelity, or the fact that he'd turned a blind eye and almost let my child be murdered?

"I can't stay here. You're sharing your bed with a girl half your age. I'm sorry. It's wrong on too many levels."

"I don't expect you to understand why—"

"Enough." I slammed my fist on the granite. "I hate the bullshit excuses. *She's pretty, she's soft. Your mother hasn't touched me in years.* It doesn't matter. You took a goddamned vow when you married her. Didn't that mean anything to you? Every time you fucked around on Mom, you hurt me. Don't you get it?"

Rocky barreled around the corner, skidding to a stop by hooking an arm around my thigh. "I love your house, Tango. It's big. You could fit a pet dragon in here."

"Ready to go?" I scooped him off the floor. "We have to beat your mom home."

"Can I come back sometime and go swimming?" Rocky asked, bouncing in my arms.

"Anytime you want," Dad said, grabbing Rocky's hand and giving it a firm shake. "Goodbye, Rocky James Mason. It sure was nice to meet you." Dad clapped a hand to my shoulder. Avoiding my gaze, he whispered, "I'm sorry, T."

"Bye," Rocky shouted.

Small fingers curled into my back, holding tight, filling my heart and head with fierce, gut-wrenching emotion. I nodded a farewell to Pop, and carried my son out the door, unsure when, or if, I'd return.

CHAPTER 13

TANGO HADN'T KISSED ME AGAIN. In fact, he'd grown colder, more distant, focusing solely on Rocky. I ached for his touch. A brush of his finger, a bump of shoulders, anything. He gave nothing. Not a smile. No friendly glances. Nothing but forced politeness.

I tiptoed through the door and locked it behind me, denying myself a final glance at the man sleeping on my couch, and the little boy tucked against his side. Happy as I was that Rocky had his dad, the fear of losing them hovered, a perpetual shadow of dread, nipping at my heels. Their bond had been immediate, undeniable, and natural. I'd become a ghost in my own home, present and vexing, but invisible. I couldn't help but feel an exorcism was on the horizon.

Regardless, I was thankful. I'd rather be ignored than rotting in a prison cell.

I pulled my dollar store shades over my eyes and started for the Truck Stop. Dew clung to the grass, birds sang their good mornings, and the sky boasted an inspiring shade of blue, sucking the heavy fog of woe from my bones. My morning walks to work had always been my favorite time of day.

At the halfway point of my trek, where my modest neighborhood ended and the stretch of lakeside homes came into view, my phone rang from the deep abyss of my hobo bag. By the time I retrieved my cell, it had stopped ringing. I didn't recognize the number on the screen and decided to worry about it later. When I reached the diner, I'd forgotten about the call. Wasn't hard to do, considering the ambulance and three police cruisers surrounding the joint.

"Oh no. Oh no. Oh no." I sprinted across the parking lot and made it to the red and white van, heart racing, as they were about to lift the bed inside. Bile rose in my throat. *Kim.*

"Oh my God, what happened?" I reached for her with trembling fingers. Face bloody and bruised. Hair matted with red, muddy goo. One eye—swollen shut. She stretched a finger toward me, her mouth working in vain, releasing nothing but a wet gurgle.

"Miss Mason. You need to step back." Someone grabbed me from behind.

"What happened?" I yelled, turning to face a wall of blue.

I recognized the man holding me as one of the officers who'd responded when The Stop had been broken into a few weeks ago.

"Come with me, please."

"Sure," I squeaked, and followed him between two police cruisers to the north side of the building. "What happened? Was there another break in?"

"No," he said, voice gruff and thick. "She was attacked before she entered the building." He paused before we rounded the corner. "I have to warn you; this is hard to see."

I skirted his thick body. Then I squeezed his arm, hard, so as not to fall over. Because when I saw the carnage, all the blood drained from my body.

Overturned recycle bins. Dumpster askew. Blood-stained ground. Chunks of long red hair. A bloody smear on the wall next to Kim's purse. The words, *Hi, Blondie*, spray painted in red across the whitewashed bricks.

The blood didn't bother me so much. What horrified me was the torn panties lying next to one of her shoes.

Oh God. No. No. No.

I didn't ask. I couldn't ask, because I knew. I knew and I didn't want my fears vocalized. *This can't be real.* Not in our town. Not in my Truck Stop. Not Kim.

I heard the ambulance drive away, its siren a low drone before breaking into the high-pitched wail that warned people to get the hell out of the way. My hand started to cramp, and I let go of the officer. "You okay, Miss Mason?"

My stomach protested. "Yeah, yeah," I mumbled, turning from the gruesome scene and running to the tree line in time to purge my breakfast.

When I was able to stand, Officer Williams stood in wait, offering a handkerchief, and a sympathetic grin. "It's never easy to see. When you've got your bearings, I have a few questions."

I shook my head no. "I need to go with her. To the hospital. I need to go. Can someone drive me?"

"I'll be happy to drive you. We can talk in the car." Squashing my chance to argue, he wrapped an arm around my shoulder and guided me back around the corner.

Charlie stood at the back door, brows worried, eyes liquid. I ran into his open arms and hugged him tight.

"I wasn't late, Slade. I wasn't late. She never gets here before me. I don't understand."

"I know, Charlie. It wasn't your fault. I'm going with her to the hospital. I'll keep you updated."

"Good. Good." He shook his head in approval and wiped his cheek with the back of his hand.

"Charlie." I pulled away and cupped his shoulders. "The diner will stay closed today, but do you mind hanging around to keep an eye on things?" I knew he'd worry himself crazy if he didn't have something to do. "Make sure the officers have coffee and breakfast."

"Of course. You go and take care of our girl."

"I will. I'll call you as soon as I know anything."

I hugged Charlie one more time and followed Officer Williams to his car. The drive to Whisper Springs Medical Center took less than fifteen minutes. Williams took advantage of our alone time, squeezing me for information about Kim. Unfortunately, I hadn't much to offer. She had just turned forty-six. Divorced. No children. Dated occasionally, but nothing serious, and nobody recently that I'd known of. Then again, I'd been too wrapped up in my own drama to pay much attention.

When he'd asked me about the words, *Hi, Blondie*, painted on the wall, I told him the truth. I hadn't a clue what it meant, and we'd had issues with graffiti in the past, and maybe that was all it was. He didn't seem to believe that was the case.

I sat in the waiting room for three hours. Three hours to hear the bad news. Kim had slipped into a coma.

I waited several more hours, with Kim's mother and Margie. We held hands, we prayed, we cried. When more of Kim's support system showed up, including her brother and Pastor Davies, I headed back to The Stop.

Charlie had chopped, minced, and diced every available vegetable. The floors had a new coat of wax, the windows sparkled, and the stainless steel appliances had been buffed and shined. He must have locked up and gone home before I arrived. I stumbled into my office and collapsed on the ratty couch.

"Come in, Blondie. Join the party." The large, hairy man held an open bottle of beer toward me.

His stench made me retch. BO and dead skunk. His bloodshot eyes told me all I needed to know about the state of affairs inside the trailer home.

"No." I turned my head, desperate for a whiff of fresh air. "I'm just here for Addy. I'll wait outside." I backed away from the trailer door and retreated down the three wooden steps of the makeshift porch.

I silently cursed myself for not being more careful. The only reason I'd come to the front door was because there were no cars or bikes around. Had I known Walter was home, with visitors, I would've told Addy to meet me down by the river.

Thick fingers wrapped around my bicep and yanked, turning me around, and slamming me against an oily leather vest. "That wasn't a question, cunt." The man stood on the bottom step and leered down at me. "Don't be fuckin' rude. Your little friend inside learned that lesson the hard way." He tossed his beer across the yard and adjusted his crotch. "In fact, she's very accommodating now that she's learned her place."

Nausea roiled inside me.

The man held me in place but hopped off the last step, his feet landing on either side of mine.

I wanted to scream. I wanted to kick and punch and scratch and fight. My limbs wouldn't move. My mouth wouldn't open.

He walked me backward until I bumped against the wall of the trailer. He shoved his free hand between my legs and rubbed with violent, clumsy strokes.

Oh God. This wasn't happening. Why couldn't I scream for help?

"Fuck," he grunted. "That's prime pussy right there."

The man released my arm and tangled his fingers in my hair, fisting and pulling tight.

He leaned closer, rubbing his nose against my head. "The brothers have been asking 'bout you. Wondering when Dane was going to share." He thrust his hips against me. Pinning me with his sweaty body. "But now that I've seen you up close, I think I'll keep you for myself."

The world around me blurred, and I slammed my lids closed. Fight, damn you. Fight.

I heard a dull thunk. Felt a rush of air. The man released me. I couldn't open my eyes. Until I heard a familiar voice.

"Jesus fucking Christ, Blondie. How many times have I warned you to stay clear of this hellhole? What the fuck are you doing?"

Dane.

I collapsed in relief, landing on my knees in the dirt. Violent green eyes glared down at me.

"Get up. Walter and the others will be here any minute." He spit at the unconscious man next to me. "I gotta deal with this shit-for-brains before they get here." He pulled me to standing and held me at arms' length, studying my face.

I watched his Adam's apple rise and fall. I watched his eyes soften, then darken. Then he shoved me toward the dirt road. "Start walking. Better yet, run. I'll get Addy, have her meet you at the junction. If you know what's good for you, you'll take her away from here. Don't ever fucking come back, Blondie."

Tango

Hi, Blondie. Hi, Blondie. Hi, Blondie.

The painted words taunted me. Despite the late July heat, the scene chilled me through and through.

"How's Kim?" I asked, teeth gritted.

"Coma," Charlie mumbled, roughing a hand over the top of his head. "Whoever did this, beat her something fierce."

That could've been Slade's blood spilt on the ground. "Cops have any leads?"

"No. Nothin' yet." He offered nothing more than a vacant stare aimed at the wall.

Words weren't necessary with the level of rage we shared.

It took everything I had not to punch a hole through the fucking bricks. "Thanks for letting me know she was here, Charlie. I'm gonna head inside."

He waved me off. "I'm heading to the hospital. Catch ya' later."

Measuring my breaths and steadying my pulse, I watched him retreat. Slade hadn't called. I'd have been furious if I weren't so damn relieved she was okay. Couldn't blame her, though. I'd been a jackass, giving her the cold shoulder for weeks.

I stormed through the back door, and down the hall, pausing at her office door. It was slightly ajar and through the crack, I could see her thin frame curled on the sofa. Relief swirled through me. Seeing her alive and well evaporated some of the simmering anger.

It could've been her. It could've been Slade in the hospital, fighting for her life.

My arms itched to hold that sweet, soft body. It would've been so easy to go to her and take what I needed. To touch, taste, and smell. Reassurance that she was living, breathing, flesh and blood, and mine. All fucking mine.

Only, that wouldn't be right. Because so much of me still wanted to punish her. I didn't trust myself not to mark her in some way. So I didn't go to her, like I needed, like she needed. Instead, I stayed a safe distance and watched her sleep.

When the urge to join her became unbearable, I headed to the coffee machine. The pot had just finished brewing when I heard, "Where's Rocky?"

Oh fuck. I loved the sound of her voice.

I didn't make eye contact, because I knew I'd lose footing on my moral high ground, and I wasn't ready to quit climbing that mountain just yet. "He's with Marion."

"Oh. Good."

I heard her slide onto one of the barstools. I poured two cups of java and slid one across the counter.

"What are you doing here?" Her fingers stretched around the cup. I imagined those soft delicate hands on me. Then I pictured them bloody and broken, like Kim's, and I remembered why I'd come.

"You didn't call. You didn't come home last night, and you didn't call." The words came out harsher than I'd intended.

Slade's eyes lifted to mine, exhausted and wary.

I attempted to tone down the raging caveman vibe. "Don't do that again."

"I'm surprised you noticed," she snapped.

She wanted to pick a fight. Couldn't blame her. I knew all too well what it was like to need an outlet.

"I was worried." I leaned my ass against the counter and lifted the cup to my lips.

Slade sighed, her shoulders slumping. "I only wanted to lie down for a minute. I didn't mean to fall asleep. I'm sorry I worried you."

"Rocky missed you last night."

"He did?"

"Yeah. I had a hard time getting him to bed."

"Thanks." She slid off the stool and walked to the window. "I needed to hear that. I feel like he doesn't need me anymore."

Because I'd done everything in my power to make her feel that way. Fuckin' jackass. "You okay?"

Slade shifted nervously from foot to foot, gaze focused out the window. "I could've ended up like Addy, you know."

I followed a trail of jet fuel hanging in the blue sky. I couldn't look at my beauty. I hated seeing her so out of sorts. "You were nothing like her."

"She didn't choose what happened to her."

"She had a choice every time she lied."

"That's not what I'm talking about." Slade shook her head. "They used her. Her body. Before I took her to Montana. Hell, for years before that. That's why she used you. I get it now. She was desperate. Thought you could save her."

Fucking hell. What was her deal with Addison? "Do you hear yourself? You're making excuses for the sick games she played."

"They would've used me, too. If it weren't for Dane, I might've ended up just like her."

Fury slammed me back a step. "The fuck you talking about?"

"One of them tried." She paused, swallowed hard, wrapped her arms around herself. "It's funny. I'd always thought that if I found myself in a dangerous situation, I'd fight my way out of it. But when he grabbed me, and touched me, I froze. My mind went blank. My body numbed. I couldn't move or scream. I just stood there." She wiped a tear from her cheek. "Dane came out of nowhere, and next thing I know, I was running home." Slade turned her head my way, chin dropped to her shoulder, and gave me a brave smile. "Anyway. I never told anyone about what happened. I never saw Dane again. Addy and I left for Montana two days later."

I was rage. My blood acid. My skin shards of jagged glass.

Slade stared over my shoulder. "I wonder if Kim fought, or if she froze, like I had."

I couldn't hear another word. I grabbed her wrist and slapped my keys into her palm. "Take my Rover home. I gotta get the hell out of here."

"Tango. Wait," she whispered, voice broken.

I was seconds from losing my shit. She'd seen enough horror. I couldn't show her what I was about to turn into. "I need to get away from you right now," I said, throwing my hands up and backing away. "Go straight home and don't fucking go anywhere alone."

I turned on my heel and sprinted out the back door. Then I ran. Across the gravel lot. Up the embankment. Across the old highway. I headed for the base of Hangman's Hill and sprinted up the old hiking trail.

My thighs were rubber, my lungs, fire. I pushed higher. Higher. Higher, until sweat weighed down my clothes. Until my vision blurred and I couldn't pull in another breath. Until I collapsed on hands and knees in the layers of rotting leaves, and crunchy pine needles.

I screamed, releasing my rage, and anguish, and self-loathing. I screamed because I hadn't been there to protect her. I screamed because I'd thrown away six years. I screamed because I had no face to bloody, no heavy bag to absorb my anger. I screamed because I had no choice. I screamed because I had no one to blame.

No one to blame, but me.

Hoarse, and winded, I lay on the forest floor, next to my heart and soul, and guts. An empty vessel submerged in a river of truth, filling fast with razor-sharp wisdom; to be the man I wanted to be, I didn't need absolution from Slade.

I needed to forgive myself.

Only, I didn't know how.

Slade

I didn't know how to ask Tango to leave.

Wasn't sure if I could.

What I did know, was that I couldn't live the way we'd been living anymore. He was everywhere and ever-present. I ached for his touch, but he was always out of reach. I craved his smile, his laughter, his kisses, but he reserved those for Rocky. I yearned for his shoulder to lean on, his ear to voice my worries to, but he only offered his back.

His presence, consuming and beautiful as it was, would eventually destroy me. He had to go so that I could get busy moving on with my life. My life alone.

Through the kitchen window, I watched the boys play catch, silently cheered for Rocky as he made futile and adorable attempts to tackle Tango, and cringed as they wrestled in the spotty grass. Father and son, sweaty and sun-kissed, carefree, and beautiful, and slowly, torturously, breaking me.

From the kitchen table, my cell announced a caller. I'd already spoken to Kim's mother; there hadn't been any change. I had checked in with Tucker earlier in the day. I didn't care to speak with anyone else. So, I ignored the phone, rinsed the last dish, poured the sudsy water down the sink, and rinsed my sponge.

Rocky's raspy giggles boomed outside, making me smile.

He was in good hands. The best hands. Hands I knew too well. The very hands that had the power to carry Rocky out my door, possibly forever.

That was the reason I hesitated asking Tango to leave. Because I couldn't risk losing the boy I loved with all my heart and soul. My son, who was never mine at all. And so, instead of retreating to my room as I'd done every night since Tango had claimed my couch, I pulled three frozen fruit pops from the freezer, joined the boys in the afternoon heat, and pretended, for Rocky's sake, and perhaps mine, that the three of us were a happy family.

To my surprise, Tango sat next to me on the back porch, on the second step from the top, and let his thigh fall against mine.

It was shameful, really, how that simple, unconscious gesture, filled my soul with hope, spiked my internal temperature, and jolted my heart rate.

"Thanks," he said, snatching the white-colored pop from my grip. He ripped the plastic with his teeth and peeled it free from the treat. Then he handed it back to me. "Coconut is your favorite, right?"

Oh God. He remembered. I blinked my burning eyes and nodded.

He grabbed the others from my hand and freed them from their casing the same way. Then he handed Rocky the blueberry splash, and he slid the raspberry rapture between his own lips.

Fire licked my thigh, where our bodies touched, and for a brief moment, I started to believe that maybe, possibly, by some miracle, we could be a family.

"Mom," Rocky interrupted my fantasy. He stood at the bottom of the steps, bouncing up and down on his toes, blue juice staining his face and hands. "Tango is taking me to his dance studio tomorrow. Wanna come?"

My insides did a funny dance of their own. I braved a questioning glance at Tango.

Preoccupied with his icy treat, he offered nothing more than a shoulder shrug.

Heat blasted my cheekbones. I'd rather roll in hot lava than step foot in that mirrored dance hall from hell. Tango probably hadn't a clue what his father was doing with the new instructor. "No, Rock, I can't go with you tomorrow. I have to work, sweetie."

"Aw." He scuffed the bottom of his shoe back and forth on a rock. "You always have to work, Mom."

Not for long. Soon, I'd be unemployed. "I know, baby. But it's fun hanging out with Tango, right?"

"Yeah." Rocky climbed the three steps between us and bumped his hip against my knee. Chin tucked, he leaned in and whispered, as quietly as a five-year-old could whisper, "I wish he was my dad instead of my babysitter."

The air surrounding me thickened. Tango leaned forward, elbows to knees, head dropping low.

Eons passed in nauseating silence before he looked over his shoulder at me, eyes liquid and stormy, communicating his frustration and disappointment. I wanted to slink away from the scrutiny, but it was the most emotion he'd given me in weeks, so instead, I absorbed his glare, and lapped up the attention like a love-starved child.

When I thought I couldn't take another blast of his fiery gaze, and I coiled to flee, he hooked an arm around Rocky, grunted, "C'mere, kiddo," and pulled his mini-me between his massive arms into a bear hug so full of love, it could've ended wars.

Again, I watched from the sidelines, while father and son shared an intimate, bonding moment. Oddly, their private exchange, their unspoken communication, didn't open any fissures in my heart. Instead, a veil lifted, revealing a truth. A truth I'd known but had tried to ignore. Tango and Rocky belonged together. Father and son needed each other. More than they needed me.

It was right.

It was how things should've been all along.

And I knew that moment was the beginning of another end.

CHAPTER 14

Slade

I STOOD OUTSIDE the front door, fighting an epic battle with my tear ducts, watching my boys laugh, dance, and make a complete mess of my entryway. Wood pieces, a tool box, and sawdust littered half the floor. A drop cloth, paintbrushes, and two gallons of paint surrounded the staircase. Rocky wore more of the happy yellow color on his body than he brushed on the banister. Tango wore a smile brighter, and hotter, than the sun beating down on my back.

I stood alone, absorbing the scene, mostly Tango's bare chest, for ten minutes. My feet ached, and my bladder was about to burst, but I couldn't bring myself to disturb their progress, or their fun.

Paint fumes reached my nose through the closed door. The thump of the stereo's bass reverberated the boards beneath my feet. Rocky's infectious giggles tickled my ears. I feared my ribcage wasn't large enough to contain the rapidly swelling muscle it housed.

That, right then, right in front of me, was a perfect reflection of the future I'd envisioned before my world had been uprooted and replanted.

What a cruel tease my life had turned into, dangling what-could-have-beens in front of my nose.

Tango would move on. Then what? Could I? Was my heart open to the idea of loving another man? Was marriage in my future? The thought unnerved me. For now, I'd focus on surviving the upcoming days, easing Rocky into the truth about his father, and I supposed, coming up with a parenting plan.

There hadn't been any more Slayer sightings. Still, I kept my eyes open. Stayed on high alert. I had planned on discussing my worries with Tango, but the timing never seemed right. Or, more accurately, our conversations never consisted of anything beefier than, "Good morning," or "Have you seen Rocky's shoes?" or "We'll see you at dinner time."

"Whatcha doin'?" Something brushed my shoulder.

I screamed, whirled around, and smashed into a solid chest.

"Sorry. Shit. I didn't mean to scare you." Tucker pulled me into a hug and chuckled.

"What are you doing here?" I mumbled into his shirt. Stiff linen scratched my cheek. "Why are you dressed up? Got a date?" I rubbed his collar between my thumb and forefinger and took in the rare sight of my brother dressed in anything other than flannel or graphic tees.

"I'm having beers with your Mr. Rossi." He straightened his button-down shirt.

"*My* Mr. Rossi? No. Afraid you've got that wrong." I looked over my shoulder. Rocky waved yellow hands at me through the glass. He turned and pointed to the half-painted staircase, raising his brows and mouthing something to me.

I opened the door to greet my boy. Tango knelt, tapping a lid onto one of the cans. When he looked my direction, heat blasted my insides. Sweet mother of mercy, what a sight. Eyes glowing with pride, playful grin, muscles rolling, bunching, teasing me from beneath his skin.

"Mom, Uncle Tuck! Look what I did today." Rocky pointed at the banister. "I hammered it and it doesn't wiggle anymore." He started toward me, only to be blocked by a massive arm.

"Wait, kiddo. We need to clean up first." Tango disappeared with Rocky down the long hallway toward the back entrance. The screen door slammed, the garden nozzle squeaked, and Rocky squealed, presumably from the shock of a cold shower.

Tucker huffed, his cheeks puffing like an overzealous chipmunk. "Yellow, huh?" he asked, pressing a finger to the fresh paint.

"He remembered." I stared, in awe of the perfectly bright, obnoxious color.

"Remembered what?"

"My mom liked a dark house. Curtains, paint, furniture. Tango and I used to tease her and threaten to paint every room a happy, blinding yellow. She'd laugh and say, 'Okay. Only the stairs, please. I suppose every house needs one bright spot.' It's silly, I know." I shook my head. "I can't believe he did this."

Cocking his head to the side, he stated, "I can't believe you don't see how in love with you he is."

If Tucker held a rabid rat to my chest and let it gnaw through my breastbone and feast on my beating heart, it would've hurt less. "Don't say that, Tuck. We can't go there. Not after everything we've been through. Not after what I've done."

"You could be a family," Tucker stated, crossing beefy arms across his chest.

A furnace lit behind my cheekbones. I jammed my index finger into his shoulder, to make him listen, to take out my frustration, hell, I don't know. Maybe I needed to vent. "No.

No. No. He hates me. He has his life, his fancy house, and now he has Rocky. There is no scenario, no possible outcome to this shitty soap opera where I come out the winner."

"Winner of what?" Tango asked, sauntering toward us, wiping his bare chest with a towel. His grin faded when he noticed my scowl. It took tremendous will power to keep my gaze fixed above his chin. I would not look at his ridiculous abs. I would not.

"Nothing," I groaned, throwing my arms in the air. I turned to retreat up the stairs, hoping to unleash the tempest of frustration and anger on my pillow, or some unfolded laundry. I stopped before stepping on the wet paint, growled my disapproval, and headed for the downstairs bathroom instead. "And put on a damn shirt," I yelled before slamming the door behind me.

"What's wrong with Mommy?" I heard Rocky ask.

I reached behind me and pushed the lock.

What was wrong with me? Well, that was a no-brainer. I was breaking, despite having convinced myself I would survive this whole nightmare. I loved Tango. I loved him so deep, and his parts were so tangled with mine that uprooting any bit of him would tear me apart from the core. I was headed toward unavoidable demise.

I plopped my ass on the toilet and cried. Angry tears. Ugly, face-contorting, giant, burning tears. I reached over and turned on the ancient, squeaky bathroom fan so nobody could hear my sobs.

I had to get this ridiculous, fanciful hope out of my system. Tango would never be mine. The fates made that perfectly clear. I needed to grow the fuck up and let him go. I could do this. Or at least pretend. I'd faked it for the past six years. What was sixty or seventy more?

I was damn lucky to be sitting on my toilet and not in a jail cell. I could focus on my freedom. Be grateful that I could still call Rocky my son. I'd given Tango his child. He'd granted me immunity—from the lies, fear, guilt, and constant uncertainty.

I had my whole life ahead of me. A whole life of blank pages. It was solely up to me how to fill them.

Tango

My life had been one giant blank page since I left home all those years ago. I had tried to cover its blinding glare by burying myself in my studies. When that hadn't worked, I'd turned to fighting, and sex. For a short time, I had fooled myself into believing I was writing some kind of epic story for myself. Despite my misguided efforts, every morning I'd wake to one blank page after another. Empty. Lonely. Pointless.

Today had been different. When I woke to a little boy stretched across my chest, drooling on my shirt, the glare was no longer there. The page was filled with laughter, and smiles, and sticky fingers. Burps and stinky feet. Wild blonde hair, enormous blue eyes, and flip-flops. There were so many words, so many stories, it made my head spin.

I couldn't stay angry. I couldn't spend another day keeping Slade at bay, while I tried to make sense of her decisions, my parents' refusal to accept my child, or the fact that I had fallen blindly into parenthood.

I had committed crimes to forget my girl, done heinous things born of self-loathing and hate. Slade Mason had committed crimes to remember. Everything she'd done had been for love. Plain and simple. She'd risked her life to save my son. Strangers had risked their lives for him. I owed the

Slade family everything. For now, I'd start with the selfless, heartbroken girl crying her eyes out on the other side of the door.

I plopped my ass on the floor against the wall and waited. Waited. Waited some more, my nerves buzzing harder with each passing minute.

After what seemed an hour, the knob turned and I jumped to my feet. When she opened the door and her eyes met mine, I had no choice but to wrap my arms around her skinny frame. The past few weeks had been torture—keeping my distance while I'd battled the war of emotions, and resisted the urge to make her hurt as I did.

"I thought you were going for drinks with Tucker," she mumbled into my chest, gripping my hips and squeezing tight.

"He offered to take Rocky, for a sleepover."

"Why?"

"Tucker insisted that we have alone time. I couldn't argue with his logic."

"I don't understand," she said, raising her head and stepping back.

I braced my arms on the wall, caging her, blocking her attempt at escape. "I should be mad at you."

Her chin dropped. "Tango. Please. I can't do this right now."

Ignoring her plea, I continued. I would burst if I waited another second to tell her how I felt. "I have every right to hate you, but I don't. It's impossible for me to feel anything other than gratitude."

Slade stared at the floor. I tapped a finger under her chin, urging her to look up. I needed her eyes on me.

When she raised them, I sucked in a breath. "I love you. More than I ever have. I love you for protecting him. For what you sacrificed. I fucking love you. I never stopped, and now…" I stepped back, dropping my arms to my sides. "Now I have a son. A family. Goddamn, Slade. You're the only family I ever wanted, and … and…"

I couldn't continue. My own words burned. First my lips, then my throat, liquid fire scorching my insides and settling behind my ribcage.

Slade buried her face behind the shield of her hands. "You can't love me," she mumbled. "How can you say that after what I did?" Tears cascaded down her chin, wetting her shirt. Shoulders heaving, she folded into herself and gave in to her own emotions.

My strong girl was falling apart before my eyes.

I alone was responsible for the decisions she'd been forced to make. My sin. My selfish act. I could never rewind the clock, and dear God, how I wished I could go back to that night and be the man she deserved.

My own mother had cast aside my child, her grandson, her very flesh and blood. Slade had laid her life on the line for him, even after I'd sliced her open and left her to bleed. If that wasn't love, I didn't want to suffer another breath on this wretched Earth.

"I love you fiercely. And you love me, too. I know you do." I fell to my knees and pulled her with me. "You loved me enough to save my boy. I wasn't brave enough to face you after what I'd done. I ran away. Left you to clean my mess."

I didn't know if she could hear me through her sobs. I pressed my lips to her ear. "I'm so fucking sorry, baby. I was a coward, and you. Shit. You were my warrior. You don't have to be strong anymore. I'm here. I'll be your rock. I'll take care of both of you."

I held her steady through the tremors, fighting my own damn tidal wave of emotion. I didn't have a fucking clue how the following days would play out. I only knew that we had to let things play out, and I owed her everything. Everything.

Slade Mason had carried the weight of my sin for far too long.

When the sobbing slowed, I lifted her off the floor and set her on her feet. I grabbed a handful of tissues from the bathroom and dried her red, puffy eyes. "Are you about finished?" I asked, tipping her face up to mine. "I really need to kiss you now."

Slade

I really needed him to stop kissing me. My nose was stuffy on account of the crying, making it difficult to inhale. Which was ridiculous, because for the first time since he had come home, I had room to breathe.

And I loved his lips. I loved how he loved me with his lips. I wanted those big, soft lips on every inch of my body. With great reluctance, I pulled away.

He combed a hand through his hair and slumped against the wall. "Sorry. I got carried away."

"We have a bad habit of doing that, don't we?" I hooked my finger into the waistband of his jeans. The taut muscles of his abdomen twitched under my touch, and I couldn't contain my smile.

I pressed my back to the wall next to him. It wasn't close enough. I looped my arm around his thick muscled bicep. Still too far away. I slid my hand downward and forced my fingers between his. "What now?"

Tango sighed, lifted our joined hands to his lips, and kissed my knuckles. "We'll take it one day at a time."

I had one more truth to reveal, and had I not cried myself dry already, I would've burst into tears again. "Tango?"

"Yeah, babylove?"

"I sold the restaurant."

His fingers tightened around mine. "What?"

"To your dad."

"No." He looked down at me, as if waiting to hear, *Ha, ha. Just kidding. Gotcha.*

I nodded. "Yes."

"No." He pushed off the wall and paced the hallway up and back. "Please tell me this is a joke. You love that place. Rocky loves it. It's yours. You can't. I mean, shit. You didn't, did you?" He stopped in front of me and cupped my face. "Why?"

Gulp. I raised my eyes to meet his, and sucked in a breath of courage. "I was running."

His face crumpled. "From me."

"When you said you were moving home, I thought I needed to disappear." I expected him to get angry all over again.

Instead, he stepped back, shoulders slouched, and kicked at something invisible on the floor. "Fuck."

"I wasn't only running from you, though." I rubbed my raw eyes. "On the night Rocky was born, when we pulled Addy out of the cabin, her uncle showed up. I hit that disgusting bastard in the head with a bat. He wasn't supposed to be there. I was so scared, and angry, and I hit him. There was so much blood. I was sure I'd killed him."

"Slade," Tango whispered, voice cracking.

"I just found out he's been in prison. I didn't kill him. Which is good, right? But what if he told the Slayers it was me who took Addy that night? What if they're coming for me? Or worse, Rocky? I keep seeing them around town, and I'm scared. I'm so scared they know it was me who tried to rescue Addy."

"Baby." Solid arms wrapped around me, chasing the shivers from my body. "You don't have to worry about the Slayers. They don't know it was you."

"You don't understand. I haven't seen them around town for years. Now, they seem to be everywhere."

His chest rose and fell. "I ran in to Dane."

"Oh God. Dane?" I wiggled free of his embrace. "Is he okay? I haven't heard from him. I've been so worried."

Tango's mouth opened, then closed. He rubbed the back of his neck, then pinned me with a glare. "Why would you worry about that sick fucker?"

"He's the reason we got Addy out of there. He's the reason your son is alive, and here with us. He risked his life to save Addy. He loved her, Tango. Like a sister. He helped us get her out. And then he disappeared. I never heard from him again."

"He never disappeared, babylove. He's had eyes and ears on you since day one. Made sure you and Rocky were safe."

I didn't ask how he knew, or where he'd run into Dane. I suspected the fading bruises on his face had been a result of their meeting.

Tango closed the short distance between us, framing my face with his warm hands. "But I'm here now. Got it? I'm here. I've got your back. Nobody is touching you or my boy."

There was something so savage in his promise, so possessive in his gaze, I felt owned. Protected. A little frightened, too, and I jerked away, shocked by the emotion.

Tango cussed under his breath and headed for the living room, pausing halfway to the couch.

"So you sold The Stop. The deal is done?" he asked, shoulders bunched, hands fisted at his sides.

"It's done," I mumbled, feeling my first twinge of regret about selling.

"Dad's been after your property since before we were born."

"I know. It's his now. I broke the news to my employees today."

"That would explain your fragile emotions." He scratched his head and turned to face me. "How'd they take it?"

"There were a lot of tears, mostly from Charlie."

That earned me a smile. "We had our first kiss at The Stop."

I laughed. Charlie had caught us kissing against the walk-in freezer. "I remember."

"Our first official date."

"I know."

"Had my first fight in the parking lot. Do you remember? I kicked Riley Smith's ass, defending your honor."

"How could I forget. You almost got carted to juvie."

"Good thing your mom and Officer Granger were fuck buddies, huh?"

"Not funny." I stepped around him and headed for the kitchen. All the crying had made me thirsty.

Tango followed. While I poured the water, he snagged the ice tray out of the freezer and popped the cubes into a bowl. "He's going to tear it down and build condos." Plop. He dropped ice into my drink. "I can't imagine this town without The Stop."

I poured him a glass, and we leaned against the counter in silence until adequately hydrated.

"What will you do?" Tango asked, after draining his glass for the second time.

"I don't know." My plan had been to take the money and run. Since my need to flee no longer existed, I was free to do whatever I wanted. Except leave. The leaving option had been taken away, but I was okay with that. I was so freaking okay with that.

Tango took the drink from my hand and set it on the counter next to his. Then he reached around me, pressing his shirtless chest into my shoulder, and fiddled with my iPod. Before I could move out of his way, he snatched my hand and pulled me against his bare skin.

"Have you danced today?"

I melted into him. Oh, how I'd missed those words.

Shakira's "Hips Don't Lie" blared through the speaker, but Tango rocked back and forth, slow and graceful, arms around me tight.

He was here. He was home and holding me. We were dancing. And there were no more secrets. I was free to hold him back. No guilt. No shame. No fear.

His hand slid up my neck, and into my hair. Then he tugged the elastic band holding my messy bun and worked his fingers through the tangles.

I closed my eyes, absorbing the tenderness, the care he put into splaying the unruly curls down my back.

Enrique Iglesias came on next. "Bailando." One of my favorite hip-shaking songs. I spun free of his arms, shook the rest of my hair loose, and danced away from him, spinning, shaking my ass, and teasing, yes, teasing Tango Rossi.

Tango stared at me, one hand tucked into the pocket of his jeans, the other rubbing the stubble on his chin. His tongue made a slow drag across his bottom lip. He smiled. I was done for. My boy, my beautiful man, chased me around the other side of the table and coiled an arm around my waist. He captured my right hand, held it shoulder high, and spun me across the kitchen floor.

He led. I followed. We danced. Hips grinding, chests bumping, laughter, smiles, heavy breaths. Oh God. My heart could burst.

Was this real? Did I have my Tango back? My mind was too jumbled to process anything. I stopped thinking and gave in to his lead, to the moment, to the pure bliss that launched me higher than I'd believed possible.

I was spinning and spinning and soon my feet were off the ground, and I was in his arms, and he was carrying me through the living room, and laying me on the couch.

The weight of his body pushed me into the cushions and our mouths crashed together. I locked my arms around his neck, my legs around his waist. I never wanted to let go. I would never again let my man go. He was mine. He was mine. He was mine.

As our chests heaved, and we kissed, and clawed at each other, the weight of my world evaporated, floated upward, and disappeared into the ceiling.

Tango raised his head and hovered above me. Perhaps to catch his breath. Every time he inhaled, his erection pressed harder between my legs, decimating every nerve, filling me with unbearable need.

"I love you, Slade Mason." His voice was ragged and raw. He dropped another kiss on my lips and rolled his hips against me. "I never stopped. Not for one second."

My eyes burned, and I blinked away the salty moisture. I pulled him closer and whispered, "I love you, too."

"So, you're mine, and I'm yours. Forever."

"Yes, please. Forever."

He kissed a trail down my neck, across each shoulder, and lower, toward my breasts. He manipulated the buttons of my work pants. I couldn't breathe. I couldn't keep up. *I can't do this.*

"Tango. Wait." I tangled my fingers through his messy hair to stop his descent.

"We've waited too damn long, babylove."

Yes. He was so freaking right about that. I was a ticking time bomb. There was no easy way to say what I had to say. "I have to tell you something."

He stopped pulling at my waistband. "Can it wait?"

I gripped the sides of his face. "I've never made love."

Tango

"I've never made love, either." If I didn't get her naked, and soon, I would self-combust. "I've only fucked, Slade. Love had nothing to do with it."

I couldn't think straight. Christ, why couldn't I get her damn button unfastened?

"Wait. You don't understand." She pushed at my chest. "I don't mean it like you mean it."

"Don't mean what?" I mumbled, giving up on the pants and going for the shirt and bra.

She laughed, and I suddenly felt like the world's biggest dope. "What's so funny?"

Her eyes sizzled and shined, highlighted by the pink in her cheeks. "You're not listening to me."

I sat back on my heels, a tad curious, mostly frustrated. "I'm listening."

"I haven't had sex." Her cheeks glowed.

"In a long time?"

Slade rolled her eyes. "No, Tango. At all."

"How is that possible?" Slade was deadly sexy, and I had found the dildo hidden in her closet. Plus, she'd made no effort to hide her birth control. "Why are you on the pill?"

"To regulate my periods."

"Shit. Are you fucking with me right now? I hope you're not messing with my head, because that's just about the best goddamned news I've ever heard. Seriously? Nobody?"

Releasing her bottom lip from between her teeth, she whispered, "I've been busy."

Busy, as in saving and raising my child. While I'd been busy rage-fucking my way through the cream of the crop in the underground fight scene. I didn't believe it was possible for my love to grow any deeper, my heart to expand any further, but it did. Fuck, it hurt, but I welcomed the burn.

"Well, then." I tugged her shirt back over her stomach. "That changes things."

Her delicate hand covered mine. "Please. Don't stop. I want you. I want this. More than I've ever wanted anything."

"Slade," I huffed, sitting back on my heels. "I don't want to fuck things up. I need to do this right."

She wiggled into the sitting position, a storm brewing in her blue beauties.

Holy shit, she was going to fight for us.

I watched in awe, and shameful anticipation, while she rose to her feet and pulled her shirt over her head. Our eyes locked, and she smiled. Sweet mother of mercy, her smile. The truest thing I knew, was that if you were on the receiving end of Slade's smile, you were the luckiest bastard alive.

If there was ever a time to stand up and be a man, that was it. That was the moment to prove my worth. Fall to one knee, beg her to be my bride, marry my girl. Then, and only then, would it be right for me to take her virginity. I knew, to the very depths of my soul, that was the right way to handle the situation.

Chivalry.

Slade deserved nothing less.

Except, when she reached behind her back, unhooked her bra, then let it fall to the floor, I lost my sense of reason.

"Come here," I ordered, rising to my feet and offering a hand.

As she stepped closer, her full, round breasts bounced and swayed. Dark pink nipples puckered tight. I was lost. A goner. Brain cells decimated. I had to have her.

Slade Mason was mine. Had always been, would always be, mine. As far as I was concerned, we were already married, mind and spirit. The *body* part? Hell, I would take care of that right-fucking-now. Legalities would come soon enough.

"Are you sure about this?" I said, pulling her close, smashing her beautiful breasts between us.

"Don't make me wait," she begged, breathy and so fucking sweet. "I'll die if you make me wait." She shivered against me.

I looked at the freshly painted staircase, then the couch. No way in hell was our first time going to be on her sofa.

As if reading my mind, Slade looked at the stairs and back to me. Shrugging her shoulders, she asked, "Think it's dry enough?"

"Fuck it." I grabbed her hand, and we ascended the steps two by two.

Slade didn't stop at her bedroom door. She pulled me toward the bathroom.

"Where do you think you're going?" I asked, delirious with lust.

"I stink. I need a shower."

"Like hell." I crouched, scooped her over my shoulder, headed back to her room. After setting her on her feet next to the bed, I took a step back to admire the view. A teasing grin spread across her face as she shimmied free of her khakis and underwear.

"Sweet Jesus," I mumbled, ogling her from head to toe.

Her hungry gaze traveled from my face to my crotch.

My dick was diamond hard, and there was no way I could move without injuring myself. Slade stepped closer and unbuttoned my jeans. I was helpless to do anything but watch and feel.

She slid her hands under the waistband of my boxers and around to my ass. My heart skipped a beat when she pressed soft kisses across my chest. The right side, then the left. She pushed my clothing down past my hips and my erection fell free. I moaned and braced my hand on the bedpost. As she slid the fabric down my thighs, her hair brushed my cock and I nearly ejaculated.

Sweet, fucking torture.

I was losing control, and shit was about to get embarrassing.

I cupped her shoulders and pulled her upright. "You're killing me right now."

"You're taking too long to get naked!" Lifting her knee, she slid her foot between my legs and pushed my pants to the floor.

"What's the rush?" I asked, cupping her cheeks and pulling her face to mine. "We have all night."

Her wild, fiery eyes filled with nervous anticipation. "Kiss me," she begged.

I obliged, working her mouth—soft, slow, unrelenting—until she relaxed.

Her lids fluttered open. "Pinch me."

I slid a hand down to her ass and pinched. "It's not a dream, babylove."

"I'm scared to death I'm going to wake up and you won't be here."

"I'm here. I'm real. I'm yours. I'm all yours." I kissed her again, this time locking my arms around her waist and lifting her off the floor.

Her legs curled around my hips. Fuck, I loved when she did that. I walked to the bed and carefully laid her down beneath me. On reflex, I swept her hair off her face. That fucking gorgeous, perfect face. Round, and soft, and turning a lovely shade of red, for me.

I danced my fingers over her shoulder, then down her arm. Touching, exploring, savoring the perfect moment, her flawless beauty. Shivers wracked her body when I lightly brushed my knuckle over the curve of her breast. When I flicked my tongue over the pebbled nipple, she bucked beneath me, arching her back, begging for more.

I slid between her legs, and she tensed, one hand gripping my hair, the other fisting the sheet at her side.

"Relax." I kissed her belly and teased my finger through the neatly trimmed pubic hair.

I moved down further, anxious to taste her arousal. Eager to memorize the one part of her body I'd never had the honor of fully exploring. I kissed the spot above her clit and she gasped and trembled. Then I pressed harder, inhaling deep and slow.

Sweet mother of mercy. Her musk made my head spin and my cock swell.

I was barely hanging on as it was, and when she tilted her hips and ground her pussy against my face, I lost control.

Slade

I was out of control. Out of my mind. Completely, unabashedly unfettered. I ground against him, greedy, craving more. Tango Rossi made love to me. With his mouth, his tongue, his moans. Sweet Jesus, the man worked me into a frenzy.

Licking, swirling, biting, sucking. He devoured me, driving me to the brink before backing off, slowing down, leaving me delirious with want. He shoved his hands under my thighs and clamped one around my hip, pinning me to the bed. I grabbed his other hand, lacing our fingers, squeezing, holding tight to keep grounded.

He latched on to my clit and sucked hard. My hips jerked off the mattress, my body no longer under the control of my brain, but one hundred percent responding to Tango's unspoken commands.

He released me, and cool air replaced his wet, warm tongue. I stared at the ceiling, then squeezed my eyes closed and drew in precious oxygen.

"Look at me," he rasped, crawling over me.

I met his gaze as he reached between my legs and swirled a finger through the moisture. "Mmm. You are so ready."

I'd never been more ready. For anything. Ever.

"I don't have condoms, Slade. I'm clean. But if you want to stop, we'll stop." He dropped a cinnamon bun kiss to my lips. Warm and sticky and so damn sweet.

"Don't stop. Don't stop."

"Thank fuck." His erection bobbed against me, and my body reacted as it always did in his presence, arching into him, seeking more. He reached between us, and positioned himself, rolling his hips, coating himself in my moisture, teasing my clit with the head of his cock.

My eyes wandered downward, but his words stopped my perusal. "Have you used the ridiculous dildo that's hiding in your closet?"

Heat slammed my cheeks. I nodded yes.

"Pleasured yourself with it?"

"Yes."

"Fucked yourself?"

Oh God. I would have been humiliated had I not been so turned on, the way he worked himself against me while he questioned. "Yes," I somehow managed to mumble.

"How many times?"

"I don't know."

"Once a week, twice a week, five times a week?"

"Tango. Please. You're killing me."

"Tell me, babylove."

"A couple times a week." I was a vibrant young woman. A woman with a hearty sexual appetite who believed she'd never have a man to share her bed with.

Was it pathetic that my only experience had been with an anatomically correct piece of rubber? I didn't think so. I sure as hell wasn't going in search of mindless sex with any guy just for the sake of sex. Like I had time for that, anyway.

"It's been inside you?" he asked with a throaty groan.

"Tango. Stop."

"Don't be embarrassed. It's so fucking hot. I'm gauging how careful I need to be. I don't want to hurt you." He leaned closer, tickling my ear with his lips. "Who did you think about when you pleasured yourself?"

Oh, jeez. Such a man. He knew the answer. He knew everything about me. I snapped my hand around his neck, tangling my fingers in the hair at the base of his skull. "Like you don't already know. It's always been you. Now shut up and fuck me already."

Holy shit. His eyes darkened. Jaw clenched. In one stroke, or slam, rather, Tango Rossi filled me. Deep. Full. Thick. Hot.

Definitely not my vibrator. Nothing like it. Not even close.

I cried out, and he swallowed my moan with a kiss. The weight of him, the heady weight of the moment, the fullness, the burn and stretch, it was too much. It was not enough.

He didn't move, only studied my face, lips parted, eyes molten. The sting of rising tears threatened to ruin the mood. Until his own tear landed on my cheek. Then another.

I wiped my eyes with the back of my hand, then brushed his away with my thumb. "Tango."

"Shh," he silenced me. "No words. Please. Just let me feel you. Let me love you. No words."

I pulled him down for another kiss, losing myself in the way he loved me, worshiped me, with his tongue and lips. He started moving, pulling out the slightest bit, pushing back in, deeper each time. Slow. Gentle. Moving his hips in his signature style. Making love, with lips and fingers. I softened and relaxed beneath him, giving in to the burn. The pain. The sweet, sweet agony.

"Are you okay?" he asked, voice raspy and thick with emotion.

"Yes," I whispered. "I've never been more okay. Don't stop." *Please God, don't ever let him stop.*

His thrusts grew stronger, and he caught my hand and stretched our arms over my head, squeezing tight, rocking, thrusting, loving me.

My free hand smacked to his tight ass, and I loved the way the muscle flexed and rolled under my fingers. He danced his lips down my neck, behind my ear, licking, sucking, nibbling.

And then he whispered to me in Spanish, words that sounded beautiful and heartfelt. Words he struggled to speak through hitched breaths and moans of pleasure.

I'd conquered the pain and started moving with him, as much as I could with his heavy body pinning me, grinding me into the soft mattress. With every down stroke, he struck my clit, twisting and rolling and sparking waves of ecstasy.

My hands were everywhere. Tango was everywhere. Exploring, caressing, teasing. Making amends for every day we'd lost.

Our eyes met briefly—his liquid, mine leaking down the sides of my face. Then he was gone, sliding down my body. He sucked hard on my clit. Swirled his tongue around and around the hypersensitive bundle. He sucked again, nearly killing me. I exploded, died, arched off the bed, trembling, spasming against his mouth, ripping at his thick hair.

Before I crashed from the high, he was back, pounding into me, hard and fast.

His elbows braced my shoulders, his hands in my hair, his forehead to mine.

Thrusting. Rocking. Fucking. Oh God. I was finally, finally making love to my Tango.

Trembling hard, he captured my mouth with his and kissed me, devoured me, and came undone, came inside me with a deep, guttural moan.

When he collapsed at my side, sweaty and spent, he cupped my cheek, turned my face to his, and continued to love me with his eyes. Communicating everything he couldn't verbalize.

We lay naked. Breathing. Burning. Crying.

We were beauty—raw and bleeding, regretting wasted years, grateful for what lay ahead. He cried, I cried. We purged, and apologized, and promised. Forever, forever, forever.

CHAPTER 15

"I'M GOING TO MISS YOU something terrible." Maurice shook his head. "Who will I share my mornings with now?"

"I know where you live, Maurice. Maybe I'll come to you for coffee from now on."

"I would love to continue our morning visits. And I'll hold you to it." He pursed his lips and pointed a shaky finger at me. "What will you do with yourself? Work a regular nine-to-five? Get a new place?"

I topped off his java and parked my butt in the seat across the table. "I'm not sure. I love this place. It's my home, ya know? I'm sad, but it's kind of exciting, too. Sky's the limit. I could go back to school, or maybe find a smaller place, open a coffee shop. I've got some soul searching to do, that's all I know for sure."

"That's my girl."

"Anyway. I've got time to figure it out. Mr. Rossi has wanted to get his hands on this property for decades. He paid more than I was asking. Wanted to make sure I didn't consider other offers. I never have to work again if I don't want to."

Maurice chuckled. "You're the hardest working person I know. I can't imagine you would last long without something to do."

"My house needs some major repairs. That could keep me busy for years."

Maurice tore open a sugar packet and emptied its contents into his cup. "How's our Kim doing?" he asked, swirling his spoon through the hot drink.

"She hasn't woken up yet." I rubbed at the gnawing ache in my stomach. "Her mother said Kim was on a date the night before her attack. Some guy she'd met online. I don't know if the police have questioned him."

My gut tightened when I registered the growl of motorcycle engines outside. I hated that I still had that reaction after all these years. I shot a glance out the window, and my world stopped spinning. It was the man again. Tatted, skinny, dark glasses, leather vest.

Flanked by two larger bikes carrying gargantuan and grotesquely hairy men, he appeared small and deficient, somehow, but intimidating nonetheless. They didn't get off their bikes. Didn't turn off the engines. Only studied the building for what seemed an eternity, then drove away, no drama, no trail of dust. Slow and steady.

"Slade?" Maurice asked, voice stronger than normal. "You look like you've seen a ghost. Do you know those men?"

I sucked in a sharp breath. "No. No. Just don't like seeing them in our town. They're bad news."

Prickly bumps covered my arm. When Charlie's deep voice travelled over my shoulder, I damn near jumped out of my pants.

"They came in here a couple days ago," he chimed in, placing Maurice's muffin on the table. "Said they were traveling through. One of 'em looked familiar, but I couldn't place him."

I looked up to find Charlie wiping a leaky eye with his apron. He hadn't stopped crying since I broke the news about selling. Charlie was family; he'd helped raise me, and he couldn't understand why I'd sold The Stop. I could never tell him, either. He'd have no trouble finding another job. It was no secret he was the best chef in town.

"Did they cause any trouble?"

"Yeah. One of 'em hit on Margie, grabbed her ass. That's when I took over servicing their table. They didn't like that. The smaller one said he wanted to talk to the owner. I told him I was the boss and he could talk to me. They left." He shrugged his shoulders. "Guess they didn't want to talk to me." Charlie scratched his chin. "By the way, got a strange call earlier. Guy asked for you by name. You weren't in yet, so I asked if he wanted to leave a message." He picked up a menu and fanned himself.

"And?" I asked.

"He yelled a few profanities, then said, *Tell Blondie to answer her fucking phone.*" His deep dimples came out to play. "I let him know what I thought of his message. He yelled some more, then hung up."

I wanted to jump up and hug the big, protective lug, but I knew that would trigger more tears. I didn't have the heart to put Charlie or my customers through such a scene. I laughed, until it dawned on me what Charlie had said. *Tell Blondie to answer her fucking phone.* Blondie. Oh, fuck a duck.

Dane was the only person who'd called me Blondie. In a panic, I had tried to contact him when Tango had first come home, and when I'd started seeing Slayers around town. I had given up after twenty or so attempts. Figured his number had changed. Maybe it'd been him trying to call my cell, the number I'd ignored because it was unfamiliar. Unease slithered through me like an oily snake. I patted down the pocket in my apron, searching for my phone. It wasn't there.

Rocky burst through the door. Messy hair, dirty face, two different colored socks. "Mom!" He skidded to a stop and held his palm in the air for a high-five. "Hey, Charlie."

"Hey, Rockster." Their hands met in a loud clap. "I need help in the kitchen. Did you read my mind?"

"Just came to see Mom. Tango said we had to say hi before we went to the beach." Rocky wrapped his tiny digits around Charlie's chunky forefinger and pulled him toward the back. "Can I make a milkshake?"

"Sure, kid. Long as you make me one, too." He chuckled, and they disappeared behind the swinging door.

I unfolded from my seat just before Tango entered. Unfortunately, when Tango Rossi entered a room, I was safer being seated, on account of the wobbly knees and all, and I was forced to grip the back of my chair.

He wore a faded graphic tee, moss green, that dialed-up the heat factor of his eyes by a few thousand degrees. Khaki-colored cargo shorts hung low on his waist. Our eyes met, and he smiled, warming my soul. I could swear, angels sang when he smiled.

Several different voices called out greetings to him as he came my way.

"Hey T!"

"Tango, how are you doing, man?"

"Good to see you, Rossi."

I didn't look to see who was talking because I couldn't peel my eyes from the beautiful beast stalking me. A man on a mission.

"Babylove," he half growled, pulling me into his arms and tucking his face into my neck for a nibble.

Tingles of pleasure, and plain-old, silly, girlie giddiness tickled my skin, head to toe.

"Have you danced today?" he asked and connected our hands before twirling me around once and lifting me completely off my feet to kiss me deep. In front of everyone.

Oh God, there went my legs, clamping around his waist like they had a mind of their own. My arms followed suit, snaking around his neck. Heat filled my face, but I ignored the applause, the lewd words of encouragement, while Tango carried me to my office, kissing me dizzy, announcing to the world, or at least our little corner of it, that he was mine and I was his.

He kicked the door shut behind us and reached back to turn the lock. Then he spun and slammed my back to the wall. "Good morning."

"Good morning, Mr. Rossi."

"How are you feeling?"

"I'm tired, but happy as—"

"That's not what I meant," he interrupted, sliding a hand under my butt, his fingertips grazing the sensitive spot between my legs. "Down here. How are you feeling? Are you sore?"

Gulp.

I fought to maintain composure. "You can't strut into my diner, carry me away from my customers, then feel me up in my office. It's very unprofessional."

"Aw, hell. We gave 'em a good show. You'll probably get better tips. And FYI, I plan on feeling you up every day. Several times a day. Now, you didn't answer my question."

"What was the question?" I asked, grinding my hips against him.

His lips quirked in a wicked display of pleasure, and he pressed me harder against the wall. "Let me rephrase. How does your pussy feel today, Miss Mason?"

My heart pounded a sporadic rhythm."Mmm. Dirty talk. I like it."

"Careful, babylove. You're being a tease. Dangerous territory." He pressed a kiss to my neck then nibbled a path up my jaw.

All at once, my office became too hot, too small, and void of oxygen. I was happy. Euphoric. I didn't know what to do with so much joy. I couldn't possibly process this overload of bliss, and I feared I'd burst, splattering tiny pieces of myself all over the walls and furniture.

I coiled my arms around Tango's head, clung to him, and mumbled into his hair, "Is this real? Please tell me this isn't a dream."

"Slade." He wiggled free from my vice.

I cupped his face, brushed my thumbs across his cheekbones, marveled at the flesh and blood beneath my fingers.

Tango closed his eyes and sighed before opening them again. "You are all I've ever wanted. I finally have you. I'm never letting go."

Tango

"Oh crap. Let me go." Slade wiggled free.

"Mom. Mom. Let me in." Rocky yelled from the other side of the door. "Tango. Open up. I made you a milkshake."

I held her for a few heartbeats longer before relinquishing control. Slade dropped her legs, sliding down my body, rubbing me wrong in all the right places.

I straightened her shirt and dropped a kiss on her nose before opening the door. My heart burst at the wonder in the giant green eyes that greeted me.

"All right, buddy," I said, clapping, then rubbing my hands together. "Let's do this. Beach, then the football field. You get to play with the big boys today."

"Yay!" Rocky jumped up and down.

"Big boys?" Slade asked.

"I promised Brett I'd watch a practice. Thought Rocky might have fun."

"Brett?" she asked, eyebrows quirked.

"He's assistant coach at WS High. You didn't know?"

Her gaze sliced to the floor, then back to me. "Yeah. I heard. Just haven't seen him since..." Slade forced a smile. "Well. You know."

Yeah. I knew. Would never forget. Guilt was a nasty bitch to shake. Slade had sacrificed so much. Too much. Her youth, college, friends. All for my son.

"We'll pick you up at six."

"It's fine. I can walk home."

Over my cold, dead body. "I'll pick you up. No arguments." Shit, had she forgotten what happened to Kim already?

Chewing on her bottom lip, Slade conceded with a nod. We had just reached the front door when her soft fingers wrapped around my arm. "Tango, wait."

I turned, and she lifted up on her toes, pressing a soft cheek to mine.

"I am sore," she whispered against my ear, so soft I barely heard the words. "Every time I move, or bend, I feel you between my legs. Think about that while you play at the beach."

Fucking hell.

Slade bent to kiss Rocky on the head. "Bye, sweetie. See you tonight." The back of her hand brushed my cock as she turned before sauntering to the counter.

I dodged a group of sun-kissed teenagers piling through the door, scooted my son and his milkshakes to the car, and hoped like hell nobody noticed the tent in my shorts.

The day flew by. Swimming. Eating. Football. Eating. Home. Eating. Rocky was a bottomless pit. If only I could get his mom to eat the same way. Through the rearview, I could see he had passed out, clinging tightly to his football. He'd played hard, and it was obvious by the slack jaw and faint snore that he slept hard, too.

As I turned onto Lakeview Drive, I noticed a Harley, slowing almost to a stop in front of Dad's house. The driver's arms were heavily tatted, his identity hidden behind a half-helmet and dark glasses. When I turned into the driveway, he tore down the street before I could get a look at his cut.

There was something wrong about the way he looked at the house.

I slammed the vehicle into park, snagged my phone off its dock, and dialed.

Tito answered on the first ring. "Tango. What's up?"

"Your friend with the sixty-niners MC still alive and kicking?"

"Yeah. Just released. Spoke with him yesterday."

"Can you get some intel?"

"I can do that. Won't be cheap."

"Money is not an issue."

I gave Tito the low-down on the Satan's Slayers and Slade's involvement with them. "Find out who this territory belongs to. Let me know if the Slayers are making to move west." Fuck, I hoped my gut instinct was wrong.

I itched to get to my girl, but I had a meeting with Dad to get through first. I called her cell anyway, because it'd been six hours too many since I'd heard her voice.

My call went straight to voicemail, as I'd assumed it would. Just hearing her sweet words calmed the raging storm that biker had stirred up.

"Slade. Hey. We're heading over to Pop's. Rocky is out cold in the back seat. Played hard today. Ate like a champion. Misses his mom. Not as much as I do, though." I paused and shook my head. Shit. *Look at me all domesticated.* "See you soon, babylove."

As I maneuvered the Rover through our cobblestone driveway, toward our ridiculous, lakeside home, Kaylee passed in her silver Honda, heading away from the house. Rage billowed in my gut. Fucking Dad.

As she drove by, her tinted window lowered and she stuck her hand through the opening, flipping me the bird. Not sure why, but her gesture made me chuckle.

Dad must've seen me coming. He waited on the front stoop, drink in hand, dress shirt unbuttoned at the collar, tie missing, hair disheveled.

When I lifted a sleeping Rocky out of his car seat, Dad's face cracked, and he smiled. Fucking smiled. I hadn't seen him beam like that in ... shit. I couldn't remember the last time.

"How are my boys?" he asked, breath fragrant with the scent of liquor. Dad clapped my shoulder and turned to open the front door.

"Everything all right, Pop?" I asked, pausing to meet him eye to eye.

He lowered his gaze to the floor, turned, and headed to his office. I followed, laid Rocky on one end of the leather sofa, and planted my ass on the other.

Dad poured another drink. When he looked up, I was surprised to see joy on his face, highlighted by newly carved wrinkles around his eyes.

"I ended things with Kaylee."

Damn, miracles did come true. "Good."

"Wasn't pretty."

"Can't imagine it would be."

"Cutting her loose has cost me an arm and a leg. I bought her a building downtown. Perfect for a dance studio, small school, maybe. It was the only way I could get her to leave me alone."

"It was the only way to ease your guilty conscience."

He tapped his fingers on the desk. "I suppose you're right about that."

"What about Mom's studio?" I asked.

"I've got a few ideas. Unless of course you want to take over her classes?"

"Hell no," left my lips faster than I could wince. Dad and I laughed.

"When are you coming to work with me, T?"

"That's what I'm here to discuss."

"You're still not sure."

"I have a family now. They're my priority. I need to know you're going to accept Slade with open arms."

"I think the question is, will she accept me?"

"You're Rocky's grandfather. My dad. She loves you by default, that's her nature. All she ever wanted was for you and Mom to embrace her the way I did. No one loves harder than that girl."

"I have a newfound respect for Miss Mason. She negotiated one hell of a deal. Not only did she get almost double what the property is worth, I also have to pay her employees their salary for a year, and guarantee them jobs with the company if they haven't found work by the time the condos are built."

"Shit." I laughed. Couldn't help it. "She outfoxed the silver fox."

"Yeah, T. She did," he chuckled, running a hand through his thick, graying hair. "She's a keeper."

Dad's acceptance of Slade, his pride in her business savvy, brought a sting to my eyes and conjured a thick lump in my throat.

He slammed the rest of his drink and crossed his arms over his chest. "What do you say, kiddo? Partner with your old man?"

Forgiveness was not an easy thing to give, especially when I'd collected and stored away a lifetime's worth of offenses all filed under the name Carlos Rossi. Having been the recipient of undeserved forgiveness, I found it absurd to hold on to any grudges. Dad was human, just like me. He'd made mistakes, just as I had. For my son, I needed to forgive my father, because I, too, would make mistakes. I was responsible for teaching Rocky how to be a man, how to forgive, how to love and live as a man should.

I rose to my feet and met Dad eye to eye. Man to man. Father to son.

"I'd love nothing more than to work with you, Dad. Under one condition."

Pop quirked a brow, choking out a laugh. "Let's hear it."

I could tell by the gleam in his eyes, he already knew what I was going to ask. The Truck Stop was Slade's home. Rocky's home. I couldn't let my father take it from them.

"It might sting a bit."

Slade

"This is going to sting. Are you ready?"

Rocky nodded, sucking his lips between his teeth. I poured peroxide over his knee and dabbed at the blood and bubbles dribbling down his leg. "You okay?"

He sucked air through his teeth, wiggled in my lap and sung through the pain, "It's cold. It's cold. Ow, ow, ow."

After his wound was dry and bandaged, I watched him run across the lawn and pick up his fallen bicycle. The dynamo hopped right back on and continued his quest to conquer all the bumps and valleys of our unkempt backyard.

My phone buzzed in my back pocket, and before looking at the screen I knew it was Tango. He had made a habit of calling or texting every hour, on the hour, since joining the family business. It'd only been a week since he'd started working with Carlos. One week since I'd closed the doors at The Stop for good.

"Hey, handsome."

"Babylove. How are you holding up?"

Demolition on the diner had been scheduled to start that morning. I'd had an emotional meltdown during breakfast. Tango had held me until it'd passed.

I rolled my eyes. "I'm fine. I promise. You can stop asking."

"What's my little guy up to?"

"He's tearing up the yard with his new bike." The Diamondback Venom Tango had brought home the same day he'd decided to work with his father.

Tango's deep laugh billowed through the receiver. "He's ready to take on the track. That's my boy. An overachiever like his mom." Tango laughed again, then fell silent before whispering, "I miss you."

I closed my eyes and sighed, absorbing his words, loving that he missed me. "Hurry home," I muttered back and ended the call.

While he hadn't officially moved in, Tango had continued to sleep on my couch. His clothes hung in my closet, and he'd crowded half of the bathroom vanity with his shaving gear. I had tiptoed down the stairs many mornings to find Rocky fast asleep, sprawled across his father's chest.

I didn't have room for jealousy, my heart too swollen with joy and gratitude.

Marion yelled a hello from her rose garden. I waved and made my way to our shared, waist-high, white picket fence. It was the prettiest part of my yard.

"Morning, Marion. How's your mom?"

She hugged me, squeezing tighter than her norm. "Mama's great. The home is taking good care of her. She's even walking on her own."

"That woman is going to outlive every one of us, isn't she?"

"I wouldn't put it past her." Marion's hearty chest bounced up and down with her laughter. "Can Rocky hang out with me today? I've missed my buddy."

His bike fell at my feet, the handle bar scraping my leg on its way down. "Can I, Mom? Please, please, please." He snagged his football off the ground. The kid never left home without it.

"Sure, honey," I said, rubbing the growing welt on my shin. "But you have to be a big helper."

"Yeah, Mister, I need your strong arms today," Marion chimed in. "I've got to pick some berries and bake a cobbler. I need someone to help me stir and test the batter." She shot me a wink.

I helped Rocky unbuckle his bike helmet and lifted him over the fence. "Thank you, Marion. I've got some errands to run, will that be okay?"

"Sure, honey. Take as long as you need." She nodded toward the blue sedan that had been parked out front all week. "Any idea who owns that beast?"

"No." I chewed the corner of my thumbnail, trying to ignore the feeling of dread creeping up my spine. Every morning, the car had been parked in a different spot across the street. I'd only paid attention because the windows were unusually dark.

Marion chuckled, her whole body bouncing with the effort. "Dollars to donuts Lorraine Bentley has a new boyfriend. Not a man on Earth can resist that woman's culinary skills."

She was probably right. Still, despite the swelling temperature, I shivered, unable to shake the feeling that I was being watched from behind the tinted glass of the Chrysler.

I said my goodbyes and parked Rocky's shiny new bike next to my refurbished, vintage, pink two-speed.

My phone buzzed in my back pocket. "Hello?"

"Slade?"

I recognized the voice immediately. "Maurice. How are you?"

"Tired of eating alone. Wanna keep an old man company for a while?"

I'd missed his warm, leathery timbre. "I would love nothing more. You make coffee, I'll bring muffins?"

"Perfect."

"I'll see you soon."

I suspected his call had nothing to do with being lonely, and everything to do with the demolition. The Truck Stop had been as much a part of his history as it had been mine. I couldn't think of a better way to spend this bittersweet day than with the man I'd shared almost every morning with for the past six years.

CHAPTER 16

Tango

"ARE YOU INSANE? You can't take them on." The rumble of an amped crowd echoed through the speaker of my cell. I could almost smell the sweat and alcohol, the sweet stench of tobacco that hung so thick around the perimeter of the arena.

"You've read the file. You know what those fuckers are capable of. You saw what they did to Addison Reynolds. I won't allow that shit anywhere near my family." I fell into my desk chair and pulled the document back up that Tito had emailed earlier.

"You wanted out. You're out. You do this. You're back in for life. Luciano loves you like a son, but he doesn't do favors. Be smart here, cousin."

I dropped a fist on my desk, making the empty styrofoam cup dance and tip over. "They're a threat to *my* son. If I gotta dance with the devil to keep Rocky safe, then I dance."

"Fuck. This is fucked. Christ. Listen. I've got a fight tonight. Let me deal with that freak show, then we'll talk this through. Swear to fuck, cousin, if you make a move without me, I'll kill you myself."

"Tito..."

He ended the call.

Damn. Tito had nailed it. Things were fucked.

The Satan's Slayers, who had formed in Montana in the early sixties, were slowly spreading their poison west. My guess was they wanted to use the retired highway to move their growing meth operations through the mountains and eventually expand their reach, either by taking over or forming an alliance with Idaho's prominent gang, the Brothers of Banshee. One word from Luciano, and the Slayers would stay away from Whisper Springs. One word and my family would be safe. I, however, would be indebted for life. Luciano Voltolini would own me.

A knot twisted in my gut when I checked the time. It was nearing ten, and Dad still hadn't shown up for work. Pop was never late.

I dialed his number again only to get his recorded voice. My skin vibrated with agitated nerves, and I paced my office twice before heading to the front desk.

"Morning, Lisa."

Lisa continued tapping her keyboard, brows drawn tight. "Mr. Rossi."

"Please, Lisa, just Tango." I hated that formal shit. Dad demanded respect from his employees. I hadn't earned it yet.

Lisa sighed and lifted her big brown eyes to me. "Good morning, Tango. Can I get you anything? Coffee? Breakfast?"

"No, thank you. Have you heard from Dad?"

"I haven't. I've sent him several messages, but haven't heard back. He missed a conference call this morning. Should I cancel today's meetings?"

Shit. What was he up to? "Yes, please. Cancel everything for today. Reschedule if you can."

Our eyes locked, and I knew we were thinking the same thing. Something was terribly wrong.

Lisa forced a smile. "If anything happened, Maria would've called you."

"I think I'll drive by the house anyway." I jogged into my office and grabbed the keys. Shit, my heart threatened to pound a hole through my chest.

Lisa's worried brows didn't help my rising panic. "I'll let you know if I hear from him," she shouted as I passed her.

I sprinted to my car, ignored most of the stop signs on my drive home, and narrowly dodged a squirrel when I tore into our driveway. The front door of the house swung wide open. Broom in hand, Maria smiled wide when she spotted me.

"Tango. Hi, sweetie. When are you bringing that beautiful boy back? I have a gift for him."

"Hey, Maria." I kissed her right cheek, then her left. "Dad still home?"

"No. He left early this morning. Said he had to meet someone before heading to work."

"He didn't say who?"

"No, but it wouldn't surprise me if it were that Kaylee girl. She hasn't stopped calling the house since he gave her the boot." Maria swung the bristles across the marble with more aggression than necessary. "I swear, I don't know what got into your father, fooling around with a girl half his age. Serves him right, the grief she's giving him."

Her eyes snapped to mine, full of hellfire and fury. "Tell me you're taking care of that lady of yours, Tango Rossi, because so help me, if you muck things up again, I'll—"

"Maria. Breathe." I pulled her into a hug because I didn't know how else to shut her up, and I needed to find out where Dad had disappeared to.

She chuckled against my chest, then patted my back. "Oh my, I've overstepped. Forgive me."

I let go and drew a deep breath. "Dad didn't happen to leave his phone, did he?"

"I haven't seen it lying around. But I haven't been in his office yet today."

"I'll go check." I dashed past the staircase, down the hall, and into his sanctuary. The phone was nowhere, but next to his computer sat a tumbler, half filled with amber liquid and oddly, ice cubes that hadn't melted, leaving watermarks on the mahogany desk. I'd never known him to drink earlier than noon.

Fuck, Dad. What are you up to?

I fired up his laptop and rifled through his neatly stacked papers. There were no early morning appointments written on his desk calendar, none entered into his Google calendar.

Aside from the drink, the only thing I found out of the ordinary was a framed picture of Rocky. He must have taken the photo when we'd visited last week and Rocky had made Pop chase him through the rose garden.

Dad had insisted things were over with Kaylee. He'd even seemed embarrassed for his lapse in judgment. I didn't believe he was seeing her again, but it was the only other clue I had. Deep down, I knew something was wrong. Kaylee's new dance studio seemed the best place to check next.

I kissed Maria one more time, hopped into the SUV, and headed back toward town.

When the blare of sirens vibrated through my closed windows and flashing lights came in to view, my heart dropped to my gut. Black and whites surrounded the building that housed Kaylee's new studio—the building Dad had purchased to silence her. The street was blocked, but from my viewpoint, I watched paramedics wheel a body into an ambulance. Blonde hair hung over the side of the gurney. Blonde, matted with blood.

The front window of Kaylee's studio was shattered, a billion dazzling pieces on the sidewalk, sparkling like the lake at midday. Dad's Mercedes sat untouched by the devastation like a *fuck you* to the hardworking blue-collar workers who fueled that area of town.

Shit, Dad. Not you. I can't lose you, too.

Before I realized what I was doing, I had breached the police tape and an officer half my size barreled toward me with his hand up, yelling words I couldn't register.

"Tango. Step back. You can't be here."

I reined in my panic and focused on the man standing in front of me. Roger Caldwell. We'd played football together. Decent halfback. Good guy.

"Rog, what happened here?" I tried to step around him.

Roger hooked his thumbs in his belt and stood his ground. He'd put on a good twenty pounds since I'd seen him last. "Break-in. Someone hurt her bad. Carved her face up."

"Kaylee?" I asked.

"Yeah."

"Anyone else in there?"

"No, T. It was just Kaylee."

"No one else inside? You sure?"

"No one." He shook his head and placed a hand on my shoulder. "Rossi, I need you to step behind the tape."

"Anyone see what happened?"

His dark eyes assessed me for a moment. He looked over his shoulder, sighed, and pointed behind me to the building across the street. The Rooster Crow Bakery was as old as Whisper Springs. Family owned and operated for damn near one hundred years.

"Lily Crow says a man driving a Harley sat inside the bakery one morning, about two weeks ago, ordered coffee and a pastry, stared out the window toward the dance studio. Lily thought he looked familiar. One side of his face was grotesquely scarred. She'd tried to strike up a conversation, but he blew her off. After that, he would drive by several times a day. Sometimes park across the street, have a smoke, then leave. She'd called us twice because the guy gave her a bad vibe."

"And?"

"And nothing. He didn't break any laws. Lily didn't like his tattoos. You can't arrest a guy for wearing ink."

"Tats on his arms?"

Roger nodded.

"Wearing a cut?"

He pulled off his glasses. Rubbed his eye with the back of his hand. "No. She didn't mention a vest."

"Fuck." Fear-fueled rage sunk its nasty claws into my flesh. I paced, seeking something to punch. The streets, the buildings, the people blurred around me.

Hold your shit together.

My unease rubbed off on Roger. He shifted from foot to foot. "Something you need to tell me, Rossi?"

"No. No." I clapped a hand on Roger's shoulder. "Thanks, buddy."

Slade

"Thanks, Maurice." I pressed a kiss to his cheek and hopped down the porch steps. When I hit the bottom tread, I turned to face him again. "Your coffee is a million times better than mine. Can we do this again, soon?"

He chuckled. "It's a date. Bring that boy of yours, too. I haven't seen the little guy in ages."

"Absolutely. He'd love it here." Maurice's front yard, as enormous as it was immaculate, boasted a swimming pool with a slide, a tire swing, and a well-manicured lawn that overlooked the bay. The Rossi mansion, visible from the back deck, sat across the water, a castle dwarfing the surrounding homes.

I heard construction noise coming from the property at the bottom of the hill. The real estate that was no longer mine. I refused to look that direction.

"Tomorrow?" I asked, hoping he'd say yes.

He gripped the railing for support. "I'm looking forward to it. And Slade?"

"Yeah?" I asked, gripping the handlebars and bumping the kickstand with my heel.

"I have something important I'd like to talk to you about. Perhaps you could bring Tango, too."

I'd never seen Maurice smile so wide. Sometimes, when his eyes lit up with joy, like they had just then, he reminded me of my mother. She had the same blue-gray eyes as Maurice. Same dimple on the left side of her face, too.

"Stay cool." I waved goodbye and threw my leg over the bike seat.

"Watch for potholes," he warned.

I looked over my shoulder one more time before rounding the corner and heading down the winding dirt road. Maurice stood on his porch and watched me leave. I waved. He waved. My heart swelled. I needed our daily visits as much as I suspected he did. He'd been a staple in my life, like Charlie, always watching over me.

There would be scant amounts of shade on my journey home, and the temperature had hit the unbearable mark about an hour ago. My legs still screamed at me from the earlier exertion of pushing my bike up his hill. At least getting home was a downhill trip.

I maneuvered, quite impressively, around the potholes and stones of Maurice's long driveway. I concentrated so hard on not crashing, I hadn't noticed the man waiting for me at the bottom until I was too close to dodge him.

My limbs numbed. My foot slipped off the pedal. I hit a rock, and the handle bars jerked out of my grip. I didn't remember the fall so much as the embarrassment of wrecking in front of an audience. Pain tore through my right thigh and up the side of my body. When I felt the warm tickle of blood dripping down the side of my face, I knew I was in trouble.

When the man standing over me chuckled, squatted to my level, and removed his glasses, I panicked.

That face.

"Blondie," he said with a wheezy rasp. "You made this too easy."

I tried scrambling away, across the dirt and stones and through the fear paralyzing my muscles. I tried.

Walter Reynolds raised his fist and struck once. It jarred my brain, my neck, my spine. He struck again, and the world went black.

Slade, you fucking bitch. They'll kill you.

Metal. I tasted metal. Razor-spiked tongues licked my body, head to toe. Pressure squeezed my head like a vise, tightening, releasing, and tightening again.

They'll kill you.

One eye opened, allowing a painful intrusion of light into my optical nerves. The other throbbed, swollen shut, no doubt because of the beating it'd taken. My bright yellow banister came into focus. A sigh escaped my lips when I recognized my surroundings.

Rocky. Oh my God. Rocky.

I lay on my floor, afraid to move. I heard the shuffle of feet somewhere to my left. The floor bounced beneath me as the footsteps drew closer.

My whole body vibrated in fear. Addison's mangled face, her ugly words, her dead eyes, snapped through my memory like a wonky slide show.

"Happy to see me?" Walter, Addy's uncle, the man I'd beaten unconscious the night I'd tried to save my best friend and her unborn child, straddled my waist and squatted. He squeezed my chin and pulled, forcing me to look at him.

The right side of his face looked like the Walter I used know. Weathered and worn, but still the same—emaciated, beady-eyed, high, pointy cheekbones. The left side, however, brought bile to my throat, choking me. I rolled to my side, coughing and fighting to gain my bearings.

"What's the matter?" he asked with a sneer. "Do I scare you?" He pressed his nose to mine. "It's a work of art, don't you think?"

From the top of his bald scalp to above his ear, his head was concave. The skin stretching through the depression was puckered and discolored. His left eye was a milky gray. The corner of his lip pulled sideways, stretching into a wide scar that almost reached his cheekbone. Dear God, what had happened to him?

Weaving his fingers through my hair, he laughed, then squeezed tight. "I have you to thank for the dent." He tapped his index finger to his head. "You've got a great swing, sweetheart."

They're going to kill you. Kill you. Kill you.

Addison's voice played on repeat in my head.

"P-p-prison," I muttered. "You were in prison."

Walter leaned closer, crushing my chest. "I got out." He pressed a wet, threatening kiss to my mouth. "Now I'm home, and I've come to collect what's mine."

His breath reeked of tobacco, flooding me with memories of wasted days with Addy.

"Put those back," I warned. "Walt will kill you."

Addy plopped her butt next to mine on the creaky wood steps leading up to her uncle's trailer. "Walter is too fucked in the head to know he's missing a couple of smokes," she replied, rolling her eyes and lighting up.

She offered one to me, and I shook my head no.

"He's completely off his rocker now. I think he's sampled too much of his own product." Her leg bounced incessantly. "Think I can stay with you tonight?"

My heart dropped to my toes. "Those guys still hanging around?"

Eyes filling with liquid, she nodded yes. I ached for her. Addy no longer tried to hide the bruises.

"You can stay as long as you need to." I stood and brushed the dust and chipped paint off my bottom. "Let's get your things before they get back."

Walter's palm met my cheek with a crack.

"No dozing off, sweetheart. I need you awake." The right side of his mouth lifted in a perverted grin. He reached behind his waist and slowly brought his hand back into view.

When he flashed the knife in my face, blood beat a death march in my ears, a deafening countdown to Walter's inevitable retribution. I didn't feel the drag of the blade as he trailed it down my throat and circled my left nipple over my bra. I didn't hear a word he spoke as he cut the straps on my tank. I heard nothing, until he spoke Kim's name.

"Kim?" I mumbled, choking on the tang of blood. "It was you?"

"Oh. Your little waitress. She was a firecracker. Did you like my artwork?"

"What do you want?" I mumbled, hoping to buy some time.

"An eye for an eye." He cocked his head to the side, his gaze dropping to my chest. "I'm going to have fun with you first, while you're still pretty."

I heard Tango's rich voice.

I was a coward. You were my warrior. You don't have to be strong anymore. I'll be your rock.

Ha! I was my own goddamned rock.

Fuck life and its ugly teases. Fuck fate and her twisted sense of humor, dangling a beautiful future in front of my nose, only to lead me, once again, toward a dark pit.

Vile, repulsive rage welled in me, pushing the paralyzing fear away, numbing the crushing pain. I would not meet the same fate as Addy. I would not be roadkill. I would not leave my boys without a fight.

You were my warrior.

I thrashed like a woman possessed between Walter's skinny legs. Ignoring the slice of the blade as it sunk into the skin above my breast, I bucked and kicked, punched and screamed. Somehow, I knocked the knife away.

His fist met my face, slamming my head against the floor. The room around me darkened. I pushed through the fog, grunting, screaming, crying.

Walter rolled off me, then tangled his hands in my hair. With a hard yank, he dragged me across the rough wood.

"Stupid, fucking cunt."

I managed to flip to my stomach and push up on my hands. He pulled, I crawled, desperately scrambling to get to my feet. When I did, I was halfway through the kitchen door. Walter released my hair. When I found my footing and lifted my head, I screamed at the scene before me.

Dane. A larger, darker version of Dane, sat at my kitchen table. Face bloody. Arms pulled behind his back. Head drooping forward. He was fighting to stay conscious. Walter stood next to him, rummaging through a black bag. His eyes darted to mine before he removed a syringe and laid the needle down next to the satchel.

I swayed and took a step back. My right leg wouldn't cooperate, and I fell against the doorjamb.

"You can run. You won't get far. My brothers are waiting in the van outside." He turned the burner knob on my gas stove to high, picked a cigarette out of his breast pocket, and lit it on the blue flame.

They're going to kill you.

My warrior. You are a fucking warrior.

The scream that tore from my throat startled even me. I charged, not sure of my intentions, and threw my body against his, throwing him off balance.

His flailing arm tangled in my gingham curtain, tearing it, along with the rod, off the wall. When he straightened, and swung to strike me, the curtain fell across the stovetop. His fist made contact yet again with my face, and I hit the floor. I blinked up, before giving in to the black void, to see orange flames eat the red and white fabric and spread up the wall, devouring the ancient wallpaper.

Walter's boot raised above my face, as if to stomp. A loud bang shook the floor. Walter fell backward toward the flames, and the darkness swallowed me whole.

Tango

Darkness surrounded me, suffocated me. I fought against the arms pinning me to the ground. Watched in horror as Slade's house disappeared, crumbled, disintegrated under command of the black smoke and horrid flames.

"They're in there," I cried. "Let me go. Let me fucking go. I have to get them."

Someone lifted me by the shoulders and dragged me backward, across the street, and through someone's lawn, before setting me on the ground behind an ambulance. Forcing an oxygen mask over my face, a man ordered me to stay.

I heard a woman yell, "Behind the house. Hurry."

Life pumped back into my veins. I watched the scramble of bodies disappear behind the smoke. Searched wildly for her face. Time stood still. The voices faded to muted noise. The scene played in agonizing slow motion.

I ripped the mask off my face and rose to my feet, desperate for a better view.

"Tango! Tango!" Rocky's voice was a faint sound winding through the commotion.

Was I hearing things?

"Tango."

Someone squeezed my shoulder, and I jumped.

"Where's Slade?" Tucker asked, fear strangling his voice.

I couldn't answer. I couldn't say the words out loud. I wouldn't say them because speaking them would make the nightmare real.

"Tango!" I heard Rocky yell again. Was I hallucinating?

My knees gave out, and I screamed into my hands. Tucker came down with me, offering a supportive arm. "They're in there," I cried. "They're in the house." I raised my eyes to Tucker's.

"Tango. Rocky is with me." He turned and pointed down the street.

Rocky sat in the backseat of Tucker's Jeep, waving, smiling, pointing at the fire trucks. Marion stood next to his door, one hand covering her mouth, her head shaking back and forth as if refusing to accept the scene playing before her.

I folded into myself and cried into my palms. My son. Thank God. My son was alive. I gave in to the emotion, briefly, before wiping my face and pushing to my feet.

"Get him out of here." I forced the words through clenched teeth.

Tucker stepped back. "Tango."

"Get him away from here!" I yelled. "He can't see this. He can't see her..." Another sob escaped. I forced my lungs to draw in oxygen. "Get him the hell away from here."

Tucker pulled me close, a quick embrace, before jogging back to my son.

Commotion near the burning house drew my attention away from Rocky. Two gurneys were coming my way. Paramedics shouted commands and someone pushed me to the side.

"Is it her?" I asked, rushing forward. "Is it Slade?"

"No pulse," someone said.

My heart stopped beating. I watched as they scrambled past me, my guts twisted in knots, my vision blurring in and out of focus.

It wasn't Slade. Maurice McReary lay lifeless on the stretcher, skin ashen, face hollow. They lifted the bed into the back of the ambulance.

I sprinted to the other vehicle as they lifted another victim inside. "Wait. Jesus Christ, wait!"

As I stepped closer, as Slade's bloodied hair and mangled face came into view, a fissure tore wide open, somewhere deep, flooding my psyche with blood rage.

"Is she alive?" I whispered, curling my fingers into the hair at my scalp. Nobody heard me.

I grabbed the closest man in uniform, lifting him by the collar, bringing him nose to nose. "Is she alive?" My arms trembled. Control slipped further from my grasp.

The man shrugged free. "Yes. She's alive, but we need to get her to WSMC. She's lost a lot of blood. Stab wound."

Stab wound? What the fuck had happened?

The man shrugged free of my grip. I stood amidst the chaos, the smoke, the wail of sirens. I stood, trembling, shaking with vile, vile rage, the red seeping in around me, through me, penetrating deep, to my marrow.

I stepped closer to the heat, shedding the layers of hope, vulnerability, pride. The man, the boy I used to be, had hoped to be again, burned away layer by layer, charring to ashes along with the house, the home I loved. I willed my old self to burn with it.

I couldn't make allowances for the old Tango, not when I had murder on my mind.

I only hoped she could love the new me. The real me.

Slipping the phone from my back pocket, I headed toward the blue sedan parked behind my Rover.

I dialed the number I'd hoped I'd never have to use. Luciano Voltolini answered on the second ring.

"Tango, my boy. Good to hear from you. How is your father?"

"He's gone. I can't find him."

"What do you mean?"

I stepped up to the car with the dark windows.

The man I had hired to watch my family, to keep them safe while I was away, unfolded from his seat, met me nose to nose. "I stayed with the boy, as you'd instructed. I saw nothing to cause alarm, or I would've called you immediately."

"Luciano, forgive me, I just need a moment," I said into the speaker. I set my cell on the hood of the vehicle, balled my fists, and struck. Once, twice, three times, and the man fell to the ground. It wasn't enough; it wouldn't be enough until he shared my pain, but Luciano Voltolini was waiting, and he was a man you never put on hold.

"I no longer require your services," I said to the bloody heap at my feet, tossing a roll of bills on his chest.

I grabbed my phone, brought it to my ear, and headed to my SUV.

"I need help," were the only words I needed to speak.

Three words. Three words and I'd pledged my life, my loyalty, my soul, to the devil himself.

CHAPTER 17

Slade

"BABYLOVE."

Soft lips warmed my forehead.

"Mom," a sweet voice whispered. Tiny fingers brushed my cheek. "Mom. Wake up. Grandma and Grandpa came to see you."

Rocky.

I needed to get to him. I had to find him.

"Mommy," he whispered. "I haven't danced with anyone. I'm waiting for you."

Darkness, heavy and warm, weighed me down, enticed me to stay. Pain accompanied the light. I had to find Rocky. I had to hold him. I had to dance.

Bright green, brilliant eyes met mine when I blinked the room into focus. Rocky threw his arms around my neck and squeezed tight.

"Ow, ow, ow," I both laughed and cried. My face felt like one giant, throbbing bruise.

"Whoa, buddy. Take it easy." Tango lifted Rocky off my body and set him on his feet next to the bed.

Soft, cinnamon bun lips landed on mine, caressing like a soothing breeze. His hands slid up my neck, his eyes searched mine, he smiled, and released a hot breath. "You scared the shit out of me."

"Did they get him?"

Tango tilted his head, studied my face. "Who?"

"Walter. Walter Reynolds. He was going to kill—"

He shut me up by pressing a finger over my lips. His gaze darted to Rocky, then back to me. "Hey, Rocky. Come here." Tango walked to the door, stuck his head out, and caught the attention of a nurse. They exchanged a few whispered words.

"Lina is going to walk with you to the waiting room. Can you tell everyone your mom is awake and they can come and see her soon?"

Tango nodded to the nurse, who took Rocky's tiny hand and led him out the door.

When he turned to face me, the harsh lines framing his eyes made me shiver. "Tell me what you remember."

I told my story, wincing at the painful parts, crying when I remembered my kitchen in flames. When I told him the part about Kim, his face paled, his large body trembled, and he excused himself to the small bathroom. He came out minutes later, eyes glassy, and stood at my side, brushing a knuckle down my cheek.

"How bad is it?" I asked.

"To put it gently, your face looks like you lasted three rounds. Thankfully, he didn't break any bones. The doctors said you'll be fine. The knife didn't hit anything vital, your leg isn't broken, just beat to hell."

I raised my hand to stop him. "I meant my house. How bad is my house?"

"Oh." Tango scrubbed both hands over his face, drew a deep breath, then sandwiched my hand between his. "It's gone."

Salty liquid stung my eyes. "How did I get out?"

"I'm not sure." Lips pinched together, he focused his gaze on our hands. His face contorted, as if fighting back his own tears. "They found you and Maurice in the back yard." He shook his head and huffed. "Someone must've pulled you out of the house."

"Maurice?" I shook my head. "I don't understand. How? I mean. He wasn't there."

I remembered the loud bang and Walter falling backward before I had passed out. Had it been a gunshot I'd heard?

Tango choked back a sob. "He didn't make it, baby. Heart attack."

I sought his eyes, for comfort. "Maurice is dead? He can't be. I promised to visit him tomorrow. I was going to bake his favorite muffins." I cried. It hurt my chest, my face, my lungs. Hard as I tried, I couldn't stop the release, couldn't stifle the pain or tuck it away.

Tango leaned over the bed, wrapped himself around me, and held me tight while I bled.

When I finished, he wiped my face, held the tissue as I blew my nose, then called the nurse for more pain medication.

"What about Dane?"

"They didn't find any bodies in the house." Tango paced back and forth across the small space. "I spoke with the fire chief an hour ago."

"What?"

"That means the fucker is still out there." His face darkened three shades. He looked everywhere but at me. "I have to go. Not sure when I'll be back. Rocky will stay with Tucker tonight."

"But—"

He raised a palm to cut me off. "Your family is anxious to see you. The police are waiting to question you, too. Tell them everything, baby. Everything you can remember, even if it doesn't seem important."

"Where are you going?"

Squeezing his eyes closed, he ran a hand through his hair, then down to the back of his neck. I didn't recognize the man who met my gaze. His dead eyes sent a shiver down my spine.

He leaned forward and pressed a kiss to my lips before whispering in my ear, "He'll never hurt you again, I promise."

"No. Don't go. Let the police handle this." I grabbed his wrist, but lacked the strength to hold on as he backed away.

"They can't protect you like I can."

"Tango. This isn't you. You can't..." I tried to sit up, misjudging the effect the pain meds had on my muscles. "Just don't. Please," I begged, knowing, by the strain on his face, that it was already too late.

Tango reached back and wrapped his fingers around the door handle. He banged the back of his head against the door, then dropped his chin.

Silence poisoned the air between us.

Dread crushed my chest. He wanted me to tell him it was okay. He wanted my approval. I couldn't do it. Not because I didn't want Walter Reynolds to suffer, but because I didn't want the man I loved anywhere near those dangerous criminals.

"I love you," he said before slipping out of sight and leaving me breathless.

Tango

Breathless and bloody, Walter Reynolds arced his knife one more time through the air. Pathetic really, his ineptitude with the weapon he wielded. And here I'd thought I was in for a good fight.

He hadn't been hard to find. Would be easier to take down, which I planned to do as soon as I finished playing. I had a fuck ton of rage to burn off before I put this piece of shit out of his misery.

The morbid dance had started inside the dilapidated trailer home he owned north of town, along the river. Wasn't much room to move, so I'd thrown him through the door ten minutes ago. The dogged bastard bounced right back to his feet and continued to come at me.

He swung and missed; I punched and struck hard. Walter charged, and I dodged, striking him to the ground with a blow to the back of his head.

His recovery took a bit longer this time. I waited, bouncing on the balls of my feet, throwing punches at the night air. With one arm snug around the haphazard bandage on his torso, he pushed off the ground. Walter was slowing down; I was just warming up.

Sirens wailed in the distance. Slade must have talked to the police already. Walter's home would, of course, be the first place they looked.

I widened my stance. Dropped my fists. "They're coming for you, Reynolds. They can find you alive or dead. It's up to you." I had no intention of sparing his life, let alone handing over the pathetic piece of shit, but I wanted him scared, desperate, and begging for mercy.

His working eye searched the darkness. "You won't do shit except get me out of here."

I hadn't expected that reaction.

Okay, I'll bite. "What makes you think I'd do anything for you? You've done nothing but ruin people."

On wobbly legs, he stood, hunched and huffing. "I've done nothing but collect what I'm owed."

"What exactly might that be?"

"An eye for an eye." He tapped the tip of the blade to the corner of his milky peeper. "The Mason bitch stole my niece from the club. I owe them a girl and a ki—"

I struck so fast and hard I felt his jaw shatter against my knuckles. Before he could spit any broken teeth out, I wrenched his knife free and held it to his throat. Red lights flashed through the thick of pine trees, casting eerie shadows across the dirt lot.

"I wanted to kill you slow. Seems there isn't time for that. Too bad."

"You won't kill me," he mumbled, half-laughing.

Slade's bloody, swollen face was still vivid in my mind. Death was the least of his worries. I leaned closer. "Tell me. Why shouldn't I cut you wide open, right here, right now?"

He struggled to breathe. "I die, your father dies."

Fucking hell.

I was out of time. I yanked him to his feet and pushed him toward the Impala I'd stolen. He fit all too easily in the trunk. I had disconnected the safety release, but I used my fist to render him unconscious anyway. One can never be too careful. Besides, the fight had ended too soon. I had more steam to blow off. For a little fucker, he could take a beating. A skill he'd no doubt perfected in prison.

The police would find evidence of a fight. They would find the knife that Walter used to stab my girl. They wouldn't find Walter. Pieces of him, maybe.

While I drove along the undeveloped stretch of river road, I dialed Tito. I ached to see Slade, hold her, and tell her everything would be okay.

But that would be a lie.

I wouldn't face her again until I made it truth.

Things would change. The life I'd hoped to settle into was nothing but a pipe dream. I belonged to Luciano now.

A worthy sacrifice if it meant keeping my family safe, and running the biker shit heads out of my town.

Tito sounded groggy when he answered, "Cousin. Everything all right? You get the fucker?"

"I have him. Change of plans, though."

"What's that?"

"He has Dad."

"What the fuck?"

"My thoughts exactly. What time does your plane land?"

Tito huffed into the phone. "Had to reschedule. Bad shit went down at the fights. Fill you in later. Right now I have a meeting with Voltolini. He'll go ballistic when he hears the Slayers have your Pops. Text you my flight schedule when I have it."

"Yeah. Thanks, Tito."

I ended the call. Luciano would lose his fucking mind when he heard the latest development. He loved my dad like a brother. Had tried to recruit him early on, but Dad had initiated his own plans for world domination. Plans that hadn't included New York, or Voltolini's brand of violence. Although, recalling the stories Luciano used to share with me, Carlos Rossi could hold his own in a knock-down-drag-out.

I knew what the Satan's Slayers were capable of. Trusted that my father could handle himself for a short spell. Convinced myself that he was still alive, or Reynolds wouldn't have played his *I have your father* card. They had Pops for a reason. I suspected it was money. It always came down to money.

Slade

"I promise, I don't need money. I'm rolling in dough." I tried to laugh, but every inch of my body screamed in protest.

"Honey, if you and Rocky need to stay with us, you're more than welcome." James kissed the top of my head and rested his hand over mine.

"Thank you. That means the world to me." I pinched my working eye closed, determined to hold the tears at bay. Even that slight movement proved excruciating.

Lettie peeked her head through the door. Her whole face lit up when she looked at her husband. "Am I interrupting?" she asked.

"Of course not."

She settled her handbag on the wide windowsill and came to stand at my side opposite James. She placed a red shopping bag near my feet. "I brought you some new clothes, sweetie." She bent to kiss my forehead and before I could offer gratitude, she continued, "I bumped into your doctor outside. He says you can go home this afternoon."

I no longer had a home. I forced the sadness down, burying it somewhere between grief and anger. I was alive. A house didn't matter. My family celebrated my life while Maurice ... *Oh, God, Maurice's family.* I imagined them gathered in his big, beautiful house, mourning, planning his funeral.

How in the world had he been sucked into my nightmare?

I had slept for the past twenty-four hours. I had vague recollections of Rocky and Tucker storming in and out, hugging and kissing me. Lettie and James sitting at my side, whispering, holding my hand.

I'd refused pain meds, or at least anything stronger than ibuprofen since that morning. I hated the effect narcotics had on my body, how, when under the influence, I couldn't distinguish dreams from reality.

What I hated most, was that I hadn't been able to talk Tango out of going after Walter. He hadn't come back, and his absence hurt, deeper than the physical pain. I refused to let my trepidation show. I knew why he hadn't returned.

Part of me wanted to tell someone, so they could stop Tango from doing something he might regret. Most of me wanted Tango to succeed. All of me wished I had killed Walter Reynolds the night I'd saved Rocky. If I'd swung the bat harder, hit him one more time, Tango wouldn't have cause to hunt him down. Maurice would still be alive. I'd have a house to go home to.

It wasn't fair, considering the horrors Walter had put Addy through, that he continued to breathe. How unjust that Walter's actions had turned me into a monster who would take pleasure in another man's suffering.

"Honey?" Lettie gently stroked the top of my head. "You okay? We lost you there for a sec."

"I'm fine," I whispered, blinking up at her. "I just. I just can't believe Maurice is gone. I'd like to attend his funeral, but what if they don't want me to come? What if they blame me?"

"Don't be ridiculous. Nobody could blame you for what happened," James chimed in. He looked down at me with enormous blue eyes full of compassion. Full of love. Bursting with fatherly concern.

"What if they catch Walter and he tells them what I did? What if they investigate and figure out my connection to Addy and Rocky?"

"Shh." He patted my hand. "Walter won't speak to the police. He's a career criminal. And one thing I know, despite how fucked up those bastards are, they'll die protecting their club. Walter tells the police about the history you share, he'd implicate his brothers. So unless he's got a death wish, his lips are sealed. Hell, he'd bite his own tongue off before talking."

Lettie reached over the bed to pinch James's cheek. "Honey, you've been watching *Sons of Anarchy* again, haven't you?" She shook her head and rolled her eyes. "Your father is obsessed with Kurt Sutter."

My father. I wasn't sure if it was a slip. Lettie had never referred to James as my father, or Tucker as my brother. I needed to hear her acknowledgement. Needed to feel like part of a family, whether she meant it or not.

I slumped against the scratchy pillow, buried my anxiety under the blankets, and enjoyed the company of my father and his wife.

Five hours later, I settled into Tucker's king-sized bed, in his seventh floor, downtown condo, with a full view of the lake. He'd insisted I take his room. I hadn't the energy to argue.

Rocky wiggled and squirmed next to me. "Mom?" he whispered, even though I'd sworn over and over that I was okay and I didn't need to sleep anymore.

"Yeah?"

He rolled to his side and blinked his big dewy eyes at me. "I saw our house on fire, and I was really scared."

"I know." I swallowed the thick lump in my throat.

"And Tango was scared and crying. Tucker said I couldn't watch anymore because we needed to let the firemen do their jobs."

Grunting through the pain, I rolled to face him, nose to nose, and brushed a chunk of hair off his face. "He was right. It wasn't safe for you to be close to the house. Fires are very dangerous."

"Tango got to stay."

I cupped his hands between my own. "He did. But the firemen made him move way back."

Tucker had mentioned that Rocky refused talk about what had happened. I was overjoyed that he was opening up to me.

"He wanted to save you. I saw him try to run into the house, and he fought with the firemen and everybody was yelling. They tackled him."

Oh God. I hadn't heard those details yet.

"Tucker made me stay in the car by Marion, and he tried to help Tango, but he came back and he was crying, too."

"Oh, baby. I'm sorry. I'm sorry you were scared, and I'm sorry we don't have a house anymore."

"It's okay, Mom." He sat on his knees and pressed a small, sticky hand to my cheek. "I like Tucker's house, too. It's right by the beach, and the park, and downstairs he has a swimming pool that's warm like the bathtub."

Such a boy. "That is pretty cool, huh?"

Rocky scooted to the edge of the bed and looked around the room. "Are you sad that our new stairs got burned?"

"Sure. I'm sad about everything. But we'll be okay. We can buy new things. I'm happy we're both safe."

He hopped to the floor and ran to the chair in the corner of the room to rifle through the stack of new clothes Tucker had bought for him. "I'm glad I had my football with me." He held his favorite toy in the air.

Definitely his father's son. "Me, too."

"Tango said we can't practice for a few days."

My heart skipped a beat. "Oh. Did you see Tango?"

"He called and said I have to give you lots of hugs."

"He called you?"

"Yeah, on Uncle Tucker's phone."

Relief washed over me. If he'd called, he was alive and safe.

Rocky wouldn't understand why Tango hadn't been around. The fact that he'd called to reassure his son made me love him even more. It did absolutely nothing to soothe the burgeoning ache, though.

I missed him.

Tango

"I missed you, baby." Aida's moist lips pressed against mine, sticky with red goop.

When I didn't reciprocate, she dropped her arms and stepped back, rubbing her belly.

No. No. No. Not happening. Aida Voltolini, in my town? Hell had officially frozen over.

A red glow highlighted her high cheekbones. "Daddy didn't tell you, did he?" Aida snapped her red-tipped fingers in my face. "Tango, darling, say something."

"Fuck me," I managed to declare.

Tito's massive arms choked me in a tight embrace, breaking the tension. "Cousin. Sorry about the surprise. I couldn't tell you over the phone."

I clapped his back, still too stunned to form a coherent response.

I studied the petite brunette. Stunning as always. Enormous brown eyes. Full red lips. Impeccable hair and make-up. She'd always been curvy, but there was no mistaking the new curve. Especially under the tight black dress she wore. She was either bloated, or ... fuck.

Math was never my strong suit, but I ran the numbers in my head. I hadn't been with Aida for over six months. And fuck that idea anyway, because I had never dived into her pool without a wetsuit.

"How far along are you?"

Aida's deep, raspy laugh grated my nerves. "Shit. You should see your face right now." She reached up and patted my cheek. "Don't worry. You're not the daddy."

"Who? What are you..." I glanced from Tito, to Aida, back to Tito. Luciano would never send his pregnant daughter away. I needed to hit something. "What the fuck's happening here?"

A beefy, bald man in a sharp, navy suit carried luggage down the steps of Luciano's private jet. He made no attempt to hide the Glock tucked into his belt holster. Tito gave him a chin nod and grabbed the suitcase handle. I snatched Aida's luggage and pulled it behind me as I led them to the car.

Fuck. Fuck. Fuck. What the fuck was she doing on my turf? How the hell would I explain her to Slade?

After helping Aida into the passenger side, Tito claimed the seat behind her, leaning forward to pat my shoulder. "It's great to be back in Hicksville, USA."

I turned the key and found my voice. "Explain, Tito."

He settled back against the leather. "Listen. I would've called to warn you, but Luciano's got a mole. Phones aren't safe."

"Okay."

Aida reached over and placed her hand on my thigh, stretching her pinky toward my crotch.

"Not gonna happen." I lifted her fingers and set them back in her lap.

She pretended to pout, then laughed. "You were right, Tits. He's got it bad." Aida patted my cheek, then pinched hard and whispered, "Just fuckin' with ya, pretty boy."

Tito chuckled behind me. "Luciano made a few calls. Your suspicions were spot on; the Satan's Slayers have been looking to branch out, run their shit through the hunting roads and retired highway, hoping to stay off radar."

"And?" The inside of my car filled fast with Aida's fruity musk. A scent I used to enjoy, that now left a bad taste in my mouth.

"T. Man. Luciano had words with the chapter president. Guy by the name of Butler. He insisted that they didn't know what Reynolds was up to. Tried to convince Luciano that the guy is working on his own. Claims to know nothing about your pops."

"You and I both know that's bullshit."

"Yeah, but they don't want a war. They probably thought this would be a quick and clean abduction. Now that Voltolini has jumped into the mix, these dipshits are scrambling. He made it clear to them, if one hair is out of place on Carlos Rossi's head, he won't only wage war, it'll be a biker, butt-fucking genocide."

Aida made a tsk sound. "Boys. Language. Please."

"Whatever you say, princess." Tito shook his head in mock irritation.

"So, you know, if they don't already have your dad, they're frantically searching. Wanna get their hands on him before we do, make sure your dad is returned safe and sound. Is Reynolds secure?"

"He's secure."

"That takes us to princess bun-in-the-oven, here."

My intestines knotted.

Aida stared out the window. Nothing in her expression gave away her state of emotions. I was almost fooled into thinking she wasn't worried until I heard the familiar *Click, click, click. Click, click, click* of her acrylic nails tapping against each other. The sound made me shiver. It was her one tell. On the outside, Aida was cool composure, a stone-cold beauty. On the inside, the girl was a ball of nerves wound tighter than the cha-cha.

Christ. Shit was bad.

"Princess got herself into a bit of trouble. Needs to lay low. Nobody knows she's here aside from you, me, and the big guy we left on the jet."

"Poor bastard," Aida huffed.

Translation. *Neither the pilot nor the big guy would make it home alive.*

My life sentence had begun. My heart sunk. No. It shriveled. I had hoped to have more time with my family before the ugly side of my life seeped through the cracks. "Luciano is calling in his favor already."

"You're the only one he trusts. Nobody would expect him to let her out of his sight, let alone hide her across the country."

"Lucky me, now I'm playing babysitter." To the girl I used to fuck while trying to get the girl I should've been fucking out of my system.

I had dodged a bullet, I supposed. Luciano could've ordered me to New York, thrown me back into the ring. Aida's fuck-up may have just saved me from having to leave my family.

Click, click, click. Click, click, click.

"Hey." I merged into the carpool lane and set the cruise control.

Click, click, click.

I flattened my hand over hers. "Aida. I don't know what kind of trouble you're in, and I don't want the details until I get Pops home. You're safe here. Got me? Nobody is going to touch you."

Aida dropped her head against the seat and rolled it to the side to look me in the eye. "Thank you, Tango. I promise, I won't cause any trouble for you and your girl."

My girl. My rockstar. My warrior.

Slade needed me, and I needed to deal with this shit so I could get back to her arms. I was empty. Desolate and angry without her.

After settling Aida into a guest room at home, introducing her to the staff, and leaving her in Maria's care, Tito and I left to dispose of Walter Reynolds and bring Pops home.

CHAPTER 18

I CLOSED MY FIST AROUND the colorless napkin bearing the Rooster Crow Bakery logo and squeezed hard, willing my nervous energy into the tiny ball of recycled pulp. When adequately smashed, I placed it on the red formica and flicked, aiming at the space between the sugar jar and napkin holder on the opposite end of the table.

"Miss Mason."

The deep, rich voice drew my attention from my goal line to the man standing at my side.

"Hi. Um. Jason, right? Good morning." I shifted to stand, but the man put his hand on my shoulder.

"No. Please. Don't get up." He slid into the seat across from me.

Jason McReary was tall with solid shoulders. Wrinkles framed his soft brown eyes. When he smiled, it warmed his face and the very air around him.

"How are you feeling?" he asked, tucking sunglasses into his breast pocket.

How was *I* feeling? I wasn't the one who had just lost his father.

"The truth?" I asked, tapping my toes under the table. "The bruises will fade. It's my heart that hurts, for you and

"

your family. I'm a mess. I feel like this is my fault somehow." I swallowed the lump in my throat.

Jason leaned closer and patted my wrist. "How could this possibly be your fault? You were brutally attacked."

"I don't know why your dad was at my house. I had just said goodbye to him. We had coffee and a long visit." I pulled my hand free, sat back in my chair, and dabbed the moisture on my cheeks.

Jason rested his elbows on the table and nodded when the waitress asked if he wanted coffee. He waited for her to leave before continuing, "Slade. I have some things to tell you. My brother wanted to be here, too. Unfortunately, he had another family matter to take care of. We wanted to talk to you personally. Our lawyer advised against us meeting you without him, but considering your long history with Dad, I thought this would be better."

Oh crap. Lawyer? They wanted to sue me. It *was* my fault Maurice was dead.

My intestines seemed to take on a life of their own, moaning, groaning, twisting, and tightening. I was going to vomit, or faint. God, what I wouldn't do to have Tango by my side.

You were my warrior.

I inhaled and released the air, nice and slow, forcing my eyes to dry.

"Christopher and I have known about you for years. When we confronted Dad the first time, he denied it, but he had never been a good liar."

Okay. I was lost. "Known about me? I don't understand. Lie about what?"

He smiled again, and I noticed the dimple, the same as his father's, the one that reminded me of Mom.

"I know why Dad was at your house."

My heart sunk and shriveled.

"And it wasn't your fault. It was mine." Jason ran a hand over his balding scalp.

I took note of his wedding ring, it's thick gold band, braided with a thin vein of platinum. Solid, and sturdy, much like he appeared to be. So why was he talking like a crazy man?

"Jason, I don't understand."

"He called me right after you left his house. Said he was going to tell you the truth the next time you came to visit. I told him not to wait. I told him to get in his car, go to you, and tell you everything. He'd waited too damn long already."

"Tell me what?"

Thump. Thump. Thump. I placed my hand over my chest, to keep my heart from breaking through its flesh and bone cage.

Jason pulled a worn photo from his wallet and pushed it across the table with his forefinger. I looked at the image without touching it, trepidation freezing my limbs, tearing my heart to bits.

The man in the black and white snapshot looked to be in his late teens, early twenties. He stood in front of the Truck Stop. Proud. Tall. One hand on his hip, the other pointing to the OPEN sign hanging on the door.

Off to the side, three women stood in capri pants, aprons, and button-down blouses.

"Dad carried this in his wallet." Jason tapped the photo, drawing my eyes to the woman in the middle. She paid no mind to the camera. Her face, her eyes, her body language, seemed to be aimed at the man with the giant smile. "Do you recognize her?" he asked.

I looked closer. She could've been my mother. She could've been me.

"Is that…" I couldn't finish my thought.

"That's Dad." Jason's bottom lip curled between his teeth while his head bobbed up and down. "He worked at the Truck Stop for a couple of summers. Dishwasher."

"And that's my grandma. Oh my God." I covered my mouth with a trembling hand.

My grandmother had lived across the lake, until she'd died when I was nine. I'd never known who my grandfather was. Mom had never mentioned that Grandma had once worked at The Stop.

Jason only nodded, waiting for me to play catch up.

My insides warmed a thousand degrees as I played back Maurice's advice about regret and lost love.

His daily visits.

His twenty-eight cent tips.

My daughter was born on the twenty-eighth. You aren't the only one with secrets.

"Mom's birthday was October twenty-eighth," I whispered, holding back a sob. "He always left a twenty-eight cent tip. Every day. Every single day."

"Sounds like something Dad would do."

"Are you saying? I mean. Are you telling me? Jeez." I dropped my elbows to the table and rubbed my temples. "I can't even say it."

"Dad was your grandfather. That's what he wanted to tell you. That's why he was at your house."

Once again, life, the evil bitch, had thrown me a bone, only to snatch it away and bury it. This time, quite literally, six feet deep.

Emotion I couldn't decipher welled inside me.

Suck it, life.

Jason McReary cleared his throat. "Listen, Slade. I'm sorry to dump this on you, considering what you've been through. We just thought it was important for you to know. You're allowed to mourn him the same way we do. The memorial service is the day after tomorrow. Christopher and I would like very much for you to be there."

I stared at the photo still lying in front of me, putting pieces together in my head.

Maurice had cheated on his wife, with my grandmother. Grandma had died alone. James, my father, had cheated on his wife, with my mother. Mom died, a drunk. Carlos Rossi cheated on his wife, repeatedly. Marta died, bitter and angry, by her own hand.

How could people so easily ignore the trail of destruction left in the wake of their selfish acts? Why was it the women who suffered most? There was a pattern, yet people chose to ignore it. Infidelity equals devastation. Broken homes, poisoned children. Wash, rinse, repeat.

My hands trembled. "Does the rest of your family know?"

"Know what?"

God, I was angry. It wasn't Jason's fault, but I couldn't hold the ugly words in. "That I'm the granddaughter of his mistress. That I'm the daughter of the town whore Maurice was too ashamed to claim as his own. Who else knows?"

Jason's kind eyes disappeared behind his thick lashes. His thumb tapped a rhythm on the handle of his coffee mug. "My brother and I are the only two people, besides you, who know the truth. The rest of the family know you as the girl my grandfather had a soft spot for. His favorite waitress from his favorite diner. I can't remember one conversation I've had with him over the past ten years where he didn't mention you."

"Oh," I mumbled, as the boiling rage reduced to a slow simmer. "I'm sorry. I didn't mean to take my anger out on you."

"You've been through hell. No need to apologize." He drew a deep breath and pinned me with a hard glare. "There's one more thing."

I opened my mouth to speak. Jason stopped me with a palm in the air.

"I need you to understand that Christopher and I, hell, the whole family are one hundred percent okay with this. The last time Dad updated his will was over five years ago. This wasn't a last minute, rash decision."

Will? His will? My heart raced, frantic and erratic. I couldn't speak.

"Dad left you his house."

Tango

That house. It physically hurt to look. I studied the charred remains of the few bones left standing. The base of the stairway, once a bright and hopeful ray of sunshine, now mocked me, black and ugly, from beneath the ash and rubble pile.

So many memories. Growing pains, stolen kisses, pointless fights, study sessions, refuge, laughter. Dancing. Planning.

I offered God a silent thank you, for keeping my family safe. Then I fell to my knees and silently begged forgiveness for what I'd done to cause this devastation, for what I was about to do to make it right.

Tito blew a low whistle between his teeth. "Damn, T. I can't believe you let the guy live."

I cleared the emotion from my throat. "I didn't know fear until I stood here and watched it burn, believing they were inside."

I'd wanted to burn with them.

"You're a stronger man than I am." Tito smacked my back. "Shall we?"

I stood, rolled my shoulders, and shook off the funky vibe. "Let's get this over with."

The flesh beneath my skin itched. On the surface, I burned. Twitchy and irritable, I pumped my fists, closed my eyes, called my monster to the surface.

One more time, I told myself. One more trip to the dark side. Only then could I face Slade, look her in the eye and tell her, with one hundred percent certainty, that she was safe. That I'd protected her. That, from now on, I would be her warrior.

We headed back to the van. Tito rounded to the front door and claimed the captain's chair. I threw the back door open, jumped inside, and pulled it closed behind me.

Walter Reynolds rolled his working eye up at me and mumbled through the gag in his mouth.

I made a show of pulling on the latex gloves and working them over my wrists.

"This is how it's going down." I glared into Walter's wild eye. "I made a call, talked to your prez." I tilted my head. "Nice guy. Although, he's none too happy about the heat you brought down on your brothers. You cost them a chance at absorbing this territory."

Walter thrashed against the chains that bound his wrists and ankles, stretching him from one side of the van to the other like a human X.

"Butler wants you back." I lifted the lid of my black tool box and held up the rongeurs, twisting, turning, giving him ample time to study my favorite bone cutter. "Until you tell me where my father is, we'll send him a piece at a time."

I pulled the goggles over my eyes, pulled his index finger straight, and cut off digit number one.

Walter screamed into his gag, shaking his head from side to side.

"You got something to say?" I ripped the duct tape from his mouth and pulled the rag from between his teeth.

"I'll fucking kill you, like I did your mother, you piss-ant piece of shit. Like I'll do to your father."

As if blindsided by a Mack truck, all oxygen left my lungs. Rational thought scrambled to hide. I struck hard, between his spread legs, with the tool still in my hand. With equal force, I shoved the rag between his teeth to quiet the scream.

Face to face, I waited for him to work through the pain, catch his breath.

"Did I hear you right? My mother?"

The lunatic laughed. "Eye for an eye. That cunt and your father helped put me away. Bitch already had the drugs. Made my job easy."

"Aww, fuck." I heard Tito say.

The metal under my feet vibrated as the engine roared to life. The small space shrunk around me. I turned my back to hide the flash flood of emotion tearing me apart.

Mom hadn't killed herself.

She'd died by Walter's hand. Not her own.

"T. Uh. We have a problem," Tito yelled over his shoulder.

I hadn't mourned her. I hadn't shed a tear, because I'd been too angry. I'd been furious at her for quitting, after raising me to believe, beating it into my bones, that quitting was never an option.

My lungs shriveled. A sheen of sweat formed on my skin. I needed air.

"Tango. Man. You hearing me?"

I tore off the gloves and goggles, twisted the handle on the back door and jumped onto the pavement. The bastard killed my mother, almost killed my girl, my son. My father.

Although I had beaten people to the brink of death, I had never taken a life.

Thanks to Walter's confession, that would change.

As soon as I could breathe. As soon as I could see straight.

I pounded a fist against my head. *Pull your shit together.* I paced, shaking the tension from my arms, staring at the hot asphalt.

You're doing this for Slade. I would end that man, stop him from hurting anyone else, so I could hold her again. This was for her, but when I crossed the line between violence and playing God, would she still love me? Would she still have me, knowing what I'd done for her?

Could I risk losing her again? Would I survive without my heart?

"Tango?" Slade's soft, sweet voice reached my ears.

I whipped around, hoping that it'd been my imagination, falling to my knees when I realized it wasn't.

"What are you doing here?" Wrapping her arms around my head, she held me against her abdomen.

I hugged her, clinging to her hips, her waist. "He killed her, baby. Son of a bitch killed my mother, almost killed you. He has Pops." I unleashed, clinging tight to the one person who could quiet my demons, bleeding my soul all over the front of her shirt.

She stroked my hair, curled around me, protective and comforting, slaying my demons one heartbeat at a time.

"Tang ... Oh. Um. Hi, Slade. Long time no see."

"Tito?" she said, arms tightening around my head.

I forced my hands to Slade's hips and pushed her back a step, wiping my face as I stood.

"What's going on?" she asked, looking at me, the van, and then Tito.

"What are you doing here?" I asked. "You're supposed to be in bed."

Slade pointed over her shoulder. "I had a meeting. Borrowed Marion's car. I was just returning it." Her eyebrows dropped low. She started to cross her arms, winced at the pain, sucked air through her teeth, then fisted her hands at her sides. "What are you doing here?"

I had never lied to her. I wouldn't start now.

"Taking care of Reynolds."

"Oh." Her gaze dropped to the ground. She kicked a pebble. Shifted. Rubbed her chest.

When she raised her eyes to me again, they were cold and vacant, not their signature brilliant and shiny. "Is he in the van?"

Tito shook his head at me in slow motion, silently begging me, *Don't do it, man. Don't do it.*

"Yes," I whispered.

Tito mouthed a "fuck" and threw his hands in the air.

"Is he alive?" Slade asked, rubbing a circle over her chest with a fisted hand.

I nodded, studying her face. Damn, I wanted to put a bullet in Reynolds's head for putting those horrid bruises on her perfect skin.

She turned on her heel, and, before I could stop her, she pulled the van door open. Her arms dropped to her sides. Her shoulders rose and fell with each sharp breath.

Walter thrashed against the chains, bloody, broken, and one hundred percent insane.

My shoes stuck to the road. I wanted to shield her from the ugliness. Instead, I stood stone still, awaiting her response, her verdict. Could she live with my monster?

Her head dropped low, and she closed the door. She didn't turn around. "He hasn't suffered enough."

Tito's head snapped up. Our eyes met, and equal parts shock and relief washed over me.

"You saw what he did to Addy. My god, what he did to Kim. He would've done the same to me. And what if he'd gotten his hands on your son?" Slade turned to face me. "For Rocky, for Addy, Kim, your mom, make that man suffer. Make him beg and scream and cry and bleed. Make sure he never hurts another living soul."

She stepped closer and splayed an open palm over my chest. "Do what you need to do, Tango Rossi, then get your ass back to me and Rocky, where it belongs."

The fierce tremble in her hand shot adrenaline through my core. I'd do this for her, and only her. So I would never again have to see fear in those eyes.

Rising on her toes, she pressed a kiss to my jaw and whispered, "I want to dance. Please come back to me soon."

Slade turned and walked away.

My heart stopped. It beat too fast.

I had never loved harder than I did in that moment.

Slade

In that moment, as I turned my back to the violent scene, trusting Tango to make things right, any doubt about his love, his commitment, any fears of losing him again, simply vanished. Because in that moment, Tango revealed his soul in its darkest state, the depth of depravity he would suffer to make the world right, to make life right, for me, for us. In doing so, he ripped his still beating heart from his chest and offered it to me, in all its gruesome beauty, naked, and vulnerable, trusting that I, too, would accept his sins, as he had mine, and make his world ... right.

My heart grew wings and fluttered in my chest. I didn't turn around. I walked across the street, up Marion's steps, and let myself in. I didn't look out the window when I heard the van drive away.

Marion and I made potato salad. We talked about my plans for the future. She gave me advice about Rocky's first day of school, which was quickly approaching. She told me where to get the best back-to-school bargains, and we debated homemade lunch versus school lunch.

I refused to let worry consume me. Marion tended to my wounds with her homemade remedies. Tucker and Rocky picked me up on the way home from their early morning fishing excursion.

After we'd tucked Rocky into Tucker's bed, I collapsed on the couch next to my big brother. When he wrapped a solid arm around me, I snuggled close and let my head fall against his shoulder.

"Are you worried about him?" Tucker asked, pointing the remote at his sixty-five-inch flat screen.

I shook my head no. Then nodded yes.

"He won't kill Reynolds." He continued to click through the channels.

"How do you know?" I asked, gnawing the skin on my thumb.

"Tango Rossi is not a killer. He's tough as shit, and I wouldn't go head to head with him in a fist fight, but he doesn't have a murderous bone in his body." Click. Click. Click.

A week ago, I would have agreed with him. Nonetheless, Tucker's words sunk in. I hadn't told anyone where Tango disappeared to. "How did you know he had Reynolds?"

Click. Pause. "I know people, sis." Removing his arm from behind my shoulders, he leaned forward, elbows to knees. "I would've hunted the fucker down if he hadn't." Click.

"Oh." I sat up and turned to face him. There was still so much to learn about my brother. "What exactly does that mean ... *you know people*?"

"That's a conversation for later." He set the remote on the arm of the couch and pushed to his feet. "Popcorn?"

"Only if you're going to pick a channel and keep it there for longer than five seconds."

"You pick something," he yelled from the kitchen.

I fell asleep halfway through *Magic Mike*. Tucker ordered me to bed, and I passed out next to Rocky the moment my head hit the pillow.

Sometime later, thick, warm lips woke me from slumber.

"You're here," I moaned, stretching and curling my toes under the sheet.

"Shhh." Tango pressed a finger over my mouth and folded the blankets off my body. "Come with me." He offered a hand and helped me rise.

"Where?"

"Shh. Come on." He laced our fingers and led me out of the bedroom, through the living room, where Tucker snored like a boar on his couch, then through the front door.

The moment it shut behind us, he pinned me to the wall. Leaned close, then closer, and nuzzled my cheek before touching his lips to mine.

His lips.

Sweet mother of mercy, those lips.

They teased my mouth, danced along my jaw, skimmed my neck. I couldn't get a kiss in edgewise, so I stopped trying and instead hooked my fingers in his belt and exposed my throat, absorbing his wet, hot affection.

Tango worked his mouth to my ear with ragged breaths. When his strong hands cupped my jaw and tilted my face, I forced my lids to raise. Dear, sweet Lord, the hunger, the promise churning in the depths of his eyes.

"I missed you." He brushed his thumb, with a stroke lighter than an angel's kiss, under my bruised eye. "Does it hurt bad?"

"Everything hurts when I'm not with you," I said on a sigh.

He joined our hands again and walked me toward the elevator. When inside, he pushed the button for the rooftop garden.

"How did you get in?" I asked, admiring the sight of him. "This is a secure building."

"Tito and his mad hacking skills."

I rolled my eyes. Boys. "You know, I'm sure Tucker would've given you a key. Or there's this thing called a doorbell. It's quite handy. I've used it myself a few times."

His lips quirked. "Where's the fun in that?"

When I stepped off the elevator, clean, crisp air hit my skin, sending a shiver through me. Tango tucked me against his side and led me toward two lounge chairs settled against the balcony wall.

He leaned against the railing, stretched his neck over the side, and drew a deep breath.

I looked out over the lake, blue and dark and eerie under the moonlight.

Tango turned to me, his face masked in shadow. "I'm sorry I didn't stay with you at the hospital."

"I understand why you weren't there, and I don't need an apology."

Tango lifted his hands, slid them over my jaw, then curled his long fingers in my hair, tilting my head. "You're safe now. Walter Reynolds can never hurt you again. I won't let anything hurt you again." He leaned closer, showing me the truth in his eyes. "I swear to you, on my life, *I* will never hurt you again."

I gripped his wrists to keep from collapsing under the weight of his words. "I know, Tango. What you did—"

"What you saw today," he interrupted. "What I did to Walter, it's part of who I am. I can't change the past, but I can promise that ugly side of me will never touch you or Rocky. I understand if you can't live with that, knowing what I'm capable of."

"Shut up, Tango." I pulled away from his grip and pushed him until he dropped into the chair behind us. "What you did today was to protect your family; you fought for me, for Rocky, your mom and dad. You loved me in a way nobody else could. And don't call it ugly ever again. Because if you're ugly, then I'm ugly, too. I tried to kill Walter the night I saved Rocky, and I've never wanted anyone dead more than that horrid man."

Tango's arms snapped around my waist and he pulled me into his lap, settling me between his legs. "What a pair of fucked up, white trash asses we are, huh?" He lay back, and I settled against him.

"I'm white trash," I reminded him. "You're just an ass."

Curling his arms around my neck, he peppered my head with kisses.

I studied the sky, the stars, and listened to his breathing. We stayed that way, silent, sleepy, and together until Tango cleared his throat.

"I didn't kill him."

Unexpected relief washed through me, followed by a wave of fear.

"Where is he?"

"Tito is with him. I have to get back soon. Tomorrow we're handing him over to the Slayers in exchange for Pops." His arms tightened around my chest. "That's all I can say on the subject. I came tonight to tell you that you're safe."

Tango never lied. If he said I was no longer in danger, he meant it. I trusted him, and I wouldn't push for details. He had always been protective, and I appreciated his effort to shield me from the grisly specifics.

I rubbed my hands up and down his solid thighs. God, it felt good to touch him. "Are you okay?"

"Mmm," he hummed, lips in my hair. "I am now."

If I only had him for a short time, I didn't want to waste a second. I pushed up and off the chair, then turned and offered my hand, my heart pounding a thousand beats per second. "Have you danced today?"

Tango sucked in a sharp breath. His face crumpled and recovered so quickly I almost missed it. When he pushed to his feet, all corded muscle and predatory leer, I stumbled backward.

Faster than I could recover, I was between his arms, lighter than air, and spinning under a blanket of happy, twinkling lights.

I never wanted the night to end.

Tango

I couldn't wait for the day to end. I needed to see my boy, hold my girl.

"That prick had some cojones, huh? Hiding your pops in his own cabin. Fuckin' genius." Tito's leg bounced incessantly. Guy was wired, which made him dangerous, and exactly where I needed him to be in the event things went south during our transaction.

Three bikes and one van came into view when I maneuvered the last curve of the private road leading to our mountain cabin.

Tito leaned forward and tucked a blade into each of his boots. Then he turned to me. Game face on. No doubt he had at least three other weapons hidden on his person.

There was nothing more impressive, or anyone more intimidating than Tito when he was in the zone, whether he was hacking databases, or going full charge into battle. Hand to hand, hands to keyboard, didn't matter. When his expression fell stone cold focused, you steered clear, or found yourself neck deep in a shit quarry.

I executed a three-point-turn and backed the van to the front porch of the cabin. Dane stood in wait at the front door. Worn jeans. Nothing but ink under his cut. Bruises. Bloody knuckles. Singed beard.

"Pretty boy," he said, giving me a nod as I strode his way. He gestured to the back door of the van. "He in there?"

"What's left of him." Missing fingers. Shattered kneecaps. Half a tongue. Walter wasn't going anywhere without assistance. "Where's my dad?"

Tito came around the corner and flanked my left side, arms crossed, glare set tight.

Dane gave him an apathetic once-over. "'Sup." His gaze sliced to me. "Your old man is out back. Putting the fishing gear away."

"Fishing gear?"

"That's what I said," Dane growled, rubbing the bare patch on his otherwise full facial fur.

I scratched the tingle at the base of my skull. "What the fuck's going on here?"

"Couple of the guys took him fishing while I disposed of Riggs." Dane slipped a quick glance at the white van, not dissimilar from the wheels I'd jacked, parked between two bikes. "Couldn't have any witnesses."

Tito piped in, voice low and charged. "And this Riggs, he was working with your dad?"

"Don't call him my dad. Fucker ain't no father to me." Dane spat. Dropped his head. Huffed. "Yeah, they were working together. The two of 'em brought your old man up here. Thought they could force him to sell this property. Used his girlfriend as bait. Jumped him at the dance studio." His glare darted between me and Tito. "How is that girl, anyway? She gonna live?"

"Yeah. She's gonna live." I had checked on Kaylee that morning. While her physical wounds were superficial, I didn't envy the emotional scars she would suffer.

"What the hell does your club want with this property?" I asked, gritting my teeth, struggling to tame the rage brewing in my gut.

Dane hopped down the steps and pounded a palm on the back door of the van. "Wasn't us who wanted it."

Tito shifted next to me, radiating tension. "Let me guess. Riggs wasn't a Slayer."

"Fuckin' weasel was a Banshee. Aryan fucking twat." Dane turned, crossed his arms, leaned against the van, one foot hitched on the bumper. "The two of 'em hooked up on the inside. Walt gave up intel for protection. Swore loyalty to the Brothers of Banshee. Our enemies. We've been looking for him since his release."

"How the hell you end up in Slade's house the night of the fire?"

"Finally caught up with Walt at the trailer. Fucker stuck a needle in my neck. Next thing I know, I'm tied up in Blondie's kitchen. Crazy bastard wanted me to watch him carve her up, like he'd done with Addy." Dane shook his head, releasing a grunt. "That old man came out of nowhere, wavin' a damn pistol. Got Walt in the gut. He tried draggin' Blondie out the back door. She was too heavy for him. He cut me loose and keeled over, clutching his chest. I ended up haulin' both their asses out the door. Didn't see Walt slip out."

How close had Slade come to burning in that fire? Fucking Dane had saved her again. That knowledge hit me something fierce, like an F5 tornado. "Then you found Riggs. Followed him here?"

"Somethin' like that."

"And now you're fishing buddies with my dad."

Dane pushed away from the Chevy and stuffed his hand in the front pockets of his denim. "Cool guy. He was happy to see us. Happier to watch us take down Riggs. Fuckin' Banshees roughed him up a bit, but he's good."

"I'd like to see for myself."

"First things first," he said, kicking at a stone, then raising his eyes to mine. For the first time, he looked human. "How's Blondie? She gonna be okay on the other end of this mess?"

Fuck. I wanted to slice this guy to shreds. He'd clearly never gotten over my girl. "Slade is none of your concern. But yeah. She's a tougher shit than I thought."

"Take care of that boy. He's the only blood I got left. All this shit'll be worth it if he gets to grow up right." It cost him to say those words. Evident by the tight pull of his lips, the tick in his jaw, and the way he obsessively checked the door, as if to make sure no one else was listening.

Made him almost likable.

"You have my word," I promised.

At that, Dane Reynolds rubbed a hand over his head, met me eye to eye and nodded his approval.

"We done? Can I see my dad now?"

He chuckled and put some space between us. "Don't suppose you wanna help me get Walt to the other vehicle?"

I tossed him the keys to the van I'd "borrowed."

"Keep this one. I have no use for it." My Rover was parked halfway down the mountain.

We shared a stare down. Could have been my imagination, but under his beard, his lips twitched, as if he were fighting a smile. I nodded. He nodded back.

"We good?"

"We're good."

Tango

"Now, be a good girl and hold still," I whispered against her neck.

Slade shivered and raised her chin, granting me access to that soft porcelain skin.

"Someone might see us," she whimpered, curling her fingers around my shoulders.

"No one is coming up here, baby. It's two in the morning."

We had fallen asleep, her in my lap, on the lounge chair in the rooftop garden. I had woken a short time later to Slade wiggling her ass against my cock, pretending to stretch.

Swear to my maker, waking up against her curves, breathing her vanilla scent, knowing she trusted me with her life, our boy, her body, it was the headiest damn feeling. A drug. An addiction. Obsession. I could take on the fucking universe.

Nothing else in the world mattered. None of the bullshit in my head—Dad, his infidelities, our violent past. Mom and her greed, her betrayal, her cold, superficial personality. None of it fucking mattered.

Slade Mason, my soft, my sweet, my cushion, my rock. She was my laughter, sunshine, mischief, and truth.

My girl.

And right then, on the rooftop garden, under the soft rays of the moon, she was naked, a priceless work of art, on display for my own private viewing. I kissed her neck, her shoulder, and down to her chest, pulling a tight bud between my teeth.

Slade writhed beneath me, arching into my body. I slid a hand down her firm abdomen, mindful of her bruises, and brushed my fingers against the soft folds between her legs. She parted her knees, completely trusting, definitely wanting, and I groaned, overwhelmed by her beauty.

I stroked her, sucked and licked her nipple, pressed my thumb against her clit, rubbing in slow circles. Fucking hell, the way she moved with me, whimpered, the way her hair fell over the sides of the chair. Slade was soft and pure and pink and mine. All fucking mine.

Parting her pussy lips with my middle finger, I pushed inside, only far enough to feel that she was wet and warm and ready. Ready for my cock. For me.

I climbed over her, parting her lips with my tongue, taking her mouth. Tasting her. Loving her.

When I reached down and pulled her knees higher, she broke the kiss and cupped my face. When I pushed inside her ... *Fuck, fuck, fuck,* when I slid inside the liquid silk, the tight warmth, it was death, it was life, it was heaven. And hell, she owned me. Owned me.

Her hands still on my face, her eyes locked with mine, she shifted her hips, urging me to move. I pulled out and pushed back in, shivering with pleasure. I pumped again, slow, controlled, and dropped my head to claim her mouth again.

Slade moved with me, curling her legs around my waist, raking her nails down my back. I rolled my hips, grinding her clit on the down-stroke, pushing deeper. Her pussy. Sweet Lord, it was perfect, gripping me tight, sucking me in.

Knowing mine was the only cock to caress her sacred flesh, it did things to me, unnatural things, otherworldly things, and I couldn't get deep enough, or close enough, and I wanted, needed, to push harder, hold tighter, make love to my sweet, soft angel until our bodies fused, until we were one, until my parts became her parts.

Slade arched beneath me, and I knew she was close. Throwing her arms over her head, she gripped the back of the chair, bucked her hips. "Oh God, Tango. Oh, shit. I'm coming," she breathed against my ear.

Her words, her voice, pushed me over the edge, and I buried my face in her neck and came hard, loud, trembling. I thrust again and again, deeper, harder until the last tremor, until I hadn't a solid bone in my body, until I collapsed at her side—breathless, sweaty, and with a dumb-ass smile on my face.

CHAPTER 19

Slade

THE SUN TOOK EXTENDED BREAKS on the day of Maurice's funeral, hiding behind billowy gray clouds, sneaking a peek every so often as if checking to make sure we were all okay.

I met my new family—cousins, aunts, uncles. I made small talk, smiled, cried. Tango held my hand, held me upright. Even made me laugh when I seemed to get lost in my grief. Christopher had introduced me as *the diner girl* and everyone seemed to know exactly who he was talking about. Someday, maybe, I would feel confident enough to come out as Maurice's bastard granddaughter. When the time was right. Not today. Not in the near future, but someday.

Tucker came. As did Charlie and Margie. No Kim. Not yet. But I had high hopes for her. I wished I was seeing my ex-employees under different circumstances. Nonetheless, it made my heart happy to hug them.

When the service was over, when the last of the mourners ducked into their cars and drove away, Tango asked me to walk with him.

"Where we going?" I asked, grateful to be alone with him.

"You'll see," he said, smiling and squeezing my hand.

We cut through the manicured grass of Whisper Springs Cemetery, past rows of headstones and flowers, until Tango found what he was looking for—the gravestone that read, *Marta Rossi. Beloved Wife and Mother.*

Simple, yet elegant.

Tango sat in the grass next to his mother's final resting place and pulled me down beside him. "I haven't been here yet." He turned to look at me. "I couldn't do it. Not until you were with me."

My heart, already soft and mushy, liquefied.

"I'm sorry you lost her the way you did."

"Me too," he mumbled. "I was angry, you know. Not at her as much as myself. I only talked to her once a month when I was away. How pathetic is that? All I had to do was dial the phone, say hi. Let her know I cared, let her know she still had a son who loved her. I'd give anything to hear her voice one more time."

"She was proud of you. Loved you hard. That was obvious."

"We had our issues, but I loved her, too. Mom was cold, and strict, and hard. That's how I knew women to be. Until you jumped off my dock, anyway. I pulled you out of my lake, and you were warm, soft, and nothing but laughter, smiles, and positive energy. I couldn't get enough. Soaked you up like a damned sponge."

He shot me a sideways glance, then rested his arms over his knees with clenched fists. "I hate what she put you and Addy through. Hate that she turned away my baby. I wish I knew why she did it. I wish I could understand, or tell her how angry I am, how much she hurt me. I wish I could ask her why."

"We'll never know why, and we can't waste our precious time or energy trying to figure it out, but Tango, you need to forgive her. You need to make your peace and let it go. You are not your mother, but you are who you are because of her. And who you are is everything to me. And the man you are means everything to the little boy who's waiting for you to go throw a football with him. And some of Rocky comes from her. That's why you need to forgive. Let go of the hate, so your heart doesn't harden like your mother's."

I watched his face crumple, his Adam's apple rise and fall, his head nod in agreement.

What he needed to do, he needed to do alone. I pushed to my feet and kissed the top of his head. "Take your time, I'll meet you at the car."

He swiped a tear off his cheek.

Hard as it was, I walked away.

Twenty-five minutes later, Tango found me leaning against his Rover. When his blotchy red eyes met mine, I wrapped my arms around his waist, pressed my cheek to his chest, and hugged all the love and support I could offer into him.

His arms coiled around me, one high, one lower on my back. He rocked me, with his cheek pressed against the top of my head, and I melted against his hard planes.

"This is my favorite place in the world," I mumbled against the silk of his dress shirt.

"The cemetery?" he asked with a chuckle. "That's creepy."

"No. This space, right here, between you and the rest of the universe."

The rocking stopped. He didn't lift his head from mine, nor did he loosen his hold on me.

After clearing his throat, he whispered, "I used to think I was the one taking care of you. That was never the case. It was always you, making me laugh when I wanted to drown in my own self-pity, standing ready with your pin to pop my inflated ego when my head got too big. You never let me get caught up in the bullshit of my privileged life. And if I tripped and fell, you always picked me up with that magical smile and a bucket full of cold hard truth."

Tango pulled away from me. I cringed when I saw the makeup stains on his shirt. He wasn't paying attention to the shirt. He was melting me with the heat of his gaze. His lips parted and his tongue darted out to wet them.

My heart palpitated.

He lowered his gaze to my chest and lifted his hands to my shoulders, pausing briefly before sliding them up to cup my face. "This is my favorite place in the world." He tapped my temples with his thumbs. "This space under that gorgeous head of hair, hiding inside that thick skull. The things you have going on in there. Shit. Blows my fucking mind every day."

Speechless. Only Tango Rossi could talk about someone's brain and make it sound sexy.

He wrapped his arms around me one more time. "I'm keeping you inside your favorite place so I can protect my favorite place."

Swoon. Yes, I swooned. Then I pushed up on my toes and kissed his recently moistened lips. "We are so weird."

Tango

"Why are you acting so weird?" Slade asked, following me out of the elevator of Tucker's condominium.

I'd invited her and Rocky to come and stay at my father's house with me. She'd refused. I couldn't blame her. Too many bad vibes. Didn't matter. Maurice's house would be ready soon. Then, we'd start our new lives together.

"Tango." She snapped her fingers in front of my nose. "What's wrong with you?"

Christ. The last thing I wanted to do was introduce my future wife to my ex-fuck buddy who I was obligated to protect because I had needed to rescue my father from a deranged biker.

Halfway to the car, I stopped and turned to her. "I couldn't talk in front of Tucker or Rocky. I have something important I need to tell you. Something you're not going to like, but it is what it is and there is nothing I can do to change it."

Her eyebrows quirked. "Ohhh ... kay."

I turned and continued toward the SUV. Her flip-flops smacked behind me. It was my third favorite sound, Slade's laughter being my favorite, Rocky's raspy giggle being second.

"Are we going to the movies, or not?"

"No." I pushed the key fob, and we both climbed into the Rover.

"You're starting to scare me. What's going on?"

I started the engine and rolled out of the parking garage. "We're going to Pop's house."

"You just left your dad's house."

"I know."

Slade twisted in her seat, hoisting one knee up so she could face me. "Tango Rossi, you better start talking right now."

Christ, why was this so hard? "I did things in New York that I'm not proud of. I've told you that already."

Slade nodded, chewing on her bottom lip.

"Luciano sent me home when Mom died, free and clear of any debt, any allegiance. Then I needed his help to find

Dad and to make sure the Slayers stayed clear of Whisper Springs."

"Okay," she said, confusion drawing her browns together.

"When you ask a favor of Luciano, he owns you."

Slade shook her head. "Nobody can own you."

"Trust me. Luciano grants you a favor, he owns you."

She straightened in her seat, then dropped her leg back to the floor, to face forward again. "Now I'm scared."

"Anyway, like I said, I didn't like who I was in New York. I ... um..." Shit. No nice way to put this. "I fucked around. Mostly with one girl. Aida. Luciano's daughter. He pushed her my way. I think he hoped we'd work out. Needless to say, we didn't. Anyway. We had fun. Used each other to get off. It wasn't love. I guess we were friends, kind of. I bailed her out of trouble more times than I care to count. She does that a lot, get in trouble, I mean. Luciano appreciated that I had her back, when it wasn't my job, and I suppose that was another reason he tried so hard to get us together."

Slade threw her head back against the seat on a drawn out *ugh*. "You're rambling. Whatever it is, just say it."

"Sorry," I sighed.

Aida. I was stuck with her. If babysitting her brought Slade any grief, gave her any reason to doubt my faithfulness, it would kill me. If I didn't take care of Princess Voltolini, her father would kill me. We had this one last hurdle. One last mountain to conquer, and I would make Slade Mason mine, legal and binding.

"Luciano sent his daughter to Whisper Springs. To me. To protect."

I tightened my fingers around the steering wheel, bracing for impact.

Slade sat stone-still and crickets-chirping-quiet.

I kept my eyes on the road. When the silence became unbearable, I snuck a quick glance at my girl.

Her shoulders shook. Then she dropped her face into her hands.

Oh, fuck. I made her cry. "Baby. I'm sorry. I'm so goddamned sorry. I promise, she doesn't mean anything to me and you have nothing to worry—"

Slade wrapped her arms around her stomach, threw her head back again, and laughed. Hard, tears pouring down her face, laughter.

Not sure why, but I laughed, too. Hard enough that I had to pull over. When Slade cooled it enough to look at me, she threw her hands in the air and yelled, "Suck it, life."

"What?" I managed to ask, now doubled over in my own fit of unchecked hysteria.

"Fuck it! Bring her on. I can take it." She leaned forward, roaring into her knees.

We laughed for a good five minutes. I had no fucking clue what had triggered Slade's fit.

Hell, maybe we both needed to release the pressure valve.

When we'd cooled our shit, she unhooked her seatbelt and crawled halfway over the console. Her lips touched mine softly. Then she whispered, "I broke into a biker clubhouse to save my pregnant friend. I fought off a psychopath. Big, bad, scary dude. I can handle an ex-girlfriend."

The worry I'd stockpiled left me on one extreme exhale. "I could tell you an alien baby was growing inside me and you'd perform a C-section, build a spaceship, and fly that fucker back to Mars."

She smiled the smile reserved for me. "Yeah. I would do that, too."

"You are so fucking amazing. I hope you know that."

"You were so worried. I thought you were gonna have a stroke. Did you honestly think I'd freak, hearing about this woman?"

"If I had a stroke, you'd slice my head open and save my life. Probably with a bobby pin."

"Kiss me."

I did. I kissed her. Felt her up, too. Damn, my girl had perfect tits. Neither one of us wanted to stop. We climbed into the back seat and christened my Rover under a shady maple on Rockford Avenue like a couple of horny teenagers.

We pulled into Casa de la Rossi thirty minutes later. Aida floated down the stairs to meet Slade. My girl, my warrior, pulled Aida into a bear hug and welcomed her to the family.

And when I thought my heart couldn't grow any bigger, Dad came around the corner holding a bag of peas to his blue and purple eye. It may have been the pain meds, but when he looked at Slade, his cocky, *I'm the king of the world* facade cracked and tears fell like diamonds down his cheeks. He fell to his knees at her feet, and he thanked her for saving his grandson.

Then he asked her forgiveness.

Without hesitation, Slade hugged my dad and told him she had forgiven him a long time ago.

She was lying.

I didn't care.

I knew my girl would forgive him in time, because he was my pops, and that was the way she loved me.

Dad had yet to talk about what had transpired at the cabin. He covered his bruises and made a valiant effort to hide his aches and pains. He wasn't one to show weakness. I understood. I didn't push. I had my Pops. I had my girl. I had Rocky. We were going to be just fine.

That night, when I tucked my son into his uncle's bed and watched him drift to dreamland, God and I had our long overdue heart to heart.

Slade

Hearts. Everywhere. Littering the bed, a trail on the floor leading out the door, large heart shapes floating against the ceiling. Big hearts, tiny hearts, glittery, shiny, polka-dotted. Every shape, size, and color. Hearts.

I scratched my head and heart-shaped confetti fell out of my hair.

A black garment bag hung on the closet door with a note taped to it that read, "Wear me."

I unzipped the bag. The dress inside took my breath away. Ice blue, fitted, sleeveless bodice with a plunging V-line adorned with sparkling rhinestones, and a floor-length billowy skirt with layers of delicate tulle and silk. A gown fit for a princess.

"Oh good, you're awake."

I jerked around, startled by the sound of Aida's voice at the door.

"Chop, chop. There isn't much time." She pushed in, rushed me to the bathroom, and not so gracefully shoved me into the shower.

"Aida. I..." I tried to protest, but the dark-haired beauty, who I'd only known for a month, and already considered a friend, shushed me.

"No talking. Just scrubbing."

I did as told.

When I emerged from Tucker's bedroom forty-five minutes later, after Aida had worked magic on my hair and unleashed her bag of designer cosmetics all over my face, I was a princess.

Aida hugged me and whispered in my ear, "El Tango te espera." I didn't know what that meant, and I didn't have time to ask, because she shooed me down the hallway.

Tito stood at the front door, wearing a suit, no less, with his arms tucked behind his back. "Damn, girl." He shook his head. "For the first time in my life, I'm speechless."

Heat batted my cheeks.

I started to speak, again to be cut off.

"No talking," Tito ordered with a scowl, then cracked a smile. "Here, put these on." Bringing his hands into view, he presented me a pair of silver flip-flops with rubber bottoms bedazzled to the hilt with rows of sparkling, brilliant white stones.

Tito dropped to one knee and helped me slip them on. When he rose, he kissed my cheek, hooked an arm through mine, and guided me out the door.

By the time he settled me in the back seat of the fancy town car parked on the street outside Tucker's building, I was breathless, giddy, and my cheeks ached from smiling so hard.

Tito pulled a silk scarf, blue, like my dress, from his pocket, and proceeded to wrap it over my eyes and tie it, quite skillfully, at the back of my head.

He smelled like expensive cologne. Whiskers tickled my ear when he whispered, "El Tango te espera." Then he kissed my cheek and left me alone—blind, warm, and with a tummy full of jitterbug-dancing butterflies.

The car started. Tango music oozed from the speakers— the light twinkling of piano keys, the bandoneons with its airy voice rising above the tug-of-war between the violins and the Spanish guitar, each vying for attention, the bass in the background holding the notes together with its warm embrace.

I sunk into the chair and absorbed the beauty of the music, remembering the times I'd watched Tango glide across his mother's dance floor, making every woman he partnered with shine, and smile, and feel like Ginger Rogers, no matter their skill level. I remembered our private dances in my bedroom, on his dock, in the hallway between classes, in the bleachers of the football field after every home game.

Seconds after the car stopped, Tito helped me out of the seat, wrapped one arm around my waist, and guided me twenty steps forward, then through a door. His lips brushed my cheek one more time before I heard retreating footsteps.

Chills crept up my arm when a warm hand slid against mine, palm to palm, entwining our fingers. I sucked in a sharp breath when soft lips pressed to my shoulder. The scent of sun-baked skin made my heart skip a beat.

A finger traced my jawline, stopped at my chin, and tilted my head up. Tango's breath warmed my lips, but he didn't touch. He breathed, I breathed, and the only sound was a soft Spanish guitar playing on surround sound. His hand slid to the back of my head. I was nothing but gooey, melty girl held together by skin. Skin that sizzled and sparked in the arms of a man who was power, and sex, and muscle, and love.

"Have you danced today?" he whispered, so close his lips tickled mine. I felt a tug at the back of my head and the silk scarf fell to the floor. Tango stood before me in a tuxedo, lips parted, devouring me with those eyes. Those eyes, dear God, they were beauty, sensuality, claiming, adoring.

"Tango te espera," he said, coiling one arm around my waist, pulling me tight against him.

"What does that mean?" I asked, raising my hands to his shoulders.

"Tango awaits you." He kissed me. Finally. Deep, hard, and hungry. I opened for him, softened against him, lost myself to the pleasure of his tongue, his lips, his moans. When his arms coiled around me, I was weightless, and airy, and spinning, twirling, flying, dancing. Free and beautiful, and young and carefree, and in the arms of the only man I ever wanted to dance with.

Tango broke the kiss too soon. He stopped spinning and set me back on my feet. And then ... And then, I took in my surroundings. We were standing on a black and white checkered floor. Behind me, a red counter stretched almost the entire length of the room. A row of stainless steel stools boasting red, shiny vinyl seats were bolted to the floor. Stacked against the far wall were brand new tables and chairs, and as I looked around the dining room of the Truck Stop, I noticed brand new everything—appliances, windows, trim, paint, napkin holders, everything. Shiny and sparkling. Everything except one table in the corner. Maurice's table.

"You saved The Stop?" I asked, heading toward the table to get a better look.

A shelf had been mounted next to his booth. On the shelf sat a picture of Maurice and my mom, the photo that used to hang in my office. Next to the photo sat a cup and saucer. Inside the cup, a quarter and three pennies.

"It's your home. Not a chance in hell I would let anyone take it from you."

"Our home," I corrected him, and before I turned to thank him properly, something caught my eye.

In the center of the table sat a ring. A platinum band with a single, oval shaped diamond. Simple, delicate, perfect. When I whirled around to face Tango, he was bent on one knee. Lashes wet, eyes like glass, jaw set tight.

He cleared his throat, and when I swayed, he braced my hips with his strong hands. I'd never seen anything more beautiful than the warmth, the pride, the pure joy on his face as he looked up at me.

"Mikhail Baryshnikov once said, '*When a body moves, it's the most revealing thing. Dance for me a minute, and I'll tell you who you are.*'" He slid his hands higher up my waist. "Slade Mason. From the moment I watched you dance on my dock, with your wild hair, and your bright smile, I knew who you were. Carefree, funny, brave, and so fucking in love with life. I knew you. And, even at six years old, I knew that you were my destiny."

Tango grabbed my hand. I swallowed a sob.

"Life is a dance. There are beautiful, fluid moments, and there are times when limbs get tangled and we trip and fall. The important thing is to keep dancing. And Slade, that's what I love so much about you. You take hit after hit, blow after blow, and you bounce right back to your feet with that soul-gutting smile, and you fucking dance."

I half-laughed, half-cried, and wiped a tear off my cheek.

"Marry me, Slade. Dance with me, and only me, forever. Be my wife."

I bounced on the balls of my feet, and then I pounced, tackling Tango to the floor with my arms around his neck and my thighs squeezing his hips. "Yes. Yes. Yes." I kissed him hard. Teeth clashing hard. I was ready to rip his tie off, until I heard one of my favorite sounds.

Rocky's raspy laugh.

Other voices joined in, followed by applause, then whoops and hollers.

I looked up to discover we were surrounded by our loved ones. Rocky, Tucker, Carlos, James, Lettie, Charlie, Margie, Tito, Aida, and best of all, Kim. Everyone was dressed for a ball, in tuxedos and gowns. The best part? Everyone wore flip-flops.

I looked down into the world's most handsome face, a laughing, happy face, and I thought to myself, *suck it, life.*

And I meant that in the most respectful, gracious, beautiful way. Then I kissed my Tango, in my Truck Stop, one more time, before climbing off him and celebrating with my family.

And we danced.

We danced.

We fucking danced.

ACKNOWLEDGEMENTS

Thank you, thank you, thank you for reading *Truck Stop Tango.* I can't begin to tell you how much it means to me that you took the time to read my words.

SexyBoyfriend and crazy kiddos, you deserve medals. I am grateful beyond measure for your patience. Thank you for putting up with my crazy schedule. It's your love and unwavering faith that keeps me going.

Julie Trisolini, thank you for the gorgeous (original) cover. Your beauty is soul deep, and that shines through your work. I adore you.

Rebecca Zanetti, you probably didn't realize at the time, but you gave me a boost when I needed it most. Our visit meant the world to me. Your encouraging words kept me from crumbling. I still owe you a lunch!

Madison Seidler, you're a doll. I look forward to many, many more words with you.

Rob Wheeler, you'll probably never read this book, but thank you for making the best flip-flops in the world.

Robart flip-flops are real. And they are freaking awesome.
robartflipflops.ecwid.com

OTHER BOOKS BY
Krissy Daniels

TRUCK STOP SERIES
Truck Stop Tango
Truck Stop Tryst
Truck Stop Tempest
Truck Stop Titan

THE APOTHEOSIS SERIES
Aflame
Aglow

How To Kill Your Boss

If you enjoyed *Truck Stop Tango,* please share the book
with others and don't forget to leave a review.

CONNECT

www.krissydaniels.com

Facebook: @authorkrissydaniels
Instagram: krissydanielsbooks
Twitter: @kdanielsbooks
BookBub: @KrissyDaniels

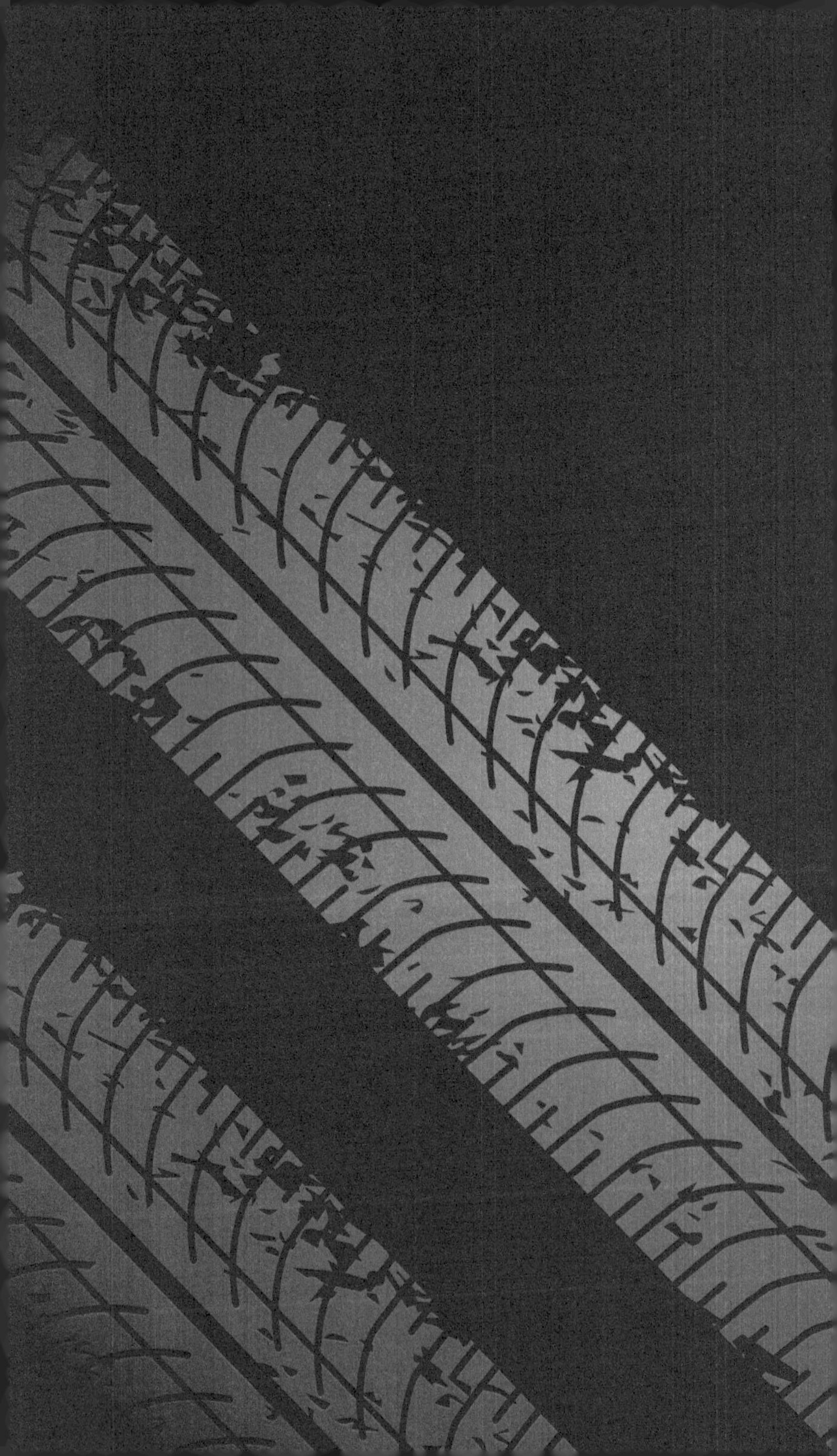